THE CONTINGENCY FACTOR

Philip Fleishman, M.D.

The Contingency Factor

This book is typeset in Times New Roman, Arial and Theodora Medium.

Edited and Interior Design and Layout by: Russell Phillips,
The Creative Source
(www.the-creative-source.com)

Cover Design by: Karen Phillips (www.phillipscovers.com)

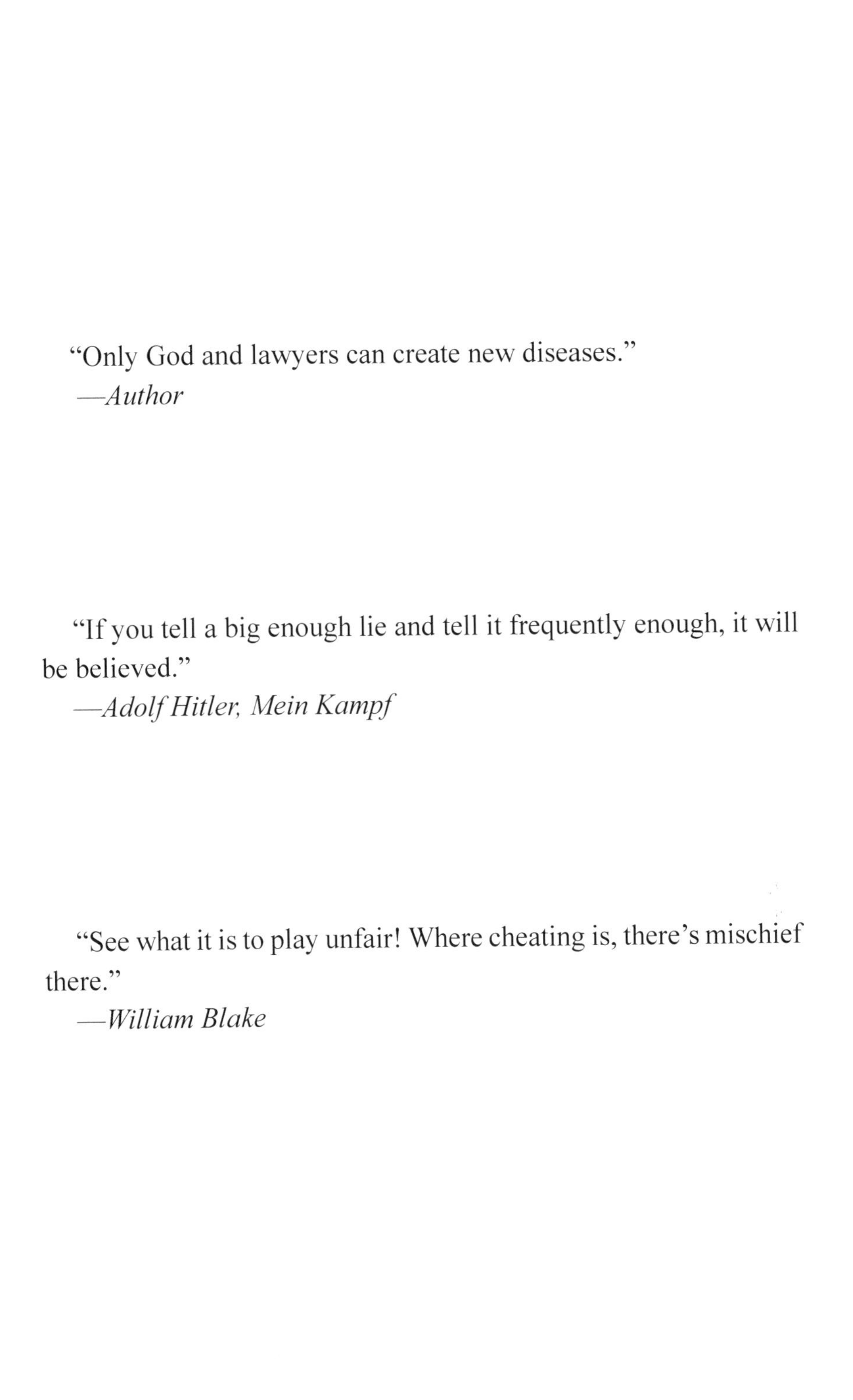

"Only God and lawyers can create new diseases."
—*Author*

"If you tell a big enough lie and tell it frequently enough, it will be believed."
—*Adolf Hitler, Mein Kampf*

"See what it is to play unfair! Where cheating is, there's mischief there."
—*William Blake*

For Michael Palmer M.D.

Michael was my mentor and friend, but most of all…Michael was a mensch, who left us far too soon.

PROLOGUE

Przytyk, Poland
Monday, March 9, 1936.

THE KILLING OF three Jews during the Przytyk pogrom on March 9, 1936, barely registered on the pogrom meter when compared to the tens of thousands of Jews that were massacred by the Cossacks in the Ukraine during the Kymelnytsky Uprising of 1648-1657, and thousands more during the Koliyivschnya uprising in 1768-1769. However, for ten-year-old Itzhak Minkowski and his four-year-old brother Naoch it was the most significant event of their young lives.

On the morning of March 9, 1936, Josek Minkowski awakens before the first rays of dawn sneak through the window of his humble cobbler's shop. His wife Chaja is still asleep, her snores sound like the back and forth of an accordion being pushed and pulled by an accordion monkey. Josek slips on his robe and makes his way down the stairs, which groan in protest over being assaulted by his two hundred pound frame. He hears the shuffling of feet outside the front of the house, followed by a violent maniacal banging on the door. It flies open, and he is confronted by a bearded glassy-eyed peasant from the village, his breath reeking of alcohol, and his mouth frothing like a rabid Rasputin.

"Pieprzony Żyd zabójca Chrystus—fucking Jew Christ killer." He raises his axe and buries it deep in Josek's chest…again…and… again. Josek crumples to the floor grasping his breached chest in a futile attempt to contain the flow of blood and the bubbling of air as it hisses through his crushed lungs.

The peasant charges up the stairs and enters the bedroom where

Chaja, now fully awake, pulls her eiderdown comforter up to her neck—as if it will protect her from the peasant's rage. Her fear is palpable. With a satanic grin the peasant drops his axe and pulls the comforter from her hands; he rips off her nightgown, exposing her sagging breasts and abdomen, scarred from the birth of her two sons by Caesarian section. A single blow to her face renders her unconscious. He unbuckles his belt and lowers his pants, freeing an erect uncircumcised penis throbbing with desire. He spreads her legs, mounts her, and violates her unconscious body.

"Kurwa suka Żyd. To jest jak człowiek pieprzy—Jew bitch. This is how a man fucks." He climaxes; his body dances as if in a grand mal seizure. Satisfied, he raises his pants and leaves the bed; he picks up his axe, and with one vicious swing her head is almost separated from her body. Blood erupts like an angry volcano. He unsheathes a knife from his belt and cuts off her breasts and throws them in a corner. He laughs. *"Nie więcej Żydzi nigdy ssać te piersi"*—"No more Jews will ever suckle these breasts."

Standing in the doorway are Itzhak and Naoch. They bear silent witness to the carnage. The peasant turns, raises the bloody axe, and then lowers it. He picks up the frail Naoch and hurls him against the wall. He throws Itzhak through the open bedroom window.

The riot lasts but forty-five minutes. The peasants leave the village, and the Jews begin to clear the rubble and start the process of rebuilding, as they have done since the first recorded pogrom in 1096, the Rhineland massacres.

A neighbor, who is the village doctor, hears the moans of a child in the yard of the cobbler's shop. He follows the sounds and discovers young Itzhak Minkowski lying in a bed of mulch that cushioned his fall from the window. After satisfying himself that Itzhak has sustained no serious injuries, the doctor carries him to his office and has his wife tend him while he returns to the cobbler's shop.

The door is open. He sees the body of Josek lying in his own blood. Blowflies have started their pilgrimage and are congregating in his sightless eyes and nasal cavities. Another procession of blowflies makes its way to and from his gaping chest wound. The buzzing sound of their vibrating wings crescendos as more and more join the procession. Upstairs he hears the plaintive wailing of a child. He ascends the stairs and finds Naoch sobbing in spurts with his eyes squeezed shut: he lies curled, as if in a cocoon, by the wall indented where his head struck when thrown by the peasant.

The blowflies are having a second convention in Chaja's chest cavity. The doctor approaches the bed, lifts the comforter, now a shroud, and covers her body.

New York Harbor, December 18, 1936.

ITZHAK AND NAOCH stand on the deck of the RMS Aquitania, each embraced by an arm of their uncle Chaim, their father's older brother, as the ship steams into New York Harbor on their way to a new life in America.

"What's that?" asks Itzhak as they approach the Statue of Liberty.

"That," replies his uncle, "is the symbol of freedom that says you can be and do anything you want without ever having to be afraid again."

Naoch asks, "But why do we have to change our names and learn to speak English?"

His uncle smiles, "*Ponieważ będzie Amerykan*—because you will be Americans. You will have American names and you will speak only English. You are no longer Polish. From now on you will be 'Neal Mink.' Neal means champion."

"What will Itzhak's name be?"

"His name will be 'Ingram,' which means hero."

"Always remember that a mink is an animal that will fight and defend its territory to the death. That will be the destiny of the Mink brothers—to be heroes and champions and to fight injustice to the death."

CHAPTER ONE

Tucson, Arizona
Wednesday, December 12, 1990.

INGRAM MINK SAT in a soft leather swivel chair surrounded by a chrome and glass desk in his ultramodern office on the top floor of the Williams Center Tower. In the palm of his right hand lay a soft, gelatinous, amorphous mass that shimmied like a mold of Jell-O. He juggled it from one hand to the other, and each time it assumed a pancake like shape as it plopped into his palm. He grasped it between his thumb and index finger and watched it morph into the shape of a teardrop. Smiling, he laid it on his desk blotter, got up, and walked to the window, which had an unobstructed panoramic view of the Santa Catalina Mountains to the north and the Tucson Mountains to the west.

He was a slight man, no more than five feet eight inches in height. His dark hair was peppered with just enough grey to give him a look of distinction. He had deep-set obsidian eyes that burned with intensity, and a slightly hooked nose that his detractors referred to as a *Jew nose*. He stood straight up, in contrast to the slightly stooped posture he assumed in the courtroom, which was an affectation purposely created to gain a measure of sympathy from jurors. His English was flawless, despite the fact he did not learn English until he was eleven years of age. However, in the courtroom he spoke with a trace of an accent, which Hispanic jurors immediately identified with. All jurors viewed him as a simple, humble man, wearing off-the-rack clothes, unlike the high-priced defense lawyers in their Brooks Brothers' suits whom he regularly decimated in court. A defense attorney saw a pit-bull, but a plaintiff saw a savior.

As he watched the setting sun play peek-a-boo with the clouds, changing colors like a kaleidoscope from a blazing red to a regal purple, he knew what he was going to do. He returned to his desk, pressed a button on the intercom and said, "Neal I need to see you in my office."

Neal Mink was the antithesis of his older brother. He was tall and fair-haired, with glacier blue eyes that twinkled constantly. Michelangelo could have sculpted his Roman nose. His casual demeanor was reflected in the way he dressed, unpretentious, but always with taste. The two brothers were polar opposites in all aspects of their lives. Ingram, a widower, was the somber, studious, serious one, and Neal was the unmarried, light-hearted, playful satyr, who at the age of fifty-eight appeared much younger, and who still attracted women like moths to a flame. But, when they worked together on a personal injury case the brothers fit like a glove on a hand.

Ingram was the litigator and Neal the researcher. Neal provided the paints for the pallet, and Ingram painted the landscape. Neal's memory was eidetic, and the database stored in his brain rivaled that of the Library of Congress. Ingram would take the facts that Neal provided him and weave a case that was unassailable. Like a chess grand master, which in fact he was, he could anticipate his opponents' moves long before they did. And in the courtroom it was always check…mate…game…match. He had never lost a case. Opposing attorneys knew that if Mink took a case to court the result wasn't if, but rather how much. When Mink took on a personal injury case the knee jerk reaction was to settle the case before it ever reached the courtroom. He was receptive to settling cases, but only if the offer started with six zeroes. The only pictures on his walls were blowups made from checks of jury awards. Encouraging to clients. Intimidating to defense attorneys. Those attorneys who balked at an offer to settle made a huge mistake.

Neal sauntered into the office and said, "Well big brother it's almost quitting time, and I've got a date tonight." He glanced at his Mickey Mouse watch and said, "...In exactly three hours. What's up?"

"Not to worry, you'll be there in plenty of time to sow your seed. Take a look at this." He threw him the gelatinous pancake.

Neal caught it and watched it mold into the spaces between his fingers. He raised his eyebrows and looked up. "Goop? Play-Doh?"

"No, my learned brother, that is the *veta madre*—the mother lode. Take a look at this." He turned to the entertainment center behind his desk, opened the flipper doors and inserted a cassette in the VCR and waited for the image to appear.

"Good evening. Welcome to Face to Face with Connie Chung. Tonight we will be talking about something that may pose a serious health hazard to millions of women. Most of us know little about breast implants. We've seen the ads; we've heard the rumors about which celebrities have them and which don't. But we don't know anything about the dangers. Since the early 1960s, some two million women have had breast implants. It's a simple device; the most common ones look like this: it has an outer shell made of silicone, with silicone gel on the inside. The operation takes a few hours, and if all goes well, the implants should last a lifetime, at least that's what most women believe, but not the women we interviewed. In fact, it couldn't be further from the truth.

"For almost thirty years, American women have been getting breast implants. An astonishing average of three hundred and fifty implant operations a day. But what's shocking is that the federal government has never approved these devices. Only now is the government looking at the dangers. For some women, it may be too late."

He played the tape until the end, and then turned off the VCR and said, "Well, what do you think?"

Neal steepled his fingers and replied, "I think we should stake a claim. Do you want me to get the mules, picks, and pans?"

"You better believe it. I want you check out everything she talked about in that interview. Find out all you can about Chung's experts and the women she interviewed. When we have assembled all the pieces we are going to know more about these implants than the manufacturers who made them. Chung said there were two million women who have had implants. I want to know if that number is just in the U.S., or worldwide. I suspect she's talking about the U.S. If only one percent have had a problem with them, it means there are at least twenty thousand potential plaintiffs who will require our services. And I guarantee that once we get started there will be a lot more women who will be convinced they have a problem.

"Once the legal community realizes the potential, they'll be lining up like runners for the Boston Marathon. We're going to have bib numbers 1 and 2."

Neal rubbed his chin and said, "Hmm, I wonder where Chung got her numbers. At first she said two million, and then she said three hundred and fifty implants a day for almost thirty years. Let's see what that is..." As if he were a savant, he calculated the numbers in his head. "Those numbers convert to three million eight hundred and thirty-two thousand five hundred. So, which one is it? In either case there's an orchard of cherry trees out there just begging to be picked.

"Miss Chung I believe you have just opened the floodgates like your colleague Ed Bradley did four years ago on *60 Minutes*, when the snowball he threw started the avalanche that almost destroyed Audi."

On November 23, 1986, *60 Minutes* correspondent Ed Bradley hosted the segment, *Out of Control*, which presented visual evidence that showed the Audi 5000 could lurch forward even when the driver had his foot on the brake. He claimed 1,200 accidents, five deaths, and 400 injuries resulted from the defective Audis. Millions of people watched the segment. Audi sales plummeted, and the lawsuits began. Even though the visual evidence that Bradley presented had later proven to be rigged, it did not stop the feeding frenzy created by plaintiffs' attorneys. It's hard to convince a shark that the dining room is closed.

Neal smiled as he rose from his chair and said, “I think I’ll send Miss Chung a dozen roses.”

CHAPTER TWO

Midland, Michigan
Two days earlier, Monday, December 10, 1990.

A VISITOR IN the 1850s to what is now Midland Michigan would have seen the riverbanks at the confluence of the Tobacco and Tittabawassee Rivers lined with many Chippewa Indian wikkiups—round huts made of bent saplings covered with skins and bark. By 1874, the Flint and Père Marquette Railroad extended through the heart of Midland to Averill, three miles to the west. The resulting booming community is what Herbert Henry Dow saw when he arrived in Midland in 1890, and this is where he settled and founded the Midland Chemical Company, the forerunner of the Dow Chemical Company, in 1897. The river would be a perfect place to dump the waste products from the bromine extraction processes performed by Midland Chemical.

In 1990, Midland had a population of about 39,000. It was the archetypal company town. The Dow Chemical Company and the Dow Corning Corporation spawned approximately eighty percent of the populace. The town was as exciting as a field of hay. In its thirty square miles could be found a marriage of industry and suburbia. Smokestacks and snakes of winding pipes carrying chemicals to massive gray storage tanks and corrugated buildings, spread out over hundreds of acres of sterile land, competed with uniform tree-lined streets and uniform sized houses with chain link fences where the worker-bees lived. The executives lived by the golf course.

The Dow Corning corporate logo—a white-lettered black bar resting on top of a matching teal blue bar—could be found everywhere, reminding everyone who was the master. The Dow Horticultural Gardens, the three timbered H.H. Dow Historical Museum, the Grace A. Dow Memorial Library, on a campus next to the Midland's Center for the Arts with a 1,500-seat auditorium, and three art galleries were all products of Dow's benevolence. Dow's largesse contributed to the building of the county courthouse, schools, churches, a community center, and a golf course. Midland was no longer an exhausted logging town with a plethora of saloons. It had been transformed by the power and money of Dow into a town of Stepford husbands and wives.

On December 10, 1990, a group of Dow Corning executives gathered around a TV in the executive conference room in the opulent corporate headquarters known as the Pink Palace. The TV was tuned to WNEM Channel 5, and at nine p.m. the face of Connie Chung filled the screen. The long anticipated episode of *Face To Face* began. Throughout the segment the men remained silent. When it was over, the towered Dow Corning headquarters building became the Tower of Babel. Everyone talking. No one understanding.

When the cacophony of sounds faded, a spin-doctor from the PR firm Briggs and Morton reminded the assemblage that they had been warned in 1985, of the potential for a *corporate media crisis*, when a San Francisco federal jury awarded $211,000 compensatory damages and $1.5 million in punitive damages to a woman named Maria Stern. The company was found to have committed fraud when it suppressed damaging information regarding health risks associated with the implants for what the court judged were *defectively designed and manufactured* breast implants.

He further reminded them that although the courts issued secrecy orders to keep damaging information from reaching the public, it was inevitable that someone would sniff it out. Pandora's box had just been opened, and Connie Chung was Pandora.

CHAPTER THREE

Tucson, Arizona
Wednesday, December 12, 1990.

ADELE GRANT WAS a thirty-year-old pert, saucy, blonde, former cheerleader with flashing brown eyes who was very much into body image. Like a balloon with a slow leak her breasts collapsed further with the birth of each of her three children. Now that her family was complete she wanted her breasts back. She sat fidgeting, crossing, and uncrossing her legs in a hand carved Jacobean chair placed in front of the most elaborate antique desk she had ever seen. The doctor's chair behind the desk was equally elaborate. It reminded her of the Coronation Chair in Westminster Abbey. On the desk sat an elaborately tooled antique brass Tiffany desk set, monogrammed with a fancy Victorian script emblazoned with the initials DP. In fact, all the furnishings and pictures looked like they came from, or belonged in a museum. She grew up in a very wealthy family, but she had never seen such opulence. She knew the operation was going to cost two months salary, but she didn't care—Devin Powers was one of the best plastic surgeons in the country. People came from all over the world to experience the magic of his hands. She lifted the mirror and was caressing its intricate scrollwork when Powers entered the office. "Ah, Mrs. Grant, I see you appreciate fine artwork."

"Dr. Powers, I'm sorry…I didn't mean to…"

"No please, don't apologize. What is the purpose of having art if its beauty can't be shared with others?"

"This desk set is beyond magnificent," she said as she replaced the mirror.

"You have an excellent eye. The set was custom designed by Charles Tiffany in 1847. It is one of only twelve sets in existence."

"1847? But it has your initials."

"Very astute. I'm impressed. A man named Daniel Putnam commissioned the set as an anniversary present for his wife Dolly. It was by sheer chance that I discovered the set in an antique shop in Kalamazoo Michigan, where the Putnams' once lived. It was as if the set was waiting for me, Devin Powers, to discover it."

Devin Powers was not the name he was born with. He was born Dariuscz Palowski, the son of a Polish peasant who fled Przytyk in 1936, a small village in Poland, for reasons that were never discussed by his family.

Dariuscz was beaten and bullied as a boy in Polish Hill, the Polish community of Pittsburgh, where he grew up. He was known as the son of *Polski Pijany*—the Polish Hill Drunk. Not that his father was the only drunk in Polish Hill, he was just the most visible. Young Dariuscz studied like a man possessed, and excelled at school. When he graduated high school he had his pick of the many scholarships that were offered him. He chose the University of Arizona. The day he enrolled, he changed his legal name to Devin Powers, thus severing the last connection to his Polish heritage.

He chose the name Devin Powers because in Gaelic Devin meant divine or perfect, and that is how he saw himself, perfect, with divine powers.

"But Mrs. Grant you did not come here to discuss antiques... what can I do to help you?"

"Well, in a way I did come to discuss antiques. My breasts. I feel like they're antiques. They were never large, but after my third child was born I felt they went on vacation and never returned. When my husband tries to touch me there, I freeze. I know he doesn't care, but I care. All I want is to have my clothes fit me again and to be able to look at myself in a mirror without cringing. They're a pair of socks that don't have any feet in them. Am I making any sense?"

"Perfect sense. I'll have my nurse take you to an examining

room, and when you're ready I'll examine you, and then we can discuss what will be the best option for you."

He lifted the receiver of an antique biscuit barrel telephone that had been modified to be used as both an intercom and a telephone. He pressed the intercom button, and when his nurse answered he asked her to prepare the patient for an examination.

His nurse took Adele into an examining room, and she was given a mauve silk half-robe that opened from the front, secured by a contrasting floral sash, not one of those ridiculous, over-laundered fleur-de-lis Johnny gowns with ties in the back that only a trained contortionist could manage.

When she was ready he entered the room and asked her to stand by the examining table and slip off her gown. She had small atrophic breasts that before she had children were probably a 34B. The right one was slightly higher than the left, and a little larger as well. The areolae were deeply pigmented.

He gently palpated each breast, one quadrant at a time, to ensure there were no abnormal masses. The movement of his fingers was almost sensuous, and her nipples responded by becoming taut and erect. His demeanor was entirely professional, but it was a rare woman who did not respond to his touch, enhanced by his movie-star good looks, penetrating malachite green eyes, dark hair, and seductive smile that revealed cavernous cheek dimples.

"Well, Adele, your examination reveals no abnormalities. Get yourself dressed and we'll talk back in my office."

This time Powers sat beside her in a matching chair. Patients always felt more comfortable when there was no desk to separate them.

"Adele, you are an excellent candidate for this operation. Your motivation and reasons for wanting the surgery are perfect. There are two types of implants that we can use, either the one we fill with saline, that has a silicone shell, or the gel type which has a inner soft gel with a silicone covering. My preference is the gel type, because if the saline-filled implants should ever develop a leak they will deflate and need to be replaced. To believe they will never leak is like saying you can buy tires for your car that will never need air."

"Are there any potential problems with the gel implants?" she asked.

"No. They will last forever. Occasionally you may develop a little thickening, or capsule formation, around the implant, which may distort the appearance and cause a degree of firmness, but that is easily corrected by squeezing the implant and breaking the capsule. It's a simple office procedure."

Neither of them had seen the Connie Chung special two days earlier, and neither was aware that registration for the draft for the impending silicone implant war would soon be starting, and that armies would be mobilized on both sides. Adele could have survived that war, but the fate that awaited her would be far worse than being a casualty in a war of words.

CHAPTER FOUR

Tucson, Arizona
Monday, December 17, 1990.

"WELL, BIG BROTHER, Chanukah's over, but I have a delightful Christmas present for you." Neal plunked a large accordion folder on his brother's desk.

"Please, you know I don't celebrate Pagan festivals, especially that one."

Ingram was a passionate student of the origin of religious festivals, and the celebration of Christmas particularly rankled him because Christmas evolved from the celebration of the Roman pagan carnival of Saturnalia. In 1466, Pope Paul II intentionally revived some of the most depraved customs of the Saturnalia carnival, first introduced by the Roman pagans. He forced the Jews of Rome to race naked through the streets of the city. An eyewitness account reported, "Before they were to run, the Jews were richly fed, so as to make the race more difficult for them and at the same time more amusing for spectators. They ran…amid Rome's taunting shrieks and peals of laughter, while the Holy Father stood upon a richly ornamented balcony and laughed heartily."

"Well, I think you'll make an exception this time," Neal countered.

"What've you got?" Ingram asked.

"Take a look," Neal replied. He opened the accordion folder and removed a document. "Read it and tell me what you think." He handed the document to Ingram.

Ingram adjusted his granny glasses, scanned the document, wrinkled his forehead, and laughed. "Only one-point-five million?

She should've owned the company."

In 1982, a young woman named Maria Stern consulted San Francisco attorney Nancy Hersh. Stern had breast implants inserted several years earlier and shortly afterwards developed extreme fatigue and arthritis that her physician believed were caused by the implants. Hersh sent an associate, Dan Bolton, to the headquarters of the Dow Corning Corporation in Midland Michigan to review the company's files on breast implants. What he discovered would turn out to be the ultimate undoing of Dow Corning. The lawyers took the case to court in 1984, and the jury awarded Stern $211,000 compensatory damages and $1.5 million punitive damages. Dow Corning appealed, reached a settlement, and the court ordered that the evidence in the case was to be sealed.

"Anything else?" Ingram asked.

"One other case. In 1977, Rich Mitthoff sued Dow Corning and got his client a one hundred seventy thousand dollar jury award for pain and suffering. Apparently her implants ruptured and she needed several operations to fix the problem."

"Peanuts," Ingram sneered.

For most attorneys those sums would have been a pirate's treasure, but not for Ingram Mink. He set the bar so high that only a very few attorneys could ever approach it. In 1970, he obtained an award of $4 million for a client who had been badly burned in a car accident, at a time when awards of six figures were considered astronomical. That verdict represented the first million-dollar jury award in Arizona and the highest verdict ever awarded in the United States. It was after that award that the idea for the creation of the Centurion Counsel took seed. He wanted to create an elite organization of personal injury lawyers that stood apart from the hordes of ambulance chasers. When anyone who had been seriously injured needed an attorney to represent him because of a doctor's malpractice, a defective consumer product, or someone's wanton carelessness, he passionately believed that person was entitled to have the best of the best to be that person's advocate. The purpose of the organization would be to share their collective experience and methods in the courtroom, which their detractors called their tactics, in order to best serve their clients.

The organization would be known as the Centurion Counsel—a group of 100 men who would be available at any time to advise an injured person of his or her rights. To become a member, an attorney had to have successfully litigated a minimum of fifty court cases with at least one jury award of $1 million. In order to ensure a balanced geographic distribution there would be only one attorney in any one city who would be allowed to be a member of the Centurion Counsel. Continued membership was contingent upon obtaining $1 million awards every year after becoming a member. As a result, lawyers who were accepted as members of the Centurion Counsel cherry picked only cases that had a million dollar potential. Single-handedly, Ingram Mink changed the course of litigation in the U.S. forever.

He selected the name because the centurion of ancient Rome was often of humblest origin, promoted from the ranks because of his bravery and military efficiency. The Roman centurion could be relied upon to lead his soldiers in every campaign and battle with dedication and commitment, even to death. He was the role model for all soldiers. A counselor was a man of wisdom and sound advice. A member of the Centurion Counsel would be a centurion and a counselor.

The symbol of the Centurion Counsel would be the Taijitu, the diagram of ultimate power. In the Chinese Taoist religion the Taijitu was the yin and yang—opposites living in harmony. Yin was the dark side, representing the wrongdoers, and yang the side of light, representing the righteous. Neal Mink said it in simpler terms, the yin were the defense attorneys, and the yang were the plaintiffs' attorneys.

Coincidentally, another reason for its choice was that the mirror image of the Taijitu bore a striking resemblance to two intertwined number sixes, the number of zeros required in a jury award in order for a lawyer to be a member of the Centurions.

Ingram, ever the strategist, the chess grand master, saw immediately how to proceed. "We go for punitive damages. That's where the money is. Let's hit the deep pockets. What's the net worth of Dow Corning?"

"Billions. Their net profits will approach two hundred million on sales of close to two billion this year. I spoke with the attorney who represented Maria Stern in 1984. All he would tell me was that the court records were sealed as a condition of the settlement, which tells me that Dow has something so egregious to hide that if it were ever to come to light the company would be in deep shit."

"Buy them some shovels. They're going to need them. We're going to find out what they're hiding."

Chapter Five

Tucson, Arizona
Monday, December 17, 1990.

CAROL ANDREWS WAS a tall leggy blonde in her mid-forties, a three-time loser in the game of matrimony who after her last divorce had a body tune-up, which included a mini face-lift and a boob job. Now that she had all her hunting equipment in order she was preparing herself for another safari, and Neal Mink was the trophy she had set her sights on.

She wore a low cut Jovani black cocktail dress, purchased from Cele Peterson's, and a push up bra from Victoria's Secret that advertised her surgically enhanced breasts. The scars from her mini-face lift had faded and were imperceptible except to a trained eye. Her perfume exuded enough pheromones to attract a pride of lions, but she was interested only in the alpha male—Neal Mink. Her smile revealed perfectly aligned, like a sharks's, cap-enhanced, vanilla ice cream white teeth.

Neal had taken her to the Tack Room for a private party of two.

The Tack Room offered the finest gourmet dining in Tucson. In 1987, under the stewardship of David Vactor and his son Drew, it became the first restaurant in the Southwest to be awarded five stars by the Mobil Travel Guide. In its early years first time visitors would frequently miss the hidden entrance off Sabino Canyon Road. Drew realized the restaurant needed better signage, so in 1976, he commissioned artist Michael Kautza to design a sign that no one could miss; one that would be distinctive, yet not gaudy like the signs on Speedway Boulevard that gave the street the unflattering title of "The ugliest street in America." Kautza designed a 16-foot tall cowboy boot, built in two pieces in his back yard. No one ever drove by the entrance again. It became a Tucson landmark.

"So tell me Neal, how is it that a specimen like you has never been caged?"

Neal grinned, "I suppose I could say I've never found the right woman."

"Please. That is so trite, you can do better than that."

He sighed. "Do you know how many times I've been asked that question, and when it's asked I hear the six short and one long blasts that tell me it's time to abandon ship?"

She placed a finger on the back of his hand, and with slow deliberation traced a concentric circle with her blood-red, long manicured fingernail, that had the desired effect of arousing him. "Does that mean I should put on a life jacket?" A coquettish grin crossed her face. "Neal, I've no intention of trying to sink your ship," which was exactly her plan. "I've been to bat three times and have struck out each time. The last time was in the bottom of the ninth. The game is over. I'm officially retired."

He didn't believe her for a minute.

"The truth is, when I chose to be an advocate, I married my profession. I couldn't ask any woman to accept broken dates, canceled vacations, missed graduations, showing up late, if at all, for birthday parties. Marriage would've been a Catch-22 for me. I couldn't bear the thought of watching the disappointment on a child's face when I told him or her that I couldn't attend the school play because I had to interview someone in Bumfuck, Alaska. And I was unwilling to tell a client that I'd have to delay his or her case because I was going on vacation to Hawaii. Like a priest, I saw the law as a calling which didn't allow for a wife."

"But that doesn't mean you had to take an oath of celibacy," she said as her hand slipped under the table and walked its way up his thigh.

"Celibacy is definitely not part of the job description."

* * *

The valet retrieved Neal's red Ferrari. "Would you like to drive?" he asked her.

"Where would you like me to drive to?"

"I was thinking of breakfast at the Ventana room."

"Breakfast? But it's only ten o'clock at night, and besides the Ventana Room doesn't serve breakfast."

"Well, I guess we'll have to find something to do 'till then, and then have a room service breakfast," he grinned.

It was a short drive from the Tack Room to the Ventana Canyon Resort where Neal maintained a suite year round to entertain out of town clients and lady friends alike. The resort was a jewel. It was as if God had whispered in the ear of the resort's architect and told him where and how to build it—which may have been true. When Laurence Tisch, the CEO of Loews' resorts, and his architect were circling the property in a helicopter trying to decide where to build the new resort, Tisch saw water cascading from a waterfall on the side of the mountain and exclaimed, "This is it!" The 80-foot waterfall became the focal point of the resort. But, because the water only flowed during the monsoon season, a way had to be devised to make the waterfall a year-round attraction. They solved the problem by creating a 2.2 million gallon koi pond reservoir system that recycled the water back up the mountain by means of an incredibly powerful pump system. The resort was designed and built to co-exist and blend with the natural beauty of the mountains—not to compete with them.

The 600-thread count of the sheet that covered their naked bodies approximated the number of women he had bedded over the years. Each was different and each had a different story to tell. He traced his fingers, featherlike, over her right breast and gently squeezed it. She flinched and took his hand and placed it on her surgically tightened abdomen.

"I'm sorry. They're very sore and they don't feel right. I had breast implants about six months ago, and a couple of weeks ago they started to become hard and painful."

Neal sat upright in the bed and focused on her face.

"I went to see my plastic surgeon, and he told me it was no big deal—that he could fix the problem with a simple office procedure. He said he did it all the time."

"Did he use the word *problem*, and had he ever told you about the possibility that your breasts could become hard, before he did the surgery?" His mind flashed back to the Connie Chung interviews.

"I can't remember whether he did. He may have, but I was so excited at the prospect of having surgery I may not've heard him. However, he did say that there were never any problems with these implants. He said they were made of silicone, and that silicone was totally inert in the body. He said they would last forever."

"Did he tell you how he would fix the problem?"

She laughed. "He did more than that. He said the solution to the hardness was discovered strictly by accident. According to him a woman in Florida who had breast implants was at a party with her boy friend, a professional football player; they were horsing around and he picked her up and squeezed her. She felt something tear in her chest and she thought he had broken her implants, but when she felt them they were softer than they were before. She went to see her plastic surgeon the next day; he examined her and figured out that when her boyfriend squeezed her, he had broken down the scar tissue that had formed around the implants.

"When the doctor realized what had happened he called in several of his patients who had developed hardness, and he squeezed the breasts, and like the football player he broke down the scar tissue that had formed around the breasts."

"So, is that what your doctor did?"

"Yeah. He said I'd feel a little pressure for just a few seconds. *Pressure?* Ha! It was the most excruciating pain I'd ever felt, like someone had taken my breasts and put them in a vise and slowly tightened the handle. *A few seconds?* It felt like an eternity!"

Neal, ever the lawyer, mentally collated what Carol had just told him with what he had learned from the Chung interviews and the Maria Stern case.

The passion party was over.

"Carol would you be willing to come to my office next week? There's something I'd like to show you."

She looked puzzled, but agreed, nodding her head.

It would prove to be the biggest mistake of her life.

Two weeks earlier.

She wasted no words and dispensed with any niceties. "Dr. Powers, I don't understand, you said I would have no trouble with my implants. They were soft after you put them in, but they've become progressively harder." Ice in her voice.

"Carol, I think I know what the problem is. Let me have my nurse take you into an examining room where I'll check you. He pressed the intercom button on the phone. Almost immediately the door opened. "Angela, please take Carol into an examining room, I want to check her breasts."

Ungrateful bitch. I've turned her from an ugly duckling into a swan. What's the big deal? I know she likes things hard. Wasn't that why she wanted me to tighten her pleasure-port last year?

He took her chart from the holder on the door and riffled through it. *Hmm, just over six months. The induration doesn't usually appear this early. I wonder what's going on. She's the third one today, but the others didn't show any signs for almost a year.* He entered the room. She had refused a gown and was standing by the examining table, arms folded across her chest, exuding hostility and defiance.

He tried to melt the tension in the air with his seductive smile and soothing voice—to no avail. He unfolded her arms, stood back, and assessed her breasts. She stood, arms at her side, rigid as the guard at the Tomb of the Unknown Soldier. Powers placed his fingers first on her right and then on her left breast. *Right class III, a little distortion; left class II*, he thought.

He was referring to the Baker classification of the degree of severity of capsule formation associated with silicone breast implants. Class I being the least severe, and class IV being the most severe, with the augmented breast being hard, painful, cold, tender and visibly distorted.

"Well Carol, it appears that you've developed a little hardness of your breasts, but not to worry, I can easily fix that." He proceeded to tell her the story of the football player and how the closed capsulotomy treatment for the problem was discovered.

His nurse remained expressionless but thought, *a little hardness, who the hell does he think he's kidding? She's at least a class III.*

"Hop up on the table and we'll fix that in no time."

Like a lamb being led to slaughter she sat on the edge of the table not knowing what was coming next. He pulled out the foot piece of the table and asked her to lie on her back.

Without asking her permission, or telling her what he was going to do, he took her right breast between his large hands and began compressing it with increasing pressure from the heels of his hands. The pain she felt was as if she had been struck on the chest by a sledgehammer. She felt a tearing sensation in her breast…as if it were being ripped from her body. Before she could react, his hands were cupping her other breast, and this time not only did she feel the shearing of her breast, but she heard a muffled *pop!* It was over.

"There. That wasn't so bad, was it?"

She rubbed her hands over her breasts. They were sore as hell, but they were soft again. That maneuver brought back the memory of the soreness she felt between her legs the night she lost her virginity. That bastard hadn't asked her permission either. Before she could protest, her panties were pulled down, and the next thing she knew he was on top of her, and then the *pain...oh God...the pain.* He said the same goddamned thing that Powers said after it was over. Powers had the same supercilious smile on his face.

She regained her composure and returned his smile. "Actually doctor, it was pretty bad. It felt like the first time I got laid. I didn't know what to expect then either. He didn't ask me if I wanted to do it, but just like you, he did it anyway, and just like you, said, 'That wasn't so bad was it?'

"Bad? Not so bad you say! How do think you'd feel if I took your erect penis and put in the jaws of a grape press and tightened the handle with slow deliberation until you felt like it was going to explode, not with pleasure, but with indescribable pain. I guarantee that hard penis would become very soft…very…very quickly, as well."

I can't believe I just said that! She thought.

Powers' hands dropped to his side and ratcheted into fists. The smile vanished from his face.

It took the discipline of a Queen's Guard standing at attention at Buckingham Palace to keep Power's nurse from bursting into laughter.

"If you don't mind I'd like to get dressed now."

"Certainly. To keep your breasts soft, just squeeze them like this..."

She deflected his hand. "Please, they are very sore, just tell me what it is I have to do."

He cleared his throat. It had become very dry, as if someone had rammed a hair dryer in his mouth and turned it on full blast. "Very well." His teeth were clenched in rigor. "Take your breast between your hands and place your fingers at three and nine o'clock, then squeeze it and hold it in that position for one minute. Repeat the procedure with your fingers at twelve and six o'clock. Do the same with the other breast. If you do this three times a day for two weeks your breasts should remain soft."

"Three times a day? I can see doing the exercises when I get up in the morning, and when I go to bed at night. But when do you think I should do it the third time? At noon? At two? At four?

Should I just stop what I'm doing? If I'm showing a client a house, should I say? 'Excuse me for a few minutes, I have to go squeeze my tits.' Is that what I'm supposed to do?"

"I'm sure you'll be able to find a time that fits with your schedule," he winced.

"I'd like to check you again in six months." He turned and left the room. It took supreme control to keep him from slamming the door when he left the room.

He entered his office trying to control his rapid breathing. He picked up a breast implant that was sitting on his desk and threw it against the wall with the speed and force of a major league pitcher. It ruptured when it struck the wall. A gelatinous goo adhered to the wall and began to inch its way down, like the slime trail of a snail. The same thing was happening to the implants under the breast tissue of Carol Andrews.

"I'll schedule you an appointment for the first week in June, Carol," Angela said.

It was an appointment she would never keep.

Powers regained his composure. He checked his hair in the large, gold leaf rococo framed mirror on the wall behind his desk. *I can't believe that bitch. After all I've done for her. She was the one who begged me to do something with her breasts. She was the one who felt self-conscious when men tried to fondle her breasts because they were so not there. She was the one who wanted a vaginoplasty, because she felt her lovers were entering the Grand Canyon when she had sex. She was the one who wanted her face repaved because of all the cracks in the road. I made that tramp beautiful. So she thought I squeezed her breasts too hard. I don't imagine she feels that way when her cadres of lovers squeeze them. Lovers! She'll get over it. She'd better get over it!*

He sat down at his desk and saw the light blinking on his phone. He pushed the button, and Angela opened the door. "Has she left?"

"Yes doctor. I gave her an appointment for six months."

"Good. That'll give her time to cool off."

She hesitated, "...I have Louise Purcell in the waiting room."

"What's that hypochondriac doing here? I told her I wouldn't have to see her again."

"I know, but she said she wouldn't leave until you saw her. She threatened to start screaming if you didn't talk to her."

"Alright. Bring her in, but when I buzz your station I want you to knock on the door and tell me I have an emergency at the hospital."

Louise Purcell shuffled into his office in and eased herself into a chair. Her dark hair was disheveled, and her eyes red, vacant, and ringed with fatigue. She looked as if she had not slept for days. She was sick. She was only thirty-four, but appeared ten years older. Her voice was strong, and she spoke with purpose and determination. "You said the implants had nothing to do with my fatigue and total body pain."

He sighed. "Louise we've been over this many times. I've told you there is absolutely no evidence in the literature to suggest that breast implants cause any of the things you are complaining about. They're made of silicone, and silicone is completely inert in the body. There are hundreds of medical devices that are made from silicone, and there have never been any problems with them."

"Well I don't think your *literature* has ever had a breast implant. I have, and until I did, I never had any health problems. You were the one who said, 'I've never seen such a healthy specimen.' Well let me tell you something doctor, this *specimen* is anything but healthy now. I had to quit my job. I can barely make breakfast for my children. I can't have sex with my husband. It's an effort for me to get out of bed. My husband has to support me when I take a shower so I don't collapse. This is not what I signed on for when I had the surgery.

"I've seen every specialist I can think of, and none of them could find a reason for my problems until I saw a rheumatologist this morning; she told me there was no doubt in her mind that the cause of my problems is directly related to the implants. She said I probably had human adjuvant disease—an autoimmune syndrome in which the body becomes extremely sensitive to an injected foreign material—because of the silicone in my body.

"She recommended I consult a lawyer if I couldn't get any satisfaction from you."

"Human adjuvant disease? I have no idea what you're talking about," he muttered. "You weren't injected with anything."

"My rheumatologist thinks the implants have ruptured and that silicone is leaking into my body, just as if the silicone had been injected. If you don't do something I'm going to sue your ass off. If you had told me those things could happen, I would never have had the surgery."

He was trying to control the rage he felt. "Louise, if you recall, you came to see me because of the strong history of breast cancer in your family. *You* were the one who wanted your breasts removed so you wouldn't have to worry about developing breast cancer. And *you* were the one who begged me to reconstruct your breasts so you wouldn't look like a freak. And for four years you were delighted with the results.

"For the past three years when every other doctor you saw told you they couldn't find anything wrong with you, I was the only one who would listen to you, with the exception of that charlatan who convinced you that you had Lyme Disease...to the tune of...what was it...fifty thousand dollars?

"So now, all of a sudden it's your breast implants that are responsible for your symptoms. Did it ever occur to you that your problems would've developed even if you never had the implants put in?"

"Not according to Dr. Shanklin."

Who the hell is Dr. Shanklin? "I'm sorry Louise I don't know this Dr. Shanklin. Is that the rheumatologist who blames the implants for your symptoms?"

"Yes. She said she's seen other women who've had breast implants with problems like mine." Louise didn't see him push the button on his phone.

The door opened.

"Angela, you know I'm not to be disturbed when I'm with a patient."

"I'm sorry doctor, but the hospital called and said it was an emergency."

"Louise, if you want me to speak to your doctor—"

"It's too late for that. You'll be hearing from my lawyer."

CHAPTER SIX

Tucson, Arizona
Thursday, December 20, 1990.

CONFUSED WAS THE only word to describe how Carol felt after Neal turned off the VCR and ejected the cassette. "Neal, I don't understand, why did you show me that, and what do those women have to do with me?"

"Carol, I don't want to scare you, but there are some facts you should know..."

"You don't want to scare me? What you just showed me was a three-alarm-fire, and I feel like I'm right in the middle of it, and I don't have a clue what I'm supposed to do."

"We think there may be some problems with the breast implants that the manufacturers and the doctors are not disclosing. When you told me that your breasts had become hard shortly after the surgery and what your doctor did to fix the problem, I wondered how many other women were having the same problem. We need to know what's not being disclosed, and the only way we're going to find that out is to examine the manufacturers' records, and the only way we're going to get access to those records is by taking them and the doctors to court. "In 1984, a woman sued the manufacturer of her implants because she developed some medical problems that her family doctor said were caused by her implants. The jury awarded her $1.5 million in punitive damages. We don't know the reason, because as part of the settlement the evidence was sealed."

Carol was a very successful real estate agent and knew how to close a deal. She understood where Neal was taking her and she was seeing the dollar signs. "So what is it you want me to do?"

* * *

NEAL WALKED INTO Ingram's office waving a paper in the air. "She's on board. When I told her how much Maria Stern got in her settlement her eyes started flashing like she'd hit the jackpot on a slot machine. Also, she knows a few other women who've had implants put in, and she's going to talk to them and find out if they've had any kind of problems."

"Good. We're going to have to move fast. We'll need to get the Counsel involved. If we get a couple of claims started in each city Dow and the other manufacturers won't know what's hit them. We don't know how many cases they've settled without ever having gone to court, but we're sure as hell going to find out. If they think they can just settle a few cases and walk away, then they're in for the surprise of their lives.

"Once we have a few mega-awards, and believe me we will, Dow and the other manufacturers will clamor to settle, just like the Japanese did after Hiroshima and Nagasaki. It'll be an unconditional surrender. Dow has too much to lose, and I predict they'll roll over and go for a chapter eleven by the time we're finished with them. As soon as there are a couple of awards the media will take over and do the advertising for us, but we'll have to be the first kids on the block and get an award big enough to make them realize their ship is in danger of sinking.

"And as soon as *that* hits the news, women will be clamoring to sue, even if they have no problems. They'll see a lottery. There'll be no possible way to handle them all on an individual basis so we'll need to start a class action. Once we do that, the bottom feeders will be lining up to get a few crumbs of the action. Dow and the other manufacturers will sprint for chapter eleven protection, and when *that* happens the big party will be over. I wonder how much they'll offer to pony up after we drop their own napalm and Agent Orange on them?"

The irony wasn't lost on Neal. Dow Chemical was the creator of napalm and Agent Orange. He laughed. "I think we should send Miss Chung *a hundred dozen roses*."

"Let's get the paperwork started on Andrews. We'll name everyone that even looked at those implants. A wide net will catch more fish than casting a single line into the weeds. We'll start with Carol's doctor as a diversion while we prepare the heavy artillery for the manufacturers. With the doctor it'll be like shooting fish in a barrel. How long do you think it'll take to put everything together?"

For most lawyers it would take at least a month working overtime. Neal said, "Give me a week."

CHAPTER SEVEN

Tucson, Arizona
Monday, January 7, 1991.

THE RED LIGHT FLASHED at the nurse's station. Powers was ready to see his next patient. Angela escorted Adele Grant and her husband into Powers' office.

"Dr. Powers, this is my husband Greg. He wants to hear just what it is you're going to do tomorrow."

Powers smiled and gestured for them to sit in the chairs in front of his desk. He stood until they were seated before he sat down. Powers always insisted that his patients have a second consultation the day before their scheduled surgery. Experience had shown him, and statistics substantiated it, that most patients retained less than twenty percent of what had been discussed in an initial consultation. He tape recorded all his consultations, but never advised his patients that he was doing so. Arizona was a one party state, so he could legally record their conversation without them being aware of it. This practice had proved invaluable several times when patients claimed they had never been informed that a particular complication could occur, when in fact they had been informed. Lawsuits had been averted each time, except once, when a patient, Donna Rivers, had been so incensed with him that she told him she would take her chances in court. She couldn't get a lawyer to represent her, so she represented herself *in pro per*. The sum she wanted was so paltry the insurance company wouldn't even consider defending him in court. The company pointed out to him that it would cost more to defend the case than to settle it and make her go away. Powers wanted to fight the claim, but he was reminded that the terms of his policy were quite specific: If he didn't accept the company's offer to settle, and agreed upon by the plaintiff, then if the case went to trial and a jury awarded a sum that was greater than the amount offered in a settlement, then he would be responsible for the difference. Reluctantly he agreed. Rivers had developed thick, slow healing, painful scars in the folds of both breasts. Powers suspected she had been picking at the scars, and that was the reason they didn't heal properly. She claimed Powers told her she wouldn't have any scars. After the settlement her incisions healed as if by magic. She did go away, but like herpes, she would return. She had seen the Connie Chung *Face to Face* special.

"Mr. Grant I'm delighted to meet you. I suppose Adele has explained everything to you."

"I think so, but I'd like to hear it from you, and I do have several questions that I'd like to ask." He removed a piece of paper from his pocket with the questions written on it.

"Certainly. I'll explain the operation, and then if you still have any questions, I'll be happy to answer them.

"First let me show you the type of implants that I'll be using. As Adele probably told you there are several types of implants that can be used. There are the saline-filled implants, which I never use, because of the possibility that they could leak. If they did, the body would absorb the saline, but the implant would have to be removed and replaced. Statistics have shown that the failure rate can be as high as forty-five percent. Another reason that I don't use them is because some patients feel a sloshing sensation when they walk.

"The second type is the gel implant, of which there are two types. The first is the textured gel type, and the second is made with a double lumen. The inner part is the gel, and there is a second chamber in which we put a small amount of saline to adjust the size, if necessary, so the breasts will be more equal in size. But no two breasts are ever equal, or exactly in the same position on the chest wall. So to try and make them exactly equal is not necessary. If they are significantly unequal then I would make an adjustment of the smaller breast. I prefer to use the textured type because it produces the best results, and the scarring that forms around them is reduced because the irregular surface prevents the capsule, or natural scar, from forming a continuous sheet, which is more likely to create the hardness we occasionally will see." He showed him the implants.

"There are three different ways to insert the implants; through the nipple; through the armpit, or through a small incision made in the natural crease of the breast, which is the incision I prefer for several reasons. First, it is the easiest and has the least potential for problems. Should a thick scar develop there the breast will cover it, but if such a scar develops around the nipple it can be very obvious and painful. The scar in the armpit is hidden, but in the rare incidence where bleeding may occur after the surgery it would be necessary to return the patient to surgery and make an incision in the breast crease, because it's very difficult to find the bleeding point through an incision made in the armpit. It's much easier to view and stop any bleeding through a breast crease incision.

"Now I'm ready for your questions."

"You explained everything pretty well, so we'll go along with your recommendations." He checked the sheet with his questions. "Well, you answered my questions about where you'd make the cut and how big the scar would be. I just need to know if there are any problems with the gel implants."

He had not seen the Connie Chung special either.

"As I explained to Adele, occasionally, the scar tissue that forms around the implant, which is called a capsule, may become a little thickened, but it's easily corrected by a simple procedure called a closed capsulotomy, which I can do here in the office. Basically, I put a little pressure on the breast to break the capsule. It takes less than a minute."

"But couldn't you break the implant doing that?"

"That's highly unlikely, because the capsule would break before the implant would, and I know when to stop so it doesn't happen."

"Will I feel anything during the surgery?" Adele asked.

"Absolutely not. You'll be given a medication called Versed, which will cause total amnesia, and the local anesthesia will freeze the nerves. So no, you won't feel any pain." *Doesn't the stupid bitch remember anything I told her?*

"Well I think that covers everything," Greg said.

"Well then, when you leave, stop at the desk, and Angela will give you your pre-operative instructions and have you sign the consent form. Your surgery is scheduled for nine o'clock in the morning, but you'll need to be here at 7:00 a.m. I'll see you then."

He pushed the call button and stood up. The audience was over. Angela appeared and escorted the Grants from Powers' office.

"Here are the instructions and consent forms," Angela said. "Read them over carefully and tell me if you see anything that is unclear."

Adele studied the consent form. She looked up and said, "They seem pretty straightforward." She signed the form.

There was nothing in the form that said anything about the possibility that the implants could rupture.

CHAPTER EIGHT

Tucson, Arizona
Tuesday, January 8, 1991.

POWERS SAT AT his desk trying to make sense of the events of the last few weeks. He had finally watched the video of the Connie Chung show, and his reaction was summed up in one word. *Bullshit!* He thought, *visual yellow press at its finest. What do pathologists know about living breathing patients? They have their slides and microscopes, and that's it. Did Miss Chung ask a real doctor, a plastic surgeon, to present what really goes on with patients? Where did she find these women? They sounded just like that bitch Louise Purcell.*

His reverie was interrupted by a flashing red light. They were ready in surgery.

His surgery center was state of the art, designed by Stantec, the leading medical architectural firm in the country. The center had the most up-to-date medical devices and equipment to ensure absolute patient comfort and safety. A contingency plan had been provided for every possible complication…except one…human error.

* * *

"Good morning Adele, are we ready?"

"I'm a little nervous. You're sure I won't feel anything?"

"Absolutely."

He towered over her as she lay on the operating table. He was wearing a black scrub suit with his name and logo, a lotus flower—the Japanese symbol of perfection and enlightenment—embroidered in gold thread over the pocket. That was how he saw himself, Devin Powers...The Lotus Flower...Perfect...The Enlightened. The gold thread was about to unravel.

He nodded to the anesthesiologist who then inserted a syringe containing Versed, the amnesic medication, into the IV port of the tubing that snaked its way to the needle inserted in the back of her hand, and depressed the plunger.

"Good night Adele," Powers said.

She smiled and then she was gone. When she awoke she would be in the recovery room and remember nothing. He turned and left the OR to go scrub.

While most hospital-based surgeons were still using their knees to control the water handles located under the scrub sink to turn on the water, and their feet to compress the valve that allowed the soap dispenser to squeeze out foam to scrub their hands, Powers employed the latest in motion detectors to turn on the faucet and dispense the soap. He dried his hands with UV sterilized hot air. The door to the operating room was also motion controlled. He made contact with nothing that might harbor harmful microbes. He was a fanatic when it came to sterility.

He completed the hand washing ritual and entered the operating room holding out his arms to be gowned and gloved, like the pope extending his arms to bless the multitudes. After Adele was prepped and draped with sterile linens Powers approached the table and pushed down on her right breast to accentuate the breast fold. He then held out his other hand. His scrub nurse knew every step of the operation and how to respond to his every move. Talking was not allowed in the operating room. She placed a sterile marking pen in his hand, and he drew an inch long purple line in the fold. The pen was replaced with a scalpel, and following the line, he made an incision, stopping when he reached the chest wall. The punctate bleeding was controlled with an electrocautery. He then placed a retractor in the incision and lifted the skin. Using the electrocautery to separate the tissues, he created a plane between the breast tissue and the thin fibrous tissue layer that enveloped the pectoral muscle. He removed the retractor and inserted his index finger in the plane he had created and moved it back and forth, like the blade of a windshield wiper, until he had created the desired sized pocket. He then took the retractor, lifted the skin, and like a spelunker shone his headlamp into the cave, looking for bleeding points akin to a dripping stalactite. He irrigated the pocket with sterile saline, and once he was satisfied there was no bleeding he changed his gloves and raised the implant from the sterile basin with the reverence of a priest preparing the transubstantiation of the host…which, in a sense he was. A priest transubstantiated the host into the body of Christ, and Powers would transubstantiate the silicone implant into the body of Adele Grant.

When the implant lay flat it measured about four inches in diameter and its volume was 260 cc. He was going to squeeze this into the pocket created through a one-inch incision.

He took the implant, laid it on her chest, and started to nudge it through the incision. Like the back and forth motion of a bull pawing in the sand his fingers advanced the implant into the pocket until it vanished like the last traces of a lion's mane jellyfish being devoured by a pink-sea-anemone bed.

He repeated the dissection on the opposite breast. When he had created the desired pocket and was certain there was no bleeding he inserted the other implant. He then took the needle holder in his left hand and a sharp multi-toothed alligator forceps in his right, and began to close the incisions. When he grasped the skin of the right breast with the forceps he was unaware that a tooth of the forceps nicked the implant…just barely, but enough to set up a chain of events that would end in disaster.

* * *

By four o'clock in the afternoon he had completed three other augmentations and a face-lift. He was sitting at his desk reviewing the cases for the next day's surgery when the red light on his phone started flashing. He depressed the button and put it on speakerphone.

"Yes, Andrea."

"There's a deputy from the sheriff's department who says he has to see you."

"Did he say what it was about?"

"No, only that it was important that he see you. Should I bring him to your office?"

Puzzled, Powers said, "Yes, bring him back."

The deputy was a massive black man standing six-feet-five-inches and weighed about 240 pounds. To say he was intimidating would be an understatement.

"Dr. Powers?"

"Yes, officer may I ask what is so urgent that you have see me without scheduling an appointment?"

The deputy unfazed by Powers' arrogance smiled and said, "These will explain everything." He handed Powers the papers he was holding.

"Dr. Powers...you have been served."

Having the Sheriff serve the legal papers was the opening gambit that Ingram Mink often used when he initiated a lawsuit. He knew that a civilian process server would rarely get past the front desk to serve an individual. But the sheriff? It always worked, and it always raised the recipient's anxiety level. And that's what he wanted. Anxiety. The papers could be left with a receptionist, but when the named person was served directly, that person could never claim that he hadn't received them.

Mink was right. Powers was shaken. His first inclination was to file it, without reading it, and then call MICA—Mutual Insurance Company of Arizona—and let them deal with it. But he was curious to see if Louise Purcell had followed through with her threat to sue him. He wasn't concerned about her. None of her complaints had anything to do with her breast surgery. And it wasn't until she saw that rheumatologist that she had any reason to complain about her breasts. When he saw the name of the plaintiff on the subpoena… Carol Andrews, he thought, *Oh crap, she's suing me. For what? Because she hurt a little after I broke the capsule.* He read the rest of the complaint and became livid.

This is what the defendant has done to cause the damages I am claiming: (state wrongful acts)

1. Failure to inform. The defendant failed to inform me that my breasts could become hard after the surgery. Had I known this could occur I would not have had the surgery performed.

2. Assault on my person. When I visited the defendant in his office on December 1, 1990, and informed him of my concern, he made me lie down on an examining table. He examined my breasts and then told me he could correct the problem with a simple procedure, and then without asking my permission, or giving me the opportunity to make an informed decision, he grabbed my breast and squeezed it so hard I thought I would faint. The pain was indescribable, and before I could react he did the same thing to my other breast.

3. Pain and suffering. I have not felt the same since the defendant assaulted me. My breasts have remained sore and tender to the point where I have to take prescription pain and sleep medications at night.

4. Loss of income. Because of the pain I cannot wear clothing suitable for the performance of my occupation as a real estate agent. I have had to refer six clients to other agents because I could not keep the appointments. My commissions would have been approximately $350,000.00.

I am asking the court to award me judgment against the defendant in the sum of $5 *million.*

"It won't happen," he fumed, "she'll never get a nickel."

By the end of the month he had been served six more times

CHAPTER NINE

Tucson, Arizona
Monday, February 11, 1991.

"CAROL, I THINK your implant has ruptured."

"Ruptured? How is that possible, Dr. Phillips?"

"I believe that when Dr. Powers broke down the scar tissue the pressure must have ruptured the implant as well. That would explain why you have this distortion now."

"But, my breast didn't look like this after he broke down the scar tissue. It was sore for a couple of weeks, but my breasts looked normal until last week when I felt this lump in my armpit, and noticed that the skin around my right breast was getting red and sore again."

"When you called me I checked the literature, but couldn't find anything that would explain what you told me. I spoke with several other plastic surgeons in town after you called. None were willing to see you because they didn't want to get involved with another plastic surgeon's patient, especially since you were having a problem. They all said you should go back to Dr. Powers and let him take care of it. Have you discussed this with Dr. Powers?"

"No. There's no way I'll let that arrogant SOB near me again. I think that bastard actually enjoyed hurting me when he broke those capsules. And there's no way he'd want to see me anyway, since I'm suing him."

"Well, I spoke with a medical school classmate, who is a pathologist in Cleveland, and he put me in touch with a plastic surgeon, Dr. Peter Newton, with whom he works. He said he's probably the most experienced plastic surgeon in the country when it comes to dealing with women who've had problems with their implants. I spoke with him, and he's willing to see you."

"Cleveland? You mean I have to go to Cleveland to have someone see me?"

He sighed. "Carol, I don't think there are too many plastic surgeons in the country who would be willing to see you now, especially since you've filed a lawsuit against another doctor."

"But why not?"

"Because there's a very good chance that your lawyers would try to drag them into the lawsuit as well. That's how the legal system works in this country. Carol, the only reason I'm seeing you is because I've been your gynecologist for twenty-five years."

* * *

"I just got off the phone with Carol Andrews. Apparently she's developed some other problems with her breasts."

Neal explained to Ingram what Carol had told him.

"So she's going to Cleveland?"

"Yes."

"When?"

"Tomorrow. I reminded her we had a deposition with Powers scheduled on Thursday, but she said the doctor in Cleveland wanted to see her right away."

Ingram thought for a moment and then said, "Actually that may work to our advantage. We both know there's no way in hell that this case is worth five million. I just want to use it to get the defense's attention. If we were to proceed with only the damages listed in the complaint they might offer us a bone just to get rid of us, but if it turns out that she has a ruptured implant then the ante will go up significantly.

"We'll take the deposition on Thursday without amending the complaint, because if we do, it'll give them an additional twenty days to respond. I know they're anxious to defuse these cases as quickly as possible, so let's not disappoint them. Besides, Thursday is Valentine's Day. It's time for another massacre."

On the morning of St. Valentine's Day in 1929, seven men were gunned down in cold blood in a garage in Chicago, orchestrated by mobster Al Capone...The Valentine's Day Massacre. This Valentine's Day in 1991, it would be Devin Powers who would be massacred.

* * *

Ingram scheduled the deposition to be held in Powers' office because he knew Powers would let his guard down in the comfort and familiarity of his own surroundings. Let him think he was in charge. The defense attorneys were surprised that Mink suggested the deposition be held there because Mink always wanted everyone on the defense team to feel intimidated by the pictures of the jury award checks that hung on his walls. Not today. He was employing a chess tactic known as *Zwischenzug*, a ploy aimed to deceive an opponent with a surprise move made in the buildup to the real line of attack. In other words, he was setting them up for the kill. They didn't know that the claim for damages was going to be amended when Mink learned the results of Carol Andrews' surgery.

Powers was a little ruffled because three more chairs had to be brought into his office to accommodate an additional three people. It would upset the *feng shui* of his office. Like tag team wrestlers the two lawyers from MICA and the Mink brothers took their chairs, positioning themselves for the opening attack. The court reporter was the referee and Powers was the spectator. MICA always employed the law firm of Horscht and Becker to represent their clients. Neal irreverently referred to them as the Katzenjammer Kids, Hans and Fritz, the irascible characters from Rudolph Dirks comic strip of the same name. Horscht was Hans and Becker was

Fritz.

After the opening remarks and formalities were stated and recorded, Ingram began.

"Dr. Powers, thank you for taking the time to speak with us. I have only a few questions, and then you'll be able to get back to your busy practice." A hint of sarcasm coated with honey. "When Carol Andrews consulted you on Wednesday May 2, 1990, did you inform her that there was a possibility that her breasts could become hard after the surgery?"

"Of course. I thoroughly discuss that possibility with all patients. Ms. Andrews was no exception. In fact, I record all my consultations, and I have the tape of that consultation right here." He opened his desk drawer and removed a cassette.

Neal suppressed a smile. *Didn't his lawyers tell the arrogant fool that the answer to any question was either 'yes or no?' Never embellish.*

Ingram glared at Powers and then at his lawyers. "We weren't advised of any tapes in discovery. Why are we just learning about this now?"

Hans shrugged, "We didn't know either...Dr. Powers?"

"I thought you just wanted my documents."

Ingram's voice dripped acid. "No doctor, the subpoena was very clear, it asked for all records. For the record, I object to the introduction of this tape, but let's hear what it has to say."

A tape recorder was produced, they played the tape and the proper notation was recorded. Tag: Neal's turn. He had no notes. "That's interesting doctor; you said there was a slight possibility that a little hardness could occur sometime after the surgery, and that it could be corrected by a simple office procedure?"

"You heard the tape. So as you can see, her allegation that she was never told induration could occur is preposterous. I don't know why she was so surprised when it did occur."

Shmuck. Keep talking. Why don't those yo-yos tell him to shut up? "Doctor are you aware that in November, 1988, Dr. Nirmal

Mishra presented scientific studies to the FDA's General and Plastic Surgery Devices Advisory Committee with evidence that the most common, widely acknowledged problem with breast implants was 'capsular contracture,' with an occurrence rate of up to seventy-five percent of patients in published studies, averaging forty percent?"

"I have never heard those numbers before. And certainly, they're not representative of what I see in my practice."

Tag: Ingram took over.

"Well, what percentage do you see, doctor?" asked Ingram

"I don't keep track of percentages; I just know that the numbers are not that high."

Change direction.

"On the tape you said, 'there is a slight chance that a little hardness can develop around the implant, and if it does, I can correct it with a simple procedure.' Are those your words?"

Powers was becoming agitated. "Yes. You heard the tape. I believe the words you lawyers use *are res ipsa loquitur*...the thing speaks for itself."

Ingram grinned, "Oh yes doctor, the thing does speak for itself.

"Would you agree that a closed capsulotomy is a medical procedure?"

"Yes."

"And that a face lift, a rhinoplasty, a tummy-tuck, and a breast augmentation are all medical procedures?"

"Yes."

"Do you require a patient to sign a consent form for a face-lift, a rhinoplasty, a tummy-tuck, and a breast augmentation before you will perform these surgeries?"

"Of course. And if you read those forms you'll see that the details of the operation and all possible complications are explained in minute detail."

Hans and Fritz were starting to squirm. He was volunteering far too much information. Hans leaned over and whispered something in his ear. Powers nodded.

"Did you have Carol Andrews sign a consent form before you performed the medical procedure of closed capsulotomy on her breasts on December 1, 1990?"

White queen to f3...check.

Powers stammered…"A capsulotomy is not the same thing."

"No? Are you saying that a procedure in which you grab a woman's breast and squeeze it with such force that she feels like she is going to pass out..."

Fritz shook his head. "Objection! Inflammatory. Lack of foundation."

Neal wondered when they would hear from defense counsel.

"Let me go back to the tape for a minute," Ingram continued. "You said, 'There is a slight chance that a little hardness could develop around the breast implant'. Your office notes state that Carol Andrews developed a Baker II on her left breast and a Baker III on her right breast. Doctor, in the Baker classification of relative hardness of breast capsules, doesn't a class III mean the breast is firm and appears abnormal…and do you consider a breast which exhibits the criteria of a Baker III just a little hard?"

"No, but..."

"Thank you doctor, you have answered my question. So, we have a situation in which you performed a medical procedure without a signed consent, which in turn caused considerable pain and suffering..."

Hans almost rose from his chair, "Objection! Foundation."

"Well then, you failed to disclose the true incidence of capsular contracture and just stated that you did not know what percentage of your patients did develop this problem, but that is was lower than what statistics suggested...but had no documentation to prove this..."

"Objection!" Hans stammered. "Counsel is badgering and offering closing argument..."

"I have no further questions." Ingram closed his folder.

The defense attorneys couldn't believe that was all he had to ask. This was the famous Ingram Mink? If that was all he had, they were certain they could settle the case for *bupkis*…virtually nothing. They had no questions. They also had no idea what was coming next.

The lawyers all shook hands, Like in a wrestling match the apparent animosity among the lawyers during the deposition was all show. Tomorrow they would be drinking cocktails together.

Neal turned and smiled at Powers. "Dr. Powers, thank you for your cooperation. I know it's not a pleasant experience to be put on the spot with a bunch of lawyers gnawing at you, but we're just doing our job.

"Your office is stunning. These furnishings are exquisite." As he scanned the room he saw an object on the back wall that tried to coax something from his distant memory. He paused, trying to remember. After what seemed an eternity he approached the wall and touched the object. What at first he thought was a patch of rust, he soon realized was a patch of dried blood. A long time dried.

Powers had regained his composure, and like a peacock he was ready to fan his feathers. "Thank you Mr. Mink. That object you seem so enthralled with is a Polish Ceremonial Shepherd's axe. It belonged to my father."

Ingram Mink's eyes bored into the axe. He had seen it before.

* * *

After the lawyers had left, Powers had Angela remove the extra chairs and place the consultation chairs back in their original position. He stared at the summons again and then removed the six others from his desk drawer and squeezed them as if he were performing a capsulotomy. He raised his eyes and focused on the Shepherd's Axe on the wall and thought, she'll pay...they all will pay.

CHAPTER TEN

Cleveland, Ohio
Tuesday, February 12, 1991.

THE PLANE TOUCHED down with barely a thump at Cleveland's Hopkins International Airport. Carol sat in the first row, and was the first passenger to deplane. Having only a carry-on she headed directly to the taxi stand. Normally, it was a thirty-minute drive from the airport to Mt. Sinai Hospital where Dr. Newton's office was located. The snowfall of the last couple days had been cleared from the roads, so the taxi was able to get there in just over that amount of time. She decided to check into her hotel after she had seen the doctor.

* * *

"Well Carol, Dr. Phillips was correct. Your right implant has definitely ruptured. The lump you feel in your axilla is probably extravasated silicone, which means the silicone has migrated to your armpit. It's possible that the left one has ruptured as well, but I won't know for certain until I remove it. I think we should schedule the surgery as soon as possible."

Carol stuttered, "M-my plastic surgeon never told me that the implants could rupture."

"Carol, I've seen many women with this problem. Most of them had a spontaneous rupture of their implants, and some, like you, after a capsulotomy."

"But he said they would last forever. I feel so deflated." She attempted a smile, "Both literally and figuratively."

"We're going to need some special studies, including an MRI, before we do the surgery." He spent the next hour explaining what tests needed to be done and a step-by-step explanation of what the surgery would entail, and what was expected of her post-operatively.

"We should have all the tests completed by Friday, and I have an opening on Monday in my surgery schedule, if that works for you."

"It doesn't seem like I have a lot of choices, do I?"

Dr. Newton squeezed her hand. "I'll take good care of you."

* * *

When she left Tucson the temperature was a pleasant fifty-three degrees, and when she arrived in Cleveland it was a brisk twenty-four degrees. The streets had been cleared of snow, so with her overnight bag in tow, Carol decided to walk the short, less than half-mile distance to the Glidden House, the historic B&B where she was staying. Many faces passed her, but she saw no one; she was oblivious to the sights and sounds of the city. The only winter clothes she had were her ski clothes, which she wore on the plane. When she arrived she raised her eyes in disbelief. The imposing structure before her was far more magnificent than advertised.

The Glidden House wasn't a B&B; it was a mansion. Blanketed against the snow it was a Christmas card. Francis Kavenaugh Glidden, the son of the founder of the Glidden Paint and Varnish Company, and his wife Mary Grasseli Glidden constructed the house in 1910. It typified the eclectic French Gothic style of architecture that was prevalent in that once-elite residential area of Cleveland.

In 1987, it was restored to its original splendor by a group of investors. It was precise in every detail, and in 1989, it was re-opened as a B&B to serve as a unique resting place for the needs of the many visitors to University Circle.

When Carol told Neal that she was going to Cleveland, it was he who suggested the Glidden House, and it was he who reserved a suite for her, anticipating that she would be having surgery. He wanted her to have comfortable surroundings while she convalesced, and a place for a nurse to stay after her discharge from hospital. When she protested the cost, he reminded her that it wasn't she who'd ultimately be paying for her medical bills and expenses. There was nothing in the statutes that said she couldn't go first class all the way. And monies awarded for future medical expenses would be in large part determined by previously incurred expenses.

She wheeled her suitcase into the reception foyer and was greeted by a pleasant, generic, bubbly, twenty-something desk clerk. She went through the ritual of presenting her credit card, and was given a key to access her suite and the usual "Hope you have a pleasant stay with us."

Her stay would prove to be anything but.

She declined assistance with her bag and took the elevator to the top floor. There were four suites on the uppermost level of the B&B, but hers was the only one occupied. February was not a good month to visit Cleveland, and when it snowed in February, it was even a worse month to visit. Six to eight inches of snow was expected in the next couple of days, and as a result occupancy at the Glidden was at a seasonal low. Normally there was twenty-four hour desk service available, but because of the expected storm and the fact there were few reservations scheduled, only the security officer would be there to assist guests after midnight that week.

The elevator opened directly in front of her suite. When she opened the door to the Mansion Suite she was greeted by a queen's residence. She felt as if she had stepped into another era. There was a gas fireplace with a carved stone mantel. The logs were so well crafted they appeared authentic. A swooning couch was placed in an alcove with dormer windows. Carol took off her ski jacket and went into the bedroom. Like the living room it was tastefully decorated with vintage furniture. The bed was what she wanted. She was beyond tired. There was one thing to do before she crawled under the fluffed-up down comforter. She was going to call that bastard Powers and tell him what Dr. Newton had found.

* * *

"Dr. Powers I have Carol Andrews on line two. She is calling long distance from Cleveland. She wants her medical records faxed to a doctor Newton at Mt. Sinai Medical Center, or directly to her at the hotel where she is staying, the Glidden House in Cleveland, and she would like to speak with you."

"Send him the records, but tell her I will not speak to her except in the presence of my attorney."

Newton. He had heard that name before. He was the hired gun that plaintiffs' lawyers from across the country were referring patients to…the Silicone Doctor.

CHAPTER ELEVEN

Tucson, Arizona
Saturday, February 16, 1991.

HE PARKED HIS car at the long-term parking lot at Tucson International Airport even though he would be there less than 48 hours. It was the anonymity of the lot he wanted. He walked to where the Cessna 414A Chancellor was hangered. He didn't file a flight plan because he planned to fly VFR—visual flight rules—to Kansas City to refuel, and from there directly to Akron where he'd rent a car for the 40 minute drive to Cleveland. The Cessna had a range of 1,528 miles with a maximum air speed of 235 k/hr. Akron was about 1,500 nautical miles from Tucson. With the stop to refuel in Kansas City he estimated the flight would take him just over seven hours. Akron had received six inches of snow the day before, but the weather called for clear flying conditions for the rest of the weekend. He'd be back in Tucson by late Sunday afternoon.

* * *

Three days of grueling tests and examinations had left Carol exhausted. She planned to sleep in and spend Sunday reading in front of the fireplace. She wasn't looking forward to having her implants removed on Monday, and she was concerned because Dr. Newton couldn't tell her how long the surgery would take. Each case was different she was told. She tried reading for a while, but her eyelids were protesting, so she turned off the light and wrapped herself in the down comforter and was soon asleep.

When the light vanished from her window he returned to his car. He'd come back around three in the morning. He made a call to the hotel earlier, making inquiries as if he were going to make a reservation, and told the receptionist he didn't know what time he would arrive, but it would be late. The receptionist told him there'd be no one at the front desk after midnight, but assured him someone from security would be available to provide him keys if he were a late arrival. The front door was always open. He told her he would call back when he finalized his schedule. She had told him what he needed to know.

The street was deserted. His only companions were a few scattered snowflakes trying to make a statement. He parked his car on a street two blocks away from the Glidden House, inconspicuously sandwiched between two other nondescript cars. The temperature was seven degrees above zero, so if anyone were around and saw someone in a long dark coat with the collar pulled up to cover his exposed neck, and wearing a knit hat pulled down over his ears, he wouldn't have received a second glance, nor for that matter, even a first glance.

As anticipated, the reception area and lobby were deserted. He slipped behind the desk and discovered which suite had only one key on the key holder instead of the usual two keys. He pocketed the key and made his way to the stairs rather than the elevator. The whirring sound an ascending elevator might make, as it ascended, completed by a ding, announcing its arrival at three in the morning just might attract the attention of security.

The click of the door opening was barely audible. He entered her bedroom and stood by the bed. Carol was restless and not completely asleep. She sensed a presence in her room; she felt for the switch to the bedside lamp and turned it on. Her eyes struggled open and then widened in confusion. "What...what...are you doing here?" she stammered.

He slammed his fist into her face and then opened his coat and removed an axe strapped to his waist. Dazed, she offered no resistance. He ripped off her Arizona Cardinals nightshirt and then buried the axe deep in her neck. He stood back and watched the blood erupt from her severed carotid arteries. She was dead within seconds. When her heart stopped pumping he took a knife from a sheath on his belt and with surgical precision he cut off her breasts.

CHAPTER TWELVE

Cleveland, Ohio
Monday, February 18, 1991.

THE *DO NOT Disturb* sign was still in place. The maid was puzzled. It had been there all day yesterday as well. She had checked twice more in both the early and late afternoon, but the sign appeared to be in the same place. She wondered if the señora was all right. "*Debo llamar*?" Should I knock? "*Será mejor que verifico*." I better check. She opened the door. "Housekeeping!" No response. The bedroom door was ajar. As she approached the door an all too familiar odor assaulted her. It was the same smell she remembered when the FARC—Revolutionary Armed Forces of Colombia—invaded and destroyed her village. The men had all been shot. The women raped and hacked to death. She was the only survivor. She nudged open the door. "*Querida Madre de Dios*!" Dear mother of God, she crossed herself.

* * *

In twenty years as a homicide detective, Sergeant Dennis Scalpone had seen all forms of brutality inflicted on the human body, but nothing like this. The bar for depravity had just been raised a couple of notches. "So wha'd ya think?" he asked his partner Detective Mort Sadowsky.

"Wha' do I think? I think we're dealing with a fucking psycho."

"Another Torso Murderer?" Scalpone said. He was referring to the *Cleveland Torso Murderer* also known as the *Mad Butcher of Kingsbury Run,* a serial killer who terrorized Cleveland in the mid-thirties, by beheading and dismembering his victims and then scattering the remains throughout the Kingsbury Run. There were thirteen in all.

"Christ, I hope not," Sadowsky said, as he ran his hand over his hairless scalp.

The two detectives, in addition to being partners, were the best of friends. Scalpone was a short, mustachioed bull of a man, with a full head of salt and pepper hair, some of which he should have loaned to his partner. Sadowsky was the taller, irreverent one, always the joker. The two were the best detectives on the Cleveland Division of Police, and boasted the highest murder solve rate in the entire division. Because they were so effective in obtaining confessions they were referred to as the SS by their colleagues—short for Scalpone and Sadowsky—although implying the brutal German *Schutzstaffel,* the SS of World War II.

They waited outside the bedroom until Dr. Morris Fine, the medical examiner, finished his examination. When he was finished he came out and said, "She's all yours. You can release the bloodhounds." Fine was a tall, gangly, bespeckled, acerbic, curmudgeon with a razor sharp intellect.

"Enlighten us," Scalpone said.

"There's not much I can't do, but enlighten you? That's impossible!"

"All right then, how about the details, Ichabod," Sadowsky smirked.

"Mort, you know you really should wear a hat when it's this cold outside. Bald heads tend to lose a lot more heat in cold weather, and when you lose heat your brain shrinks to protect itself," he countered.

"Doc, you're the one who'll need protection if you don't get on with it."

"Okay. Here's what we've got. I think you'll agree, she bled to death. She was hacked with a very sharp object, probably an axe."

"What's with the breasts?" Scalpone asked.

"That's what's interesting. It looks like your perp waited until she bled out before he removed them."

"How can you tell?"

"There's virtually no bleeding around the excision sites. I say excision because they were removed adroitly, rather than having been just hacked off."

"TOD?" Sadowsky asked.

"Based on the core temp and degree of rigor, I would say the time of death was between two and four in the morning on Sunday."

"How soon can you do the post?" Scalpone asked.

"Oh, I can do it as soon as the body gets to morgue, but...when will I do it? That's a different question," Fine grinned.

"Excuse me, professor. When will you do it?"

"Since it's for you...I'll do the anatomical in the morning, and should have all the lab results back, except for the DNA, by the end of the week."

Scalpone thought, *He took the breasts. Trophies? Shit, I don't want to go there. If they're his trophies...then he's just getting started.*

* * *

Like a colony of army ants, each member of the CSU carried out his or her designated task, knowing what to do next, often without communicating with the others. It was if as they were following trail pheromones. When they were ready to release the body Scalpone asked Jenny Cole, the lead investigator, whether anything stood out.

"Nope. Just your everyday, routine, hatchet murder," she said. "But I'll tell you this, from the way those wounds were made, this guy was pissed off...big time."

Cole was a veteran of almost 1,000 homicide investigations

during her career with the Cuyahoga County Coroner's Office. She was smart, witty, and a five star smart-ass. What she lacked in beauty she made up for in brains. The chain-of-evidence had never been compromised on her watch. She was a lesbian, but even the most misogynistic cops, and there were many on the force, trusted and respected her abilities.

"There was no sign of forced entry, so either she knew the guy and let him in, or he had a key, or the door was not locked."

"Good call. We'll check with the front desk and see if they can account for all their keys," said Sadowsky.

"There was no sign of a struggle, but we'll bag her hands just in case. Now get out of here and go do your job, and let me do mine."

There had been only six rooms and one suite—the victim's—occupied at the time of the murder. The occupants of two of the rooms had departed on Sunday and would have to be tracked down. The others had been sequestered in the Palette Lounge, and the two detectives were planning to interview them individually in the Magnolia meeting room. The uniforms were already canvassing the neighborhood.

* * *

The Cleveland Police headquarters was a squat ten-story building. In addition to being the command center for the entire police department, it housed the Cleveland Police Museum and artifacts of the infamous and unsolved Kingsbury Run Torso Murders of the 1930s.

The detectives learned nothing from the hotel guests they interviewed, and the canvass provided no information either. Sadowsky spoke with the guests that had checked out the previous day. Same result. *Nada.* Unless they learned something from the autopsy and the CSU investigation, they might just end up with another set of artifacts to join those of the Kingsbury Run Murders.

Three business cards were found in the victim's wallet, but no *In Case of Emergency* information. One was for Dr. Peter Newton, the others for Dr. Devin Powers and Neal Mink. Both doctors were in surgery all day, and the detectives were told the doctors would return their calls when they were free. The lawyer…same thing, he was in court all day.

* * *

The first one to return the phone call was Dr. Newton. Sadowsky didn't expect the others to call until later, because of the two-hour time difference.

"Thanks for returning my call, Dr. Newton. I need to ask some questions about a patient of yours, a Carol Andrews. I'm going to put you on speaker phone so my partner can hear."

"Detective, you know I can't discuss anything about a patient without permission."

"Well doctor, I don't think she'll mind…she was murdered yesterday."

"Oh my God…that's why she was a no-show this morning. Of course…how can I help?"

"We know from the information package we found at the scene that she was scheduled to have breast surgery today. Can you provide us with any personal information that may help us track down her next of kin, and why she came all the way to Cleveland from Tucson to have surgery?"

"As I recall, Carol was divorced and lived alone. And I remember distinctly when I asked her whom I should contact after her surgery she told me there was no one. She had no family. She laughed and she said the only ones who cared about what happened to her were her lawyers."

"Lawyers?"

"Yes," he hesitated. "Well, I don't suppose it matters now.

She'd had breast implant surgery and was suing the plastic surgeon that had performed the original surgery…Dr. Devin Powers from Tucson. She came to see me because I have considerable experience in removing ruptured breast implants."

That explains the other two business cards, Scalpone thought.

"Did the lawyers refer Ms. Andrews to you?" Scalpone asked.

"No. Her gynecologist, Dr. Ethan Phillips, referred her to me. I can give you his number. He should be able to provide you with more information."

"Thanks Dr. Newton, you've been a great help. If we think of anything else we'll call you." He disconnected the call.

"So, Sherlock, whadda ya think?" asked Sadowsky.

"It's a start. We've got the usual ex-husband and undoubtedly a very unhappy doctor who might've had a reason," Scalpone said.

"The doctor? Nah, doctors consider lawsuits just part of doing business. That's why they pay those hefty premiums. I think we should start with the ex-husband."

Ethan Phillips took the call immediately. "Poor Carol. She never found happiness. She was so insecure. I advised her against having breast implants, but she thought they would make her more attractive. She was married three times. Kept looking for Mr. Right."

"Three?" said Scalpone.

"Yes. They were nice enough guys, but none could give Carol what she needed."

"Any problems that you know about?" Sadowsky asked.

"No. Her divorces were all amicable, as far as I know, and money was never a problem. She was a very successful real estate agent."

"Can you give us the names of her ex-husbands?"

"I'll turn you over to my secretary; she should have that information. If there's nothing else, I have patients waiting."

"No, that'll do it doctor. Thanks for your time."

Sadowsky said, "Amicable! Bullshit! There's always something. Divorces are never amicable."

* * *

Powers stared at the pink message slip...Detective Dennis Scalpone from Cleveland. What could he possibly want? He reached for the phone...hesitated, then dialed the number.

Three rings and then picked up. "Homicide."

"This is Dr. Devin Powers. I'm returning Detective Dennis Scalpone's call."

"You've got him doc. Thanks for returning my call. I need to ask you some questions about a patient of yours, Carol Andrews." He turned on the speakerphone so Sadowsky could hear.

"She was my patient, but is no longer. And I *do not* discuss my patients, past, present, or future, with anyone, without their consent."

Oooh! Attitude, he thought. "*Was*? That's an interesting word doctor."

"Detective, I *am not* about to engage in a game of semantics with you. Please get to the point so I can get back to my patients."

Scalpone was not someone you wanted to piss off, and Powers had managed to do just that. "Doctor, the point is Ms. Andrews was murdered yesterday, and not in a very gentlemanly fashion, I might add. Your business card with a scheduled appointment for next August was found in her wallet. Please explain to me why she would've been carrying an appointment card for next August with you if she weren't your patient any more. Did something happen between the time she made that appointment and the time she became your ex-patient?"

"Detective, whatever transpired between Ms. Andrews and me is subject to doctor-patient confidentiality, and I don't believe you have jurisdictional authority to ask me any questions. I'm sorry to hear Ms. Andrews was murdered, but her murder has nothing to do with me, and I have nothing further to say to you. If you have any further questions please contact my attorney and make an appointment."

He hung up.

"Wow!" said Sadowsky. "What an asshole."

* * *

Neal was exhausted. It been a very long day in court, and he hadn't gotten much sleep over the weekend. He removed his jacket and draped it over a down filled, tufted, Regina Andrew Design tub chair with Havana arms. A matching sofa positioned in front of an intricately carved desk, hand-made from Mexican highly figured cocobolo, separated the chair and its twin. The pictures on the walls were photographs of white mink in various postures, defending themselves from their natural predators. By one wall there was a Honduran rosewood credenza, on which stood a white stuffed mink and snow fox getting ready to do battle. Unlike the Spartan furnishings of his brother's office, his office was designed for comfort…not intimidation.

He picked up the message from Scalpone and checked the time. *Six-thirty here, eight-thirty in Cleveland.* There was no message from Carol, but he sensed this message was about her. He called the number.

"Homicide…Scalpone."

His fingers tightened on the receiver. "This is Neal Mink. You called me earlier?"

"Mr. Mink, thanks for returning my call..."

"This is about Carol Andrews, isn't it?"

How did he know that?

Ever the detective, his suspicion sense tingled. "Why do you say that?"

"Because one plus one equals two. Carol's in Cleveland and I was expecting a call from her. She didn't call, but you did."

"You're right. Ms. Andrews was murdered early yesterday morning. We found your business card in her wallet, and we're following up with every possible lead. As you said, 'one plus one equals two.' So I called you, hoping that you might be able to provide us with some information. I hope you're not going to invoke lawyer-client confidentiality."

Neal sighed, "I suppose you're right…Carol wouldn't care. Our law firm was representing her in a lawsuit. After reviewing the facts we believed that she had a legitimate cause of action against the individual."

"Dr. Devin Powers?"

"Yes, but if you already know that, why are you asking me?"

"Just connecting all the dots counselor. His card was found in her wallet as well. Can you tell me why she was suing him?"

"Well, that's an area that is off limits. We were still in the stage of discovery, and since the depositions are not yet a matter of public record, any statements in them are merely allegations. And were you to focus your investigation of an individual based on unsubstantiated allegations that originated from this office, then we would be exposing ourselves to the possibility of slander."

"I see." He really didn't see, but he knew from past experience that trying to get information from a lawyer who claimed privilege, or whatever other term he might use, was like trying to storm the Bastille with a flyswatter. "So then, can you think of any other reason why someone would want to kill Ms. Andrews?"

"I didn't say I knew *any* reason for someone wanting to kill Ms. Andrews."

This guy's smooth, he thought, and knew he wasn't going to get anything else from him. "Well, I guess that's all I've got to ask; if you think of anything that might help us with this investigation I'd appreciate a call."

"I will," said Neal, and hung up the receiver.

Scalpone drummed his fingers on his desk and thought, that's strange. *He never once asked me how she was killed.*

* * *

Neal saw the light in Ingram's office and walked in. Mink was bent over his desk scribbling like a conductor waving his baton.

"If you're writing notes on the Andrews case...forget it. She's dead."

* * *

Viewing an autopsy isn't like watching a PG movie, nor is it like watching Jason running around on Friday the Thirteenth wielding his murder instrument of the day. Movies are fiction and fantasy; an autopsy is fact and reality, and is the final act of desecration on the body of the recently murdered.

Scalpone and Sadowsky long ago had lost count of the number of autopsies they had witnessed. The only common denominator among them was that the guests at the pathologist's party had all been violently murdered...but that's an oxymoron. No one is gently murdered.

They were greeted by the deputy-chief medical examiner, Dr. Kevin Lynch. "I know you were expecting Dr. Fine to be your date, but mayor White called him to a command performance, so you'll have to dance with me. Thank God he's the politician around here."

Dr. Kevin Lynch FACP was a tall, ascetic, sharp-witted guardian of the catacombs known as the Cuyahoga County Morgue, located at University Circle, within a boring, five-story, uniformly windowed structure, befitting its purpose. He had 221 guests the previous year that were victims of homicide, and 1991 was off to a good start. Carol Andrews was his newest guest. He removed the sheet that covered her body.

"Well boys, it would appear as if someone had started the autopsy without me…and with great finesse, I might add. It looks like her breasts were meticulously removed with a surgical instrument." He scanned the lifeless body lying on the cold stainless steel autopsy table. "The wound in her neck is interesting. Probably made with some kind of axe. Look at the angle of the cut through her neck. It's a very thin, tangential, slice, suggesting a very thin-bladed narrow axe-head.

* * *

Forensics came up with nothing that would offer any clues to the killer's identity, and the canvass was equally fruitless. After two weeks of wheel spinning the detectives directed their efforts to the next murder. Because there was no next of kin, Neal Mink made arrangements for Carol to be cremated and left it to the funeral director to dispose of her ashes.

CHAPTER THIRTEEN

Tucson, Arizona
Friday, July 12, 1991.

INGRAM SMILED AFTER he read the Birmingham News article about Brenda Toole. She had just been awarded $5.4 million in her lawsuit against Baxter/Heyer-Schulte. The award was not based on any sound medical evidence that the implants caused her problems, but rather on the testimony of the plaintiff's *experts*, who divined she was at risk of developing an autoimmune disease because her implants had ruptured. He was ready to make his move. Carol Andrews' death caused him a minor setback, but he had twenty-five clients lined up with far more significant problems than either those of Carol's or Brenda Toole's. Nationwide the number of lawsuits against the manufacturers was increasing exponentially.

He opened Louise Purcell's file. She would be his Nautilus, the first atomic submarine, and the one that would sink Dow Corning and the others. The other ships in his fleet were being prepared as well, but the real strike would come from Purcell. The Armada was ready to sail. The number of women joining his navy was increasing every day.

* * *

Powers made no attempt to control his emotions. Hans and Fritz sat like statues listening to him vent. "What the hell am I going to do?" he screamed. He waved the charts in their faces. "Twenty-two of them! And I only carry $5 million in malpractice insurance.

Look at this one. He sorted through the charts. Elaine Peters. She's asking $2 million. She never had a problem until she saw that Connie Chung show and then spoke to that lawyer in Houston. Does this mean I'll have to go to Houston for a deposition?"

"No Devin," said Becker, "her attorneys will have to come to Tucson."

"So why did she go to Houston? Aren't there enough ambulance chasers in Tucson?"

"Uh...Devin...she doesn't live in Tucson...she's from Houston," said Becker.

Neither lawyer wanted to tell him that Texas had the reputation of being plaintiff-friendly. The awards were higher, and cases got to trial much faster than anywhere else in the country. And they didn't want to tell him that the lawyer she was seeing in Houston obtained some of the highest jury awards in the country. This was one case they did not want to go to trial.

He waved his hands. "No matter. And then she has the audacity to thank me and say, as she cupped her breasts, 'These babies are going to buy me a new house...it's not about you doctor...I have no complaints against you, but my lawyer said he had to name you in the complaint; he was really going after the manufacturer.' Then the bitch kisses me on the cheek and says, 'It's nothing personal Doctor.' Nothing personal? What planet is she living on?

"And look at this one. Faith Greene." He handed the chart to Fritz. "I operated on her two years ago. She wanted to be a movie star and thought that if she had larger breasts they would help her get a part. I told her the only thing I could guarantee her was that her breasts would be larger. She never had a problem post-operatively either. I saw her a year ago, and her breasts were as natural and soft as any I'd ever seen. So now she's having severe mental anguish because she's afraid to let her boy friend touch her breasts, thinking they may rupture if he gets too frisky. She claims I never told her they could rupture, that they would last forever. So she's suing me for $1 million and the manufacturer for $5 million."

Fritz...Becker...said, "I understand your concern doctor, but that first patient may be right. Our experience thus far has shown that once action has been taken against the manufacturers the individual doctors have been either discharged from the suit, or we have been able to settle the claim for a relatively insignificant sum. All your charts have been reviewed by independent plastic surgeons, and the consensus is that you had followed the correct procedure in all but ten cases. And the only point of contention in those ten is whether you provided full disclosure about the risks involved."

Hans...Horscht...added, "Yes, with the Greene woman the question is whether you disclosed that the implants could rupture. The product information provided by the manufacturer at the time you performed the surgery did not indicate the possibility of spontaneous implant rupture. So once again we are convinced the liability lies with the manufacturer...not you. Whereas with the Peters woman, at the time you performed the surgery, the product information clearly indicated that rupture could occur. And there's a problem with the closed capsulotomy procedures that you *continued* to perform after Dow Corning changed their brochure to include a caveat about performing that procedure. So you do have exposure from that aspect. Of course, unless they can prove the implant ruptured after the capsulotomy, and the only way they can prove a rupture is to have the implant removed and examined, the plaintiff would still have to prove the capsulotomy was the proximate cause of the rupture. The rupture may have preceded the capsulotomy."

Becker continued, "We will continue to aggressively pursue settlement, because we know the plaintiffs' attorneys will discover the extent of your coverage and realize that unless they attempt to attach your personal assets they'll be better off devoting their efforts against the manufacturers."

They may have been convinced, but he wasn't. It wasn't their reputation that was at stake. Did they have any idea of the hell that he experienced each time he sat through one of those depositions?

All they did was sit there and toss in an occasional "objection" while the vultures picked him apart with such efficiency that he even began to doubt the truth. They did it with Carol Andrews, and at the end they all smiled and shook hands. His attorneys didn't care about him. All they cared about was the number of zeroes that appeared on the checks. He knew what would've happened to him with the Carol Andrews case if she hadn't been murdered. No, he couldn't wait for the lawyers to play their games. He knew what had to be done. What he didn't know yet was that the all lawyers who represented the patients who had filed lawsuits against him were members of the Centurion Counsel.

CHAPTER FOURTEEN

Los Angeles, California
Three months earlier, May 1991.

FAITH GREENE WAS the typical Mid-western girl who received rave reviews for her acting ability in high school plays. After she graduated from Bullock Creek High School in Midland Michigan in 1988, she set out for L.A. with aspirations of becoming the next Meryl Streep, but then again so did thousands of other ingénues who waited tables in L.A. She was cute enough, not striking, but had a genuine smile and honest eyes. She knew, or so she believed, that she would never make it with small breasts. Directors wanted cleavage; all she had was a flat plain. Her roommate raved about Dr. Devin Powers, the Tucson plastic surgeon who did her breasts, and besides he was cheaper than the doctors in L.A., so Faith made the decision to fly to Tucson and have them done by him. Southwest had a $79 round trip special, and that's what sealed her decision. She never told her family that she was going to have implant surgery, which was ironic, because her father worked at Dow Corning in Midland and had been instrumental in the development of the silicone implants.

In 1991, two years after the surgery, she had cleavage, but the casting calls were still virtually non-existent. She was ready to give up and return to Michigan until she saw an ad in the L.A. Times from an attorney who was representing women who had problems with breast implants. She had no problems, but that didn't mean she wouldn't have problems with them in the future. She took advantage of the free consultation he offered and scheduled an appointment.

* * *

"Good afternoon Ms. Greene. I'm Albert Chiricosta and this is my assistant Georgina Donovan. I understand you may be having some problems with your breast implants and would like to know if we can help you."

Chiricosta was dressed to impress, and his deep baritone voice was carefully honed to instill ministerial confidence. His capped teeth were white, but not so white as to appear contrived. If he were selling timeshares he would have been the perfect closer.

"Yes…well I'm really not sure. I read your ad in the Times and when I saw all the things that could go wrong with the implants and the diseases that they could cause, I thought maybe I should check it out. I saw my doctor about a year ago and he said that everything was perfect and that unless I had any questions or problems in the future he wouldn't have to see me again. When I read your ad I got to wondering what he meant about *problems in the future*. So here I am."

He placed a fatherly hand on hers and said, "And that's why *I* am here.

"I don't want to alarm you Faith," which is exactly what he wanted to do, "but your doctor and the manufacturer of the implants are not telling you the whole truth. There's a very real danger that your implants could rupture, and if they do…silicone could spread all throughout your body. Our experts believe—his experts were hired guns that had impressive credentials, but could offer no scientific evidence for their pontifications—if that were to occur, you'd be at risk of developing all kinds of disabling diseases…even cancer."

Thank you Ralph Nader and Dr. Sidney Wolfe. He was thinking of the warnings issued by the Public Citizen Health Research Group, founded by Nader and Wolfe, that silicone in the body could cause cancer, but without any scientific evidence to support their claims.

"That's why we've started this campaign. To ensure that all

women who have been harmed, or who are in danger of being harmed by silicone breast implants, will have someone to represent them against these large corporations and the doctors who are complicit with them in their deceit and lies; to ensure that all women who have been harmed by silicone will receive fair compensation for any pain and suffering and future medical expenses that may be incurred." *And to ensure we get our thirty-five percent...plus expenses.*

"My doctor never told me they could rupture. He told me there was a possibility that they could get a little hard after the surgery, but if I did these exercises and massaged them, it was unlikely that the hardness would occur. And if it did happen, there was a simple office procedure he could do that would fix it."

"Faith, what you have told me leads me to believe you may have a cause of action against the manufacturer. Of course we would have to review your doctor's records to determine the extent of his involvement. In order to do that, we'll have to name him as a defendant in the lawsuit as well. I'll be blunt...the liability insurance coverage that your doctor has in force will in no way approximate that of the manufacturer. Therefore our efforts will be directed primarily against the manufacturer. In a recent jury award a patient received $1.7 million. I believe we can obtain a substantial award, or settlement for you as well."

He didn't really believe she had much of a case, but he wanted to build up the numbers. One of them could turn out to be the lottery.

"If you feel you'd like our firm to represent you, Miss Donovan will have you sign the engagement letter and explain all the details to you. Of course I'll *always* be available to answer any questions you may have."

She hesitated and wondered whether she should talk to her father, but she knew he would say the implants were perfectly safe. She needed the money. "Yes Mr. Chiricosta, I'd like you to represent me...where do I sign?"

It would be the last document she ever signed.

June 14, 1991.

Faith was feeling elated. Her attorney had called her the day before to inform her that he had received a phone call from Dr. Powers' attorneys. They wanted to talk settlement. Their initial offer had been $100,000, but he was certain that he could negotiate a higher amount. She told him to do what he thought best and she'd go along with it.

She had also received a call from her agent to let her know that he had arranged an audition for her on Monday. It was a speaking part in a movie starring Anthony Hopkins. Everything was perfect. Her roommate had gone to San Diego for the weekend so she'd have the apartment all to herself. She could spend all day Sunday rehearsing the lines. She wasn't scheduled to work until Monday, but she planned to call in sick on Monday so she could make the audition.

She didn't notice the nondescript sedan that had followed her from the restaurant, and she didn't notice it when it parked across the street as she turned into the parking lot. Bouncing like an India-rubber ball all the way to her front door she fumbled her key into the lock. Her first-floor apartment faced the street, but he already knew that. The light by the door was out. She'd call the manager in the morning to have it replaced.

She knew she wouldn't be able to sleep, so she took a Dalmane and crawled into bed.

He waited for an hour after she turned off the light and then made his way across the street. It was an older, circa 1956, well-maintained, 22-unit, two-story apartment building built in the shape of a "U." It had a grass courtyard and several scattered palm trees on the periphery. Her apartment didn't have a very elaborate locking system. He was able to slip the lock with a credit card. She didn't hear him enter her bedroom and she didn't feel the bed cover being removed, nor her nightie being cut open, and only briefly did she feel the axe when it made contact with her neck.

* * *

June Tourangeau, Faith's roommate, was worried. She had been calling the apartment all day Sunday to tell Faith she wouldn't be getting back from San Diego until early Monday morning, but all she got was the answering machine. Faith had told her she would be staying home on Sunday to rehearse for an audition, so she couldn't understand why Faith didn't pickup the phone...or at least return her messages.

* * *

When June arrived home and saw Faith's car in its parking space she felt relieved. Her relief vanished when she discovered the door to the apartment was unlocked. Faith would never leave the door open. She nudged the door open and edged her way into the apartment. It didn't take long for the stench to reach her nostrils. She gagged when she turned on the light to Faith's bedroom, and then she retched, and then she screamed. Backing out of the apartment she continued to scream and continued to retch. She attacked her neighbor's door with her fists, in a state of hysteria. When the door opened she uttered only two words, "Faith's dead!" And then she collapsed.

* * *

The first responders were from the Wilshire Station, which was just a short three miles away. They were not surprised when the one-eighty-seven was called in; the homicide rate in that area was over two hundred percent higher than the rest of L.A. County, despite the manicured, tree-lined, tranquil appearing streets.

Detectives Winston Martin and Don Saffer were sleeping when they were rousted from their beds. Martin was sleeping with his wife, and Saffer was sleeping with his girlfriend of the week. They made it to the crime scene within half an hour. Four black and whites, with lights flashing like the strobes at a disco, were already on the scene when they arrived. The coroner's van was positioned to receive its newest passenger. There were several residents being shooed away from the crime scene tape, and there were more starting to congregate in the courtyard. The uniforms were keeping the gawkers at bay, but kept them from leaving the premises. They would all need to be canvassed shortly.

The two detectives were dressed L.A. casual. At this hour no one cared whether they dressed by the book, certainly not the victim. Martin was a twenty-year veteran who settled in L.A. after he returned from Viet Nam. He figured the skills he learned in the army, which were basically how to shoot a gun and kill people, could be put to good use in civilian life, either on the side of the law by becoming a cop and shooting bad guys, or by returning to Tennessee and join the family business distilling moonshine, growing weed, and shooting good guys. He chose to become a cop. Saffer, on the other hand, grew up in L.A. and went to UCLA where he majored in criminal justice. He was the only cop in L.A. to sport three NCAA Championship rings, earned when he played basketball for John Wooden. He was spotted in a pick-up basketball game by a UCLA assistant-coach and was eventually offered a basketball scholarship. Before that, he was headed on a downward spiral with his gang affiliation where the life expectancy was just short of thirty years. The education he acquired on the streets would prove invaluable when he joined the LAPD.

The medical examiner, Dr. Ed Rogoff, was just leaving as the two detectives entered the apartment. "Well, gentlemen how kind of you to join us. I believe as the expression goes, 'You have your work cut out for you.' Or I should say, *axed out* for you."

"Axed?" said Martin. He raised his eyebrows.

"Yes. It would appear our killer was a very angry individual who dispatched the victim with what appears to be the stroke of an axe, *à la* Lizzie Borden. And the *coup de grâce*...he cut her breasts off with a very sharp knife."

"TOD?" asked Saffer.

"Based on her core temp and the size of the little white wiggling fellows that are playing tag in her various orifices and wounds, I'd say sometime between midnight and three on Sunday morning. I hope you have your VapoRub and compazine; the maggots are not just having a party, they're having an orgy."

"Thanks for the warning, you can go ride your bike now," said Martin.

Rogoff was a dry-witted, sixty-something, pedal-power-proponent, who rode his bicycle at every opportunity. While most of colleagues in the medical profession found their fun on cruise ships and the canals of Venice, his vacations were spent finding mountains to climb on his full-suspension trail bike. "I'll try to have the post party ASAP; it's been a busy weekend. The boys of the barrio had some major disputes."

Martin and Saffer thought they had seen every form of violence that could be inflicted upon the human body, but when they saw what had been done to Faith Greene they realized a new chapter had been written in the book of depravity.

Martin felt his rage percolating. Even with the massacres in the jungles of Vietnam he had not seen this degree of brutality. "This bastard goes to the head of the list," he fumed.

* * *

Los Angeles had to be the capitol of the World of Weird.

The L.A. County Morgue was a clone of the haunted house in Disneyland. The imposing structure had its birth as the sixteen-bed L.A. General Hospital, at a time when more people entered a hospital to die rather than to be cured. It was fitting then that it evolved to become an emporium for the dead. It was almost as if Lucifer whispered suggestions into the ear of the architect. To enter the building you had to climb sixteen stairs to the front doors. The building was constructed of red brick and a facade made up of rows of sixteen rectangular concrete biscuits, resembling Kit Kat wafers, and elaborate molded concrete corbels. At any one time there were sixteen stainless steel autopsy tables being used to solve the mysteries of the dead. What was it about the number sixteen that permeated this structure? To the seventeenth century mystic and theologian, Boehme, the number sixteen represented *the abyss,* or the hell, because it was the mystical number of Lucifer.

So if Lucifer had anything to do with this place, he sure had a hell of a sense of humor, because in 1993, he decided to introduce his future minions to the world of the dead by creating the first gift shop in the world to be located in a morgue, *Skeletons in the Closet*, where one could acquire a range of products including, body bag garment bags, toe-tags, and L.A. Coroner body notes. A sign in the shop warned shoplifters that when they were apprehended their next of kin would be notified.

Once you left the fun atmosphere of the gift shop and descended into the bowels of the building, you would find the remains of over 300 persons waiting to be released to their families, so they could be lowered to their final resting place. Those who were never claimed waited their turn to be delivered to the crematorium… ashes to ashes.

How do you tell a family that their daughter had been hacked to death by a savage killer? Or do you spare them the details? Martin lost the flip of the coin, so it was he who had to notify the Greene family. Faith's parents were flying in from Midland and would arrive later in the day.

In 1990, there were 983 homicides in Los Angeles, and by the time Faith was murdered on June 17, 1991, there had already been over 300 homicides committed. So although her murder was particularly heinous, it didn't raise any red flags. Time passed and priorities changed. The L.A. Detectives would soon be devoting their efforts to more pressing issues, and the Greene murder would become as cold as the morgue storage vaults.

CHAPTER FIFTEEN

Tucson, Arizona
Sunday, July 28, 1991.

THE CENTURION COUNSEL met annually in Tucson to share new ideas, experiences, past performances, and to brag about the size of the awards they had obtained. Normally the meeting was held in March, the absolute best time to visit Tucson. The temperature remained steady in the seventies, it rarely rained, and the golfing was great. So why were they meeting in July, the absolute worst time to visit Tucson? It was so hot the road kills were cooked and ready to eat shortly after impact. The rains of the monsoon were so torrential you could find yourself in another county if you were unfortunate enough to have your car stuck in a wash.

Ingram called an emergency meeting in July because he wanted the Counsel to be prepared for the number of women that would be filing law suits against the implant manufacturers. No one would have believed that by May 1995, Dow Corning would be facing over 20,000 individual lawsuits, and over 400,000 women would be involved in a global settlement, and that a fund of over $4 billion would have been set up to satisfy these claims. No one that is, except Ingram Mink.

The meeting was held at The Westward Look resort, Tucson's first resort built in the early 1900s, on 80 acres snuggled in the foothills of the majestic Santa Catalina Mountains. The resort was secluded, and offered privacy and comfortable elegance.

Mink stood at the lectern and scanned the audience. He knew them all by name. Some were good, some were very good, some were superb, and some were even better than that. It didn't matter.

They all had met the criteria for membership, but soon, even first year associates throughout the country would reach the magic one million dollar figure, and ten million would become the new one million. Until this year it appeared that the record Mink held for the largest award in the history of American jurisprudence would be unreachable. But Mink knew it was only a matter of time until awards were measured in tens of millions, and then hundreds of millions, and then billions. All he wanted at this point in his life was to be the first to reach the billion-dollar plateau. Roger Bannister would always be remembered as the first person to break the four-minute mile, and Neal Armstrong the first man to walk on the moon. Mink wanted to be remembered as the first lawyer to break the billion-dollar barrier.

Today he was not wearing his jury suit or scuffed shoes, but rather a Leonard Logsdail Savile Row suit and Berluti shoes obtained on one of his many visits to London. His hair was perfectly coiffed, razor-cut at the back. His watch was a Patek-Phillippe, but in the courtroom he wore a humble Mickey Mouse watch. This jury was not impressed by humility, but rather by confidence.

"Gentlemen," there were no women, "thank you for coming on such short notice. Before we start I would like to propose a toast to Connie Chung." He raised an imaginary glass.

The sounds of laughter and clapping were equally divided.

"Ms. Chung stated that there were over two million women who have had breast augmentations since the first one in 1962. My brother Neal, the human computer, attempted to find out how many procedures have actually been done, because Ms. Chung's report was somewhat contradictory. Despite exhaustive research, Neal was unable to discover exactly how many women have had implants. The numbers vary depending on whom you ask. Nobody keeps records. Let's assume for a minute…and yes I know when you assume you make an ASS out of U and ME…using the two million figure, if just one percent of these women were to have problems with their implants, it would mean there are potentially twenty thousand women who will have a cause of action. However, I think when all the facts are in, those numbers will be considerably higher. He paused to take a drink of water. "I'll let Neal explain what these figures mean...Neal."

Neal exchanged places with Ingram at the lectern. As usual he was casually, but impeccably dressed. Had there been any women in the audience, his smile and good looks, if not his words, would have definitely caught their attention.

"Thank you Ing." He scanned the faces of the audience. Their anticipation was palpable. "You've all seen the video. Ms. Chung interviewed five women and two *experts*. We all know that in a courtroom virtually everything that was said in that interview would be inadmissible, as being hearsay, inflammatory, contradictory, without foundation, etcetera. I verified the credentials of her experts, and they are impeccable. But I believe, as I'm sure we all do, that their opinions and conclusions would wither under a good cross-examination. But that's not the point. The point is that perception is reality. Because Ms. Chung didn't present anyone to offer a contrary opinion, there are now millions of people who watched that program who are convinced that silicone breast implants are instruments of the devil, and that the doctors who inserted them into the bodies of unsuspecting women are his minions.

"The first silicone implant was designed by two plastic surgeons, Drs. Thomas Cronin and Frank Gerow, and the first recipient in 1962, was a woman named Timmie Jean Lindsey. Since then, it's believed there are over two million women who've had breast implants. That means there are two million guinea pigs that now have breast implants. I say guinea pigs because since the first implant was inserted there've been four generations of different implants that have been used for experimentation in these women, and within these generations there've been additional modifications.

"Why so many changes in such a relatively short period of time? Because there were problems that surgeons recognized in their patients that necessitated these changes. Did the manufacturers conduct controlled animal studies on these implants to ensure their safety and efficacy prior to their release? They *did not*. If the implants were so good why did they keep making changes? What was wrong with the implants?

"Researchers use guinea pigs, rats, mice, primates, and other animals to test the safety of a device before it's approved for use in humans. Not so with silicone breast implants. The FDA essentially gave the manufacturers *carte blanche* to produce and sell these devices with no oversight. Prior to 1976, there were no Federal regulations requiring proof of their safety and efficacy. Even when the medical device amendment was adopted in 1976, breast implants were grandfathered. And despite the unanimous recommendation of the FDA advisory panel to classify these implants as class III devices in January of 1983, the FDA did not publish the final rule requiring the manufacturers to provide proof of their safety and effectiveness until April 10, of this year...over eight years later. And still, the manufacturers had an additional 90 days to respond with a PMA—pre-market approval—application, which wasn't approved until last month, and I suspect the final rule would still be bouncing around in committee if it weren't for Ms. Chung's exposé.

"Gentlemen, if the FDA weren't protected by the doctrine of Sovereign immunity I would love to sue their sorry asses. But since we can't, we'll just have to settle for the doctors and manufacturers."

This elicited some laughter and catcalls among the lawyers. Neal held up his hands. "Please bear with me as I throw some numbers and statistics at you. Their relevance will soon become clear. I'm going to briefly discuss the epidemiology and symptoms of four diseases. Lupus, CFS,—chronic fatigue syndrome—fibromyalgia, and HAD—human adjuvant disease.

"Lupus is a chronic inflammatory disease that occurs when the body's immune system attacks its own tissues and organs. The incidence can vary between four and two hundred fifty per one hundred thousand persons. It's more common in women and in

Hispanics. CFS and fibromyalgia share a lot of the same symptoms and oftentimes the two conditions are indistinguishable. Fatigue, memory loss, sore throat, enlarged lymph nodes, unexplained muscle pain, migratory pain, headaches, poor sleep, and extreme exhaustion. Human Adjuvant Disease is an autoimmune disease that occurs in response to the injection of a foreign substance. The incidence, when a diagnosis is finally made, is about two hundred thirty-five per one hundred thousand with CFS, and for fibromyalgia the incidence is anywhere between one in twenty-five to one in fifty, depending on the study. And for lupus the number is one in four hundred. If we accept the fact that two million women have had silicone breast implants, then based on proven epidemiological studies, five thousand of those women would have developed lupus even if they never had breast implant surgery; for CFS the number would be around forty-seven hundred, and for fibromyalgia the numbers would be between forty thousand and eighty thousand.

"Until the manufacturers conduct double blind studies to prove those statistics, they won't be able to convince anyone that silicone implants didn't cause those diseases."

"I think I see where he's going," said one lawyer to those on either side of him.

"Yeah, the white mink always was a numbers guy," said one.

The other grinned and said, "I wonder what the black mink's closing argument will be like."

The Mink brothers were referred to as the *black mink* and *white mink* because of the difference in their complexions and hair color. Ingram had a dark complexion with dark hair to match. Neal on the other hand was fair and had light blond hair that his hairdresser probably helped maintain.

Neal continued. "Of the five women interviewed by Ms. Chung, one stated that she had been diagnosed with lupus, six months after she had the surgery. Two others had symptoms consistent with either fibromyalgia or Chronic Fatigue Syndrome. The other two sounded like they had problems because of ruptured implants. One doctor made the diagnosis of Human Adjuvant Disease. I'll let Ing put this in perspective for you."

The brothers exchanged positions.

Ingram placed his hands on either side of the lectern and scrutinized the audience. "Gentlemen, doctors, like the military, frequently use acronyms for strange medical conditions. FUO for fever of unknown origin; GOK…God only knows. Very few are willing to say, 'Mrs. Smith. I just don't know.' I recently settled a case because the doctor did a very stupid thing. He peppered a patient's chart with medical acronyms. PRAFTOF, BMW, and CTS.

"Ah, I see some of you smiling. When I asked him, at the deposition, what those terms meant he became very fidgety and nervous. He hesitated with his answers and asked to see the entries in the chart. His forehead started to perspire.

"He said, 'PRATFOF means patient reassured and told…further options found; BMW means, back must wait, and CTS means… uh…can't take steroids.'

"After I'd reviewed the chart, before the deposition, I checked with a physician-poker-playing buddy of mine to find out what they really meant. He told me that PRATFOF is a term they use among themselves when they're talking about a patient they want to get rid of. It means 'patient reassured and told to fuck off forever; BMW… bitchy, moaning whiner; CTS…crazier than shit.'

"He swallowed the bait. His face dropped when I said, 'Doctor, don't they really mean...' His attorneys threw in the towel. They didn't want a jury to hear the real meaning of those entries. So when you run across acronyms in a chart, they may turn out to be bonus points.

"Gentlemen, the potential we have before us is unprecedented. The numbers that Neal presented to you are just the tip of the iceberg. Every woman who has had breast implant surgery is a potential litigant. It's our duty to inform these women that they have a problem, or will have one in the future because of the silicone in their bodies. Our initial course of action should be to attract all those women who have the symptoms of Chronic Fatigue Syndrome and fibromyalgia that have been bounced around like a pinball from doctor to doctor without a definitive diagnosis. To do that we must start to advertise and arrange appearances on talk shows. We must develop a pool of doctors who will testify that patients have Human Adjuvant Disease because of breast implants. Their credentials must be impeccable. And we must have a pool of scientists who will state that silicone can wreak havoc on the human body.

"Once we've started the campaign it'll be impossible to litigate every case that we get. We'll have to cherry pick those women with the greatest jury appeal. There aren't enough courtrooms in the entire country to handle the number of lawsuits that will be filed. Once the lawsuits have started, every lawyer who has ever settled a PI case will want to get in on the action. Eventually, the lawsuits will have to be settled in a mass tort.

"Let's use the women who appeared on the Connie Chung show as our case studies. It makes no difference whether their breast implants caused their problems; the only important thing is that they believe their implants have caused them. As Neal said, 'Perception is reality.' Also, Mr. Nader and Dr. Wolfe will convince women they have a problem, or will have a problem in the future. TV talk shows will feature women with problems that would draw tears from a stone. And silicone experts will be there to offer gobbledygook, 'In my opinion,' about the evils of silicone.

"We should exploit all the individuals who will unwittingly further our cause. We should direct our campaign to attract women who've developed undiagnosed chronic illnesses that had their onset after they had implant surgery. They'll stir up the most sympathy and bring the largest awards. Next, we present women whose implants have ruptured, requiring multiple surgeries to remove the silicone. It's with this group that our experts will shine. Then we address the issue of informed consent. There'll be thousands of women who will testify they were never told that the implants could rupture, or that hardness could occur. It wasn't until 1980, that Dow included in their brochures the information that implants could rupture from abnormal squeezing or trauma. And that was the only complication that was mentioned in the product information until 1985, after the Stern award. For this group we should focus our attention on the doctors, because many of them continued to perform closed capsulotomies, despite the warnings that are now included in the product information. Lastly, there's the group of women who will have absolutely nothing wrong, but will find some disease hoping to hit a jackpot.

"We should attack the manufacturers on failure to disclose and fraud. It's with them that the acronym FUBAR, that the army uses so often, applies—Fucked-Up Beyond All Recognition. Your syllabuses, that we'll hand out, will explain in full detail how we should manage this campaign. We'll need to keep a central registry of all women who have filed lawsuits in order to know what progress is being made against the manufacturers, without us having to read about it in the press after the fact. By having a central registry we'll know the status of all cases in real time and will know immediately what the manufacturers are doing to counter the suits. We'll have instant access to their strategy, but they won't know that a member of our group in San Diego will have access to information to a case in New York.

"Lastly, we'll need a dummy organization to help fund activist groups, like Public Citizen's Health Research Group, who unwittingly will do the heavy lifting for us. I'm asking each of you to contribute $100,000. I think an appropriate name would be, 'Protect All Women Now.' The acronym is PAWN."

CHAPTER SIXTEEN

Tucson, Arizona
Tuesday, December 10, 1991.

IT HAD BEEN exactly one year since Connie Chung had aired her show, and predictably the number of lawsuits and the size of the awards had been increasing. Dow Corning had been at the vanguard, and had been taking most of the casualties, but other manufacturers were starting to feel the effects as the plaintiffs' attorneys were starting to breach their defenses. Ingram Mink was preparing to make his move. He had won several of the warm-up matches, and the manufacturers were watching him closely. Of the lawsuits filed against them, his firm represented the majority of the litigants. The manufacturers were preparing for his assault and expected that he would make his move against Dow Corning, and that's exactly what he wanted them to think. They forgot or didn't know he was a chess grand master. His opening salvo would be like the Polish, or Sokolský opening, an uncommon opening among grand masters, but a radical opening designed to destroy common opening theory, and win because of the mistakes of the other player. He wasn't going to attack Dow Corning who could delay and obfuscate the proceedings for years, but rather a smaller company, Sherman-Hall. They didn't have the war chest of the other companies that would allow them to fight a prolonged battle and they didn't have the ships to protect themselves against the armada he was about to launch. But they had enough reserves to provide him with the largest judgment in history. He was going to employ the same tactics that large companies employed. They crushed small law firms that didn't have the material resources to engage in a prolonged battle, and forced them to accept pittances in settlements. Once he destroyed Sherman-Hall, the others would topple like dominos. And once the large firms realized their rearguard had been destroyed, they would discover their own vulnerability.

Check…mate…game…match.

* * *

Powers riffled through the charts on his desk. As difficult as it was for him to admit, he realized that Horscht and Becker were right, because several of the lawsuits against him had been settled for relatively small sums in a very short time. The attorneys were now going after the bigger fish. Nonetheless, his reputation and pride had been sullied. There were still a number of lawsuits that wouldn't go away. He removed two charts from the stack. *Elaine Peters. The attorneys had tried to settle the case but the bitch wouldn't roll over. She thinks she's another Brenda Toole. And this one, Joy Baker, she has no problems or complaints. Her husband's the problem. He hasn't worked a day in years, and he's been sponging off her ever since he injured his back. He thinks I'm going to be the road to easy street.*

His phone flashed.

"Yes Angela."

"That was the airport. The mechanic said he replaced the landing gear and took the plane for a test flight; everything checked out perfectly. The plane'll be ready for you in the morning."

Although many of his colleagues considered Powers to be an arrogant, intolerant, bigoted bastard, none would deny the man's generosity when it came to children. Much of his work with children was done *pro bono*. Twice a year, in December and June, he would fly to a third world country for two weeks under the auspices of Doctors Without Borders to perform surgery on children. He was leaving in the morning with his team, his nurse and her anesthesiologist husband, for the Mayan village of Panajachel in the southwestern highlands of Guatemala. The lay Catholic mission S.O.S—Sending out Servants—had discovered in the region of Lago de Atitlan a number of children with cleft lips and palates that had never been repaired. When Powers agreed to do the surgery he suggested the organization find other children from the region with congenital defects, and he would do what he could to help them. S.O.S. had found forty-six children.

But before he left there was something else he had to do.

* * *

Joy Baker was a mousey thirty-five year old mother of three girls, all under the age of ten. After each pregnancy her breasts lost a little more of their volume and started to sag. She wasn't terribly concerned, but her husband wanted her breasts to be the way they were when they were first married. He finally cajoled her into having implants, and when the lawsuits started making the headlines he bullied her into suing Powers, even though she had no complaints. Her husband was the one who orchestrated the *problems* she presented to her attorney.

She was putting the dishes away when the phone rang. The voice on the other end was muffled, but the message was very clear.

"Law suits filed against innocent people can have very serious consequences. Sulphuric acid can really do nasty things to your face. Drop the lawsuit, or you'll find out just how nasty that can be. If you tell *anyone* about this phone call…it *will* happen."

She dropped the receiver and cupped her face.

"Hey Joy, who was that?" her husband belched, his face frozen on the TV watching two steroid-enhanced kick-boxers attempt to annihilate each other.

No answer.

"Hey, I asked you a question!"

"No one. It was a wrong number…I'm going to bed now."

"Before you do, bring me another beer."

Zombie-like she opened the refrigerator and removed a bottle of Bud Light. She took it into the living room and placed it on the table beside the recliner he was stretched out in. His eyes never left the TV as he reached for the bottle and raised it to his lips.

"Son-of-a-bitch, you never took the fucking top off! Here! Open it." His eyes were still glued to the TV.

"What's the matter is your arm broken?"

"Goddamn it, you know that twisting motion is bad for my back. Just open it!"

She twisted the top off and threw it at him. "Here!"

That got his attention. "What the fuck's with you?" He turned to face her, "Holy shit, you look like you've seen a ghost. Was it that phone call?"

"No. I'm just feeling a little light-headed. I think I'm getting my period."

"Whatever. Just make sure you lock the door before you go to bed." He turned back to the TV.

She lay awake all night visualizing the picture of a woman she saw once, on TV, whose boyfriend threw acid in her face. It was still dark when she got out of bed. She went into the bathroom, flicked on the light, and stared at her reflection in the mirror.

* * *

The bacon was sizzling in the frying pan when he came into the kitchen.

"Where's my coffee?"

She poured his coffee and turned back to the bacon.

"I'm dropping the lawsuit."

"What did you say?"

"You heard me. I said I'm dropping the law suit."

Eight other women had received a similar phone call the previous night.

Houston, December 16, 1991.

Elaine Peters was an attractive redhead with no morals. Her mother ran off with an itinerant musician when she was ten, and that's when her father started visiting her bedroom. The visits continued until she was fifteen, at which time she ended his abuse by wielding an axe that ended his ability to penetrate, propagate, and urinate. He ended up wearing a bag. Since she was a minor at the time her name was never revealed to the press, and her case never went to trial. She ended up in a series of foster homes, never lasting more than six months in any of them. The Houston attorney, Lawrence Band, who represented her went on to become one of the leading trial attorneys in the country, and was a member of the Centurion Counsel. When she decided to sue Powers she immediately contacted Band.

He knew that she didn't have much of a case, but that didn't mean anything. In plaintiff-paradise Texas, a good attorney could get a million dollar judgment if your neighbor ran over your pet snake, and you could prove it was done with malice aforethought. And Band was a good attorney…a very good attorney. He took her case and dutifully reported it to the registry. Powers' attorneys tried to settle her case, but Band was determined to go to trial. Powers was a minor-league player. She was going to be a warm-up for the major-leaguers.

Elaine worked as an escort for a very exclusive and discrete service. She was used to entertaining her clients at Houston's Four Season's, not the Baron Inn. She was a little surprised when she called to find out her next date was staying at that fleabag. But what the hell, if the customer had the two grand opening bid she'd entertain him in Miss Peach's kindergarten class.

She checked the room number she had been given, and knocked on the door.

"The door's open."

She let herself in. His fist was in her face before she could react.

* * *

"Who discovered the body?" Detective Barry Berkson asked the uniformed patrol officer.

"The maid. She's in the office reciting her Hail Marys."

"Maid? I didn't know they changed sheets here. I thought they just sprayed Lysol on them between guests. Lead on MacDuff, show me the body."

Berkson was a grizzled bear of a man who defined the word cynic. One look at him and you thought of a linebacker for the Houston Oilers, not a Woody Allen-glasses-wearing-pussycat who was a lover of ballet and the opera. He stood about six-foot-three and weighed in at about two hundred thirty pounds. His pitch-black hair and Fu Manchu mustache were thought to be Clairol enhanced, because no one at the age of fifty-three was without at least one follicle of grey. He was.

The medical examiner, Dr. Brian Schwartz, was leaning over the body when Berkson came in. "Holy shit!" Berkson uttered when he saw the mutilated body. "It's Karla Faye all over again."

He was referring to Karla Faye Tucker who in 1983 had hacked a young woman, Deborah Thornton, to death with a pick-ax. In 1998, she would become the first female executed in the state of Texas since 1863. Berkson had been the arresting officer.

"She's dead," Schwartz deadpanned. He was known for his laconic way of describing life, or in this case, death. As the medical examiner he spent his days slicing and dicing cadavers and his evenings slicing and dicing various foods. He was a gourmet cook and could sew fabric like Versace when he wasn't sewing bodies.

"Oh? How can you be sure?" Berkson asked, playing the game.

"Well, the blue-bottles have been here and left their babies without a baby-sitter, and she's not breathing."

Berkson dropped the levity, which sometimes was the only way he could cope with the ever-increasing amounts of shit he saw shoveled upon his fellow man.

"When do you figure?"

"I think she bought it sometime between ten and two last night based on the size of the maggots and the degree of rigor. Temp is eighty-eight point two. Normal is ninety-eight point six. Body temp drops about one and a half degrees per hour post-mortem. It was done very methodically. Look at the right side of her jaw. There's some swelling and discoloration, and the skin's slightly abraded. I suspect she was knocked out first and then placed on the bed. And the perp's left-handed."

"I won't dispute the science of temperature," said Berkson, "but what makes you think he, assuming it's a he, is left-handed?"

"The angle of the blow. She *must* have been facing him. If he were right handed the blow would've been on the other side. As you know, when you hit somebody with a fist you have to do it with a swinging motion to knock them out. You don't push your fist into their face. He was left-handed.

"Also, look at the angle of penetration. It indicates the fatal blow came from the right side of the bed. He's a left-handed batter. Her breasts were cut off cleanly with a very sharp knife."

"Trophies?" asked Berkson.

"That's your department Berky," Schwartz said. "I can tell you when and how she was killed, but who and why...that's for you to figure out."

Berkson considered himself fortunate to have Schwartz as the medical examiner. He was one of the few pathologists in the state who was fully qualified and accredited in forensics. Texas was one of the few states in the country that didn't require medical examiners or pathologists to have advanced training in forensics. The theory was that you really couldn't harm a dead person. So anyone fresh out of internship could be a medical examiner.

"I'm outta here," said Schwartz. "Will I see you at the poker game tonight?"

"Only if I'm dead will I miss it...but if I'm dead...then I'll still see you."

Now the tedious part of the investigation would begin. The CSI team would go over the crime scene, inch by inch, hoping to find some obscure piece of evidence that would lead to the killer's identity. Berkson's team would start the canvass, but in this area of town nobody ever saw anything, heard anything, or said anything. See no evil, hear no evil, speak no evil. He'd start with the manager. His partner would organize the canvass when he arrived.

* * *

"So you're telling me that you have no idea who rented the room?"

"That's what I said,"

"Well let me ask you this. If you never saw him how did he get his key and how did you get paid?"

"He phoned earlier in the day and told me what unit he wanted, to leave the door unlocked, and leave the key on the bed. He said I'd find the money in the key deposit box."

"Didn't you find that a little strange?"

"Hey, if you've got the money you can be as strange as you want. Maybe he was a married guy meeting his mistress and didn't want anybody to see him."

You've got that right. "And how much did he leave?"

"A hun...forty dollars."

Berkson sighed, "Show me the bills."

The clerk hesitated. There was only about thirty dollars in the cash box. He couldn't tell him that he had already deposited the money in the bank…it hadn't opened yet. He reached in his wallet and removed two twenty dollar-bills.

"All of them."

He gave Berkson the other three bills. Berkson put the money in an evidence bag and labeled it. He wrote him a receipt for forty dollars and glared at him. "*Thank you* for your sixty dollar donation to the Police Boys' Club." He wrote him another receipt.

Berkson returned to the motel room just as the body was being placed in the CSI van. The techs were putting away their equipment and the first responders were talking to his partner who had arrived while he was with the desk clerk.

"Glad you could make it Murray," Berkson quipped.

"Well, somebody's got to see that this investigation is run properly," he said.

They shook hands.

Murray Fletcher and he had been partners for ten years. Murray was the quiet, taciturn, laid-back one of the two. He never raised his voice nor lost his temper. During an interrogation he was the reassuring one, whereas the explosive Berkson could scare the shit out of an earthworm. They were the perfect good cop/bad cop team.

"You saw her?"

"Yeah. Did they release Karla Faye because she convinced the parole board she really was born again, or did she escape?"

"I hear you. My mustache has been twitching. I've got a feeling this guy is just warming up."

He was almost right. Except the killer wasn't just getting started. He was in full gear, and wasn't finished yet.

CHAPTER SEVENTEEN

Midland, Michigan
Thursday, December 19, 1991.

THE REPRESENTATIVES FROM the breast implant manufacturers were seated around the conference table with the damage-control team from Dow's PR firm, Briggs and Morton. Somber was not an adequate word to describe the expressions on their faces. A mask-of-death would have been more fitting. On December 11, 1991, the Ninth Circuit Court had upheld the $840,000 in compensatory damages and $7.5 million dollars in punitive damages awarded to Mariann Hopkins, "...for injuries sustained as a result of two sets of implants manufactured by Dow..."

When everyone was seated the representative from Dow Corning introduced John Briggs, the president of Briggs and Morton.

"Gentlemen you all know why I'm here, and I'm not going to sugar-coat anything. You've been torpedoed, and my firm has been called in for damage control. I'm not a lawyer, so I won't be giving you any legal advice. The gentleman with me is Richard Lafleur, a lawyer with extensive experience in product liability. He's not here to plan strategy, but rather to answer any legal questions that you may have. Your lawyers were not invited to attend this meeting because, frankly, I believe they were instrumental in getting you into the shit you're now in.

"Did you all think that the lawsuits would just go away if you satisfied the plaintiffs by paying a pittance in compensatory damages? You're in the midst of a category five hurricane that's about to strike land, and I'm afraid a tsunami is just around the corner."

Eyeing the representative from Sherman-Hall he said, "Did you think that the punitive damages on Hopkins would *not* be upheld?" He turned to face the representative from Dow. "Did you think the court records from Stern would be sealed *forever*?" He sighed and shook his head. "Do you have any idea how much John O'Connor's law firm paid their PR firm to get interviews on *Donahue* and *60 Minutes* to discuss the dangers inherent in silicone breast implants? Well neither do I, but I do know that in 1990, Dow paid our PR firm a mere six thousand dollars for public relations. In addition, I might add, the entire proceedings of the Johnson case were broadcast on *Court TV*." He glared again at the representative from Sherman-Hall. "And your president said, according to the transcript I'm holding, 'The goals of Sherman-Hall were not to help patients, but to lead Sherman-Hall employees down the path to the good life.' I shudder to think what John O'Connor will do with that statement when he asks for punitive damages. And I freeze when I think what Ingram Mink will ask for punitively in the Purcell case. O'Connor is good, but he *is not* in the same league as Mink, and we'll know the results of those cases before Christmas.

"I want you to look at this chart and think about where you'll be a year from now if this trend continues...and I assure you it *will* continue."

He turned off the lights and turned on the projector. "Gentlemen, this PowerPoint presentation will be most informative. There's only one slide. You're all familiar with a bar chart. However, your familiarity comes from charts that represent profits and losses from sales. They have their ups and downs. This chart as you can see, represents only one thing...losses. And there's only one direction it'll be going, and that's... up...as in...more losses. Let's examine why.

"1977. Norma Corley. That's the year of the first lawsuit against Dow. Why did she win? Because the jury found that the failure of the 'form or material or performance' of the prosthesis was due to the negligence of the defendants and that such negligence was a proximate cause of the occurrence.

"1984. Maria Stern. We don't know what transpired because the records were sealed.

"July, 1991. Brenda Toole. Reason...'for injuries she received as a result of breast implants...'

"December, 1991. Mariann Hopkins. Why so much? ...'Liable on all plaintiff's theories, including strict liability, breach of warranty and fraud.'

"Gentlemen that's what happened in those four trials. Look where those numbers are headed." He paused to let them digest the numbers.

"Look again at Hopkins. What did I just say? 'Liable on all plaintiffs' theories...' *Theories*...not facts; and because you have been sitting on your collective asses you have no studies and no facts to refute their theories. Now that the stage has been set, emotion will win out every time.

"What you see is what has happened to date. You don't need your bean counters to explain their meaning, or what to expect in the future. How much do you think the award will be when Ingram Mink delivers his closing arguments next week? He has *never* lost a case in court, even when a case started out as a slam-dunk for the defense.

"Gentlemen, the plaintiffs' lawyers have set sail, and you have yet to *raise anchor.* It's been a year since Connie Chung aired her show. *Donahue* and *60 Minutes* followed up with their shows. All three shows were inflammatory, one sided, tear jerkers. Do you have any idea how many women watched those shows? I guarantee you that every woman who has breast implants has seen those shows or knows something about them, unless they've been living in caves. Your silence has been a tacit acknowledgement that something must be wrong with the silicone implants.

"Can we reverse the trend? I doubt it. But maybe we can slow it down until you can come up with some studies that'll show that those things are safe. You'll need to reach out to the plastic surgeons and have them convince their patients that implants are safe, and in turn you're going to have to convince the plastic surgeons that they are *indeed* safe. Get organized gentlemen. Get organized, and for God's sake get started on those studies.

"In closing, you should know that in 1977, there was only one lawsuit filed against Dow Corning. As of today one hundred thirty-five lawsuits have been filed against Dow alone. Of those, one hundred twenty-six have been filed by members of the Centurion Counsel, and of those, ninety-four have been filed by the law firm of Mink and Mink. Merry Christmas gentlemen, I hope you find more than a lump of coal in your Christmas stockings.

"Rich, do you have anything to add?"

Lafleur stood and made eye contact with everyone in the room. "Just one thing...do you all know what a mass tort is?"

CHAPTER EIGHTEEN

Tucson, Arizona
Thursday, December 19, 1991.

INGRAM MINK WAS wearing his blue *jury suit*, the same one he had worn throughout the entire trial. He hadn't polished his shoes and he hadn't cut his hair. Like Neal, he was wearing a Mickey Mouse watch, not the Patek-Phillippe. He approached the jury box, stooped at the shoulders, and made eye contact with each of the eight jurors, and none turned away. That was good. He was ready.

His voice was as soft and warm as a child shoveling sand into a pail. A hint of an eastern European accent was present. It was intentional.

"Ladies and gentlemen it's been a long two weeks, and I want to thank you for taking time away from your families and loved ones as we approach the Christmas season. *As if jurors had a choice.* I know you all want to get home and prepare for Christmas, bake, wrap gifts, decorate your trees, hang the mistletoe, phone your loved ones, and take a stroll or hayride through Winterhaven."

The annual Winterhaven Festival of lights was the transformation of a central Tucson middle-class neighborhood, as if by magic, into a winter wonderland of blinking holiday lights and decorations. Each home was more elaborately decorated than the next. Majestic Aleppo Pines strung with lights that couldn't make up their minds whether they should be red, green, blue, or white, as they changed colors constantly.

"Unfortunately, Louise Purcell will be unable to do *any* of those things. And why not? Because the Board of Directors of the Sherman-Hall Corporation allowed a product that was not tested for safety to be released for use *in*, not *on*, but *in* the human body. With great power comes great responsibility. Sherman-Hall is a great, powerful, corporation that did *not* exercise that great responsibility. Theirs' is an outrageous story of greed, lust, and vanity.

"Louise Purcell's story, on the other hand, is one that could be the story of any of you ladies on the jury." There were four female jurors, Mink would have preferred more, but the defense used its peremptory strikes to exclude as many women as they could. "Louise did not want breast implants for reasons of vanity; she just wanted to look normal again after her breasts had been removed. She made the difficult decision to have her breasts removed because of a strong family history of breast cancer. At the time she made that decision there was nothing wrong with her breasts. Her mother, grandmother, and older sister all had died of a highly malignant form of breast cancer in their late thirties. Louise did not want to take the chance of leaving her three young daughters to grow up without a mother, so at the age of thirty-two she had both breasts removed.

"Her plastic surgeon reassured her that he could make her look normal again by immediately reconstructing her breasts using silicone implants. He told her they were completely safe, that they had been on the market for almost twenty years, and that they would last a lifetime. What he *didn't* tell her was that they could become rock-hard and rupture, and silicone would spread throughout her body and lodge in vital organs. And why didn't he tell her that? He didn't tell her that because the only complication mentioned in the product information put out by the defendant Sherman-Hall at the time she had her surgery performed was that the breasts could become a little hard. *A little hard.* In 1978, Dr. Thomas Baker described four classes of hardness that could occur after a woman had breast implant surgery, with class four being the hardest. Yet in 1980, the product information provided by Sherman-Hall still said 'a slight degree of hardness could develop in some women.' According to her doctor's notes, Louise developed a Baker IV capsular contracture, which is described as 'hard, cold, painful, tender, and distorted.' Is this what the defendant meant by *a little hard*? Louise said she could live with the hardness because she didn't want to go through the *simple* procedure of closed capsulotomy again. That *simple* procedure was far too painful.

"It was shortly after that *simple* procedure that Louise started to have other problems. At first she'd wake up in the morning and feel that she hadn't slept at all. Then came bouts of confusion and memory loss. Pain. How many of us have *not* had pain? A couple of aspirin, maybe an occasional percodan, and the pain usually goes away. But what if the pain doesn't go away? What if the pain is with you every moment of *every* day? First in one arm, then a leg, or maybe a headache...a headache so severe it feels as if your head is being squeezed in a vise. Like the waves of the ocean striking the beach...ebbing and flowing. Never stopping until you are forced to take a pill, and sometimes not even that works.

"Weakness. Louise's six-year-old daughter Amy, asks her for a glass of milk. It's an effort to open the refrigerator door. It takes both hands to lift the milk from the shelf. It's not a gallon of milk... it's a quart. When Louise is having a good day her ten-year-old daughter Melissa helps her with the laundry. Melissa hands her the clothes to put in the washer...one garment at a time.

"Brad. Louise's husband comes home from work; the girls are spending the night at Louise's parents. It's a perfect time to have a romantic candlelight dinner... a glass of wine, but she can't have the wine because the medications she takes caution against the use of alcohol. And then do they retire to the bedroom to make love? No. The pain is far too great. It has been that way for almost four years. *Four years*. Louise is thirty-nine years old. She has a life expectancy of at least thirty-five more years. Is this way her life will be for the next thirty-five years?" Mink pauses and sees moisture in the eyes of three jurors. One is a man.

"In the past four years Louise has visited eleven different doctors. *Eleven*. Every test imaginable has been ordered, and ordered again...

and again. Normal. You have all heard the expression ASAP, which stands for *as soon as possible*. The government and doctors use letter abbreviations a lot, like the FBI, NASA, POTUS, etcetera. Those are the acronyms that the government uses, probably because it gives the people who work there a feeling of importance...'I work for the FBI!' Well doctors use acronyms a lot as well...probably to save time, and probably because anyone who tries to decipher a doctor's handwriting will have an easier job if the letters are capitalized, and those capitals stand for something specific." The jurors all grinned; the judge suppressed a smile. "ASAP…as soon as possible. When I went over Louise's medical records, I found several acronyms under Dx, which stands for diagnosis. NTAFC; CTS; BMW. Ask any doctor what they mean…here's what they mean. NTAFC…nuttier than a fruitcake; CTS…crazier than shit; BMW…bitchy, moaning whiner. Those, ladies and gentlemen, are the only diagnoses after spending thousands of dollars and countless hours that eleven doctors came up with. It would've been easier for Louise to accept if they just would have said... *'I don't know.'* Because they didn't know, it must have been because Louise was *crazier than shit*. But one doctor said, 'I know.' The last one. Her diagnosis? Human Adjuvant Disease.

"Human adjuvant disease is an autoimmune disease which results from the injection of a foreign substance into the body, and if you recall, an autoimmune disease is a disease in which the body produces antibodies against its own tissues. The learned counsel for the defense argued that implants are not injected into the body, therefore a diagnosis of H-A-D is not correct...there I go, using those acronyms." More grins. This time the judge smiled.

"My colleague is correct up to a point. He was correct in saying the implants were not injected. But the minute they ruptured they ceased to be implants. The silicone that migrated throughout Louise Purcell's body produced the same result as surely as if it had been injected by syringe. A condom does not cause pregnancy, but if it ruptures and its contents are released into the vagina...well you know what the result can be.

"Let's take a look at the history of these Human Adjuvant Disease causing silicone implants..."

"Objection! Counsel is stating as fact something that has not been proven."

"Overruled. You'll have your chance to refute when you make your closing argument Mr. Bennett. I'm interested to see where Mr. Mink is going with this. It will be for the jury to decide whether it has been proven."

Ingram was doubly delighted. He had been prepared for Judge Barry Corey to sustain the objection, but even if he hadn't sustained it, Bennett's objection would have re-enforced what he had just said. You can instruct a jury to disregard something, but you can't instruct them to *unhear* it, anymore than you can tell a person to shut his eyes and not visualize a pink elephant with blue polka dots. The fact that Corey overruled the objection was consistent with his thirty-year history as a plaintiff's attorney before he was appointed to the bench. Bennett had made a tactical error.

"Thank you your honor," Mink said, feigning humility. "Ladies and gentlemen, silicone breast implants have undergone many changes since they were first introduced in 1962. To date there have been four generations of breast implants, and within each generation there have been modifications. Why? Because the manufacturers couldn't get it right. Did they think they were dealing with soap-powder? 'Use our *new-and-improved* product. It will make your clothes whiter and softer.' Well, that logic may work when you wash clothes, but it doesn't work with a product that is supposed to be *forever,* a product that has been surgically implanted into your body. The *new and improved* implants did not make breasts softer, like soap powder was supposed to do with clothes. Nope, they continued to remain hard.

"The first generation implants were tear-drop-shaped, with thick shells, holding, or supposedly holding, the gelatinous silicone at bay. But they remained in a teardrop shape even when a woman lay down on her back. Not the natural appearance of a woman's breast. Also, they were hard, and you could feel the edges of the implants, and as the capsules around the implants developed, the breasts became distorted. So to fix this problem the surgeon would either have to cut the patient open again to release the scarring, or if the breasts weren't too hard he could rupture the capsule by taking the breast and squeezing it as hard as he could until he felt the capsule rupture, and oftentimes rupturing the implant as well, releasing the gelatinous silicone into the body.

"Well that didn't work out so well, so the defendant made the shell containing the silicone much thinner so you couldn't feel the edges, and as result the implant was much softer. But the thinner shell allowed the silicone to gradually bleed out into the body and rupture spontaneously, without the help of the surgeons who kept on squeezing those breasts to break the capsules that would not go away. So the next brilliant move, to try and keep that hardness from occurring, was to just have an outer thin shell of silicone and fill it will saline...saltwater. Water's nice and soft. But what the defendant didn't take into consideration was the possibility that these devices might just spring a leak and deflate, necessitating additional surgery and additional medical expenses. Have any on the jury ever blown up a balloon, triple-tied it, and have it keep its air? That's what the defendant Sherman-Hall believed about the saline implants. Again, they said the implants would last a lifetime. How could they say that? They never did any research to substantiate their claims. Well, saline filled implants were deflating at an alarming rate, so it was back to the drawing board. Next, they coated the implants with polyurethane...*polyurethane*, which caused an inflammation that was supposed to prevent the capsule from forming around the implants. The only problem with the polyurethane was that after awhile it disintegrated into a substance called TDA, which was known to cause cancer in animals. Back came the capsule. Was this yet another attempt at an implant that would last *forever*? It's interesting this polyurethane coated implant was named *Même,* which in French means the same. *The same.* And, the same means *no difference*. But this was supposed to be a *new and improved* implant."

Bennett bolted up and yelled, "Objection. Clearly inflammatory."

Before Corey could rule Mink said, "Yes, What I said ab*out Même* is clearly *inflammatory*. I withdraw the comment." *Withdrawn, but not forgotten.*

White queen to h5...check.

Mink was just getting warmed up. He went through the other modifications made in the second generation of implants, and those made in the next two generations, detail by minute detail.

"Ladies and gentlemen of the jury, you have listened to the tedious chronology of the manufacture of silicone breast implants. What is the one common thread that links them all?" He paused. "They were never subjected to proper clinical testing. Did the defendant Sherman-Hall ever consider following guidelines to ensure the safety of their medical devices? They did not. And why not? The answer is because they didn't have to. It wasn't until 1976, that the FDA had the authority to review and approve the safety and effectiveness of new medical devices. But because silicone implants had been on the market for almost fifteen years, they were *grandfathered*, and unlike any new devices, Sherman-Hall would not be required to prove the safety and effectiveness of their silicone implants.

"It wasn't until 1982, that the FDA proposed classifying silicone implants into a class III category, which would now require breast implant manufacturers, including Sherman-Hall, to prove the safety and efficacy of the implants. And it wasn't until June 1988, that they were so classified. So what happened? Nothing! It wasn't until July of this year that PMAs—Premarket Approval Applications—were required to be submitted. And the PMAs were required to show, with valid scientific data evaluated by the FDA, that their devices were safe and effective.

"After the manufacturers submitted the PMAs in July, the FDA had one-hundred eighty days to evaluate the safety data. Well guess what? That won't be until January of next year.

"At the beginning of my summation I said, 'with great power comes great responsibility.' Sherman-Hall is a great, powerful, corporation that did not exercise that great responsibility. This is an outrageous story of *greed, lust, and vanity*. Let us look at that statement again. Sherman-Hall is a great, powerful corporation. Did they exercise great responsibility? They did not. For twenty-one years Sherman-Hall was totally unregulated. It was as if a group of five-year-olds was given the keys to a candy store without any supervision. Greed? Make as much money as you can...take as much candy as you can. Lust? The intense craving for it all...the whole candy store. Vanity? Their own self-importance, 'we don't have to answer to anyone...we can eat as much candy as we want, and no one can stop us.' "

He paused, and eyed each member of the jury. None broke eye contact. Neal Mink, sitting in the second chair knew the best was yet to come. Bennett and his team knew the worst was yet to come. It was the best of times; it was the worst of times. For the next two hours Ingram chewed apart the prey known as Sherman-Hall. It was now time for the final course.

"Ladies and Gentlemen, you have heard evidence that the defendant Sherman-Hall altered and conveniently *misplaced* or lost records that proved they knew of the problems patients and doctors were having with their product. And what did they do when they learned of the problems? They put a different type of implant on the market, without adequate laboratory testing of its efficacy or safety, and added a smidgen more information in their patient brochures about the remote possibility of additional complications that might occur. Those implants went directly from their laboratories in Hemlock, Michigan into the bodies of uninformed women. They had no ethics.

"Ethics. Are you aware that the Greek philosopher, Socrates, a founder of Western philosophy, renowned for his contributions to the field of ethics was executed because of his ethics while trying to improve the city-state of Athens' sense of justice? He was forced to drink a cup of poison called Hemlock. *Hemlock is poison*!"

Bennett was on his feet. "Objection! Counsel's last statement is irrelevant and inflammatory."

Corey banged his gavel. "Sustained. Mr. Mink, please refrain from delivering speeches on history. Stay focused on the issues... the jury will disregard Mr. Mink's last statement."

Ingram smiled to himself. *That shmuck Bennett doesn't get it. Didn't he realize I wanted him to object? Now the jury won't be able to forget the hemlock connection. Corey only reinforced their remembrance when he told the jury to disregard.* He knew Corey appreciated what he had done, because Corey would have done the same thing when he was a plaintiff's attorney.

"I'm sorry your honor...I just got carried away. It won't happen again."

Bullshit, thought Corey, *of course it will happen again, or he's not the lawyer I thought he was. Doesn't Bennett realize Mink's just playing chess with him?*

"Proceed Mr. Mink."

"We know of the shameful way that Sherman-Hall conducted their business and their total disregard for the safety and well-being of women who accepted, on faith, that their implants were indeed safe. I quote again from the memo issued by the president of Sherman-Hall. 'The goals of Sherman-Hall were not to help patients, but to lead Sherman-Hall employees down the path to the good life.' That's what he said."

Bennett squirmed as Mink paused to let the full impact of that statement be absorbed by the jury. He knew full well that one of the basic techniques a good lawyer employed during the course of a trial was to have a jury hear an irrefutable piece of evidence presented three times. Mink had just presented it for the second time. Bennett knew the third time was coming, and when it did he knew the three members on the Board of Directors of Sherman-

Hall would end up looking like the Three Stooges.

"Ladies and gentlemen of the jury, Louise Purcell will never again walk down the path to *the good life.* She will be walking down the path to the *living hell*, and unless someone comes up with a cure for the diseases wracking her body she will be walking that path to hell for the rest of her life. And she will have to pay to walk that path. She can't pay her present medical bills; she's exceeded the maximum allowed in medical benefits provided by her medical insurance. One-million-dollars. Gone! Not one penny of those one million dollars relieved her pain and suffering. Her pain and suffering are intractable. How much will her medial care cost for the rest of her life? We can only estimate." He raised his voice in controlled fury. "The defendant Sherman-Hall has destroyed this young woman's life. The goals of Sherman-Hall were not to help patients, but to lead Sherman-Hall employees down the path to *the good life.*

"In closing, I would like to say if you, the jury, had the power to return Louise Purcell's life back to the way it was before she had breast implants, that's all she would ask. But you can't do that, so we believe the $10 million in compensatory damages, and $50 million punitive damages we have asked for are reasonable. Thank you."

The courtroom was as silent as an army of feathers striking the floor. The jurors' eyes did not hide their anger. Bennett saw it and the entire courtroom saw it. All he could hope for was that the jury wouldn't get carried away with their award. He couldn't reverse the emotional blitzkrieg with which Mink assaulted the jury, but he could minimize the damage with an effective closing. Besides, the amounts Mink was asking were preposterous and unheard of.

Corey swiveled his chair to view the wall clock and then turned back to face the jury. "We'll recess for lunch and reconvene at one o'clock sharp. Lateness will not be tolerated. Once again I admonish you not to discuss this case with anyone, not even among yourselves. Court is recessed."

He slammed his well-worn gavel on his desk as the bailiff intoned, "All rise."

Corey rose and left the courtroom. The jurors filed out next, followed by the spectators. Neal and Ingram remained standing, facing the front of the courtroom. When the courtroom had cleared Neal turned to his brother and laughed. "Should I remove the onions from under the jurors' chairs?"

Ingram grinned, "Leave them there for the next trial."

They sat down.

"I've studied Bennett's moves throughout the trial. He's maneuvered his time to ensure his words were the last the jury would hear before being dismissed for the day. I let him do it."

"Why?"

"Based on the information you provided, Bennett rarely spends more than three hours on his closing arguments. He knows Corey likes to finish on time, so I expect him to be finished by around four-thirty today. He thinks the jury will hear his words last, before recessing for the weekend.

"Corey goes to the Garlands, in Sedona, every year at this time, and would love to have the trial over by the end of today so he can join his wife, who is already there."

"And you know this…how?"

"Slater is a wealth of information."

Marvin Slater was their chief investigator, a retired cop, and former Recon Marine, who was now a private investigator.

Neal furrowed his brow, and then smiled. "But, that doesn't give you much time for your rebuttal, and…what about the jury's deliberations?"

"Watch what happens."

* * *

"All rise."

Corey eased into his chair and glanced at the clock, "Mr. Bennett, are you prepared for your closing arguments?"

"Yes your honor."

Corey nodded to the bailiff, and said, "Bailiff bring in the jury."

The jurors entered the courtroom like soldiers on parade, and when they were seated Corey banged his gavel once more. "Court is now in session. Mr. Bennett you may proceed."

"Thank you your honor.

"Ladies and gentlemen of the jury, you have heard Mr. Mink offer…"

As Mink had predicted Bennett had finished his summation just before four-thirty, and Corey didn't have to look at the clock to know the time, Bennett had appeared before him many times before, and he knew how long his summations took.

"Because of the time…" he started.

Ingram was on his feet, "Your honor, if it please the court, my rebuttal will take but five minutes."

Corey was pleased and puzzled. Bennett was not pleased, but he was puzzled. "Very well, Mr. Mink, you may proceed."

"Thank you your honor."

He approached the jurors' box, and like in a state of nystagmus, his eyes moved rapidly back and forth from one juror to another without him ever moving his head. "Ladies and gentlemen, I have nothing more to add. You have heard my arguments and those of Mr. Bennett; it's now time for you to make a decision. Based on the evidence I am confident that you will make the correct decision and find for the plaintiff, Mrs. Louise Purcell. Thank you."

This time Corey looked at the clock. It took Mink less than one minute. "Well, that was certainly a surprise Mr. Mink. Ladies and gentlemen of the jury…"

Corey was interrupted again, this time by the jury foreman. "Your honor, I don't know if it's proper to ask, but would it be okay if we made our decision today, instead of next week?"

Corey was delighted, Bennett deflated, and Mink demure.

"Mr. Mink?"

"No objection."

Mr. Bennett?

Bennett slumped in his chair, "No objection.

"Very well then…" Corey gave the jury their final instructions, and the bailiff led them to the jury room.

Sixty-three minutes later the light flashed signifying the jury had reached a decision. They were led back into the courtroom, and assumed their seats. Corey raced back to the courtroom.

"Mr. foreman, has the jury reached a decision?"

"It has your honor."

Very well then, bailiff…"

The foreman handed the bailiff the paper with their decision, and he gave it to the judge. Corey adjusted his glasses and scanned the paper. He looked up and gave it back to the bailiff, who in turn returned it to the foreman.

"The jury finds for the plaintiff in the sum of twenty-five million dollars in compensatory damages, and…one hundred million dollars punitive damages."

The courtroom erupted.

CHAPTER NINETEEN

Panajachel, Guatemala
Saturday, December 21, 1991.

PANAJACHEL, A TOWN in the southwestern Guatemalan Highlands hugging the northeast shore of Lake Atitlån, was known as the *Mile High* city of Central America, rising 5,240 feet from sea level; it was founded in the 16th century during the Spanish conquest of Guatemala. The Spaniards established a church, the façade of which still stands, and a monastery. They used the town as a center to convert the indigenous Mayans to Catholicism.

Powers and his companions were waiting outside the Casa Cakchiquel Hotel for the representative from Friendship Bridge, a medical missionary group based in Denver, to drive them back to Guatemala City where their plane was waiting to fly them to Miami on their way back to Tucson.

"A brilliant job Devin. There are now forty-two kids who'll have a better shot at life thanks to you," said Fred Landers the anesthesiologist.

"Come on Fred, you know I couldn't have done it without you and Julie."

His humility was in stark contrast to the arrogance he displayed when he was back in the U.S. Landers was never sure just who was the real Devin Powers. Will the real Devin Powers please stand up? He truly believed Powers was an insecure kid at heart, who tried to overcome his insecurities by attempting to dominate everyone around him.

"Devin, the timing couldn't have worked out better for us. Julie and I had planned to spend Christmas with her family in Miami;

the kids are already there. What are your plans? You're welcome to spend Christmas with us."

"Thanks for the offer, but I have to get back to deal with all those lawsuits."

Landers knew exactly what he meant. He had been named in two of the suits because he had been the anesthesiologist in those cases. It's a good thing the janitor hadn't been in the operating room at the time, or he would've been named in the lawsuits as well.

A vintage Land Rover decorated with dust and dents pulled up in front of the hotel and the three climbed in. Forty-two children would now be able to smile for the first time in their lives.

Miami, Florida, December 23, 1991.

He was a cop's cop, and his solve rate was the highest in the state, but a little known secret was that homicide detective Steve Lasky really didn't like the sight of blood, especially his own. A cut finger warranted a 911 call and a helicopter evacuation to the nearest level I trauma center, when actually a Band-Aid would have sufficed. The only other phobia he had was his irrational fear of dogs. A Chihuahua was an attack dog, but his son's Rottweiler, a frequent guest in his home, was a pussycat. Lasky was a transplanted New Yorker who waved good-bye to the snow when he left New York. The only snow he ever wanted to see again was in the shape of a Snow Cone. Steve was an unusual cop, unusual because he had an I.Q. of 142. He had the quickest mind and wit in the entire Miami-Dade Police Department. When his son once asked why he had a mustache, his answer was, "Because it keeps my lip warm when I eat ice-cream."

The only one in the Department who came close to keeping up with him was his partner Phil Forman. Their knowledge of trivia was legendary.

"Highest navigable lake in the world?" challenged Lasky.

"Lake Titicaca in Bolivia," replied Forman.

They had been friends for years. They were both about the same height. Lasky had a full head of hair, missing only a patch on the crown. Forman had hair on the crown and all the way to the nape, but was scant in front. They dressed pretty much the same, casual, but Lasky always had a display of his last meal on the front of his shirt. Spare shirts shared space with the spare tire in the trunk of his car.

The crime scene was a houseboat moored on the Miami River, with a backdrop of private homes dripping with dollars. There were several uniformed police officers securing the perimeter. Dr. Arnold Hollander, the medial examiner, was preparing to leave the boat as the two detectives approached. "Well if it isn't my favorite two detectives, Dick Tracy and Sam Ketchum." He was referring to Chester Gould's legendary comic strip characters. "Remind me, which one of you is the Dick?"

With a straight face Lasky said, "Hi Arnie. Say, did you ever get your mother to autograph her book for me?"

"What book?"

"You know, *The Happy Hooker*, the autobiography of the Dutch prostitute, Xaviera Hollander."

"No comment."

Hollander was quick, but no match for Lasky, a master of the quick retort.

"Is there room in there for both of us?" Lasky asked.

"I'll go. You can interview the first responders," Forman said. "What can you tell us Arnie?"

"Either she consented to being chopped up, or she was unconscious at the time. I suspect the latter, because I really can't imagine someone agreeing to being whacked with an axe. There's no sign of a struggle. She was probably sleeping when that dastardly act was performed."

Hollander was well known for his droll humor when discussing death. It masked his true feelings. His outer self belied his inner self. The inscription on the bronze star that he earned in Viet Nam defined who he was: *Heroic or meritorious achievement*. He was the most astute forensic pathologist in Dade County.

"An axe?" asked Forman.

"Yeah, you'll see for yourself. She died between three and three-thirty in the morning. I'll know for sure when I do the vitreous."

"Between three and three-thirty? How the hell can you be that precise? You know your usual fudge factor is at least two hours," Lasky said.

"Aha, detective, you're not keeping up with the latest technology," Hollander puffed.

"Alright your doctorness, please inform us."

Hollander grinned, "Because there was an eye-witness who saw someone board her boat at around three and leave at three-thirty. Now gentlemen, I really must go, and because I am imbued with the Christmas spirit, I'll fast track the post and do it this afternoon. Besides, my wife and I are leaving for Vegas in the morning."

"I thought you had a poker chip from every casino in the world," said Lasky.

"A new casino opened, and I have to check it out to see if it meets my high standards," he smiled. "Get to work gentlemen, so I can get to work."

He started toward one of the many Austin-Healeys that he had restored over the years when Lasky yelled out. "If your name is Hollander you must be descended from an Ashkenazi who was raped by a Viking when they invaded Holland. Nobody from Poland has red hair. Your mother *had* to have been the Happy Hooker."

Hollander kept walking, circling the bird at Lasky.

"Steven. I'm surprised at you, he's older than Xaviera Hollander, she wasn't born until 1943. She couldn't be his mother."

Lasky arched his eyebrows, "Really? You know that for a fact?"

"Of course. Do you doubt me?"

"Well maybe she's his sister. Let's get to work."

Forman entered the houseboat and Lasky went to talk to the first responder who took the 911.

"So what can you tell me," Lasky glanced at his nametag, "Officer Jefferson?"

He looked at his notes. "We responded to the nine-eleven called in at zero-three-forty. A neighbor in the next houseboat saw somebody leave the victim's houseboat in a real hurry, so he thought he should check on her."

"Where is he now?"

"He's by his houseboat, *The Bouncing Ball*, in the next slip, his name's Jack Ball. That's my partner talking to him."

"Thanks. I'll go talk to him."

Lasky noticed there were a lot fewer houseboats moored than the last time he was here. They used to be squeezed together as tight as a bag filled with marshmallows, but there were just these two, with about 50 feet separating them, and a couple of others about 100 yards apart. He looked over and saw a short, stout man, waving his arms, talking to the other cop. He approached them.

"Mr. Ball, I'm Detective Lasky."

He turned to face Lasky. "That's me. I was telling this policeman I seen a lotta' bad shit in Desert Storm, but nothing like what happened to that poor girl over there."

"Please start at the beginning and tell me what you saw."

"Well, I'm a light sleeper, and around three it started raining pretty hard. I woke up and got up to cover the furniture in the bow when I saw this guy boarding Brandy's boat. I thought it was weird because Brandy never has visitors that show up in the middle of the night, if you know what I mean."

Lasky nodded, and thought, *if he knows she has visitors that don't show up on her boat in the middle of the night, he must watch her boat a lot...in the middle of the night*. "Go on."

"A few minutes later he left the boat...I checked my watch... it was three-thirty. I saw him take off down the river walk, away from downtown."

"Can you describe him and what he was wearing?"

He sized up Lasky. "He was taller than you...wearing a long coat...maybe a raincoat...no hat... but it was funny, his arm was folded across his chest, like he was holding something." He paused. "After he was gone I thought I better go check and see if Brandy was all right, and that's when I saw her. Fuck, I almost lost my cookies. I've never seen anything like that. I checked her pulse, but she was gone. Christ...her neck. I was a medic in Desert Storm, and the worst shrapnel wound I saw never looked like this. And her tits! The guy cut off her goddamn tits."

"You said 'he.' Are you sure it was a man?"

"Well unless it was a woman with short hair wearing a man's coat...it was a man."

"Color?"

"Couldn't tell."

"Anything else that you noticed?"

He thought for a moment. "Nope that's all I remember."

"What can you tell me about Brandy?"

Ball filled him in on everything he knew about her.

Lasky gathered his thoughts and said. "Mr. Ball, I know it'll be hard, but I would really appreciate it if you didn't mention anything about her breasts to anyone, especially if you're contacted by someone from the press. We're going to receive a lot of crank calls from people who will claim to be the killer, and if this information is not made public, it will help us sort out those crank calls."

"I get it. Something that only the real killer would know about."

"Exactly."

"My lips are sealed. They won't hear it from me."

Lasky doubted it. The press would find out eventually, especially if this was the work of someone who had done it before, or who was planning to do it again. "Anything else?"

Ball thought for a moment. "I can't think of anything."

"Well, if you do, you can contact me. Here's my card. By the way, I noticed that there's only a few boats slipped here now, is there a reason?"

"Yeah. At first the city banned any more houseboats from mooring on the river if people planned to live on them. There were thirty-eight of us who'd been here for years, so we fought it and won because we'd all lived here for years and had nowhere else to go. All those yuppies living in those fancy high-rises, and the rich-bitches who have their houses on the riverside said we were polluting the river. The real reason was because they complained we were blocking their views."

Lasky thanked him and returned to the other houseboat. He braced himself, took a deep breath, and went aboard. Forman was talking with the two CSIs in the bedroom. There was barely enough room for two, let alone four. "Holy shit," he said when he saw the carnage. "I've seen enough. Meet me outside and we can talk."

Forman followed him out to the forecastle and let the CSIs get back to their work.

"What did you learn?" asked Forman.

Lasky repeated the neighbor's observations and added, "Brandy Evans, twenty-eight, lived alone, no family that the neighbor's aware of, ran a small fishing charter out of Bayshore with a another girl, 'Cookie' Cutter. He gave me their card. He said she had no regular boyfriend, but had a lotta guys who visited her. I'll go visit the girlfriend if you get the canvass started. We can meet at the morgue when Hollander gives us the heads up.

"Lowest lake in South America?"

Forman thought for a moment. "Laguna del Carbón, Argentina. Now get your ass to work."

* * *

"Cookie" Cutter was a thirty-something bronze blonde, baked and bleached by the sun's rays. Lasky had to support her when he told her that her friend had been murdered.

"Poor Brandy," she wiped tears from her eyes with a tissue Lasky had found. "Just when she thought things were turning around for her."

"What do you mean?"

"Well, she was always self-conscious about her small breasts, so about a year ago she went to Tucson to get a boob-job."

"Tucson? Why Tucson? Miami's crawling with plastic surgeons."

"Money. This guy was supposed to be one of the best, and cheaper than the Miami plastic surgeons. He had a place where she could recuperate after the surgery. Even with the air-fare the total cost was about a thousand bucks cheaper than having it done here. And by staying at his place she'd really be getting a week's vacation as well."

"Do you know his name?"

"I think it was Powell or Powers...something like that."

"What did you mean when you said, 'things were beginning to turn around for her?' "

"Well, she never dated a lot before the boob-job, but after she had them done she felt lots better about herself, and started seeing a lotta guys."

"Anyone in particular?"

"No, nothing serious. Sometimes she'd go out with a guy after a charter, but nobody on a regular basis."

"You said 'things,' was there something else?"

She fidgeted with the now shredded tissue. "If I tell you, you won't think she was a bad person, will you?"

"Cookie, I don't judge people. Anything you can help me with to find Brandy's killer is important."

She didn't answer for a moment, and then took a deep breath. "Lately, the charter business has been real slow, and we've had to struggle to make payments on the boat. Brandy saw this ad in the Herald from a lawyer who was getting money for women who were having health problems because of their breast implants."

"Did Brandy have any problems?"

She hesitated. "Not really, but she figured how could they prove she wasn't feeling tired all the time, and having all kinds of pain. She thought maybe she could get enough money so we could pay off the boat." Her eyes dropped.

"Do you have this lawyer's name?"

She fumbled in her purse and gave him the lawyer's card that she picked up when she went to the lawyer's office with Brandy. It read, "Donald Worthington Attorney-at-law. Charter member: The Centurion Counsel."

* * *

A morgue is not exactly a place where you would consider entertaining your friends, enemies perhaps—but not friends. However, Dade County's The Joseph H. Davis Center for Forensic Pathology is different. As you approach the building you are greeted by a balance of South Florida tropical trees, washed river stone and warm earth tones of a patterned brick design lushly landscaped with indigenous tropical shrubs and bushes. Visitors find the lobby a warm, bright, environment, befitting a luxury hotel, enhanced by a three story open staircase and atrium, capped by a skylight. The marriage and use of wood, red Georgia brick, plush carpet, and cushioned furniture create a home-like atmosphere.

Lasky and Forman met in the spacious parking lot and went directly to the morgue complex. They were shown to the autopsy room where Hollander was waiting for them.

"You know Arnie, I'm sure the only reason you were hired for this job is because your red hair is a perfect match for the red Georgia brick in the lobby," quipped Lasky.

"Careful Lasky, I could find a room for you here, and you would never be found."

He had already started the autopsy, but was waiting for the detectives to arrive, to point out some very interesting findings.

"This I what I want you to see. Look at this smooth sheet of tissue on her chest wall."

Forman leaned over. "It looks like the tissue surrounding a placenta. But what are those bluish lumps in it?"

"Very good observation. You get an A plus. Steve come a little closer. I want you to see this too."

Lasky wanted to back-peddle out of the room, but he wouldn't give Hollander the satisfaction of seeing him react. Hollander took a scalpel and cut through one of the lumps. A gooey, gelatinous, clear fluid oozed out.

"What the hell is that?" Forman asked.

"Liquid silicone. The tissue on the chest wall is the back of a capsule that always forms around a breast implant. Your lady had breast implants that had ruptured. Another capsule formed around the liquid silicone, I expect to find silicone particles throughout her body when I do the microscopic examinations."

"I knew she had implants, but her friend told me she had no problems. Wouldn't she've had some kind of reaction to all that goo?" Lasky asked.

"You saw the reaction. The capsule on the wall of her chest formed after the implants were inserted, and the capsule surrounding the liquid silicone is the secondary reaction.

"For years women had silicone injections in Japan and Mexico, and most of the tissue reaction they got was like what you see here where the silicone leaked out. When your killer cut off her breasts, he removed them very carefully. The implants went with them."

Forman turned to Lasky. "Trophies?"

"Maybe, and maybe someone wanted a lawsuit to go away," Lasky replied.

CHAPTER TWENTY

Tucson, Arizona
Tuesday, January 7, 1992.

"WELL BIG BROTHER, it looks like the manufacturers have capitulated as a result of our campaign," Neal said as he plopped down in the client's chair in front of Ingram's desk. "The head of the FDA, David Kessler, just announced all manufacturers have agreed to a voluntary moratorium on the use of breast implants until the FDA and its advisory panel of monkeys can evaluate the new information."

"Well that should certainly create a frenzy when women hear that their implants may not be safe. And by the way, speaking of women, how's it going with PAWN?" Ingram asked.

"Better than expected. We can't handle the number of calls that are coming in. We've got six doctors lined up who'll testify that silicone can cause anything from social diseases to pregnancy. Can't you just hear it? 'Oh my God, if I hadn't had those implants put in I wouldn't have improved my self-esteem, and if I hadn't improved my self-esteem I wouldn't have gotten laid, and if I hadn't gotten laid I wouldn't have contracted Chlamydia.'

"We've also lined up the participants for the seminars on breast implant litigation. There are a couple of docs who'll say they can find silicone anywhere in the body, and have the studies to back up what they say about the effects on the immune system. The acting coaches are right out of Hollywood. The jury consultants are incredible. I think the English poet William Blake said it best, 'See what it is to play unfair! Where cheating is, there's mischief there.' "

"That's true," Ingram said. "And although I hate to admit it, Hitler was right when he said, 'If you tell a big enough lie and tell it frequently enough it will be believed.' He would have been something in a courtroom."

"Speaking of courtrooms," Neal said, "by the end of the year there should be thousands of lawsuits filed. Are you gonna take a break?"

"Of course not, but it's going to take longer to get a case on the docket, the courts can't physically handle the volume. We need to work on the mass tort and of course the appeal on Purcell. We both know that it's unlikely that the punitive will hold up, and it'll take years to resolve. I understand Sherman-Hall's insurers are balking and are trying to use the fraud card to get out of paying. We'll need to tighten the screws and get them to settle before they wake up and run for a chapter eleven. Anything else?"

"Yeah, I got a call from Don Worthington in Miami, he asked me to drop one of his clients from the data base. She was murdered just before Christmas."

Ingram raised his eyebrows.

"That's not all. After he called I checked the database. She's the fourth, and there are eight others who've withdrawn their suits."

"I think we should call Slater and have him find out just what the hell is going on."

* * *

When Powers returned from Guatemala he had been greeted with four additional lawsuits. Two of the previous ones had been settled, but he was approaching a state of critical mass, and an explosion was imminent. The amount of insurance remaining in his liability policy was dwindling, and if the case against him by Louise Purcell went to court the remainder could be wiped out in the blink of an eye. However, Hans and Fritz assured him that they could negotiate the suit away because the plaintiff's attorneys would be concentrating their efforts on the manufacturers, based on the recent award against Sherman-Hall. He wasn't convinced. His personal attorney advised him to prepare for bankruptcy, despite the fact he was certain the corporate veil could not be pierced, keeping his 401K safe. That wasn't the point. It was his reputation that wasn't safe. He reached for the phone.

"I have some more phone calls for you to make."

Midland, Michigan, January 7, 1992.

It wasn't the usual post-Christmas depression that was reflected on the faces of the assemblage. They were the faces of Stalingrad. FDA Commissioner David Kessler had just lowered the starting flag for every plaintiff's attorney in the country by requesting that breast implant manufacturers place a *voluntary* moratorium on the use of silicone gel implants.

The representative from DCC—Dow Corning Corporation—rose to his feet and said, "Gentlemen, this meeting will be held *in camera*. Note taking will not be allowed. This meeting never took place.

"By April of this year the Dow Corning Corporation will no longer manufacture breast implants. And it's my understanding that Bioplasty and Bristol-Myers-Squibb will be following suit. The breast implant is only one of over fifteen hundred medical devices we manufacture, and it generates only one percent of total revenue, yet it's responsible for over ninety-five-percent of the litigation that has been initiated against our firm. That is an *intolerable* situation."

William Sherman from Sherman-Hall was quick to his feet. "That may be fine for you, but what about those of us who don't have fifteen hundred other products to fall back on? As it stands right now we'll be close to bankruptcy if the Purcell award is upheld on appeal. We relied on your assurances that you had carried out the research. We still have twenty-four cases pending with that son-of-a-bitch Mink, and financially there's no way we can defend them."

"To quibble among ourselves is exactly what the PI attorneys want us to do," said Jack Hogan, the CEO of Hogan Medical Supply. "The reality is that our collective ships are sinking. Bill, you were doomed once the Purcell award hit the news. There are law firms that are now taking only breast implant cases. Neal Mink is setting up training sessions across the country to teach attorneys how to litigate breast implant cases. There's not enough time left in this millennium, and there are not enough courts in this country to deal with what's coming down the pike.

"Class actions will be the only answers. Based on the jury awards so far, we'll have to create a fund that'll have to be in the billions, because our insurance coverage will turn out to be grossly inadequate if every case were to be litigated successfully in the plaintiffs' favor."

"I'm afraid Jack is right," said Bruce Draper, of Draper–Payne Medical Devices. "But that's only half the problem. We're being assaulted on two fronts. Our insurers are now disclaiming coverage because they claim we *knowingly and willfully committed fraud and deceit*." He looked directly at the representative from DCC.

It wasn't Stalingrad...it was Hiroshima.

Cleveland, Ohio, January 7, 1992.

The homicide department of the Cleveland Division of Police was located on the fourth floor of the Ontario Street Headquarters. Sadowsky was reading an advertisement in the Plain Dealer when Scalpone approached his desk. "I see you learned how to read over the holidays."

"Nah, I'm looking at the pictures. Take a look at this."

"What am I looking for?" Scalpone asked.

"This advertisement."

"Oh, from the Law Firm of DSH and Associates."

"That's the one." He paused for a moment. "I think those letters stand for *Dewey, Screwem, and Howe*. Those sleaze-buckets are soliciting women who had breast implant surgery, asking them to call if they have had any of these symptoms. I guess that's why they call them solicitors."

"Nah… solicitors are pimps."

"There's a difference?" Sadowsky asked.

Scalpone shrugged, "I guess not. Holy shit! It's a list of every symptom for every disease known to man. I love this line, 'You may be entitled to financial compensation.' What's the lawyer's cut these days?"

"I think it's around a third plus expenses," said Sadowsky.

"So what's your point about the ad?'

"I dunno…I just got to thinking about that woman who was axed last year and wondered if it'd had something to do with the breast implants she was gonna have removed."

Scalpone looked at the ad again and said, "Remember that doc in Tucson? Wouldn't talk to us on the phone? I hear Tucson's a nice place to visit in January…you think the boss would authorize a trip?"

Los Angeles, California, January 7, 1992.

The Police Administration Building in Downtown L.A. was considered state of the art when it was completed in 1955. In 1966, it was renamed the Parker Center to honor former LAPD chief William H. Parker. It became a household name and was identified more with the TV cop shows that were filmed there, such as *Dragnet* and *Perry Mason*, than for the real work that went on.

Detectives Don Saffer and Winston Martin were becoming inundated with ever increasing numbers of murders to deal with, and Faith Greene's file kept getting buried deeper in the pile of unsolved cases. They were sitting at their desks in the ever-shrinking space allocated to them in the homicide section of Parker Center when a call came in from pathologist Dr. Ed Rogoff. Martin picked up the call.

"Is this Dean Martin?" Rogoff asked. "If it is, put your partner Jerry Lewis on the other line, I think I may have something for you two comedians."

Martin signaled to Saffer to pick up the phone.

"Don's on the other line, go ahead Ed."

"I just returned from a meeting in Cleveland. While I was there I had dinner with a buddy of mine that I did my post-graduate training with after internship. We were playing catch-up, and he told me about a murder victim that he had posted a little over a year ago." He paused for dramatic effect.

Saffer sighed, "Get to the point Ed."

"The vic was a woman who had been chopped to death with an axe. Her tits had been cut off and…"

"And what?" Saffer asked.

"Like our victim, …she had had silicone implants."

Houston, Texas, January 7, 1992.

It had been only a couple of weeks since Elaine Peters had been murdered, but the case was already cold. No clues, no suspects, she was not a priority. Hookers rarely made the A list. Her attorney Lawrence Band had taken her case only because of his association with her when he got the charges dismissed after she eunuchated her father. And the only reason he took her case *pro bono* was because he had a weakness for underage redheaded girls. And she was a temptress who worked magic with his *bono*. The best lay he ever had.

When he found out she had been murdered he was actually relieved. She didn't have much of a case to start with, and he was always afraid that one day she might turn on him and reveal his past indiscretions with her. If she had, he would've been disbarred and probably indicted for statutory rape. The statute of limitations for statutory rape in Texas was ten years, starting the day the minor turned eighteen. She still had two years to bring charges when she was murdered. He forgot to call the registry and inform Mink of her death, and he offered no details when he called the Katzenjammer Kids to inform them he was dropping the case. The less said the better. Horscht and Becker were happy to have the case just go away and gave it no more thought. Powers had no reaction when he was informed that the suit had been withdrawn.

Detectives Berkson and Fletcher filed the case away after their initial investigation proved fruitless. They weren't about to spend a lot of time chasing the killer of another hooker, even a high-priced one. The killer was probably thousands of miles away anyway, and since he hadn't struck again it was unlikely they were dealing with a serial killer.

They were wrong on both assumptions.

Miami, Florida, January 7, 1992.

It had been just over two weeks since Lasky and Foreman started their investigation. They were no further ahead than they were after the first day. The eyewitness, Jack Ball, had nothing further to contribute, and the canvass turned out to be a massive expenditure of man-hours with absolutely nothing achieved. The crime scene was clean.

Lasky and Foreman worked out of Metro-Dade's Cutler Ridge South District Station. Foreman was penning in the New York Times crossword puzzle when Lasky came into his office. Foreman looked up. "A ten letter word for someone who mistreats women."

"Misogynist. How about something hard?"

"You want to see my dick?"

"I said something hard, not erectly challenged."

"Speaking of misogynists, did you come up with any new thoughts on our boy who axed that broad?"

Lasky grabbed a swivel chair and spun it over to Foreman's desk. "There's something about that whole scene that bothers me. While you were sloshing through the slush back in New York over Christmas, playing Santa, this Jewish kid was working overtime.

"Hollander and I went over the autopsy findings again after he got back from Vegas. This wasn't an act of passion or rage. It was just too damned neat. Just one very precise swing of the axe, and it was like a surgeon cut off her breasts. I think he's a guy with an agenda. My gut keeps telling me there's a link between the lawsuit and her murder, and I don't think he took her breasts as trophies."

"I see your point, but shit there's always at least a dozen defendants named in those lawsuits. So who's sending the message?"

"I don't know, but I think we should start with the doctor. Hollander is going to check with some of his pathologist friends to see if they've run into anything like this. We'll need to check newspapers and other police departments throughout the country to find out if there've been others."

Had Google been available then, they would have found the answers within seconds, but in January, 1992 Larry Paige and Sergey Brin, the creators of Google, had not yet started to shave.

CHAPTER TWENTY-ONE

Tucson, Arizona
Friday, April 17, 1992.

"YOU SAW THE news conference last night?" asked Neal.

"Of course," Ingram replied. "Nothing has really changed. It's a joke. The FDA banned the use of the gel implants, except in certain cases, which includes just about anyone who wants them. They can still get them for cosmetic reasons if they agree to be part of a clinical study. So how hard will it be for a plastic surgeon to convince a woman who wants bigger boobs to be part of the study?"

"Have you seen these?" Neal handed Ingram copies of the April journals of *Plastic and Reconstructive Surgery* and the *New England Journal of Medicine*.

"No. Summarize them for me."

"Bottom line, there's no increase in breast cancer if you've had breast implants."

"So Wolfe and Nader will have to find something else to crusade about. But we both know that given a choice between rumors and facts, rumors will always win out. If a woman believes that breast implants caused her cancer, try and convince her otherwise. Anything else?"

"The big three are getting out of the implant business."

"No surprise there. I'm sure the bean counters convinced them that it was in their best interests. Future projections?"

"The money will come from the class actions. There's no possible way that these jury awards are sustainable. You set the bar so high with Purcell, that everyone else is going to try and top it. O'Connor got Johnson twenty-five million, but he spent a fortune with his PR firm. He was all over the place with those interviews on *Donahue* and *60 minutes*, and the fact that the trial was broadcast on *Court TV* didn't hurt. But, just like with you, I don't think the punitive will ever hold up on appeal, and it'll be years before any of these women see a penny on compensatory. By then I expect that there'll reputable studies disproving everything we have claimed."

"It doesn't matter. There'll still be plenty of sympathy awards no matter what the science says."

"I've projected some numbers," Neal said.

"And?"

"The Counsel members alone have already filed two thousand twelve cases so far this year. By the end of the year I expect we'll pass five thousand and by the end of 1993, there should be close to thirty thousand.

"I've filed the class action, and the number I'm asking is five billion. You're one step away from the trifecta, Ing. The first million, the first hundred million, and by this time next year I expect it'll be the first billion."

"Plans for the weekend?"

"I'm going to drive to Vegas and visit a couple of casinos that my money helped remodel."

"You're not going to take the plane?"

"Nah, I need to give the Ferrari a work out, and where better than the Nevada desert?"

"Watch out for the NHP—Nevada Highway Patrol—speeders like you are an endowment for their annual budget."

Neal grinned, "The last time I was stopped the cop smiled and said, 'I've been waiting for you all day.' I told him, 'I know, that's why I raced to get here. I didn't want you to wait any longer in this heat.' He laughed so hard he let me go."

"I can't convince you to come to the Weintraubs' with me for the Seder? Passover starts tonight."

"I know, but I'm going to celebrate Easter with the Easter bunny at the Mirage."

Ingram was not religious, but he was passionate about his support for the State of Israel. He and his good friend Ron Weintraub had raised millions in scholarships for students to study in Israel and for Israelis to study in the U.S. He and Weintraub had personally established the bulk of the funding for the Department of Arid Land Studies at the University of Arizona and its sister organization the Agriculture Research Organization, Volcani Centre, Bet-Dagan, Israel.

Neal's contributions to society were less visible, but no less meaningful. He was an ardent supporter of the Boys and Girls Clubs of Tucson and Casa de los Niños, where he served on their respective boards as a powerful voice and advocate for abused children, and his wallet was always open for any organization that had anything to do with children.

"Besides," Neal added, I need a rest.

"Rest? How much rest do you think you'll get frolicking in the flannel?"

Neal laughed, "But I *will* be spending most of my time in bed."

* * *

Powers was reviewing the charts of his upcoming surgery schedule. Because of the FDA moratorium on silicone implants he had to cancel all his previously scheduled elective augmentations. He thought the FDA's decree made no sense. Saline implants, with a known high failure rate, could still be used, but gel implants, which had never been proven to cause any diseases, were banned from use unless they were going to be used for reconstructive surgery. He sighed and shook his head. He set those charts aside and looked at the other pile of charts on his desk, the lawsuits that would not go away.

He picked up the chart of Donna Rivers, the bitch who picked at her incisions so they wouldn't heal. The insurance company paid her thirty thousand dollars so they wouldn't have to go to court. Now she was suing him for mental anguish. He set her chart down and looked at another. Adele Grant. This was the case that could force him into bankruptcy, unless she could be convinced to drop her lawsuit. He threw her chart across the room, picked up the phone, and dialed a number in Hemlock, Michigan.

* * *

Neal estimated he could reach Vegas in just over five hours if he avoided Hoover Dam and went through Laughlin. His bright red 1989 Ferrari Testarossa, which Ingram referred to as his Ferrari Testosterone, certainly was a testosterone teaser. Its 12 cylinder 4.9 liter engine stabled 390 horses of pure power, and Neal was going let the car flex it's muscles at 170 MPH on the open stretches of the Nevada desert.

Fast cars, fast planes, and fast women kept him young. Despite his bravado and brilliance, he was just a frightened little boy, but he never knew why. Despite years of therapy, psychiatrists were never able to unlock the secrets that were buried deep in his psyche. They all agreed he must have experienced a devastating traumatic experience as a child, but no amount of coaxing could release it.

He had experimented with all forms of mood altering chemicals, but they did nothing for him. Permanent relationships were not possible. He was devoted only to his work and to his brother. Even his commitment to troubled and abused children was transitory. They grew up and moved on. The faces always changed. It was the same with all the women in his life.

* * *

He roared under the *porte-cochere* of the Mirage in just under five hours.

The valet drooled as he opened the car-door. It was a rare occasion when he got to park a beast like this. The bellmen were on Neal like ants. He was directed immediately to the concierge desk.

"Good morning Mr. Mink, your suite is ready. There's no need to register, everything has been taken care of."

"Thank you," he glanced at her name tag, "…Michelle."

Michelle typified the new Las Vegas that was being created by hotel magnate Steve Wynn. She was perfectly featured and perfectly groomed in her Armani suit, befitting the $650 million structure that was the most expensive and elaborate hotel-casino ever conceived. The hotel's distinctive gold windows got their gold color from actual gold dust used in the tinting process. Wynn was just getting started. The Mirage was the awakening bell for a sleeping and very tired Las Vegas.

The Tower Suite was 1,231 square feet of pure elegance. A bottle of Krug Brut Champagne, Vintage 1988, was chilling in an ice bucket; an arrangement of flowers and a basket of fruit had been placed on the dining room table. Neal stripped and went directly to the bedroom and crawled into the king-sized bed. When Vegas awoke at dusk so would he.

* * *

He had not slept well. The nightmare had returned. All he ever remembered was flying through the air and then nothing. The sheet was soaked. He unwrapped himself from its confines and sat up. The sun was just retreating behind the Spring Mountains. He wanted a cigarette, but he gave those up after the Surgeon General's report came out. A cold shower would have to do. He climbed into the shower stall, which was large enough to accommodate the starting five of the L.A. Lakers. The cold water danced over his body from jets strategically placed as if they were surround-sound speakers.

He wrapped himself in the plush terry robe provided and returned to the bedroom. The red message light on the phone was blinking. He pushed the play button and listened. The date was confirmed. She would meet him at The Onda at eight. He had an hour to fill, which he would spend at the blackjack tables.

Whenever Neal sat down at a blackjack table the spies in the sky turned their full focus on him. Security was convinced he was a card counter, but he never gave the slightest indication that he was counting cards. When he first started playing, the videotapes of every one of his winning sessions were studied. Nothing. Steve Wynn eventually told his security team to forget it. Neal brought too much business to the Mirage. The whales he brought to the casino would have given Ahab an orgasm. Neal didn't count cards…he memorized them. Every card played, and the order in which they were played, was permanently recorded in his personal memory bank.

* * *

Desiree LaPelle was her stage name. She was born Elmyre Versteeg, but for an exotic dancer in Las Vegas that name was flat-out boring. So Desiree LaPelle was born. Neal was waiting for her when she slithered into the dining room. She moved with the hypnotic elegance of a snake, and men were mesmerized when she entered a room. Tonight was no different. He stood when she approached the table. "Desiree, captivating as always. Thank you for seeing me on such short notice." He brushed the back of her neck with his lips. She shivered.

"Neal, you know I'm always available for you…no matter when you call," she teased, as she stroked the back of his hand. The $5,000 gift certificate he would give her at the end of the evening was probably the motivation that made her available on such short notice.

After most of the bottle of Bardolino and the antipasto had been consumed she touched his hand and said, "Neal I'm withdrawing from the lawsuit."

He had sensed her nervousness from the moment she sat down. "Why?"

She squeezed his hands. "I received a phone call, and the caller threatened to throw acid in my face if I went ahead with the lawsuit."

"Did you call the police?"

She shook her head. "No. He said he would do it if I told anyone."

"What about Richards?" John Richards was the Counsel attorney in Las Vegas to whom Neal referred her when she first called him about wanting to sue her doctor.

"No. You're the only person I've told this to."

He thought for a moment. "What exactly did he say?"

"He said, 'Sulphuric acid can really do nasty things to your face. Drop the lawsuit, or you'll find out just how nasty that can be. If you tell *anyone* about this phone call…it *will* happen.' "

"Desiree, it was probably just a crank call, but if you hear from him again let me know, and I'll see what I can find out. In the meantime, let's finish our dinner, enjoy the Siegfried and Roy show, and afterwards uncork the bottle of Champagne in my suite that Mr. Wynn so graciously provided me."

It wasn't a crank call.

* * *

The self-assurance and confidence Ingram Mink displayed in the courtroom and at chess tournaments were absent in his personal life. He had to constantly prove to himself that this Polish immigrant kid was an equal to the white-bread-and-mayonnaise lawyers who seemed to have been born with overdoses of confidence. He remembered his uncle's words on that ship, so long ago. "You can be anything you want to be." He believed it, but he didn't believe it. What was there left to prove? He was tired. His wife Leah died twelve years ago when the mole the plastic surgeon assured her was just an *age spot* decided to come out of the closet as a malignant melanoma. By the time a tissue diagnosis was made, it was too late. The tumor had already spread throughout her body.

Up until that time he had never sued a doctor for malpractice. After that, he became relentless in his assault on doctors in general, and plastic surgeons in particular. When he sued a doctor for malpractice, the smartest thing the insurance companies could do was to try and settle; you did not want Ingram Mink to spin his web in front of a jury. For the first time the reflection he saw in the mirror was the person he felt himself to be: Old, tired, and without purpose. He and Leah never had children, and when he died the name Minkowski would remain only as a faded scrawl on the manifest at Ellis Island of an immigrant family who came to America from Poland in 1936. Neal was his only living relative. It was time to retire. Time to teach, write, and pursue his hobby of taxidermy. He would tell Neal after the mass tort had been approved. In the meantime he had to get ready for the Seder at Weintraub's.

CHAPTER TWENTY-TWO

Las Vegas, Nevada
Saturday, April 18, 1992.

LAS VEGAS IS a city that lives by the odds. In 1991, the odds were 2:1 that you were more likely to commit suicide in Las Vegas than get murdered. It had one of the lowest murder rates, but the highest suicide rate in the country. There were 44 murders in 1991, but 1992 was promising to have more. If you wanted to get away with murder in Las Vegas the odds were in your favor, especially if you were from out of town. With over 2 million visitors from all over the world descending on Las Vegas each month it would be almost impossible to find an out-of-town killer, particularly one that left no evidence. That was the problem facing Detective Lucas "Woody" Dubois.

Dubois was a transplanted New Orleans Cajun cop. He couldn't live with the corruption that was the normal way of life in the NOPD, so when an opening arose in the LVPD he took advantage of it. Divorced and having only a tepid relationship with his grown children there was no reason for him to stay in New Orleans. Besides, he loved to play poker, and in Las Vegas he could find a legal poker game at any hour, day or night.

"Clean?" asked Dubois.

Dr. John Black, the medical examiner, known as Black Jack for obvious reasons, replied, "Except for a tiny bit of blood, clean as a baby's bottom after a diaper change."

"Tiny bit of blood? This was a fucking eruption of Old Faithful."

"Woody, it's all in how you perceive it. Gettysburg was bloody," he spread his arms, "this is nothing."

"I'm not interested in a Civil War history lesson. What can you tell me about this mess?"

"Well, she was murdered in her bed, evidenced by the absence of blood elsewhere. As you can see her head has been almost completely severed. I would say death was instantaneous, as if she had been guillotined. Her spinal cord was completely transected, probably by a very sharp, light axe, similar to a mediaeval battle-axe, and her breasts were removed by an equally sharp instrument. So if you find someone walking around in a suit of armor armed with a bloody axe, a dagger, and two breasts strapped to his belt, I would say you probably have found your killer."

"Very funny. Time of death?"

"Not more than twenty-four and not less than twelve hours. I'll give you a tighter window when I do the core temps and vitreous analysis, which I will do tomorrow. Right now I must get home for my grandchildrens' Easter egg hunt. And good hunting to you Detective."

* * *

Memories are short in Las Vegas, and although there were VCR recordings of every sneeze and cough in the casinos and hallways of the Mirage, the tapes of April 17, from the over 1,200 security cameras, were already gathering dust in the half-mile of storage shelves in the archive room. The Mirage was the first hotel in Las Vegas to employ 24-hour camera surveillance, but at the time of Desiree LaPelle's murder only a few other hotels had adopted the practice. As a result it was not something Dubois thought of checking. Even if he had, it would have involved reviewing thousands of VCR tapes, one frame at a time, to discover Desiree had been recorded entering the Mirage the night she was murdered, and that a lawyer with whom she had dinner that night was taped cashing in $50,000 in chips. Another person who would have been seen was a Tucson plastic surgeon who presented a paper at the annual meeting of the American Society of Plastic and Reconstructive Surgeons.

Dubois went through the motions. Who was he going to interview? Twenty thousand taxi drivers? Two hundred thousand hotel employees? Unless he came up with someone who had motive, means, and opportunity, he would strike out. The odds of picking a perfecta were infinitely better. It was strike three.

CHAPTER TWENTY-THREE

Tucson, Arizona
Monday, August 17, 1992.

ABOUT SIXTEEN MONTHS after she had her breasts enlarged Adele Grant started to feel sick. Her family doctor thought she probably had a mild case of the flu, and he treated her symptomatically, but her condition continued to deteriorate. She was experiencing episodes of extreme fatigue, mental confusion, migrating pain involving multiple joints, brain-fog, and most recently, extremely tender lymph nodes in her arm pit. He ordered a battery of tests which all came back normal. He was stumped. He referred her to an infectious disease specialist who briefly considered Lyme disease, but quickly ruled it out because she had not been in any areas where deer ticks were prevalent, and the Western blot test was negative. So he referred her to a neurologist, and that's when the specialist shuffle started.

After four months and seven different doctors she ended up in the office of Dr. Andrea Shanklin, the rheumatologist who had treated Louise Purcell. Shanklin quickly made the diagnosis of HAD and explained why Adele was having her problems. She then suggested that Adele contact the law firm of Mink and Mink.

Shanklin neglected to tell her that she made the diagnosis of HAD on every patient she saw with breast implants, and that she referred every new patient on whom she made the diagnosis of silicone HAD to the law firm of Mink and Mink. They in turn referred every new client, who entertained filing a breast implant lawsuit, to Shanklin for a diagnosis. She was one of the six *silicone doctors* that were on the payroll of the Centurion Counsel.

Saturday, October 31, 1992.

It was an effort for Adele to sew the Halloween costumes for the girls, but she finally finished them. She was too tired to go to the school Halloween party at Holaway, so Greg and the girls went without her. Normally Greg secured the front gate before he went out, but tonight he left it open because he didn't want to discourage any trick or treaters that might appear, even though they hadn't seen one for years. Their home was on a secluded dirt road in the heart of Tucson in an area known as Richland Heights West. It was zoned RX1, which meant only one house per acre was permitted in the subdivision. The zoning allowed for any and all forms of animals from chickens to llamas. Traffic through the neighborhood was virtually non-existent because a series of strategically placed diverters would re-route *cutters* through the neighborhood back to the point from where they started. The ubiquitous potholes in the dirt roads further discouraged errant drivers from risking a cracked axle.

The Grants had a two-acre lot, with their home set well back from the road. It couldn't be seen from the road and the road couldn't be seen from the house. There were no streetlights. Groves of mesquite trees and creosote bushes revealed only a circular driveway. The moon was only about one-third into its cycle and had not yet reached its zenith on this Halloween night. He waited in the bushes, well hidden, until Greg had left. When he parked earlier at Holaway School, two blocks from the Grant home, no one paid attention to a nondescript Honda and the costumed figure getting out. He was just another father dressed as a skeleton.

After Greg left, he waited about ten minutes before he emerged from the bushes and then approached the front door. Adele was reading in a high backed chair by the door, a basket of candy on the table beside her. He knocked and uttered a muffled "trick or treat." Adele struggled out of the chair and reached for the basket of candy. She opened the door and said, "My goodness, such a scary skeleton." By the time it registered on her that this was not a child she was on her back, dazed by the blow to her face, with the candy scattered on the floor.

He dragged her by her feet to the bedroom, lifted her onto the bed, positioned her on her back, and cut off her blouse. She was dazed, but not unconscious. As he raised the axe she managed to reach over and push the panic button beside her bedside table. The movement was just enough to deflect the full force of the axe as it crushed her chest rather than her intended neck.

The siren screeched and the perimeter lights began flashing around the house. There wouldn't be enough time to complete the ritual. Her breasts would remain. He didn't panic, and exited the house and property with the same stealth he had approached it. He returned to the school and retrieved his car, encountering no one as he backed out of the parking lot.

Lisa Rogers was the Grants' closest neighbor, her property backed onto theirs. Lisa was an emergency room surgeon, enjoying her first night off in a week. When she heard the alarm and saw the flashing lights she knew this was a true emergency. The neighborhood had a very active neighborhood watch program with a very strict response protocol. She was a block captain. An alarm and flashing lights were to be taken seriously. Central Alarm, the company that monitored security, took panic calls very seriously as well. As soon as the call was received the police were notified and a patrol unit was dispatched.

Lisa rushed over. She took her emergency medical bag with her in case she might need it. When she arrived the back door was locked. She went to the front and saw the open door. She went in and called out, "Adele!" The moans directed her immediately to the bedroom. She was greeted with a sucking chest wound and a froth of pink bubbles. By reflex, Lisa removed an occlusive dressing from her bag, placed it on the wound, effectively sealing it. She then started an IV, turned Adele on her side, and watched the cyanosis lessen. She reached for the bedside phone and dialed 911. "This is Dr. Lisa Rogers, I have a level one medical emergency." She provided the nine-one-one dispatcher with the relevant information and the paramedic unit was on its way.

* * *

Like any level one trauma center the activity in the ER of the University Medical Center was like a colony of ants in full working mode, and each ant had its assigned task. When the ambulance backed into the receiving bay the transition was seamless. Adele was unhooked from the temporary ambulance monitors and re-hooked to the ER monitors. Blood was drawn and x-rays taken. The assessment was fast and efficient. She was taken to surgery immediately. The total time from the moment Lisa entered Adele's bedroom until she was on the operating room table was forty-two minutes. If it had taken any longer Adele would have been wearing a toe-tag rather than a wristband.

"Lisa, even when you have a night off you just can't seem to get away from it, can you?" Suzie Dominguez, the ER head nurse, just shook her head, "You are really something…by the way, there are two detectives waiting to talk with you in the waiting room."

"I'll see them in my office, but I want to change first. They'll probably want these bloody clothes for evidence. Has her husband been notified?"

"He's on his way."

Lisa had been through the routine many times before. When an individual sustained a gunshot wound and arrived in the ER the bloody clothes were immediately removed. A proper examination necessitated, as the ER staff said, "*full disclosure*. Check your modesty at the door and reclaim it when you are discharged." She put her clothes in a plastic bag and labeled them with the date and time, unnecessary in this case, but protocol was protocol. She showered, put on clean underclothes and a surgical scrub suit.

* * *

Detectives Jeremiah Washington and Manny Vargas were an unlikely team. Washington was a Goliath at six feet four inches and 240 pounds, not too much of a difference from when he played football for the University of Arizona. He came from a privileged background, or as privileged a background a young black man could experience growing up at a time in Tucson when the city had not yet shrugged the shackles of racism. His father was the brilliant Malcolm Washington, chief of neurosurgery at UMC.

Vargas, on the other hand, was a product of the streets, growing up in the barrio where privilege was accorded to you only if you were a gang member. Because of his diminutive size he was known as *Little Man*, and was well on his way to the upper echelons of the Barrio Hollywood Gang, until his baby sister was gunned down in a drive-by shooting meant for him. That event and the intervention of his family priest turned his life around, and he became a cop.

"Lisa, you're as gorgeous as ever. When're you going to chuck that globe-trotting newspaper-boy of yours and take up life with a real man?" Vargas teased.

Lisa's husband was a Pulitzer prize-winning freelance photo-journalist whose pictures graced the covers of every major magazine in the country, and who was out of the country more often than he was in it.

"Manny, that'll happen only when you reach the six-foot barrier."

"Does that mean you'll stretch me on your rack? Ooh, I love it when you talk S and M." Vargas had stopped growing when he reached five-feet-eight-inches.

"Okay, you two, let's get serious," Washington interrupted in a deep baritone, just slightly higher in octave than a freight train rumbling through a tunnel. "What happened Lisa?"

"I was just getting ready to watch a movie when my neighbor's siren went off. I looked out the window and saw their perimeter lights flashing. That only happens when a panic button is activated on an alarm system. Our neighborhood watch is set up in such a way that the combo of siren and lights signifies an emergency. I grabbed my emergency kit and ran over there. Adele had been pretty sick recently, and I thought something might have happened to her."

"Did it ever occur to you that you might be running into an intruder?" Vargas asked.

"Honestly? No. I just reacted. If I had called nine-one-one and waited for the paramedics and police she would have been dead by the time they arrived. Besides, when Central Alarm receives a panic alarm they call in a ten-sixty-seven for immediate response. It all worked out."

Vargas and Washington had seen Lisa at work in many emergency situations, and they both knew if they were ever critically injured it was this pixie of a surgeon they wanted in their corner.

"The back door was locked, so I ran around to the front. The door was open, and I heard her moaning in the bedroom. She had a sucking chest-wound with an obvious pneumothorax. I stabilized her, started an IV, and then called nine-one-one."

"Did you see anyone?" Washington asked.

"No...but then again I wasn't really looking.

"To answer your next question...do I think she'll make it? Yes. And when can you speak to her? Don't hold your breath. After surgery she'll be in the ICU on a ventilator and will probably be placed in a controlled medical coma. You'll be the first to know when she can be interviewed."

Wednesday, November 4, 1992.

The Tucson Police Headquarters wouldn't win any Architectural

Design awards for excellence, but it was a functional four-story building fabricated from blah beige and grey concrete blocks that from a distance resembled a poor man's linen fold cabinet. The space that Washington and Vargas shared was called an office, but that was really a euphemism for an area that would make a janitor's closet resemble a ballroom.

They were puzzled over the assault on Adele Grant. There was nothing about it that made any sense. Why would anyone want to do this to a squeaky-clean, All-American mother and housewife? The attack appeared deliberate and well planned. If she hadn't been able to reach the panic button she would've been dead. But why? They needed to talk to her, but as Dr. Rogers had predicted, she was being monitored in a medically induced coma on a respirator until her lungs healed and could function on their own.

"Somebody was pissed at this lady. Big time!" Vargas said. "When I was with the BHG," referring to his misspent youth in the Barrio Hollywood Gang, "if you wanted to make a point, you sent a message that'd get somebody's attention. Getting whacked with an axe is an attention getter."

"Try this on," Washington said. "According to her husband, they're involved in a multi-million dollar lawsuit against a plastic surgeon and the Dow Corning Corporation. Something to do with a problem she's having with breast implants."

"Yeah, I remember reading about that other woman, here in Tucson, whose hotshot lawyer got her a multi-million dollar award because of problems she was having with breast implants. Do you think…?"

"Usually these corporations have enough insurance to cover their asses, but what if they don't? It wouldn't take too many awards like that to clean out the closet," said Washington.

"But shit, Dow Corning's a billion dollar corporation," Vargas answered.

"I know, that's why I think we should go have a talk with her doctor first."

CHAPTER TWENTY-FOUR

Tucson, Arizona
Thursday, November 5, 1992.

DEVIN POWERS WAS a plastic surgeon with a vision. In 1985, he had scheduled a cosmetic surgery procedure at Tucson Medical Center only to have it *bumped* from the schedule because of an emergency. The emergency was a gunshot wound to the abdomen sustained by a gangbanger when two rival gangs, disputing a territorial boundary, decided to settle the dispute in Hatfield-McCoy fashion. The property plat became a burial plot. Six of the gang members had been permanently evicted.

Powers' patient had flown in from Switzerland and was furious when she learned it would be at least three days before her surgery could be rescheduled. She fired Powers, and he vowed that would never happen again. He purchased a struggling resort in the Foothills and converted it into a five-star cosmetic surgery spa, where patients could have surgery performed in complete anonymity, and at the same time have a luxurious place to convalesce.

"Jesus, Mary and Joseph," Vargas marveled, when the valet directed them to the VIP parking lot. "This place sure as shit ain't like any doctor's office in the Barrio."

Even Washington who had grown up in a medical family was impressed. He had been exposed to affluence, but not opulence. This was a *Five* Seasons…not a Four Seasons.

They were greeted by a receptionist in a waiting room…no, not a waiting room, but an anteroom of a palace. A receptionist? She was a cover girl for *Glamour*.

Unflustered by the imposing pair standing before her vintage desk, she flashed a practiced smile, "May I help you gentlemen?"

Washington produced his gold shield and gave her his business card. "Detectives Washington and Vargas. We need to speak with Dr. Powers."

She glanced at the Sevres porcelain and ormalu clock displayed on a credenza. Vargas followed her eyes. He didn't know anything about antiques, but he knew her desk didn't come from Sam Levitz and the clock wasn't from Target. "Dr. Powers is consulting with a patient at the moment, but as soon as he has finished I will let him know you are here. He doesn't like to be interrupted when he is in consultation. May I get you something to drink while you are waiting?"

Vargas grinned, "Perrier smooth," he replied.

"Certainly, and you detective?"

Washington wanted to laugh. "The same," he replied. He could've sworn she smirked as she left the room to get the Perrier. "Nice try smartass. I suspect if you had asked her for *Napoleon Brandy* she would've said, 'What year?' " He scanned the room. "None of this shit is a repro. I imagine our Dr. Powers would be very motivated to spare nothing to keep this…" he flared his arms, "…intact."

The girl from *Glamour* returned with a silver tray with two crystal glasses, not just any crystal glasses, but two matched Luigi Bormioli Atelier crystal glasses. Washington was impressed. Vargas was oblivious.

Like a sommelier she presented the glasses to the detectives for their consideration. "If I can get you anything else, please don't hesitate to ask."

Washington thought if he asked for *Escargots Bourguignon* she would've been able to provide them.

Vargas knew you could tell a lot about the patients seen in a doctor's office by the magazines that were there. There were no stacks of two-year-old *People Magazine*, but rather strategically placed current copies of *Luxury Travel Magazine* and *Sotheby* catalogues.

A light flashed on the phone on *Glamour* girl's desk. She picked up the receiver. "Certainly Dr. Powers, I'll show them to your office." She looked up and said, "Dr. Powers has finished with his consultation, and he can see you now."

Both Vargas and Washington were on the same wavelength. When she went to get the Perrier she must have told Powers they were waiting. How else would he have known they were there? She obviously didn't interrupt a consultation, because there was no consultation...the first lie.

Powers was standing by his desk and greeted the detectives with a captivating capped-tooth smile. "Detectives, please have a seat and tell me how I can help you."

Vargas thought: *he's too fucking relaxed. Nobody's this cool when two homicide dicks show up at their office unannounced... he's hiding something.*

"Doctor, I'll get right to the point," said Washington. "We're investigating the attempted homicide of Mrs. Adele Grant, who I understand is a patient of yours."

"Yes, poor Adele. I read about it in the Star. Who could possibly want to harm that lovely woman?"

"That's what we are trying to find out," added Vargas. "Why is she suing you doctor?"

Powers hesitated and his eyes narrowed. The smile vanished. "Because of a huge misunderstanding. I'm just one of many named in that lawsuit, and the only reason I was named is because her lawyers told her to do so, not because I did anything wrong. But what does any of that have to do with the attempt on Adele's life?"

Washington glared at him. "With any homicide, or attempted homicide, the first thing we ask, as you said, is 'who would want to do this?' Which comes down to motive. It seems to me that someone who's being sued for a lot of money would want that lawsuit to go away."

Powers stood. "That's why I have liability insurance, and this interview is over. If you have anything further to ask me it will be through, and in the presence of, my lawyer. Good day gentlemen."

The detectives rose. "Okay doc," said Vargas, "But what if you lost and didn't have enough insurance to cover it, wouldn't you have to give this all up?" He circled his finger around the room, but he missed a very interesting object hanging on the back wall.

* * *

Marvin Slater was an excellent investigator who rarely had cause to disappoint his employers when on assignment. He had been a rising star in the Tucson Police Department, but had a major problem with discipline and regimentation. His investigative techniques did not exactly follow protocol, and none of the hierarchy of the TPD was disappointed when the maverick resigned to start his own detective agency. Erratic, tousled surfer-blond hair, faded jeans, Birkenstocks, and Grateful Dead tee shirts were more to his liking than a buzz cut, starched shirts, and a uniform.

"So Ing, what're you planning for an encore after that Purcell case?" He had been paid a handsome sum for his work on the case, and wondered what the Mink bothers needed him for now.

"I'll let Neal explain. He brought something to my attention that's very disturbing."

"It's complicated, and if it's what I think it is then we're dealing with a potential disaster," said Neal.

"Disasters are my specialty. You've tweaked my curiosity. Go on."

"If you recall, one of our clients, and a very close friend of mine, Carol Andrews, was murdered in Cleveland in February 1991."

"No, I didn't know that."

"At the time, I thought it was just a random murder and that poor Carol had just been in the wrong place at the wrong time. But on Halloween there was an attempt on the life of another one of our clients, Adele Grant."

"I read about it. You think there's a connection?"

"That's what we want you to find out."

Ingram said, "After the attempt on Adele's life I wondered if it had anything to do with the lawsuit, so I asked Neal to check the data base he had set up for the Centurion Counsel and see if there was anything that had been reported that might be helpful."

"And that database is what?" Slater asked.

"In December 1990, Connie Chung aired a TV show that opened the floodgates for lawsuits to be filed against the manufacturers of breast implants and the plastic surgeons who implanted them. I have the video if you didn't see the program. Afterwards, we knew that the Lawyers who were members of the Centurion Counsel would be deluged with calls from women who believed they had a cause of action. That proved to be true. In July of 1991, we had a meeting of the Counsel, in Tucson, at which time we agreed to set up a database for all cases involving breast implants, so we could exchange information that might prove useful to the others, rapidly and efficiently. Neal, tell him what you found."

"I searched the data base and found that nine impending cases had been dropped without explanation. I don't have the time to contact the attorneys who represented these women to find out the details, that's why we need you. You should have no trouble getting that information because you'll be representing us, and as I explained, all members of the Counsel have agreed to share information with other members."

"How long will I have?"

"This is a priority even though we've obtained a continuance because of the attempt on her life. Her case is just one of a number that we have pending, and next year the numbers will be staggering. If the Andrews murder and the attempt on Adele Grant's life are connected, then there may be other women who are in danger, so we need to find out why those cases were dropped. They're from all over the country, but the fact that the women we represented in those two cases were patients of the same Tucson doctor makes me wonder if there's a pattern."

"I'm on it. Give me two weeks. If there are any complications I'll let you know. Budget?"

"Whatever you need. Let's meet back here two weeks from tomorrow.

Two weeks later, November 19, 1992.

Slater's usual carefree attitude was anything but that when he sat down with the Mink brothers in Neal's office.

"It looks serious," said Ingram.

"It is," Slater replied. "It's much worse than you thought. Let's start with Carol Andrews. I flew to Cleveland and spoke with the detectives who investigated her murder. They didn't release all the information about her murder to the press because they wanted to filter out the crank calls by omitting one detail."

"And of course you learned that detail," said Ingram.

"Yeah, but only after I told them about Adele Grant, and the fact she had been attacked by someone wielding an axe, and that like Carol Andrews she was involved in a lawsuit."

"I spoke with one of those detectives after she was killed," said Neal.

"Scalpone," said Slater. "It took all my charm to get his cooperation, because when I told him I was working for you he wasn't overly thrilled. I got the impression you must've pissed him off somehow."

"Not really. I told him what he wanted to know about her, short of discussing the lawsuit."

"So tell us Marvin, what was the detail?" asked Ingram.

"The guy cut her breasts off and took them as souvenirs, or at least that's what Sadowsky thinks."

Neal looked puzzled...he was trying to remember something.

Ingram just nodded...he did remember something.

"They found three business cards in Andrews' purse, one was yours, and that's how they knew to contact you. One of the other two was from her doctor in Cleveland, and the other was from Powers. The Cleveland doctor was extremely cooperative, but Powers balked when Sadowsky mentioned the lawsuit. He lawyered up. Sadowsky wanted to check out Powers, but his lieutenant told him to forget it and stick to his own backyard. The case became ice. They've come up with no suspects."

"There are more aren't there?" Neal said.

Slater nodded. "Three more."

"Who are they?"

Slater took out a notebook. "Faith Greene, Los Angeles, June 17, 1991; Brandy Evans, Miami, December 22, 1991; Desiree LaPelle, Las Vegas, April 17, 1992.

Neal blanched when Slater said Desiree had been murdered. He was unaware of her murder. She had never followed up and called him like she said she would if she had received any more phone calls. He had given her no further thought, because he hadn't been back to Vegas since that night.

"They were all killed with an axe and their breasts were cut off. That's not all. There were nine other women who withdrew their lawsuits; they wouldn't tell their lawyers why they were dropping out. Only one of them would speak to me...the last one I called. At first she wouldn't talk to me but when I told her I'd make it worth her while, she reconsidered. It cost me, or I should say it cost you, five thousand dollars. She made me swear I wouldn't tell her husband.

"Her name is Joy Baker, from Phoenix. She received an anonymous phone call from a guy who threatened to destroy her face with acid if she didn't drop the suit. When she told me that, I re-contacted the other eight. I asked them if they'd been threatened with acid. Five of them just hung up. The other three were hesitant, one broke into tears and said, 'I can't talk about this.' The other two had a similar response, but without the tears.

"As far as the ones who were murdered: Faith Greene was a kid from Midland Michigan, who was represented by an Albert Chiricosta in L.A. When I asked him why he didn't report it to the Counsel that she'd been murdered, his answer was that he told his secretary to call the registry and have her removed from the list. He wasn't aware of the Andrews murder, so he didn't make any connection. He thought Greene was just another kid who got murdered in L.A. There were over a thousand homicides in L.A. up to the time she was killed, so her murder was no big deal as far as he was concerned."

Neal thought, *No big deal? Every homicide is a big deal.*

"Also, like in Cleveland, the cops in L.A. didn't release the details about Greene's breasts being cut off either."

"Did you tell them about Andrews?" Ingram asked.

"No, I wanted to find out what happened in Miami and Las Vegas first before I said anything. Also, I wanted to check with you to find out how you wanted to proceed. Anyway, the killings had the same MO in both Miami and Vegas, and in both of those the information about the breasts being cut off was never publicized. Same story with the lawyers; they just withdrew the names of their clients from the registry after they learned of the killings. They had no reason to think the killings were anything but just random murders, and the cops never connected the lawsuits and the murders, because either they didn't know about them or they didn't follow through with them. You know the drill. Unless they have something hot to follow, after forty-eight hours the trail gets cold and they move on to the next one. Under the best of conditions the homicide closure rate nationwide is just over sixty percent, and when there's nothing for forensics to work with, the numbers are much lower.

"You should also be aware that all the women who were murdered, or threatened, were represented by members of the Centurion Counsel, and they were all patients of Dr. Devin Powers."

Both the Mink brothers were silent after Slater delivered his report. Finally, Ingram said, "Excellent work Marvin. It would appear that we are faced with a dilemma. Certainly the authorities have to be informed of what you learned. The question is whom do we notify? It's apparent that we're dealing with a serial killer. So do we notify the FBI, or do we notify the individual jurisdictions and let them make the decisions as to how to proceed?"

Neal said, "If we notify the FBI, and they want to take over the investigation, which they surely will, we'll be kept in the dark and will have no involvement other than to provide them with information, but if we were to work with the law agencies in the individual jurisdictions we may be able to work out some type of accommodation. They have no love for the FBI.

"Also, I'm afraid that if the FBI takes the lead, the headlines that'll follow will create a panic of untold dimensions among women who've filed lawsuits. Can't you just see the headlines? 'Serial killer butchers women with breast implants.' I can see them calling him 'The Breast Butcher.' Marvin, Ing and I have to decide how to proceed. We may need you to act as liaison. I'll get back to you within twenty-four hours."

"That works for me. If you do decide to work with the individual departments, I suggest you start with Sadowsky and Scalpone in Cleveland. They've already spoken with you and all the doctors involved with Carol Andrews, and they're closest to making the association."

"Good point. We'll let you know."

Slater got up to leave and handed Neal a paper, "Here's an accounting of my expenses to date. I'll wait until I hear from you, and then let you know if I'll need anything else."

After Slater left Ingram said nothing. He swiveled his chair and stared out the window. Neal waited for him to collect his thoughts. With his back still turned he said, "It doesn't make sense." He got up from the chair and turned to face his brother. "Why would he kill the women in Cleveland, L.A., Houston, Miami, and Las Vegas, and just make threatening phone calls to the others?

"Because he wants to create confusion," said Neal.

"Precisely. Are you familiar with the American chess grandmaster Nigel Davies?" Ingram asked.

"No, but I suspect you're going to tell me all about him."

"As you well know, chess is a game of *deception*. Deception is a fundamental weapon in competitive chess. Davies wrote a book, *Chess for Scoundrels,* in which he shows that what appears to be obvious is anything but. He leads his opponent in an apparently purposeful direction, but which in reality is a deception. When the opponent realizes what Davies is doing, he changes tactics. It's called the *double deception*."

"Are you saying the killer is purposely pointing to himself, knowing that it's far too fetched to be true, so the police will discount the obvious and look elsewhere?"

"Something like that. Neal, I do believe we're in a chess game. Let's look at this a little more closely. Who has the most to lose, the individual doctors, the manufacturers, or both? Someone wants to stop these lawsuits and will go to any means to stop them. Anti-abortionists believe they are justified in killing doctors who commit legal abortions to prevent them from killing any more unborn babies. And at the same time they threaten and cajole young women who are planning an abortion in an attempt to stop them from going through with it. They may slow the process down, but they'll never stop it."

"There's another possibility," said Neal. "As with the anti-abortionists, there may be two separate entities involved, those who would kill, and those who would just threaten. Their goals are the same, but their methods are different. So the next question is, do we pursue this or do we turn what we know over to the police?"

"Neal, as officers of the court, you know we have an obligation to provide the police with any information we've learned that may help them with their investigation, but that doesn't mean we have to stop our own investigation. I'd like to know why all the murder victims and all those who were threatened are patients of Devin

Powers. I can't believe that if he were involved he would make it that obvious. He's just not that stupid. But then again, maybe the whole point is to make it so obvious that it makes you think that he couldn't really be involved. I wonder if he plays chess? I think we should let Slater continue with his investigation. We also should convene another meeting with the Counsel before December."

"I'll arrange that and I'll give Gary Ronstadt a call about what we've learned. Let him make the decision about who should get involved with these cases. I know he has a tremendous rapport with other police departments, and in addition to being a very good cop he has a master's degree in behavioral psychology, which could prove helpful in him figuring out what's going on. And I'll tell Slater to keep digging."

CHAPTER TWENTY-FIVE

Tucson, Arizona
Thursday, November 19, 1992.

THE HISTORY OF the Ronstadt family in America began when Freidreich Ronstadt emigrated from Germany to Mexico where he became a naturalized citizen. The origins of the Ronstadt legacy in Arizona began when Freidreich's son, Federico José Maria, immigrated to Tucson in 1882, from his birthplace in Delicias, Sonora, Mexico, to learn blacksmithing and the wheelwright trade. He founded the F. Ronstadt Wagon and Carriage Company, which eventually evolved into the F. Ronstadt Machinery and Hardware Company, the company that sank most of the water wells in Tucson and surrounding communities. He was the patriarch of a family dedicated to service and community.

Gary Ronstadt was a third generation Tucsonan who followed the tradition of many of his forebears. He dedicated his life to law enforcement. He was a brilliant student, multilingual, and could have been a success in any field he might have chosen. At the age of thirty he became head of the homicide division of the Tucson Police Department.

He was at his desk reviewing the reports of the attempted murder of Adele Grant when his phone rang. He picked up the receiver. "Ronstadt."

"Gary, it's Neal Mink. I have some information that may be relevant to the assault on Adele Grant. I think we should meet as soon as possible."

* * *

Compared to the space assigned to Vargas and Washington, Ronstadt's office was a gymnasium, but still not a very big one. The walls were lined with a pictorial history of the Ronstadt family. On his mesquite desk was the usual clutter of files and a very old hammered silver frame with a picture of his wife, three daughters, and two golden retriever puppies. A computer occupied the remaining free space. A matching mesquite sofa was by the back wall. Two armchairs were in front of the desk. Ronstadt's grandfather handcrafted the furniture from mesquite harvested from the trees on his ranch.

At precisely 9:15 a.m., Ronstadt's secretary escorted Neal Mink into the office. He was carrying a coffee from Bentley's and was wearing faded blue jeans, deck shoes, and a Debra Torres, short sleeve, Guayabera shirt. "Gary, thanks for meeting with me on such short notice." He wasn't surprised to see Vargas and Washington sitting on the sofa, which appeared oversized for Vargas and undersized for Washington.

The acknowledgements from Washington and Vargas were not much warmer than shaking hands with an ice cube. Washington had an inbred distrust and dislike of PI attorneys, stemming from some of the less than flattering stories he heard from his neurosurgeon father when he was growing up. Vargas's antipathy toward any and all lawyers grew from the crap he heard gushing from the mouths of criminal defense attorneys when he testified in court, but today there would be a truce at the behest of Ronstadt. If they had to work together after today they would smoke the sacred pipe of peace.

"Well Neal, I see you're not going to court after you leave here, " said Ronstadt.

"No, I'll be flying down to Guaymas for the weekend with a friend for some shrimp, mariachis, and margaritas."

Ronstadt didn't have to enquire the friend's sex. Mink's reputation preceded him. "It's your show Neal, so why don't you begin?"

Neal positioned himself so he was facing the three men. He repeated verbatim everything he had learned from Slater.

Vargas said, "So what you're saying counselor, is that women are bein' axed to death all over the country and gettin' their tits cut off, and nobody knows nothin' about it except you, your brother, and that turd Slater?"

Vargas had no love for Marvin Slater. They had been cadets together at the Tucson Police Academy, and although Slater excelled at every test and obstacle thrown at him, no one felt comfortable partnering with him. He was very good at what he did, but he was very unpredictable. He couldn't adjust to being part of a team. Like a jaguar, he preferred to hunt alone. It worked for a while, but once, because he did not wait for backup as dictated by protocol, his partner almost lost his life. After that incident he became a pariah, and no one would partner with him. No tears were shed when he left the force.

"That's right. We only learned this from Slater yesterday."

"And you believe him?" Vargas sneered.

Neal rose from his chair and approached Vargas. Without crowding him he said, "Detective Vargas, I don't know and I don't care what your fucking problem is with Marvin Slater, but he is the *best* investigator I've ever worked with, and the information he has provided me over the years has been one-hundred-percent dead on accurate."

Washington straightened and said, "But you have to remember you're a civilian, as is Slater, and you can't just run around playing policeman and interfere with an ongoing investigation. I'm concerned that your Mr. Slater chose *not* to share this information with the respective police departments when he learned of the probable links."

Neal had returned to his chair and collected his thoughts before he responded to Washington. "Detectives, first let me say that Slater didn't reveal what he discovered to the police because he wanted me to make that decision. He was acting as my agent, and I agree wholly with his decision. Despite what you may think of lawyers in general, and me in particular, let me remind you that I am first and foremost an officer of the court. It's my sworn obligation to promote justice and effective operation of the judicial system. I have an absolute ethical duty to tell the truth, avoid dishonesty and evasion concerning all matters pertaining to the judicial system. I know that may seem hard for you to believe, but it's the mantra by which I live and practice law. We want to work *with* you, not against you. Our only involvement will be to gather information and coordinate the sharing of that information with you."

Vargas didn't back off. He clapped his hands and said, "Nice speech counselor, but what makes you think we can't do this without your help? We're trained detectives, and that's what we do…we detect."

Ronstadt finally intervened. "Neal's right. It's time we put aside our differences. We'll need all the help we can get to solve these cases. Manny, we have a choice, we can work with Neal and his team, or we can turn the whole goddamned thing over to the Feds, and you know how much cooperation we'll get from them. We'll end up as their fucking water boys, and I won't let that happen. There are resources that Neal has that we don't have. Would you rather deal with all the lawyers, or have him do it? Our goal is the same, to stop this bastard before the whole country ends up in a panic."

Vargas rubbed the web of skin between his right thumb and index finger, a habit he acquired when he was thinking. It was where the number 28 had been tattooed, which represented the numbers of the alphabet for the letters B and H—Barrio Hollywood. He had it removed by laser when he left the gang. It still itched. "Alright counselor, how do you suggest we proceed?"

"I don't Manny. That's my point. How you conduct your investigations is entirely up to you. All I propose to do is provide you with any information I come up with that may be useful.

For example, as you may know, my brother Ingram founded the Centurion Counsel, a group of one hundred lawyers from across the country. We meet regularly and exchange our experiences and ideas. In light of what's been happening, we've scheduled an emergency meeting of the Counsel next week at the Westward Look."

"Will we be able to attend?" asked Washington.

Mink thought for a moment. "Not the *in camera* sessions, but you're welcome to be present at the general session where I'll be delivering an overview of what we're facing."

"And how'll that help us?" asked Vargas.

"Let me explain this one more time. So far, we know of four women that have been murdered and nine that have been threatened. The Counsel maintains a central registry of all lawsuits that have been filed by members of the Counsel on behalf of women who believe they have a cause of action because of injuries resulting from breast implant surgery. By doing that, we can determine which cases have similar elements without having to do extensive court record research. If a woman should withdraw from the lawsuit, that fact is noted, but not the reason for it.

"There may be more suits that have been withdrawn that haven't been reported. We'll know that when we poll the members next week at the meeting. And yes, there may be other murders that haven't been reported. If that's the case, then there's no way for us to know unless we stumble upon the facts. Until we have a central reporting data base it will remain discovery by serendipity."

"I agree," said Ronstadt. "I recently took a profiling course at Quantico. The FBI is working to make their ViCAP program available to all law enforcement agencies across the country, but they're still several years away from achieving that. Until then, we'll have to do it the old fashioned way. Neal, you've certainly given us a starting point. We'll call the detectives in the four cities. Perhaps we can arrange a meeting here in Tucson."

"One thing I might add," said Neal, "Right now the Centurion

Counsel represents most of the women who've filed lawsuits. By this time next year there'll be thousands more cases, and unless you catch the killer before then, there'll be more killings and threats that'll be untraceable."

Manny grinned, "I don't think our killer's too smart."

"What do you mean?" asked Neal.

"In another life, when I was a member of the Hollywoods, if you really wanted to get a message across, you cut the leader's head off. Soldiers reproduce like rabbits."

"I see where he's going," said Washington. If you kill a few women and threaten a few more there'll always be plenty to replace them, but the leaders are the lawyers...and as Shakespeare said in *Henry the Sixth*, 'The first thing we do, let's kill all the lawyers.' "

He was being prophetic.

CHAPTER TWENTY-SIX

Tucson, Arizona
Saturday, December 12, 1992.

NEAL TAPPED THE microphone on the lectern to get the audience's attention. Ingram sat in the front row. The droning of voices abated. He offered no preamble.

"Thank you for coming. There are ten who couldn't be here. I'll speak with them personally. Let me get right to the point, because you all know why we're here. Since the first lawsuit was filed, four of our clients have been murdered and nine were threatened with extreme physical harm if they didn't drop their lawsuits. There may be more of each that haven't been reported to the registry. As far as we know, all the murders and threats have been restricted to clients of the Counsel. And all of those have been the patients of one doctor, Devin Powers, a Tucson plastic surgeon. And I shouldn't have to remind any of you that his name should never be repeated outside this room."

Lawrence Band couldn't remember whether he reported that Elaine Peters had been murdered in Houston. He thought about it and was sure that he hadn't. He also didn't know whether his secretary notified the registry to withdraw her name. *I'll speak to Neal after the meeting.*

Neal continued. "Up until now the only information we have requested for the registry is the client's name, attorney's name, date of filing, and cause of action. If a client withdrew her complaint we asked only that you report the withdrawal, but not the reason for doing so. We'll now need to add that item to the list. The reason will soon become very clear.

"I'm now going to turn the lectern over to Sergeant Gary Ronstadt. Gary is head of the Tucson Homicide Department. He has a master's degree in behavioral psychology and has extensive training in criminal profiling."

Ronstadt assumed the lectern and adjusted the microphone. "Thank you Neal." He scanned the audience and waited until he had everyone's attention. "I'm sure most of you are wondering why Neal invited a cop to attend and speak at this meeting. I understand a number of you practiced criminal law before becoming involved with civil litigation, so you'll understand what I'm about to discuss. For the rest, I don't want to sound patronizing, nor do I want you to think I'm lecturing to you, but I must explain the broad picture from a law enforcement perspective.

"When Neal first contacted me several weeks ago and shared the information about the murders and the threats to your clients I was caught off-guard. At the time, we were investigating an attempted homicide of a young woman. We had no knowledge that Ingram Mink's client, Carol Andrews, had been murdered in Cleveland. And only after we learned of similar murders in Los Angeles, Miami, and Las Vegas did we realize someone was deliberately and systematically killing women who were involved in breast implant litigation."

Holy shit, thought Band. *They don't know about Elaine Peters.*

"I'm not at liberty to discuss the details of the murders other than to say the weapon in all cases appears to be the same, and the women were all mutilated in exactly the same fashion."

Like a hive of agitated bees responding to a threat, the buzzing in the room became louder as people started speaking to one another. Arms with waving hands started to rise throughout the room. A voice from the back of the room called out, "Are you saying there's a serial killer out there?"

"Please let me finish and I'll answer all of your questions." He waited until the room quieted. "We're being faced with a series of killings and threats for which we have absolutely no evidence linking anyone to those crimes. In any homicide investigation we look for three critical elements: motive, opportunity and means. Who has a motive in these killings? You could theorize that every defendant who is being sued has a motive. Look at any one of the lawsuits that have been served and see how many defendants are named in each suit. Opportunity? Until we know who we should focus our investigations on, how can we look for opportunity? Finally, means. Just about anyone has the means to commit these crimes.

"The question was asked whether there's a serial killer out there. By definition, the answer is yes. Three murders committed in the same fashion, by the same individual, categorizes that individual as a serial killer. However, most serial killers operate within a narrow comfort zone. These four murders were committed in anything but a narrow geographic comfort zone. I'm also afraid that we're not going to be successful in developing a profile on this individual any time soon.

"Let me pause here and I'll try to answer your questions." Ronstadt pointed to a hand raised in the first row.

"Jack Kerrigan, Seattle. If you believe you're dealing with a serial killer why hasn't the FBI been notified? Aren't they supposed to assume responsibility when state lines are crossed? Surely they have far more manpower and infinitely more resources than all your individual departments combined."

"I agree. And there may come a point where the FBI will have to be involved. The problem with turning the investigation over to the FBI is that once that happens the local law enforcement agencies will effectively be excluded. The FBI doesn't like to share its information with the locals, but it expects them to continue to investigate and turn over anything they have learned to them. Consider this hypothetical situation Mr. Kerrigan. You're a small law firm that has carried out extensive research and discovery in a particularly complex litigation. You've expended considerable monies and man hours on that file, but found it necessary to consult with a large law firm, and were told, 'We'll take it from here. Keep working, and we'll let you know how things turn out.' I don't believe that would sit well with you. Also, if we were to involve the FBI at this point...Neal why don't you explain what you believe would happen."

Neal rose. "What Gary is saying is that the minute the FBI becomes involved a potential sieve will be introduced into the equation. Leaks will spring up everywhere. 'Highly placed sources have revealed...etcetera.' When that happens the results will be predictable. Most of you are too young, and some of you were not born when the movie *Panic in the Streets*, starring Richard Widmark, was released in 1950. Widmark played the role of a public health medical officer who realized he had forty-eight hours to find the carrier of the microbe responsible for spreading Pneumonic Plague. He had to convince the city officials of New Orleans not to let the press learn of the potential, because reports of plague would result in a mass panic. Similarly, by restricting information to the press we *hope* to avoid a panic.

"All of us in this room have committed not to discuss these proceedings outside of this group. Sergeant Ronstadt has assured me that he can offer the same guarantee from his team. Gary, please continue."

"Obviously we wouldn't be dealing with a panic of the magnitude that Neal described, but if the press were to learn the details and connections of the killings, and I guarantee you they would if the FBI were involved, then we'd be deluged with crank calls from people claiming to be responsible for everything from the sinking of the Titanic to the assassination of President Kennedy. By keeping a small, tight unit, we hope to prevent that possibility from occurring. Later today I'll be meeting with the investigators from the four cities where the murders occurred. We'll be establishing a command center here in Tucson. The purpose of today's meeting will be to collate every available piece of information and establish guidelines; we'll meet as often as we need to down the road." He pointed to a waving hand in the middle of the audience.

"Barry Waters, New York. Your proposal makes sense for the limited number of murders that you're dealing with, but what if the killer isn't finished, and I seriously doubt that he is, how are you going to coordinate with other jurisdictions that'll become involved?"

"Our presumption is that the killer is targeting only clients of your Centurion Counsel at this point, and that's where you all will come in. You'll be our eyes and ears in the streets. Sadly, I agree that there will be more killings; we think we know the *how*, but not the *when* or *where*. We'll be asking you to report to us anytime someone drops an implant lawsuit...for any reason. Also, we'll be contacting the homicide divisions of every city where a Centurion lawyer practices. If a murder occurs in any of those cites we'll then invite the involved investigators to join our group. Ideally we'll be able to respond with the flexibility of a Delta Force as opposed to the inflexibility of mobilizing a division, which I believe would be the case if the FBI were involved." He pointed to the back of the audience. "Hand in the back."

"Jerry Cooper, Minneapolis. Do you think the murders and the threats are being carried out by the same individual?"

"Good question. We don't have enough information at this point to come to a conclusion, but the *modus* leads me to believe we're dealing with different individuals."

Ronstadt answered questions for another thirty minutes before Neal approached the lectern and said, "We have time for one more question before Gary has to leave."

Ronstadt acknowledged a hand patiently waiting in the second row.

"Aston Nelson, St. Louis. Detective Ronstadt, you seem to have strategized your quaint Delta Force analogy based on an assumption that the perpetrator, or perpetrators, will restrict their activity, or activities to clients of the Centurion Counsel. I'm not convinced that that will always be the case. What if the next victim is *not* a client of a Counsel member?"

Ronstadt stared long and hard at the questioner. "Then sir, the FBI will be notified, and we *will* have *Panic in the Streets*."

* * *

The lawyers were filtering out of the meeting room as Band squeezed his way in the reverse direction to the front of the room. The Mink brothers were talking to Ronstadt who was getting ready to leave. Band caught their attention.

"Larry. Good to see you," said Ingram.

"I have something that I need to tell you. Sergeant Ronstadt you'll want to hear this as well."

If the three men were surprised by Band's revelation they didn't show it.

"It was a year ago, and really didn't get a lot of press. Elaine worked as a high priced hooker for an exclusive escort service, so I suspect her murder wasn't prioritized. There were over six hundred murders in Houston in 1991.

"I first met Elaine when I practiced criminal defense law. She had been abused by her father since she was a kid, and when she was fifteen she took an axe and converted him into a job seeker for a sultan's harem. He spent five years as lead soprano in Houston State Prison after she chopped his dick and nuts off. I represented her. She was never indicted."

Without revealing anything to Band about how the axe was used on the current victims Ingram said, "An axe. An interesting choice of weapon."

"Mr. Band, do you know the name of the investigating officer?" asked Ronstadt.

"Barry Berkson. He's a hell of a good cop. Do you want me to contact him?"

"No," said Ronstadt. "That's the whole point of my being here today. We'll make contact and deal with the police. We need you to keep us apprised of any women who have changed, or who are considering changing their minds about continuing with their lawsuits."

"I really feel badly about dropping the ball on this one," said Band. "I hope I didn't mess things up."

"Don't," said Neal. "That's why we're meeting here today, to see if there have been any other cases that slipped under the radar."

"Neal's right," said Ronstadt. "We're just getting started with the task force. If anything, Berkson will provide us with additional resources if he chooses to get involved."

"There's one other thing," said Band. "The surgeon she was suing is Dr. Devin Powers."

CHAPTER TWENTY-SEVEN

Tucson, Arizona
Twenty-four hours earlier, Friday, December 11.

EARLIER THAT WEEK Ronstadt had contacted the detectives in the four cities where the murders had taken place. They weren't surprised when he called because Slater had hinted that Ronstadt might contact them when he had met with them. All were intrigued and excited when Ronstadt outlined his proposal. Sadowsky and Scalpone were ecstatic because it meant they could rediscover what a blue sky looked like. In Cleveland, the sky color *du jour* was gunmetal grey. Slush would be replaced by sun. All the detectives from the four cities were beyond surprised when they learned they wouldn't have to beg for expense money to cover the cost of the trip. Ronstadt explained that the non-profit Mink Foundation, the charitable foundation established by the Mink brothers, would pay all expenses. Discretionary funds were available for projects such as this one.

Ronstadt made arrangements for them to stay at the centrally located Arizona Inn, a fourteen-acre oasis within the heart of the city. The pink stucco retreat was created by Isabella Greenway, Arizona's first elected congresswoman, who served as a bridesmaid at the wedding of Eleanor and Franklin Delano Roosevelt. She built the Inn in 1930, to fund the financially troubled Furniture Hut, where disabled WWI veterans found work— one of her many philanthropic ventures. Today there is an on-site master craftsman who constantly restores the original furniture and builds new to blend with the old. The Inn was added to The National Register of Historic places in 1988.

The first to arrive were Sadowsky and Scalpone. Their plane touched down at Tucson International Airport just as the sun was starting to play peek-a-boo with the Tucson Mountains in the western sky. "Holy shit!" Sadowsky exclaimed, "the sky's on fire!"

For someone who had never seen a Tucson sunset before, the sky might well indeed have appeared to be on fire. How does one describe a kaleidoscope of red, purple, gold, and smoky black clouds, constantly changing appearance and position in the sky, except as a sky on fire? The taxi ride was a short twenty minutes to the Arizona Inn. Check-in was smooth, and they were shown to their room. In any other hotel it would have been called a suite. The furnishings were eclectic, from Edwardian to early twentieth century contemporary, all handcrafted from cherry-wood and walnut, not faux grained compressed cardboard. Original Audubon prints graced the walls.

Scalpone devoured the room with his eyes and said, "I'm impressed." He opened the note left by Ronstadt at the front desk. *Dinner in the private dining room at eight o'clock*. He checked his watch and turned it back two-hours.

Lasky and Foreman were the next to arrive. When they entered the reception area they were immediately swallowed and transported back to another era. Ever the irreverent, quick-witted, sharp as a shard of glass, Lasky said, "Just like mid-town Miami, but where are the Flamingos?"

Las Vegas was just a hiccup away from Tucson in terms of flying time, and when Dubois arrived he thought he really hadn't left Las Vegas. The terrain was virtually identical, and the mountains surrounding the city were almost the same. Because he and his partner were actively involved in another homicide only one of them could make the trip to Tucson. Dubois won the coin-toss.

Sometimes it took Martin and Saffer longer to drive to work in Los Angeles than it did to fly to Tucson. They welcomed the respite. Los Angeles was experiencing the highest number of homicides in its history. Over 2,500 and still counting—enough to fill Los

Angeles's downtown Ahmanson Theater to beyond capacity—and with three weeks still left in the year.

* * *

Shortly before eight the detectives started toward the dining room. Dubois went there directly. Scalpone and Sadowsky stopped briefly in the lush courtyard and savored the varieties of plant life. Lasky and Foreman exited through the French doors of their room and passed by the casita-enveloped swimming pool. Saffer and Martin detoured by the open-raftered ceiling library that was furnished with books and fine furnishings from Mrs. Greenway's homes in Santa Barbara and Farmington, Connecticut.

Ronstadt, Washington, and Vargas were waiting when they arrived in the dining room. After the proper introductions were made Ronstadt addressed the group. "Thank you all for coming. Dinner will be served shortly, at which time I'll explain everything I've learned about these cases and how I believe we can help one another. In the meantime help yourself to drinks. He gestured toward the fully stocked credenza.

"Gary, I've got one question before we get started," Martin said. "Do you have any openings in your department?"

Ronstadt grinned. "This *Brigadoon* will last only for this weekend." He was referring to the legend of the charming escape into the sweet fairytale of the Scottish highland village, Brigadoon, which appeared for one day once every hundred years, swept up in romance, excitement and enjoyment. "After that we'll all be back to our real lives."

During dinner Ronstadt and his two detectives brought the visitors up to date on everything they had learned. "Adele Grant is recovering nicely," Ronstadt said. "When we were finally able to interview her, she was unable to provide us with any useful information. We checked out all the costume shops here and in

Phoenix. A lot of skeleton costumes had been sold, but those we were able to trace to buyers dead-ended. Besides, I wouldn't have expected the assailant to purchase that distinctive a costume locally. He's far too intelligent to do something that stupid."

"Is she going to proceed with her lawsuit?" asked Saffer.

"Yes, the judge granted a continuance, and the trial will start in the middle of April. He checked the time and said, "We can reconvene here at noon tomorrow. I have a meeting with the Centurion Counsel in the morning, so when we meet at noon I'll have an update on what is going on with the lawyers. Enjoy the morning and just sign for anything you may need."

"A year's lease on one of those casitas?" quipped Sadowsky.

"Except that."

Saturday, December 12, 1992.

Several of the out-of-town detectives spent most of the early morning reviewing their files and wandering the grounds of the Inn. After a light breakfast Lasky retreated to the library, and Saffer took advantage of the workout room. When Ronstadt arrived they were all prepared to move onto the next phase of the operation. The meeting room they were assigned was decorated with antiques, high-beamed ceilings, and French doors which opened into a flower garden. Washington and Vargas arrived shortly after Ronstadt. When they were all seated around the oval conference table Ronstadt informed them of the murder of Elaine Peters, in Houston, exactly one year previously.

"I spoke with Houston detective Barry Berkson this morning immediately after the Counsel meeting at the Westward Look. He was able to get a flight out of Houston, and should be able to join us by mid-afternoon. If that lawyer hadn't come forward with the information when he did, I don't know when we would have found out about the Peters murder. Houston had over six hundred homicides last year, and Elaine Peters got shuffled to the bottom of the deck, probably because she was a hooker, albeit a very high-priced one. She just wasn't a priority. We'll know more when Berkson gets here.

"Attorney Neal Mink, who has been my liaison, will find out if there are any other surprise 'endings' that haven't been reported to the Counsel data base." He explained Neal Mink's role and how the Centurion Counsel became involved.

Lasky was the first to speak. "Last night I went over everything you told us about the four murders, trying to determine if there was some kind of pattern. When you mentioned Berkson and Houston I felt something connect. I think we can all agree that the motive is definitely connected to the lawsuits. I asked myself, of all the women who have initiated lawsuits, why were these five women murdered? The two common factors are the facts they were all represented by lawyers from this Centurion Counsel, and they were all patients of the same doctor. The same is true of the women who received threats. It's all too convenient, especially the fact that there's only one doctor involved. It's too much of a coincidence that the available evidence points to one person. Look at the cities where the murders took place. Cleveland, Los Angeles, Miami, Las Vegas, and now Houston. Last year there were twenty-four thousand seven hundred murders in the U.S…the highest number since records have been kept. This year the number is damned close. With the exception of Las Vegas, those cities had the either the highest number of murders, or the highest murder rate in the country."

"So what's your point?" asked Vargas.

"I think I see where Steve is going," said his partner, Phil Foreman. "I'll bet these cities, in addition to having the highest numbers, had the lowest closure rate."

"You've got it," said Lasky.

"Hang on a minute," said Dubois. "You included Vegas in your stats, but we're not in the top in any of those categories."

Saffer said, "In L.A. we're drowned by the sheer numbers. Compared with the rest of the country our clearance rate sucks. But if I wanted to kill someone, and have the best chance of getting away with it, I'd do it in Las Vegas."

"It makes sense," said Scalpone. "Woody, you have what, two million visitors a month? If I wanted to off someone in Vegas, how hard would it be? I go there, do the job, and then leave. Go ahead and find me."

After Berkson arrived they dissected and re-dissected every scrap of information, like in anatomy lab, in order to come up with a working hypothesis. The conclusion they came to at the end of the day was that in all likelihood the killer was not from any of the cities in which the murders took place. And despite the all too convenient dropping of breadcrumbs leading to Powers, he would still have to be thoroughly investigated, because as Martin pointed out, perhaps the intent was to make Powers look so obviously guilty that that very fact would direct attention away from him, when he may indeed be the perpetrator. At any rate, they all felt Powers had to be involved in some way. The consensus was that the acid threats were coming from another source. As far as the attack on Adele Grant, in Tucson, they theorized that someone didn't want the case to go to trial because of the similarity to the Purcell case and the potential of a similar award, especially since Ingram Mink represented her. That put the manufacturer of the implants in the center of the cross hairs as far as motive was concerned. At the end of the session they all agreed some progress had been made. They would reconvene in the morning to map further strategy. Ronstadt invited them all to a barbeque at his ranch.

* * *

With the exception of Dubois, whose Las Vegas was topographically almost identical to Tucson—minus the slot machines, neon lights, and taxi cabs—the detectives from the other cities marveled at the laid back informality they had experienced in Tucson. For men who lived in cities where living space was measured in square footage directed vertically ever upward in the form of towering high-rises, it was a welcome treat to see the changing faces of the majestic mountain ranges that mothered The Old Pueblo in their bosoms, unchallenged by glass and concrete behemoths. A traffic jam meant it would take twenty minutes to get across town, not twenty millennia like in Los Angeles. For formal occasions you left your horse or truck at home and traveled in a four-wheel-drive SUV.

Washington escorted the detectives from the concrete jungles of Los Angeles and Miami to the ranch in his Ford Explorer, the others followed with Vargas in his Jeep Cherokee.

Ten minutes from the inner city retreat of the Arizona Inn they were snaking their way up Campbell Avenue into the foothills of the Santa Catalina Mountains, where Ronstadt's *modest* five-acre ranch was located. The main house was set back from the road on a knoll with a commanding view of the city and the mountains. Giant saguaro cactuses, the guardians of the desert, were ushering in another sunset in the western sky. When they arrived, Ronstadt was kneeling and stoking embers in a mesquite fire pit. Two blonde-haired little girls were standing on either side of him, and on either side of them was a golden retriever. Their backs were turned. When they heard the guests arrive the girls and the goldens turned their heads. Ronstadt concentrated on the fire. Lasky, who was a battalion photographer when he was in the army, saw a Kodak moment and wished he had a camera to capture the backdrop of the sunset dancing through the wisps of the girls' golden hair. Ronstadt stood up and turned to face his guests. The girls each wrapped their arms around a leg, and the dogs tightened and assumed a protective stance beside the girls. A low growl churned from the alpha dog.

"Relax girls," he commanded the dogs. "Despite their attempts to appear tough, they're really wimps."

Sadowsky couldn't help staring at the girls. "I'm seeing double," he said.

Ronstadt grinned. "They're identical twins."

"And the dogs?"

"They're litter mates." He introduced the detectives to the girls and the dogs." Okay girls, time go help your mother and Anna set the table."

They scampered off with the dogs glued to their sides, but not before Sassy, the alpha dog, turned and stared at the group, just to remind them she was watching.

Martin took in the surroundings and said, "Like I said yesterday, do you have any openings in your department?"

* * *

The Westward Look Resort was chosen to host the meetings of the Centurion Counsel because of its seclusion, privacy, and five-star service. Built in 1912, six months after Arizona became the 48th state, as a family home for William and Maria Watson under the watchful eye of architect Merritt Starkweather, it became a guest ranch in 1920,when the Watsons added 15 cottages so visitors to Tucson could share the ranch experience. The Watsons' original living room, complete with a stone hearth, fireplace, a warm hand-hewn mahogany-planked hardwood floor, and wrought iron chandeliers, became the engaging focal point of the resort.

In 1940, it became a thriving dude ranch operated by Bob and Beverly Nason, and the name, Westward Look, was adopted from Winston Churchill's 1941, emotionally packed speech to the British Nation when the gray clouds of war blanketed the European continent. He quoted 19th century English poet Arthur Hugh Clough, "...in front the sun climbs slowly, how slowly, but westward look...the land is bright."

After dinner in the Gold Room, Lawrence Band shared cocktails with a group in the original living room, now known as Vigas Room, because of its exposed viga log ceiling. They discussed his revelation of the Peters murder. As the group dissipated he decided he would explore the grounds. The moon was ninety percent full, and together with the unpolluted glow of the stars, the trails would be sufficiently illuminated for him to explore the area without getting lost. The temperature had dropped to 50 degrees, so it was unlikely he would encounter any rattlesnakes or other desert denizens that might challenge his trespass of their territory. He took a flashlight for backup.

The saguaro trail was a 2/3 mile unpaved trail, which divided into two loops, the Coyote Loop and the Javelina Loop. He took the Javelina, and halfway into the trail he stopped at the Palo Verde Ramada to absorb the twinkling of the stars and lights of the city competing with one another for dominance in the night sky. He thought he heard a rustling sound behind him, but he continued to gaze up at the night sky, so he didn't see the figure emerge from behind a giant saguaro. When his name was called out he turned and felt the axe embrace his neck. The last thing he saw was a shooting star fade into darkness in the western sky as the light from the stars in God's marquee was turned off forever.

* * *

Ronstadt waited until the taillights from Vargas's Cherokee faded into the night before he strolled over to the cooler and rescued a longneck Dos Equis that was shivering on a bed of ice. He climbed the short rise to the gazebo that was positioned to give a 360-degree view of the city and the mountains. He sat facing the city with his boots propped up on the railing. A gentle breeze tickled his back and he detected the faint aroma of Pacifica Mexico Cocoa Perfume sneaking up on him from behind. He turned to see Elena moving with the stealth of a panther toward the gazebo, balancing in one hand a frosted salt-rimmed margarita glass, its contents trying to climb over the edge. In the other hand was its supply ship pitcher.

"Hey cowboy you look like you could use some company." She eased into a wicker chair beside him and docked the pitcher on a matching wicker table. "Didn't spill a drop," she beamed.

Ten years married and she still stirred within him the same indescribable desire he felt the first time their eyes locked. Her eyes were so black they made coal look like snow, and her teeth so white they made snow look like coal. Her hair was the color of pitch. The Mexican fiesta dress she wore tried, but could not hide the curves of a body that would make Michelangelo salivate.

He smiled in the darkness. "When you show up with a pitcher of margaritas I know I'm in for more than a hand holding experience. What's on your mind?"

"Am I that transparent?" she asked.

"You, transparent? Never."

"Gary, I listened to all of you expounding your theories tonight, but tell me why you are so involved with these murders in other cities? Granted, there was an attempted homicide in Tucson, but you don't know if it had anything to do with the other murders, and even if it did, surely Manny and Jerry are more than capable of dealing with it. What if there are more killings like these in more cities? Are you going to get involved with them as well?" She shook her head. "I really think the FBI should take over the investigation."

No one could ever say Elena was anything but direct.

"We addressed that possibility earlier today. I know what we're trying to do doesn't follow any accepted police protocol, but I can't escape the feeling that the answer to the murders lies here in Tucson. I believe we're dealing with a different kind of serial killer. He knows exactly who his victims will be and where and when he will strike next. These weren't opportunistic murders. So far the killer has attacked only patients of one doctor, and the victims were also clients of lawyers who are members of the Centurion Counsel.

The first murder victim, Carol Andrews, lived in Tucson although she was killed in Cleveland. And, as far as we know, Adele Grant was the last attempt, and she is a Tucsonan. That's why we're involved."

"Are there others who aren't patients of this doctor and clients of these lawyers?"

"At this point there's no way of knowing."

She held out her glass and said, "*una más, por favor.*"

As the liquid gurgled into her glass she said, "Are you looking for zebras?"

Elena had a unique talent of visualizing a landscape if she were shown a bouquet of flowers. She could take a few unrelated facts and create a logical working hypothesis. Ronstadt often felt she was the real detective in the family. She was always thinking outside the box.

Elena continued. "When I hear hoof beats I think of horses, not zebras. Why complicate things? The answer may be so obvious that you're walking right past it. I think your killer knows a lot more about all of you than you know about him. I think he's purposely misdirecting you, and I agree the answer will be found in Tucson.

"Now mi amor, let's go to bed and finish this party with some real fireworks."

CHAPTER TWENTY-EIGHT

Midland, Michigan
Saturday, December 12, 1992.

THE REPRESENTATIVES FROM the breast implant manufacturers were all gathered once again in the executive conference room of the Pink Palace, and once again there was no pre-Christmas cheer to be found. John Briggs the PR spin master from Briggs-Morton said, "Gentlemen, I have your numbers for the year to date. They're not pretty." He read from his notes. "As of today, December 12, 1992, there have been 3,532 individual lawsuits filed against Dow Corning alone. As I predicted last year, the numbers have increased exponentially. When we met last time the Purcell case had not yet been resolved. Not even I would have predicted the numbers that Ingram Mink was able to squeeze out of the jury. It made this year's highest award of twenty-five million dollars by John O'Connor's firm pale in comparison, and since then O'Connor has filed hundreds more lawsuits. And I understand that Mink has another client with almost identical problems to those of Louise Purcell. So how much do you think the award will be in that case?

"I'm sure most of you are familiar with cartoonist Walt Kelly's lovable comic strip character Pogo." He paused to judge their reaction. Some smiled or nodded, others looked puzzled. "Well, Pogo the 'possum was also a philosopher, and in one sentence he summarized the dilemma you are all facing. He said, 'We have met the enemy...and the enemy is us.' And just why is the enemy *us*?

"Here are the sad realities why the enemy is *us*. The Congressional Medal of Stupidity goes to...all of you. And the citation reads, '...awarded for the biggest cluster fuck in corporate history.' You hired my firm for damage control, but it was too little and too late." He directed his gaze at the representative from DCC. "Did anyone from your organization think, when your CEO put to paper the words, 'The issue of cover-up is going well from a long-term perspective,' that that memo would not come back to bite you in the ass? No, not bite, but rather chew your ass right off, so the only part that remained was your asshole. Did you think when you settled those early suits that the sealed court records would stay sealed forever? Well, they are public records now, and they're going to be used to feed a mass of previously starving lawyers and increase the belt size of some very fat ones, particularly that odious group of one hundred...The Centurion Counsel. Last year I told you what would happen when your memo about your *goal* became public," he said glaring at William Sherman, the chairman of Sherman-Hall. "Your partners in this whole mess, the plastic surgeons, screwed up in their own way. The monies their society assessed their members for a PR campaign helped pay for the expenses to Washington D.C. for the woman who *volunteered* to testify before the FDA about how happy she was with her implants. She was to be their spokeswoman.

"Well, their spokeswoman torpedoed them and I quote, 'my doctor told me to lobby the FDA to keep implants.' Instead, she attended so she could describe the complications she had suffered with her implants following a double mastectomy four years previously.

"To further compound this fuck-up, with the exception of Mentor, you have all announced that you'll discontinue making and selling breast implants. What's the credo of success in business? 'Timing is everything.' When you all threw in the towel it couldn't have come at a worse time. By doing so you've all tacitly admitted there is something wrong with the implants. Which brings us to the final chapter. *The class action.*

"As you are painfully aware, the class action has been approved by the Judicial Panel on Multidistrict Litigation, and God only knows how many billions you're going to have to bring to the table.

As painful as it is to admit, Ingram Mink's a fucking genius. I take my hat off to him. He can lay claim to initiating the largest mass tort in history.

"Before I continue, are there any questions?"

William Sherman stood up. "So while all of you come together and work out your tidy little agreements, my company is left to hang out and dry all by itself. Is that your intention?"

"Bill," Bruce Draper said, "to use your own words, 'Our goals are not to help patients but to lead our employees down the path to the good life.' You put yourself on the clothesline."

The representative from Squibb rose and said, "Mr. Sherman, with all due respect, if and when the Purcell case is settled you'll be lucky if you have enough cash left to buy a roll of asswipe. So please don't feel you've been slighted because you weren't invited to participate in the settlement discussions. Collectively, we'll have to come up with what is projected to be over four billion dollars. How much do you think you'd be able to contribute to the fund?"

Sherman remained silent.

"That's what I thought." he sat down in disgust.

Sherman stood up and said, "You all may think you'll be able to buy your way out of this mess, but there are other ways to settle these frivolous lawsuits." He gathered his papers and left the room.

"You're better off without him," John Briggs said. "There are two other issues that need to be addressed," he continued. "First let me give you our projections. Based on a chi factor of eight, our actuaries came up with the following projections, confirmed by the computers at the University of Michigan. There will not be enough money in your collective vaults, after you have exhausted your insurance coverage, to cover the claims. We anticipate, as mentioned earlier, there will be close to one-half million women who will sign up for the class action once the terms have been approved by Judge Pointer. That means approximately one out of four to five women who have had breast implant surgery will be involved in the class action, and we feel Pointer will approve a settlement of around four and one half billion dollars." He paused to let the numbers register. No one seemed particularly surprised. "Paradoxically that works in our favor; the more women who sign up, the smaller the slices of the pie. Some women will opt out and pursue individual suits, but bankruptcy will make them go away. Applying the numbers I've quoted, at this point you're looking at a maximum of ten thousand dollars per claimant unless they come up with some other kind of structured formula. After the lawyers take their cut the maximum the plaintiffs will receive is about six thousand dollars, and if the payouts are structured to the type of problem they claim to have, then some could end up with less than two thousand dollars.

"It's time to take your fingers out of your asses and take the offensive. We've already contacted the Mayo Clinic and they've started to percolate numbers and should have their study ready for publication by 1994. Also, *The New England Journal of Medicine* should have a study ready as well. We'll need to publicize the studies that will prove conclusively that breast implants do not cause cancer. Those studies will effectively neutralize Nader and Wolfe. The greatest fear that women have is that their breast implants can cause cancer. Once they learn that they don't have to fear cancer, I expect the panic over that issue will abate.

"Consider the next step to be a military operation. Until reinforcements arrive in the form of legitimate medical studies, which will prove there is no relationship between the diseases and the implants, you will have to slow things down by delaying litigation. Once the sums for the mass tort are approved and the vultures realize there's no flesh left on your bones to feast upon, the lawsuits will stop, or at least slow down to a trickle. Those who choose to opt out and pursue individual claims will find the bones have been picked dry.

The representative from DCC said, "We're the largest and have the most exposure, so there's a strong likelihood we'll go chapter eleven once we see the numbers."

Briggs nodded. "Those details you'll have to work out with your legal departments. All we can do is bring you the supplies to fight with. Once the studies are in, even the most skeptical jurors will be more likely to believe our experts who will have unassailable credentials, rather than some hack from Podunk Mississippi who's on the payroll of the attorneys."

"But what if the studies don't prove our case?" asked the representative from Paine.

"Based on what we've learned, that won't happen, but if in the remote possibility it were to occur, then I'd suggest you fill out your CVs and look for a new job.

"There's one final point to cover before we leave, and this may have far greater implications than anything you've faced so far.

"We have a contact within the Centurion Counsel, and I've learned that the Counsel maintains a central registry that contains all the relevant details of all the lawsuits that have been filed by members of the Centurion Counsel. That means any member, at any time, has immediate access to the details of any case. The registry is based with the law firm of Mink and Mink. According to the information I have, the one hundred members of the Centurion Counsel represent seventy-six point five percent of all women who have filed individual lawsuits, and the Mink firm is spearheading the class action. What this all means is that the Mink brothers are probably directing the whole show, and of those one hundred lawyers the Mink firm has the highest number of clients, followed by the law firm of Lawrence Band. There are several others that are in the front of the field, and then the rest of the suits are fairly evenly distributed. I don't know how they've set this up, but you can be certain that it's Ingram Mink who has choreographed the entire show. He's a chess grand master, and I suspect he sees this whole thing as just a big chess game. The Counsel is meeting in Tucson as I speak.

"What I'm about to reveal hasn't hit the news media yet, but I'm sure it will shortly. There have been four murders and one attempted murder of women who were breast implant litigants; all of them had the same surgeon and were represented by attorneys who are members of the Centurion Counsel. In addition, there are a number of women who have withdrawn from the litigation because of threats of bodily harm if they were to continue with their lawsuits."

"I wonder if that's what Sherman meant when he said there were other ways," said Payne.

"Don't even go there," said Briggs. "My investigators are on top of this, and right now my informant tells me the lead detectives from all the murder cases are meeting in Tucson, and they have been working with the Centurion Counsel to keep the press from learning about the connection between the murders. I just hope for your sakes that nothing leads back to any of you in this room, because if it does, then the breast implant litigation will become as significant as a game of ping-pong compared to the scandal that will follow. That's all I have for now. If you want to ask any questions call me individually. I don't want any of you to have knowledge of what anyone else had said if it should ever come up in court about what transpired here tonight."

CHAPTER TWENTY-NINE

Tucson, Arizona
Sunday, December 13, 1992.

RONSTADT HAD THE receiver in his hand after the first ring. He glanced at the display on the bedside clock…5:20 a.m. "…Give me half an hour."

Elena rolled over. "Where?" she asked. She knew instinctively when the phone rang before dawn on a Sunday that it wasn't an invitation to a tea party. As head of the homicide division of the TPD Gary was called for only one reason at that hour.

Ronstadt was out of bed. "The Westward Look. The Centurion Counsel lawyer from Houston was murdered there last night."

"Why you? That's the county."

"That was Neal Mink. He's staying at the Westward Look with the other lawyers from the Centurion Counsel. He went out for an early morning run and discovered the body.

"Why would Mink be staying there? Doesn't he live close to the Look?"

"Yes, but when they have these high power think sessions these guys frequently sequester themselves at the meeting hotel so they'll be immediately available if something comes up."

"I suppose. Can I make you some coffee before you go."

"No. I'll grab a quick shower and get something there."

* * *

The drive from the ranch to the Westward Look took Ronstadt

only ten minutes. When he arrived, there were three sheriff's cruisers and a CSI van in the parking lot. He waved to the medical examiner, Dr. Phillip Alexander, who was obviously finished with his examination and was getting into his truck, ready to leave the scene.

Alexander was an imposing man. He looked more like a linebacker for the Arizona Cardinals than the Pima County Chief Medical Examiner. He stood six-four, weighed two hundred forty pounds, and kept his hair tied in a ponytail; he was a full-blooded Apache. In his faded jeans, denim shirt, boots, and a Stetson, he looked ready for a rodeo. "Gary? What brings you here? Business slow in the city?"

He explained the reason for his appearance.

"Interesting." Alexander got back out and shut the truck door. "I'll walk back with you."

The perimeter to the Javelina Trail had been secured with yellow crime scene tape. Two detectives from the sheriff's department were talking with Mink when they arrived. Klieg lights gave an unnatural luminance to the scene. Standing by the body directing her CSI team was Amanda Suarez, the diminutive five foot zero head of the team. She was spewing bullets in Spanish with the rapidity of a Gatling gun at one of the techs who apparently neglected to follow proper protocol for something or other. She had the reputation of being able to stare a rattlesnake into slithering back into its den when she was pissed. She was definitely pissed at the cowering tech. She whipped her head around when Alexander called out.

"Well, to what do we owe this honor, Sergeant Ronstadt?"

Alexander explained and asked her to tell Ronstadt what they had learned.

"He was last seen in the Gold room around ten last night. Neal Mink discovered the body at four forty-five this morning, so our time frame is pretty clear. We're checking the entire area, but so far nothing. Impressions will be a nightmare because there are so many shoe and boot prints on the trail. There are some tracks by the saguaro where the body was found, but I don't think we'll learn much. The assailant may have been behind the cactus waiting for him to appear, and surprised him, or sneaked up on him and struck him without warning, because there are no defensive wounds, one blow...virtually decapitated. It looks like the blow came from a very sharp thin-bladed axe. Of course when my boss man does the post he'll give you more precise times and details." She looked at Alexander to see if he had anything to add. He shook his head.

"Are you going to be involved with this Gary?" she asked.

"I'll talk with Sherriff Dupnick and see how he wants to handle it, but I believe the answer'll be yes. There may be an association with the attempt on that woman's life on Halloween. I can't give you any more details at this point, but it needs to be priority one, keep the lid on about the axe."

She nodded. "My team knows the drill. There'll be no mention of the axe."

Ronstadt said to Alexander, "Phil, I think you should come with me to a meeting at the Arizona Inn this morning. Let's get some breakfast and I'll explain. Let me talk to Mink for a minute and then we can go. How about the Blue Willow?"

"I'll meet you there."

* * *

The Blue Willow restaurant was one of the few restaurants in Tucson where fresh home cooked food meant exactly that. It was originally a home built in 1940, when Campbell Avenue was a two-lane dirt road with open fields and scattered ranches. As the fields vanished and the potholes gave way to pavement, the tree-lined street gradually became speckled with offices and mini-strip malls. The home became a rental for the University of Arizona and changed faces from a mechanics' garage to a pre-school with an attached antique shop. In 1978, Louise Seidler changed its face once more to create The Blue Willow Restaurant, a cozy adobe restaurant and gift shop, which proudly maintained the building's original architecture and unhurried tranquility from another era.

When Ronstadt arrived, Alexander's muscle truck was already occupying a space meant for two vehicles. Alexander was seated in the main dining room, the former master bedroom, nursing a cup of freshly brewed coffee with another waiting for Ronstadt.

"You have my full attention Sergeant Ronstadt."

"I told you of the attack on Adele Grant and why Mink called me. There's a lot more to the story." During a breakfast of *huevos rancheros* he told Alexander the entire sequence of events.

"Interesting. And what role do you see me playing in this investigation?"

Ronstadt looked at his watch. "I'll explain that at the meeting. We should get over there, we' re scheduled to start at nine."

* * *

When they arrived at the Arizona Inn everyone was present except for Vargas. He made his way in as Ronstadt was setting up the green board. After everyone was seated Ronstadt introduced Alexander to the group.

"I'll get right to the point. We have a new development. Last night one of the attorneys from the Centurion Counsel was murdered at the Westward Look Resort." He looked directly at Berkson and said, "It was your Lawrence Band. He was nearly decapitated with a single blow...apparently from a sharp axe."

"Holy shit!" Berkson said. "Now it's the lawyers. It's becoming a whole lot clearer now. If nothing else, it seems to confirm what the bastard's motive is."

Lasky said, "If that's true and this guy is now going after the lawyers, then he's got a whole flock of lawyers to choose from and a whole hell of a lot of women who have signed up with them.

We're talking about several thousand potential victims. Logistically it's impossible to protect all of them. Are we supposed to warn these guys that they could be next, and then have them warn their clients?"

"The starting point has to be Tucson," said Ronstadt. "The first woman murdered was Carol Andrews. Although she was murdered in Cleveland, she was from Tucson. Adele Grant is from Tucson, and Lawrence Band was murdered in Tucson. Is there a connection to these three people beyond what we already know?" He walked over to the green board and wrote as he spoke. "The common factors are the Centurion Counsel and Dr. Devin Powers. What are we missing?"

"Look at the women who were murdered and how much they were suing for," said Scalpone. "The first four weren't suing for a huge amount compared to Adele Grant. After Mink got that judgment in the Purcell case the stakes went up. From what Gary said, Grant has similar medical problems to those of Purcell. Potentially she could expect a similar award since Mink is her lawyer. Eliminate her and you eliminate a potential windfall. So the next step is to get rid of the lawyers who provide the greatest threat."

"That would certainly explain why Band was murdered. He is, or I should say he was, the most well known PI lawyer in Texas. Odds are he had a huge number of lawsuits percolating, and with some of them he was probably demanding the sky and the stars in it," said Berkson.

"If that's true why not go after Mink?" said Sadowsky.

"Maybe the guy will," said Martin. "Like Barry said, go after the high profile lawyers. Gary, I'm sure your friend Mink can give us a list of names and size of demands."

"Is it possible that the answer's simply that this Powers guy is just offing these women and that's it?" asked Saffer.

"It's possible," said Ronstadt," but I think we're dealing with something more complex. What bothers me is why just the threats with Powers' other patients? There has to be more than just one person involved."

The rest of the morning session was spent discussing how to identify and focus on those who would be the most likely targets. If they were right, then the logistics of offering some degree of protection would be greatly simplified. Alexander told them he would speak with the pathologists who had performed the autopsies on the murdered women to see if there were any unusual findings that may have been a common factor among the five autopsies. It would be a formidable task but he would then contact the medical examiners of the cities in which the Counsel members practiced and provide them with details of what to look for should they be involved with similar murders. The detectives agreed to divide up the same cities and contact the homicide investigators in each city and provide them with the information they had put together. By doing so they could create a database similar to that of the Centurion lawyers. It was unanimously agreed that Ronstadt should be point for the investigation. They broke for lunch and agreed to reconvene at one o'clock for the final session. They all checked their cell phones for messages as they left the room. Dubois had a message to call his partner in Las Vegas.

* * *

After they reassembled for the afternoon session Dubois announced he had something to report. "Before we started yesterday, I remembered something about the LaPelle case. When we searched her apartment after the murder we found shit for evidence. I verified the contents of her purse with the CSI team. There was the usual girlie crap, but there was also a five thousand dollar gift certificate from the Mirage. It was new and hadn't been taken out of its sealed envelope. I didn't think anything of it at the time, but when I was trying to figure out just what went on that night, the three cherries clicked in place. I wondered what this broad was doing with a five-K gift certificate. She was an exotic dancer, and I thought she might've been hooking on the side.

"I called my partner and asked him to check it out. He found out it'd been bought with cash the night she was killed. There was no record of the purchaser, but he found out the purchase had been recorded on videotape. He contacted security at the Mirage. They keep all their tapes for a year, so he was able to review the tapes for that day. There was a recording of two five thousand dollar gift certificates sold on April 17. One was sold to a woman, and the other was sold to a well-known patron of the Mirage. He's totally comped when he stays there. They reviewed all the tapes that this guy appeared in, and at eight o'clock on April 17, he was dining at the Onda, and guess who joined him? Desiree LaPelle. After dinner they went to the Siegfried and Roy show. They entered his suite just after midnight, and she left just after two in the morning. The ME placed her time of death between 4:00 and 6:00 a.m. She was supposed to be at rehearsal at noon, but when she didn't show up the director called the apartment manager where she lived and asked him to check on her. That's when her body was discovered."

He looked at Gary. "It was your friend Neal Mink. And there's one other thing. I remembered. That week there'd been a lot of hype in the news about the fact that for the first time *The American Society of Plastic and Reconstructive Surgeons* was meeting at Caesar's Palace. It was a big deal because there were hardly any rooms available in town because of the number of docs that showed up. Yesterday, when you told us this guy Powers had operated on the murdered women, I wondered if he could've been at that convention. My partner checked and found out Powers had reserved a suite at Caesar's."

Four months earlier, Las Vegas, Nevada, April 17, 1992.

As Powers was leaving the Onda he saw her sliding into the

booth beside a very familiar face. He watched them exchange what was much more intimate than a lawyer client greeting. He wondered what she was doing with Neal Mink…Mink was not her lawyer. Puzzled, he left the restaurant to look for a pay phone.

In the lobby he phoned Hemlock, Michigan. "It's about LaPelle, I thought you said you had spoken to her." He explained what he had just seen.

"Relax Devin, we just may have to speak to her again. I assure you, there's nothing to worry about."

"That's what you said the first time I called you. If I can't rely on you I may just have to take care of it myself."

CHAPTER THIRTY

Tucson, Arizona
Monday, December 14, 1992.

WHEN RONSTADT ARRIVED at his office Vargas and Washington were waiting. They had already discussed how they felt they should proceed. They agreed the weekend meeting with the other detectives had been fruitful. The consensus from the meeting was that Ronstadt should be the one to direct the investigation because they all were convinced the answers would be found in Tucson. The other detectives would continue to be involved, but they would play a supporting role. It made little sense for all to be duplicating their efforts. However, they would be apprised of Ronstadt's progress on a daily basis, as if it were a briefing within their own departments.

Ronstadt gestured the two into his office. His secretary had already brewed the coffee. He filled his cup, sat at his desk, and said, "You first Manny."

"We've already discussed it. We think we should tag-team Powers after we find out as much as we can about where he was on the nights in question. I don't know if we have enough to subpoena his phone records yet, but if he's the one, then we don't think he was working alone."

"Jerry?" Ronstadt said.

"We've got the murders and the threats. You're the expert on profiling, but I can't see a serial killer just making threats to one group and then killing another. I suppose it'd be possible if we were dealing with a small group, but we don't know how many women have been threatened, and we won't know that until Mink polls the attorneys in the Counsel to find out if there were other women who withdrew from the litigation, and if so, whether they'd been threatened. Which brings up the question of Neal Mink who's now a player. We think you should be the one to handle him."

"I agree. I've given a lot of thought to what we learned yesterday. Neal Mink is far too intelligent to be so obviously involved. Are they just coincidences? Think about it. Carol Andrews, the first victim. He was her lawyer. The fourth one, Desiree LaPelle. He wasn't her lawyer, but he had a tryst with her. The last one, Adele Grant. He *is* her lawyer. And he was the one who discovered Lawrence Band's body. You know how I feel about coincidences."

"When everything was pointing to Powers we said it was too obvious for it to be that simple. We can now say the same thing about Mink," said Washington. "The conundrum is that the answer may just be a simple one."

"Like I said, Mink is far too intelligent not to see the connection, and he knows that I'd never miss it, so there's no point in me trying to ignore the obvious. If I were to try and keep it under the radar screen he'd know it immediately. No, I'm going to talk with him and lay out everything out on the table," said Ronstadt.

* * *

"Well Gary, it's been quite a week. Can I get you something?" asked Neal.

"Diet Coke if you have one."

Mink walked over to a motel-sized refrigerator that was built into a teak cabinet and removed a frosted red and silver can of diet Coke. "Glass?"

"Straight up'll be fine."

Neal returned to his chair, leaned back, and laced his hands behind his head. "This visit isn't about our mutual investigation, is it?"

Ronstadt returned the intensity of Neal's stare. *I never realized how blue his eyes are, it's no wonder women can't keep their hands off him.*

"You know it's not."

He sighed and let the chair come forward. "So, am I a suspect or just a person of interest?"

Ronstadt smiled, "That'll depend whether my nose starts to itch when you tell me your story."

"Ah yes, the famous Ronstadt nose for the truth. I've heard of it, but I never thought that one day I'd be the subject of its scrutiny. Tell me Gary, have you ever suspected that there was someone you were one hundred percent convinced was a stone-cold-blooded killer, but couldn't prove it, and had to let the killer walk?"

"Only once, but I wasn't a cop at the time."

"Your friend Amy Carter, if I remember correctly."

"Let's drop that and get to the issue at hand."

It happened two weeks after a confrontation in the corridor of Tucson High, with Theodore Aragon III. The three had just finished a course in Japanese culture when he heard Amy cry out. "Stop it Theo you're hurting me." Ronstadt found her struggling to get break free from his grasp. He would never forget his words. "Pain? You don't know what pain is." Two weeks later her body was found beaten and raped near Gates Pass. Her killer was never found, but Ronstadt would never be convinced that it was anyone but Theodore Aragon III.

"On the other hand, Gary, have you ever interviewed someone whom you were convinced was as innocent as a lamb who was really the wolf in disguise?"

Ronstadt wasn't sure how to interpret his smile. "I suppose I'll be able to answer that at the conclusion of this investigation." His smile needed no interpretation.

"I fully expect you to verify everything I tell you, and I'd be disappointed if you didn't, but I assure you there *will* be no inconsistencies."

"I'm aware of your legendary memory…eidetic, I believe is the term. Let's start with Carol Andrews."

Neal shrugged. "She started out as a date. My first and only sexual encounter with her was on December 14, 1990. We had dinner at the Tack Room and afterwards we spent the night at Ventana Canyon. During the post-coital phase of our encounter I learned she had breast implant surgery done by Devin Powers." He recited their conversation verbatim. "After Carol agreed to become a client our relationship was completely professional. The only time I saw her after that was in our offices. When she told me she was going to have surgery in Cleveland I made the arrangements for her to stay at the Glidden House. I learned she had been murdered when Detective Scalpone called me. And where was I the night she was murdered? I was home in bed, 1,503 nautical miles from Cleveland. Can I prove it? No."

"Who else would've known she was going to Cleveland?" asked Ronstadt.

"Other than Ingram, I have no idea."

"Tell me about Desiree LaPelle."

That caught Neal off guard, but he showed no reaction to the statement. *I wonder how he learned that I was with Desiree that night.*

"As you well know, I love to play high-stakes poker and blackjack, and I usually go to Vegas every few months to play. It also gives me an opportunity to exercise my Ferrari in the Nevada desert. I met Desiree several years ago when I was playing blackjack at Caesar's Palace. She was watching me have a very good run, and laughing asked me if I would place a bet for her. I was stricken with her beauty and thought she'd be an excellent companion for the rest of my stay. 'This one's for you,' I told her. The one thousand dollar bet I placed for her became fifteen hundred with a blackjack. One thing led to another, and after that she became my companion whenever I went to Vegas."

He explained how he became involved with her lawsuit and

detailed to the minute the time they had spent together the night she was killed. The remainder of the interview was spent explaining how Adele Grant became a client and how he discovered the body of Band.

"So, am I a suspect?"

"Neal, you'll have to admit you've given me a shit-load of coincidences to sort through."

"Yes, I know, and you don't believe in coincidences. Does this mean I'll have to recuse myself from participating any further in the investigation?"

Ronstadt thought for a moment. "No, but I'm afraid it's going to have to be a one-way street from now on."

"You mean I provide you with everything I learn, but you tell me nothing about your investigation?"

"It would have to be that way in any case."

"Seems reasonable to me. I'm as anxious as you to see the killer apprehended." His charm had returned.

CHAPTER THIRTY-ONE

Tucson, Arizona
Tuesday, December 15, 1992.

AS BEFORE, THEY arrived unannounced at Powers' emporium. "Detectives Washington and Vargas. Dr. Powers is in surgery and he will be there for at least two more hours."

Both were impressed that *Glamour* girl remembered their names.

"You're welcome to wait…I can get you something to drink if you'd like. Detective Vargas? Perrier… smooth I believe."

Vargas was now even more impressed. "No thanks. Just tell Dr. Powers we'll be back at…" he looked at his watch, "one-thirty."

When they returned, after a brief wait, they were escorted back to Powers' office. Powers was seated on his throne as if he were getting ready to grant an audience to his subjects. Seated in one chair by his desk was a new player whom they assumed was Powers' attorney. From the way he was dressed and the self-assured, over-confident way in which he assessed them, they correctly assumed this was not a junior associate. David Glover was the senior partner in the law firm of Glover and the six names that followed his.

Powers was wearing a surgical scrub suit, and appeared relaxed and ready for anything the detectives might ask, especially since the lawyer was going to run interference for him. Powers flicked his wrist, indicating the chairs that had been placed for Vargas and Washington.

"Detectives, the last time you intruded my office without the courtesy of a phone call I told you if you wanted to speak with me again it would be in the presence of my attorney. David, these are the two detectives I told you about."

"Gentlemen, I am David Glover, and as you have gathered I represent Dr. Powers." His voice was polished and practiced. "Let me establish the ground rules..."

Washington was out of his chair and squared himself in front of the lawyer. He glowered as if he were getting ready to admonish a teenager who had broken curfew. He towered over the man, and Glover had to crane his neck to make eye contact with him. The sound that came from Washington's mouth was a boom box turned to maximum volume and bass.

"Counselor, *there...will...be no...fucking ground rules*. We'll be asking your client some questions. Your function will be to either shake or nod your head if there's a problem with a question. He may confer with you before he answers." He turned to Powers. "And, doctor, we're extending you a courtesy by *intruding* your office. Your other option is to come to our office, and I assure you it would not be an *intrusion* on us."

The rage Vargas saw percolating in Powers eyes was a volcano threatening to erupt. Powers' entire demeanor was wrong. When two snarly cops, especially homicide cops, confront innocent people the normal reaction would be to fidget and be a little afraid. Sociopaths, on the other hand, showed no fear, but could be extremely volatile if they felt they were not in full control at all times. He had just described Powers. Glover, on the other hand, was completely unfazed by Washington's outburst. In fact his eyes twinkled with amusement. This interview was going to be interesting.

Washington sat down, the crescendo his voice had reached returned to lullaby level. "Dr. Powers, we're investigating a series of murders and one attempted murder. The one common link to all of them is *you*. Five women have been murdered, and an attempt was made on the life of a sixth. They were all patients of yours. They all had silicone breast implant surgery performed by you, and they all were suing you. In addition, the attorney who was representing one of those women was also murdered. A bit of a coincidence wouldn't you say?" He directed his eyes to the attorney whose look of amusement became one of curiosity.

"As you well know, counselor, in any murder investigation we look for motive, means, and opportunity. You'll have to admit, from our perspective, your client certainly had the motive..."

" I am *not* willing to concede that point, but please continue," said Glover.

Vargas glided into the questioning. The look of amusement returned to Glover's eyes. He knew what the detectives were trying to do. *All the world's a stage.*

Vargas did not sing a lullaby. "It's really quite simple, *doctor,* no matter what your lawyer thinks you sure as shit had a motive to off these women and the lawyer as well. They were suing your ass off, and if that's not a reason to be pissed off at them then I don't know what is."

"You're not talking to one of your low-life animals from the street, so I would appreciate it if you were to address the doctor with a modicum of respect," said Glover. "Also, I'm unaware of any murders, other than that of Mr. Band and the attempted murder of Mrs. Grant, that occurred in Tucson."

"We're talking about a series of murders across the country…all patients of your client," said Washington.

"Oh really? Unless you have magically become the FBI you have no authority to ask my client about anything that occurred outside your jurisdiction. So please restrict your questions accordingly."

"Then I'll make it simple doctor," said Washington. "Can you account for your whereabouts on the nights of October 31, and December 12, of this year?"

"And I'll make it simple for you detective. Unless you are charging my client with the murder of Mr. Band and the attempted murder of Mrs. Grant then he is not required to answer any of your questions, and it is my advice that he refrain from doing so."

Powers stood. "If you'll excuse me I have surgery scheduled… and if you ever show up again in my offices without a warrant you will be asked to leave."

"What's the surgery doc…tits or ass?" Vargas asked.

Powers' glare knifed into Vargas. He said nothing and left the room.

"Glover stood and said, "I'm going to speak to your superiors and request that you stop harassing Dr. Powers."

"You know counselor, you're an obfuscating asshole just like your client," Vargas sneered. "Yeah, sometimes even us barrio babies can use big words. And you know what else? Anyone who commits murder is a low-life animal from the streets, even if the zip code where he parks his Mercedes is 85718."

CHAPTER THIRTY-TWO

Detroit, Michigan
Thursday and Friday, December 24-25, 1992.

MOST FACTORIES CLOSED early on Christmas Eve day. In Detroit most factories had closed permanently, long before this particular Christmas Eve day. However, there was one factory that continued to thrive. In fact, this factory's production line was at a near all time high. It was the murder factory. What was once the automotive capital of the world was now the murder capital of the world. The number of murders peaked at 714 in 1974, fell off for a while, and then rebounded to 615 in 1991. So far, in 1992, the number was 562, but when that number was adjusted for the ever-dwindling population, the per capita murder rate was the highest in the nation. On December 25, 1992, another murder would be added to the list.

Charles Henderson's office was located in the ten story Lawyers' Building in Cadillac Square in downtown Detroit. It was built in 1922, by John J. Barlum, and was one of the few buildings of the time that strove for modernism over ornamentation. It was constructed with reinforced concrete and steel, faced with terra cotta, featuring regular bays with wood casement windows and metal spandrel panels. It was the finest, nearly unaltered, Chicago-style high-rise in Detroit, and that was why Charles Henderson refused to flee Detroit's decaying downtown to the suburbs, as did so many of Detroit's lawyers.

Cadillac Square was not virtually deserted…it was completely deserted. The temperature was twelve degrees Fahrenheit, but the wind-chill factor brought it to below zero. Henderson had worked late and was going to be alone for the holidays. He was estranged from his children, and his wife was too busy cavorting with her latest lover in Hawaii to miss him. The potentially largest lawsuit of his career was scheduled to begin after New Year's, and he was working non-stop to ensure his presentation would be perfect. If one were to look up the definition of *workaholic* in the Webster-Merriam dictionary you would probably find a *cf. Charles Henderson*, which explained why he was estranged from his children and why his wife screwed every man who would buy her a drink. He spent more time in his residence suite at the Book-Cadillac Hotel than he did at his home in Grosse-Pointe Farms.

Henderson wasn't a tall man, and if you looked closely you could see the tell-tale signs of a hair-transplant. He was a snob and an asshole. His nails were polished and manicured weekly, his transplanted hair scissors-cut bi-weekly. The only jewelry he wore was a ring with a Taijitu in the center, surrounded with diamonds, a ring worn exclusively by members of the Centurion Counsel. You could see your reflection in his Testoni shoes. Like Dorian Gray his face never aged, thanks to the incredible hands of the world-famous Brazilian plastic surgeon Dr. Ivo Pitanguy. It was necessary for him to go to Brazil for surgery because his reputation as a plaintiff's attorney precluded the possibility that any plastic surgeon in the country would go near him with a scalpel, unless it were to cut his throat.

After his Hermie grandfather clock had chimed twice he realized he should get some sleep. It was now Christmas morning. He closed the file he was working on and smiled. DCC would pay through the ass on this one, and doctor Devin Powers would learn an expensive lesson as well. *Yes, Virginia there is a Santa Claus.* He clicked off the light of his Tiffany desk lamp, walked over to the hall tree and slipped on a cashmere coat purchased at J.L. Hudson before the flagship of Detroit's downtown business community locked its doors for the last time. When he locked the door to his office it would be for the last time as well.

In early English folklore the witch's teat was believed to be where the devil suckled when he came to bed his faithful servants. Modern usage of the phrase came to mean something of a cold or foreboding nature. Henderson had no idea when he stepped outside his office that the devil was waiting for him, but not to suckle him. He opened the door and was immediately assaulted by a freezing cold wind. "Shit, it's colder than a witch's tit," he shivered. He looked around; there was no sign that humans ever existed in this once proud city. It was as if a cancer was metastasizing, and each boarded-up and vandalized building represented the result of the insatiable appetite of the cancer, ever spreading without pause. He was more likely to find a space shuttle at this hour than a taxi, but it was a just a short walk to the Book-Cadillac along Michigan Avenue.

Preoccupied with his upcoming case he was unaware that he was being followed. When he entered Campus Martius Park, his tracker closed the distance between them, and when he reached the Michigan Soldiers and Sailors Monument he heard his name called out. He turned to see a short-handled axe seeking out his neck. The blade was swift and the scream was short. Only the stars, a new moon, and a derelict, who was repositioning himself in a makeshift cardboard lean-to behind the monument bore witness to Henderson's execution. The derelict's rheumy eyes widened as they tried to focus on what they had just seen. Henderson's body fell backward as the blood erupted from his severed carotid arteries. A new fountain had been created in the park. The executioner wiped the blade of the axe on Henderson's coat and then left the park without paying attention to the lean-to.

The derelict waited until he was sure the axe-man had left the park before he crawled out from under the cardboard. A corona of blood extended from the almost severed head, but there was surprisingly little blood on the coat. "Shee-it, this guy don't got no more use for this coat," he said. He rolled the body over and peeled off the coat. Next, he removed the Cartier watch and slipped it on his wrist. He riffled through the wallet and counted three hundred thirty-two dollars. He then slipped the wallet into a pocket of his new coat and returned to his box where he finished his bottle of Night Train to celebrate Santa's largesse. He fell asleep in a drunken slumber as visions of Night Train danced through his head.

* * *

A dead body in a park in Detroit was not an unusual sight, but a dead body with a barely attached head was not an everyday occurrence. Jay Lambrecht the co-owner of the Fountain Bistro located at the edge of the park discovered the body. He was going to spend his Christmas preparing food for those who didn't want to cook Christmas dinner. Usually, the normal response time to a 911 call in Detroit would be a qualifying time for the Boston Marathon. In this case it only took thirty-six minutes for the police to make the five-minute drive from the Central District headquarters because it was early Christmas morning…the slowest time of the year for crime. The screeching sirens awakened the derelict, Elijah Craig, as they entered the park. After a while he crawled out of his lean-to box and staggered over to the two policemen who were interviewing Lambrecht. "Wha's happening?" he mumbled. It didn't take a forensic expert to determine that the blood-decorated cashmere coat that Elijah was wearing belonged to the dead man. Craig was well known to the two policemen. They had lost count of the number of times they had removed him from the park, but like herpes he kept coming back. Every cop in the Central District knew him simply as ninety-four, because he had the same name as the premium 94-proof Elijah Craig Kentucky bourbon, and because at any given time his blood alcohol level was probably hovering close to 94-proof.

"Oh shit, ninety-four, what the fuck have you done?" said Ira Blue, the officer who had just finished taking Lambrecht's statement. His eyes followed the blood trail, like an elevator, up and down the length of the coat

"I ain't done nuthin," said ninety-four. "But I done see da guy who offed dis dude."

"Really? And did he say after he offed the guy, 'Hey boy, you look cold, why don't you take his coat? He's not going to need it anymore.' "

"Dat not be wha' happened." He wrapped his arms around himself, still cold, despite the cashmere coat that didn't warm the bare skin that was climbing out of the holes in his grimy T-shirt.

Blue heard, before he saw, the unmistakable roar of only one car.

"Don't you move from this spot, because if you do I'll sew your lips shut, and the only way you'll get your Night Train will be through the garden hose I shove up your ass."

"No sir, I ain't going nowhere."

The car screeched to a halt. Only one person drove a 1976 red and white Grand Torino, and it wasn't Starsky or Hutch, but rather homicide detective Bob Denney. He was a gruff twenty-five year veteran who had not seen it all...he had seen more than it all. When he first joined the DPD he was an idealist, but now he was a cynical realist. His idealism vanished in 1967, when he was one of the first responders to the 12th street riot, which broke out after the police raided an unlicensed blind pig bar. What started out as a confrontation became the deadliest and most destructive riot since the New York City draft riots of the Civil War. During the four days of the riots, 43 people lost their lives, 1,189 were injured, over 7,200 were arrested, and more than 2,000 buildings were destroyed. Among the dead was his best friend, Jerome Alshove, the only policeman killed during the riot. After the riot, finally quelled by federal troops, the carillon sounded and the bells tolled for the beginning of the end for the city that was once the proud showcase of American industry.

Because of Denney's size he was affectionately compared to the cartoon character Yogi Bear. He wore no hat and his peppered hair, sprinkled with salt, was combed straight back. Despite the cold, he was wearing only a Detroit Tigers jacket over a bulky cable knit sweater. Dress code protocol was not followed by Denney. He didn't give a shit. In three months his twenty-five years would be completed, and he'd be moving to Texas. Perhaps that's why he missed the pink message-slip that found its way to the bottom of the pile on his desk. It was from Detective Scalpone, in Cleveland, asking him to call if there had been any axe murders in Detroit, and by the time he found it another lawyer would have been executed in Atlanta.

Denney and Blue approached the body. Denney recognized the victim. He shook his head and smiled. "Where's his coat?"

Blue pointed to ninety-four who was shivering in the exact spot where he was told to stay. Blue repeated what ninety-four had told him. Denney walked over to ninety-four and said, "Did you do this?"

"Nossuh. Like I tole the officer here, I jes' took his coat."

Denney saw the watch on his wrist when ninety-four pointed to the body. "And what else did you take?"

Ninety-four hesitated, and then raised his wrist to show the watch. "Dis."

"That's not all, is it ninety-four?"

He removed the wallet from the coat pocket and held it out for Denney, as if it were a peace offering. "Dat's all, I swear on my momma's grave."

Denney removed two Ziploc bags from his jacket and said, "Drop them in here."

"Can I keeps da coat?"

"Yeah, for now. You're lucky I don't have a bag big enough, or I'd stuff both the coat and your sorry ass in it. Now tell me what you saw."

"Well I was tryin' to get comfur'bul cuz da wind was blowin' hard, so I moves my box behind da statue, you know, so's I kin gets away from da wind, and jest as I is getting comfur'bul I sees dis guy walkin' toward da statue so I hides so he can't see me. Den I see a nudder guy comin' up behind him..."

"How could you see them if you were hiding behind the statue?"

"Da first guy was whistlin' so I peeks out…but he can't see me. Den da second guy he yells out a name and da first guy turns around, and dat's when da second guy swings dis big axe right into the guy's neck. He looked around, but he didn't see me, and den he put da axe under his coat after he wiped it off on dis coat. He den turned around and he went back da way he comed from."

"Do you remember what name he yelled?'

Ninety-four shook his head.

"Did you see his face?"

"I didn't get a real good look, but he was a white guy and he was smilin."

"Tell me about the coat he was wearing."

He thought for a minute. "Id was long and black, jes like his hat."

"Hat?"

"Yeah, you know, da kind dat sits on you head and comes over you ears."

"A ski hat?" asked Denney?

"Wha's dat?"

"Never mind. Anything else that you can think of?"

"I knows it was long a long time after da bells stopped ringin'."

He was referring to the carillon of bells from the Woodward Avenue Presbyterian Church that rang in Christmas at midnight.

"Keep going ninety-four, you're on a roll. How tall was he?"

"Kinda tall like you, mebbe, but a lot skinnier den you."

Denney was six-feet-two and built like a fullback.

"Das all I 'member, honest."

"Well my man we're going to take you to the station, and you're going to be on stage, because you're going to repeat everything you told me in front of a microphone, and you're going to describe this guy to a police artist. And guess what? You're going to get a turkey dinner for your efforts."

"Ken you keeps me in jail for awhile in case dis guy comes lookin' fer me...you know likes in pertectiv' custody?"

Denney was astounded that this sot whose brain he was convinced floated in alcohol rather than cerebro-spinal fluid could think that fast and knew what protective custody was. "Yeah, we could do that for awhile," but he knew that axe-man was long gone, and there was about as much chance of finding him as there was of Livernois Avenue ever becoming the Champs-Élysées. Livernois Avenue was razed during the 1967 riots and was never fully rebuilt. This once proud avenue was home to all of Detroit's car dealerships that during the riots became a Dresden, the German city destroyed by allied bombing during World War II. "You stay right where you are ninety-four." Denney turned toward Blue and pointed to Lambrecht who was still talking to Blue's partner. "I assume that's the guy who found the body. What time was it?"

"Just before six. He's the co-owner of the Fountain Bistro and was on his way to the restaurant when he saw the body."

While they were talking, two other cars arrived simultaneously. One was the medical examiner, Dr. Raymond Cadieux, and the other was Denney's partner Bob Gormley, the second half of the team referred to as the *Bobsey Twins*, or *Yogi Bear and Boo-Boo*, depending on who was doing the referring.

"Well, it's about time you two got here, I thought I was going to have to solve this case by myself."

"Well if I drove the pace car for the Indy 500 like you, I'd have been here much earlier," said Gormley.

Cadieux chuckled. "While you two are trying to decide who should be the alpha-dog for the day, I'm going to do what I am grossly underpaid to do." He walked over to the body, and like Denney, recognized him as well. He gave the body a cursory look and returned to the detectives. "He's dead!"

That fact would have been obvious even to a blind man, but Michigan law stipulated that only a medical examiner could make that pronouncement.

"When the CSI team gets here you can bag him and get on with you investigation. Are you two going to devote your full and undivided attention to determine who dispatched this poor humble man to the great beyond?" he smirked."

If David Letterman had a top ten for the most reviled lawyers in Detroit Charles Henderson would have been number one, if the police brotherhood and the medical community had a vote. He made his millions by suing physicians and the police at every opportunity. Even the medical examiner's office was not immune. How could you harm a dead person? Henderson would find a way. Toe-tags misplaced on the bodies of two individuals once resulted in mixed-up burials. What was the problem? They were just as dead and just as buried. The jury didn't see it that way. Cadieux was at the top of the food chain in the ME's office, and it was he who was named as the miscreant in the lawsuit. A million dollars wasn't bad for having to shed a few more tears and for having to attend a second funeral.

"Well, every doctor and cop who has been sued by the bastard certainly had a motive," said Denney. "But unless we come up with something from pickle-brain, I expect this case will join the cold-case file faster than a fresh-frozen ham. This was a professional hit. I'm sure the killer's long gone." He was right. At that moment a 414A Cessna Chancellor had been cleared for takeoff at Detroit Metro Airport.

* * *

Ninety-four was booked into the old Wayne County Jail on the charge of taking property from a human corpse. Denney doubted that he'd be a guest of the county for very long. After all, who was going to make a complaint at his arraignment? Certainly not Charles Henderson. Besides, most of the cells at the jail had been designed for single occupancy, not double. Ninety-four wouldn't qualify for VIP status. They needed the cells at the jail for more important dignitaries, like rapists and drug-dealers. The public defender would ask that he be ROR—released on own recognizance—and Denney would testify on his behalf. Slam-dunk. No harm no foul.

Denney was sitting in the interrogation room with the police artist when ninety-four was escorted in. "So, ninety-four, did you get your turkey dinner?" asked Denney.

"Yassuh, wid cranberries an' mashed potatees."

"Good. Now that you've been well fed I want you to tell me everything you saw and heard again, only this time I'm going to record it, and then I want you to describe the man you saw to the police artist."

Denney was surprised that ninety-four's recollection was pretty much the same as what he had told him in the park, but he had no idea whether the man he described bore any resemblance to the killer. It would turn out to be a reasonably accurate description.

CHAPTER THIRTY-THREE

Tucson, Arizona
Wednesday, December 30, 1992.

THE MINK BROTHERS and Marvin Slater were seated in the conference room. "Well Marvin, what have you learned since our last *tête-à-tête?"* asked Ingram.

"Let me start with our good doctor." He flipped open his spiral notebook. "I had to call in a lot of favors, so I'll have to replenish the bank. For starters, I'll need your tickets for next year's UCLA and Duke basketball games. I promised them away for some telephone records." He was referring to the *always* sold out regular season U of A basketball game with UCLA and the exhibition game with Duke. It was almost as difficult to get tickets for these games in basketball frenzied Tucson as it was to get tickets for the Super Bowl, and scalpers could get almost as much for these tickets as they could for Super Bowl tickets. "But I assure you they're worth it."

"Both of ours?" Neal asked.

Slater nodded.

The brothers were both rabid University of Arizona basketball fans. Neal could recite every basketball statistic since Arizona joined the PAC 10 in 1978, and Ingram, the master strategist, could have made a career as a basketball coach. Such was his knowledge of the game.

"Go ahead, it better be worth it," said Neal.

"Let's start in Cleveland. Powers was there when Carol Andrews was killed. He was scheduled to speak at a banquet sponsored by the *Cleveland Plastic Surgical Society* on Saturday night February

16. He flew his plane to Akron where he rented a car and drove to Cleveland."

"I wonder why he didn't fly directly to Cleveland," said Neal.

Slater shrugged. "Weather perhaps. Cleveland had a lot of snow the day before. Akron's only a forty-five minute drive, and the weather was clear there."

"So how did he know that Carol was there?" asked Ingram

"The answer to that is what cost you two basketball tickets. On February 12, 1991, his office received a telephone call, which was charged to Andrews' bill from the Glidden House earlier that day."

"So he knew she was in Cleveland, and he was scheduled to be there the night she was killed. We know he certainly had the motive, and now we can show the opportunity. I think I should tell Ronstadt about that," said Neal. "

"Wait, there's more," said Slater. "That's what cost you the other two basketball tickets.

"It seems our doctor has been making phone calls to, and receiving them from, the head of security, a Thomas Dufour, at Sherman-Hall Medical."

"And the point of that is?" asked Ingram.

"The calls were made the day before those women received the acid threats. And here's the most interesting thing. A call was made to Dufour from a payphone at the Mirage the night LaPelle was murdered. I can't prove it was Powers who made the call, but if you find elephant shit you shouldn't be looking for tigers. Powers was attending the annual meeting of the ASPRS—*American Society of Plastic and Reconstructive Surgeons*—that weekend."

"And how did you learn about that phone call?" asked Ingram.

Slater smiled. "That's why I have to replenish the bank."

"I'll have to call Ronstadt with this information," said Neal.

"I thought you were out of the loop," said Slater.

Neal looked at Slater, and hesitated before he answered. "No, my agreement with Ronstadt was that I would provide him with any information I learned relevant to the investigation. Because of my involvement with some of the victims he has to rule me out as a suspect before he'll tell me anything that's going on with the investigation."

"So what's next?" asked Slater.

"The Grant trial. Because of her injuries, we were granted a continuance until the end of April. She's recovering nicely. For a while she was reluctant to continue, but Ronstadt assured her that it was unlikely the attempt on her life would be repeated."

"Oh?" said Slater. "What made him so sure of that?"

"Right now she's under police protection, and next month she'll be going to stay with her parents on their farm in Kentucky. They raise thoroughbreds, and have quite a security system, which they put in after someone broke in and vandalized their home. I'm going to ask you to fly her there when she's ready to go. Once the trial starts she'll be sequestered here with police protection, and once it's over there'd be no reason to go after her."

"Makes sense," said Slater.

"Anything else?" asked Ingram

They both shook their heads

"Well, since someone has to watch the office while you two gadabouts are out playing, I'll be here working on the Grant file and will be meeting with the jury consultants on Monday. So what are your plans for New Year's?"

Neal said, "I'll be driving up to Vegas for the weekend, and I'll be back late Sunday night."

"Neal, since you're driving to Vegas do you mind if I use the plane?" Slater asked. "One of my SOC—special operations capable—recon buddies asked me to spend New Year's with him in Savannah, but all flights were booked."

Slater had been a Force Recon Marine and served in the elite SOC forces, which provided essential elements of military intelligence to the command element MAGTF—Marine Air Ground Task Force—which accounted for his uncanny ability to uncover details and information that would tax the abilities of the best FBI agents.

He was also trained to fly any fixed wing aircraft. As a Recon Marine he was conditioned to be an independent thinker, and that's why he could not function as a police officer. When he left the Marines his jacket was sealed, and no one knew why he resigned his commission…but there were rumors.

"Feel free to use it," said Neal.

CHAPTER THIRTY-FOUR

Tucson, Arizona
Wednesday, December 30, 1992.

RONSTADT WAS PACING in his office when Vargas and Washington arrived. It was an idiosyncrasy of his, almost a ritual, indicating he was deep in thought trying to resolve a perplexing problem. Some people doodled…he paced. It was like the cage stereotypy that large animals caged in a zoo exhibit when they are stressed or frustrated. He was both.

"If you keep it up Gary you'll have to replace that floor along with your shoes," Washington said.

He looked up. "Oh, hi Jerry. I didn't see you come in."

"If you didn't see me then for sure you missed this pipsqueak with me."

Ronstadt made a gesture for them to sit. "I just got off the phone with Neal Mink." He sat down, swiveled his chair, and placed his feet on his desk.

"Hey boss, Jerry was right...you've got a hole in your shoe."

Ronstadt lifted his foot and looked at the sole of his shoe.

"Ha! Gotcha! What's up Gary?" Vargas asked.

"We need to have another talk with Powers. And this time it will be here. When you questioned him two weeks ago did you say anything about the LaPelle murder in Las Vegas, or Andrews in Cleveland?"

Washington thought for a moment. "No, I just asked him if he could account for his whereabouts on the evening of October 31, and the night of December 5. His lawyer dummied him up and wouldn't let him answer unless we were going to charge him. I did mention that there were a number of women who had been murdered throughout the country, but I didn't mention Las Vegas or Cleveland specifically."

"Yeah, and his pasty-assed lawyer said we didn't have any authority to ask him anything about any murders outside our jurisdiction unless we were the FBI. What a prick!" added Vargas.

"Well, it seems Powers was in both Cleveland and Vegas on the nights when Andrews and LaPelle were murdered." Ronstadt repeated what Neal Mink had told him.

"Gary, did I hear you correctly...Powers flies his own plane?" Washington said.

"Yes."

"Which means he can fly anywhere, anytime, without his name ever appearing on a passenger manifest on a commercial airline. And which means he could have been in L.A., Miami and Houston, at the times of those murders as well, without being at a convention. No airport security to worry about if he were carrying a weapon."

"Yeah, but wouldn't he still have to file a flight plan?" asked Vargas.

"Not if he were flying VFR—visual flight rules—and the only time he'd have to speak with an air traffic controller would be at take off and landing, which means there would be a tape recording of his conversations. So even if he didn't file a flight plan there'd be a time stamp of him arriving in the other three cities," said Washington.

"So now we've got both Neal Mink and Powers in Las Vegas at the same time as LaPelle was murdered. I wonder where Mink was the nights of those other murders," said Vargas. "Hey, this is getting fucking interesting."

"I can see Powers having a motive, but what would Mink's motive be?" Washington asked.

"That's why I was pacing when you two walked in. This is turning into a real conundrum. In case you didn't know, Neal Mink pilots his own plane as well. And you're right Jerry…it's conceivable that

Powers and Mink could've been in any of those cities at the time of the murders.

"What we'll need to do now is trace the movements of both of them on those dates. I'll leave that to the two of you. You'll probably have to speak to the investigators in the five cities, and have them get the records for all flight arrivals and departures around those dates to see if there's a record of either of our boys having flown into those cities. I don't know how much we'll be able to get done the rest of this year, so let's meet back here after New Year's, say on Tuesday. Same time."

Tucson, Tuesday, January 5, 1993.

Vargas was pouring coffee and Washington was reading the sports section of the Arizona Daily Star, excited that the Arizona Wildcats were ranked number fourteen in the nation in basketball with a real shot at the final four, when Ronstadt arrived. He threw his jacket on the couch in frustration. "It's been almost two years. You'd think we'd have a little more to show for our efforts."

"Well maybe we have," said Washington.

"What've you got?"

"We can place Powers in every one of the cities, or somewhere nearby, at the time of the murders."

"Go ahead."

"We already knew he was in Cleveland and Vegas at the time Andrews and LaPelle were murdered. He had filed flight plans for both. He flew IFR—instrument flight rules—to Cleveland and VFR to Vegas. Here's the rest." He opened a spiral notebook and began reading. "On December 9, 1991, he filed an IFR flight plan to Houston. Elaine Peters was murdered on the 10th.

"It turns out this arrogant asshole is a real Dr. Jekyll and Mr. Hyde. Twice a year he spends two weeks operating on kids with deformities, like harelips, in third world countries. That's why he was in Guatemala. He does the *Doctors without Borders* thing, the rest of the year he spends being a prick."

"Which gives him a plausible reason for being in Houston," said Ronstadt. "When Elena and I went to Guatemala, several years ago, we made our connection to Guatemala City in Houston. So that leaves L.A. and Miami. What did you find out about them?"

Vargas answered, "On December 21, 1991, he spent the night in Miami. I spoke with Lasky, and he found out there were two others with him on the flight, Dr. Fred Landers and his wife Julia, who were the anesthesiologist and nurse team that work with Powers when he does his charity shtick. I spoke with Landers, and he said Powers flew them to Miami because they were spending Christmas there with their family. Powers left Miami on the 22nd, flew to Houston to refuel, and then back to Tucson. Lasky said Brandy Evans was murdered early on the 22nd."

"What about L.A.?" Ronstadt asked.

"There was a meeting of the *California Society of Plastic Surgeons* the week of June 15, 1991, and Powers was at the meeting. Faith Greene's body was found on the 17th."

"Bring the fucker in," Ronstadt said.

"Do you want us to call his lawyer first?" asked Washington.

"No, let the bastard stew for awhile. Powers can call his lawyer when he gets to the station."

"There's one other thing," said Washington. Did you know Powers has a Cessna 414A registered to his corporation?...and so does the law firm of Mink and Mink."

CHAPTER THIRTY-FIVE

Tucson, Arizona
Wednesday, January 6, 1993.

DAVID GLOVER STORMED into the interrogation room. "Just what do you think you are doing? Do you have any idea how disruptive this uncalled-for arrest will be to Dr. Powers' practice?"

"We didn't exactly arrest him counselor. We just brought him in for questioning," said Washington.

"Why wasn't I called first?"

Washington slapped his forehead. "Gee, it must have slipped our minds. Besides, we told you the next time we interviewed your client it would be in our humble surroundings. You're here, so consider yourself called. And now that you're here we can get the party started. Dr. Powers' patients will have to live with their tiny titties for just a little bit longer," said Washington.

Ronstadt watched from behind the one-way glass and could see Powers relax from his initial state of rage to an air of smug self-assurance. Ronstadt entered the interrogation room and sat down, focusing on the lawyer.

"Mr. Glover, we can do this the easy way, or make it very uncomfortable for your client. As you know, five of your client's patients have been murdered and an attempt was made on the life of a sixth. They all had filed lawsuits against him, and he was physically present in those cities at the time of the murders and the attempted murder," said Ronstadt. "So you tell me, as an experienced trial lawyer, don't you think that's just a little bit odd?"

"Pure coincidence," said Glover.

"No, coincidence is when you meet the first girl you fucked, at a dinner party, on the arm of your best friend in Chicago." Ronstadt rarely used vulgarities, but as a trained psychologist he knew by doing so he might ruffle the feathers of these two prissy assholes. "Again, as you well know, there are three things we look for in any murder investigation. One, motive; two, opportunity; and three, means." He turned to Powers and said, "Doctor Powers, you certainly had the motive and opportunity to kill these women, and I'm sure the means as well."

Powers sneered. "And I'm sure as *you* well know, there are three things you must have to convict a person. One: a witness to the killing. Two: evidence to link a person to the crime. And three: a murder weapon. Other than the fact I was present in these cities at the time these events occurred, I suspect you don't have a shred of evidence to suggest that I was the perpetrator, because if you had, I'd be under arrest."

"*Events*? Is that what you fucking call them?" Vargas screamed. "Those *events* were the calculated, barbarous, butchering of five young women who did nothing wrong except getting involved with you."

Glover flinched, but Powers showed no reaction to Vargas's outburst. Ronstadt gave a barely perceptible nod to Washington. The three detectives had previously rehearsed this whole act.

"Well then Dr. Powers, if what you say is true, help us by telling us where you were at 7:30 p.m. October 31, and the night of December 5, of last year—the same questions Mr. Glover wouldn't allow you to answer when we interviewed you in your office on December 15," Washington said. "And this time," he glared at Glover, "I expect an answer."

Without pausing to think, Powers said, "At 7:30 p.m. October 31, I was in my office reviewing the chart of a patient for an upcoming deposition the following Monday, and on December 5, I was in my office reviewing a number of charts of children I would be operating upon during the subsequent two weeks in Guatemala. And no, I can't prove I was in my office anymore than you can prove I wasn't there. Besides, what is so important about my whereabouts on those dates?"

"October 31, is the date an attempt was made on the life of your patient, Adele Grant, and December 5, was the date when Lawrence Band, a lawyer from Houston, who represented your patient Elaine Peters, was murdered at the Westward Look."

Glover placed his hand on Powers' arm, as if to say, "Stop adding to your answers."

Ronstadt made eye contact with Powers and resumed his questioning. "Do you know someone named Thomas Dufour?"

Powers couldn't control the reflex dilation of his pupils that occurs when a person is caught by surprise. Ronstadt saw it and knew that Powers had just swallowed the hook. Other than that, Powers showed no reaction to the question, but he realized Ronstadt knew something.

"Yes, I believe I do."

"Just believe you do? Or in fact do you know him quite well? Perhaps you can tell us what it was you talked about the night you called him from a payphone in the lobby of the Mirage Hotel on the night of April 17, 1992."

How the hell did he know that? Powers thought. *How do I answer that*? He looked at Glover, who nodded. He was just as interested as the detectives. Apparently, Powers had not told him everything. "As I'm sure you're aware, Mr. Dufour works for Sherman-Hall Medical, and sometimes I use their breast implants in my surgery. We had some issues to discuss about the implants."

Bingo! He just admitted he made the call. "You discuss issues about breast implants with the head of security? Why would you do that? I should think if you had questions about the implants, you would be discussing them with quality control, or product development, not security," said Ronstadt.

"Detective Ronstadt, I don't see what relevance that conversation has to these murders, and I am instructing my client not to answer anything further about that conversation."

"Oh really? Was it just another coincidence that Desiree LaPelle was murdered less than twelve hours after that call was made? And was it just another coincidence that nine women dropped their lawsuits against Sherman-Hall and Dr. Powers after being threatened with disfigurement to their faces shortly after Dr. Powers had placed a phone call to Mr. Dufour on December 10, 1991?"

Glover looked at Powers whose face was as inscrutable as the Mona Lisa. He turned to Ronstadt. "Are you charging my client?"

"Not yet, but if and when we do, you'll be the first to know… excuse me, the second to know…the grand jury will be the first to know."

"Then I think we are finished here. Devin…a word with you."

* * *

"So?" asked Washington.

"It's all too neat," said Ronstadt.

"Shit, what more do we need?" said Vargas. "The guy's guilty."

"Maybe. But why would a guy who's as bright as Powers leave such an obvious trail? He's arrogant and obnoxious, but he's not stupid. Jerry what do you think?"

"Gary, none of us believe in coincidences when dealing with a murder, but something's bothering me. The reasons for him being in those cities are unassailable. And I'm sure we'll find that it wasn't a last minute decision for him to be in those places…Vegas for example. He presented the results of a clinical study there, and I know when my father presents a paper at a scientific meeting it takes years of preparation. First, you have to compile your statistics and then submit your study for review by a panel of experts. After that, the process can take more than a year before your work is accepted for presentation. So his being in Las Vegas was anything but a last minute decision. He made no attempt to conceal his activities, evidenced by filing flight plans for every city he visited, but then again as you said before, maybe that's the way it was set up to be. It's definitely a conundrum."

"So, are you saying that it's possible somebody is trying to set him up? But why? What about those calls he made to that guy in Michigan? They sure as hell weren't planned years in advance," said Vargas.

"I agree that doesn't fit. It would be nice if we had a source in Michigan to check out Dufour," said Ronstadt.

That source would soon make his presence known.

"Gary, we're getting all this information from Neal Mink. We never would've known about those phone calls between Powers and Dufour if it weren't for him. I wonder what else he knows that we don't," said Washington.

"You're right. Mink is very much involved, perhaps too much. I think it's time I had another chat with him."

CHAPTER THIRTY-SIX

Tucson, Arizona
Friday, January 8, 1993.

THE NORWEST BANK Tower was the tallest building in Tucson, stretching twenty-three stories into the sky, topping off at 330 feet. The original plans called for two sister towers, but lack of interest in office space in downtown Tucson squelched the plan. The law firm of David Glover and the six names that followed his occupied the entire top two floors. And when you entered Glover's personal office there was no doubt who the senior partner was.

Powers wasn't accustomed to be sitting on the other side of a desk, and he wasn't accustomed to be kept waiting. And he definitely wasn't accustomed to be playing the role of a supplicant. Today two men whose egos were higher than Mount Everest would be colliding. Glover purposely kept Powers waiting to let him know who was alpha in this office.

Glover entered the office and made no apologies for being late. He went directly to his desk, made from Mozambique Blackwood, arguably the most expensive wood in the world.

"Devin I'll get right to the point." He opened Powers' file and uncapped a Crew 60th white gold Tibaldi fountain pen that retailed for $43,000. "There are two issues we have to address. The first issue is your mouth. Do I have to send you to training school to learn when to speak and when to remain silent? Every time you offer gratuitous information to the police you are potentially offering them information they may not've been aware of. The last thing you need to do is help them build their case. You may be a brilliant surgeon, but you don't have the slightest clue how police interrogation 101 works. That's why you have me. Secondly, I find it intolerable to learn information about a client from the police that that client has not divulged to me. And you know exactly what I mean. Why didn't you tell me about your conversations with Dufour?" His tone was that of a headmaster disciplining an errant student as he prepared to whip him with his cane.

Powers remembered the last time someone spoke to him in that tone of voice. Only it was his father, not a headmaster, and it wasn't a cane that he slapped from one hand to the other…it was a Polish shepherd's axe…

Dariuscz Palowski was born in 1950, to Ania and Januscz Palowski. Thirty-year-old Januscz had fled Poland in 1936, just before the policja were about to question him in connection with the murders of Josek and Chaja Minkowski. He arrived at Ellis Island on the RMS Aquitania eight months before the arrival of the two sons of the man and woman he had murdered in Poland. He found his way to Pittsburgh and settled in Polish Hill, a small neighborhood within the heart of Pittsburgh. Januscz married Ania, late in life, when he was forty-two. After thirteen years of beatings and abuse, Ania just vanished, leaving Dariuscz to be raised by Januscz. The beatings and abuse were then directed at Dariuscz. On his eighteenth birthday he was packing his meager belongings, as he prepared to leave for Tucson, when his father staggered into his room wielding the shepherd's axe.

"Too good to work in the steel mills; too good to get your hands dirty eh?" He slapped the handle of the axe in his hand. "I think it's time for another lesson." He raised the axe, prepared to strike Dariuscz with the handle, as he had so many times in the past, when Dariuscz grabbed the handle and twisted it out of his father's hands. Januscz fell on his back, and Dariuscz stood over him with the blade pressing on his neck.

"You will never *beat anyone with this axe again." With the slightest pressure he drew the blade across his father's neck until a trickle of blood oozed out from under the blade.*

"Please...please don't kill me."

Dariuscz raised the axe as his father's eyes widened, and his bladder and bowels emptied. He brought the axe down and buried it in the floor just beside his father's head.

"Kill you? Why would I do that? It will be much more satisfying to know that your body will rot away one cell at a time, to know that you'll have no money to buy toilet paper, and will have to wipe your pathetic ass with newspaper, or your fingers, after you shit your pants." He removed the axe, picked up his duffle bag, and left his father blubbering on the floor.

"...First of all, I did not tell Dufour to kill or threaten anyone, if that's what you're thinking. And secondly..." he stared at Glover with the intensity of a cobra about to strike. "You *will—never* talk to me in that condescending tone again. You work for me, and don't you ever forget that."

"No Devin, I do not *work* for you...I represent you, but only if I choose to do so. You should understand if Ronstadt charges you with murder, and there's a very good chance that he will, then you will need me because you'll need a good lawyer. No innocent person that I have represented has *ever* been sent to prison, but a number of guilty persons have gone free. I have *absolutely* no need for you, and don't you *ever* forget that. And I will talk to you in any way I choose, because in this office I am the Captain of the ship. That may be your role in your operating room, but this is my operating room."

Powers was ready to explode, but took a deep breath instead and said, "Do you really think that I'm involved with those murders?"

"What I think is unimportant. In thirty-five years I've never had a client who admitted to being guilty. My only concern is to see that a client gets the best representation possible, and that's why they say, 'I get the big bucks.' And you should know that if you *are* charged, the trial could cost well over a million dollars to defend, and there's a very good chance that you could be remanded without bail because you pilot your own aircraft and could be considered a flight risk. Which brings me to the second issue. My fees. I would require a $250,000 retainer with incremental draws of $100,000 as needed. You'd be required to put $1,000,000 into an escrow account. I know you are just about at the limit of your professional liability insurance, and the next step will be to attach your personal assets if your insurance is depleted. Can you raise the money?"

"If it comes to that, it won't be a problem…do you give discounts for cash or bearer bonds?" he smirked.

Glover stood, indicating the meeting was over. As Powers was leaving he turned and said, "I noticed your Tibaldi fountain pen…I give them away as Christmas presents."

CHAPTER THIRTY-SEVEN

Atlanta, Georgia
Saturday, March 6, 1993.

SCARLETT O'HARA WAS not the first to watch Atlanta burn as Sherman's hordes reduced it to ashes. Only it wasn't known as Atlanta the first time. In 1821, Standing Peachtree was a Creek Indian village located where Peachtree Creek flowed into the Chattahoochee River, and it was Lieutenant Andrew Horton who led the charge that forced the Creek Indians from their ancestral homeland as part of the systematic removal of Native Americans from Northern Georgia between 1802 and 1825. And it was to Lieutenant Andrew Horton that Andrew Horton IV traced his ancestry. Andrews II and III were prominent attorneys, who played important roles in the naissance of present-day Atlanta, and who became rich—very rich, during the process. The fourth Andrew continued the tradition by becoming an even richer attorney. Andrews II and III became rich by acquiring land and properties. Andrew IV did so by acquiring clients who had been injured, or who claimed to have been injured, by doctors, defective products, and a variety of other causes. His client list included a woman for whom he recently obtained a judgment of $10 million from a manufacturer of silicone breast implants. And there were more clients, so many more, who were skipping down the yellow brick road; only he saw it as the yellow gold road.

Andrew IV was all that a genteel Southerner was supposed to be, and he had the credentials to prove it. Southerners didn't trace their ancestry to the Mayflower. Where they came from originally didn't matter. All that mattered was that their ancestors were there when the South was born. That's why the first Andrew could be forgiven for being a butcher. A butcher who gleefully massacred Indian mothers and fathers along with their babies and babies yet to be born in the wombs of their mothers, all because they chose to defend their sacred lands rather than accept forced relocation. As a lawyer, Andrew IV had the proper credentials as well. He was an active member of The Lawyers Club of Atlanta and the Commerce Club. And of course his offices swallowed the entire fiftieth floor of 191 Peachtree Tower. The other credential that set him apart from all other Atlanta lawyers was the ring he wore with the symbol of the Taijitu identifying him as a member of The Centurion Counsel. He was a blueblood among bluebloods, except that his blood was not blue, as he would soon discover.

His mansion on West Paces Ferry Rd. was a stunning European masterpiece embraced and surrounded by a variety of Sourwood, Clustering Hawthorn, Fringe, and Devil's Walking Stick trees. And before the night was over he would be embraced by a different kind of Devil's walking stick.

The wrought iron gates responded to the signal from Horton's Jaguar and yawned open as the car approached, which allowed his uninvited visitor enough time to slide in without being seen. A light snow was falling, so Horton chose to park in the garage. His wife was attending her bi-monthly meeting of the Daughters of the American Revolution, so he wouldn't be greeted by her incessant yammering about how hard it was to find decent help, or whatever her charitable cause of the month was about. Thank God for Alicia—her magic tongue and bedroom gymnastics made life tolerable with the fat cow. His three daughters, clones of the cow, were making the lives of their husbands just as miserable as his. Finally, a night alone. The snow began to fall with increasing intensity so he didn't see nor hear the form approach from behind the massive Devil tree. When he took out his keys to open the front door he heard his name called out. He spun around, and before he could react the axe blade was buried deep in his neck. His last act on this earth was to create a giant snow cone flavored with his blood.

* * *

The snow had settled into a steady rhythm by the time Virginia Horton arrived home. As the gates creaked open she was surprised to see that the house was dark. Andrew was supposed to be home. Surely he had not yet retired, he always worked long after she had gone to bed. As her car neared the front she saw a snow covered mound blocking her way to the garage. She got out of her car to see what it was. She bent down. Her screams were louder and longer than Miss Melanie's as she gave birth at Aunt Pitty Pat's during the siege of Atlanta in *Gone with the Wind.*

* * *

The woman had to be sedated...and fast. Homicide detective Bill Shea would not get any useful information from this incoherent mess. The paramedics were trying to calm her down—without success. Shea waited until the medical examiner flagged him over.

"Whatcha got?" asked Shea.

"An almost cut off head," said Dr. Cornelius Cobb, the medical examiner, whose parents must have hated him from the moment he was born. Why else would they curse him with a name that would haunt him throughout his life? They didn't even grace him with a middle name that he could use instead. No, he would always be known as *Corncob*.

"Come closer. Take a look."

The snow had been cleared to reveal the body. The crime scene was useless, as far as retrieving any helpful information was concerned. A heavy snowfall like this did have that effect.

"I'll know more when I do the autopsy, but it looks like it could've been done with an axe."

Shea remembered the phone call he had received from that detective in Tucson a couple of months earlier. He'd call him on Monday.

CHAPTER THIRTY-EIGHT

Tucson, Arizona
Monday, March 8, 1993.

RONSTADT WAS CARESSING the frame displaying his life's greatest treasures—his wife Elena, holding Jennifer, and the twins, Elisa and Sara, who were holding their golden retriever puppies, Sassy and Rosie—when the intercom flashed.

"I have a detective Bill Shea, from Atlanta, on line two. It's about a memo he received a couple of months ago," said the administrative assistant.

"This is Gary Ronstadt...I see…" He absorbed what Shea said, and when he learned the victim was a lawyer he asked whether he was wearing a ring that had a symbol resembling the flag of South Korea. He described the symbol. Shea confirmed that he was.

"Bill, if you don't mind I'd like to come to Atlanta. What's happening is very involved, and I'd much rather explain it to you face to face." He thumbed through his appointment book. "I can be there on Friday. In the meantime could you fax me what you have? And one other thing...could you find out whether a Cessna 414A Chancellor filed a flight plan from Hartsfield to Tucson Saturday or Sunday?"

* * *

Hans and Fritz could have been stand-ins for funeral directors, if their funereal faces were any indication, as they sat down in Powers' office. They had come to bury Powers.

"What do you mean I have no more liability insurance?" he raged.

Horscht avoided eye contact with Powers and shuffled the papers he held. "Mr. Becker will explain."

Powers did not intimidate Becker. "The terms of your policy are quite clear. You have a $500,000/$5,000,000 policy, which means..."

"I know what it means, are you telling me that the entire five million is gone?"

"I'm afraid so. We were able to settle the one judgment against you for the $500,000 maximum, but the other settlements depleted the remainder. You still have a number of outstanding cases for which there will be no insurance, and of course there may be additional cases in the future."

"And," added Horscht, "you will be personally responsible for all additional legal expenses incurred with the cases that haven't been resolved."

"Let me understand this. Are you saying you will no longer represent me because I have run out of insurance?"

"No, we're not saying that. You must remember that it was your insurance carrier that retained us to represent you, and you agreed to our representation. Since they will no longer carry the burden of payment, it becomes your responsibility for all future expenses. We'll be more than willing to reach an accommodation with you."

Powers stood. "I'll get back to you."

The two lawyers needed no encouragement to leave. They collected their papers and left.

Powers wasn't concerned about the money. Any future judgments against him would be meaningless. His offshore accounts were untraceable, and his IRA was protected. The corporate assets were the spa and its contents. If those were attached he couldn't practice, and if he couldn't practice then there would be no cash flow to satisfy any judgments, but if he were to sell the spa, before any more judgments came down, then those vultures would not see a penny. Aragon would buy it in an instant. But Powers' reputation would be destroyed and his hospital privileges would be revoked if he were without liability insurance. The negative publicity would be intolerable. Everything he had worked for would vanish like a sand castle at high tide, as the waves lapped at its foundation. All because of those ungrateful bitches and their greedy lawyers. He smiled. What he was going to do next would shock them all.

* * *

Ingram was studying a chessboard when Neal entered his office. He sat down and watched, saying nothing. Finally Ingram looked up and smiled. He gestured toward the chessboard. "What do you see?"

Neal knew almost as much about chess as did his brother, and had the potential to be a grand master as well, but the game really held no great interest for him. He was an analyst, not a strategist. He focused on the position of the pieces. "You're white?"

"Of course," his brother replied.

"You've opened with the Stonewall attack and are setting up the Dutch defense with black," he grinned. "Just like our implant cases." The Stonewall was one of the most aggressive of all chess opening gambits, and the Dutch defense was frequently employed to counter it. "So, what's your next move going to be?" Neal asked.

"We're going to attack the parent company…Dow-Chemical."

Neal raised his eyebrows.

"The mass tort is in place. Despite the agreement, John O'Quinn, in Texas, is getting opt-out settlements of $1 million, just on the cases he has scheduled for trial. It's only a matter of time before DCC is forced to file for bankruptcy. When that happens we draw in Dow-Chemical."

"It'll never fly," said Neal."

"We'll see. In the meantime, what's happening with your friend

Ronstadt? Has he made any progress with his investigations?"

"I think he's desperate. He cut me out of the loop because he thinks I may be involved. His prime suspect is still Powers, but he's suspicious of me because I screwed Carol Andrews, was in Vegas when LaPelle was murdered, and was the one who discovered Band's body. He sees too many coincidences.

"There's something else. I just received a phone call from Andrew Horton's office in Atlanta...he was murdered over the weekend."

"Unfortunate, but what's that got to do with you?"

"I was in Atlanta when he was murdered."

* * *

Vargas and Washington were at their desks when Ronstadt entered the central office. He told them about the call he had just received from Shea. "Meet me in my office…I've got to take care of something first."

He asked his administrative assistant to make a reservation to Atlanta for Friday. As he was giving her the details her phone rang. "Go ahead and answer it," he said.

"Homicide, this is Pat, how may I direct your call?...one moment please." She pressed the hold button and raised her eyes to Ronstadt." It's for you...another long distance call...Detroit.

"I'll take it in my office."

Washington and Vargas had already positioned themselves in their usual seats when Ronstadt returned to his office. He pointed to the phone and said, "Let me take this call.

"This is Sergeant Ronstadt."

"Hi, my name is Bob Denney, soon to be a retired homicide detective. I was cleaning out my desk, today is my last day on the job, when I came across this memo that you had sent a couple of months ago about an axe murder. Somehow it got sandwiched in a pile of papers, and I never noticed it until today. We had a murder on Christmas Day that fits your description."

Denney's name was familiar to Ronstadt, but he couldn't place it. "Detective Denney, I'm going to put you on speakerphone, hold on for a second, I want my detectives to hear what you have to say."

Denney explained the details of his investigation, and when he told them there was an eyewitness and that they had a composite Ronstadt's pulse accelerated, Washington leaned forward and Vargas's eyes widened.

Ronstadt told Denney about the other murders and why he was point in the investigation.

"Holy shit," blurted Denney after Ronstadt told him about the killings. "Another fucking serial killer. I thought I was finished with that crap. Are you familiar with the Woodward Corridor Killer case?"

Between December 1991, and August 1992, Benjamin Tony Atkins murdered eleven women in Detroit. Atkins was the most prolific serial killer in U.S. history, in terms of numbers within such a short time span. Ronstadt had a keen interest in the study of serial killers and was familiar with the case. He remembered where he had seen the name Robert Denney before.

"Aren't you the detective who solved those murders?"

"I didn't solve them, I just got the guy to confess. This is really fucking weird. I was just getting ready to go on vacation when they brought the guy in. They had a wit who ID'd him but he kept denying it was him. The Feds who were interrogating him at the station knew jack-shit about how to conduct a murder interrogation, so I asked if I could take a crack at him. All it took was a few cheeseburgers, a giant coke, and a few sympathetic nods about how he must have been fucked over as a kid, and he opened up like a breached dam.

"Now this. Another serial killer, and me getting ready to leave in an hour, just like back then, only this time it's for good. Talk about coincidences.

"Are you getting any cooperation from the Feds?" Denney asked.

"We've managed to keep them out of the investigation so far, but if we don't come up with something fairly soon we may have to get them involved."

"If you're smart you'll keep them out. They're always trying to build brownie points and don't give a shit about cooperating. It's always about what's good for them.

"Hey, I just had a thought. Since you're working as liaison between all the other departments, how would you feel if I joined your team? Since I'm retiring, I'll have a lot of thumb-twiddling time on my hands, and I might be of some help. I won't be able to do anything in an official capacity, but that might make it easier since I won't have to go through channels."

Ronstadt thought about his offer and said, "How would you like to go interview a guy in Hemlock Michigan?" He explained the connection between Powers and Dufour and the women who had been threatened.

"When do you want me to go?" he asked without hesitation.

"I have to go to Atlanta at the end of the week, so I'll get back to you when I return. In the meantime, could you fax me a copy of that composite?"

"Consider it done."

Ronstadt ended the call. "So what do you think?"

"Two calls on the same day? Too much of a coincidence," said Vargas. "Two more lawyers? What the fuck is going on here?"

"I agree, it's weird," said Washington, "but look at it as manna from heaven. We've been trying to figure out how to get someone from Michigan involved, and this guy Denney appears to be the answer."

"I'm starting to feel some good vibes for the first time since this investigation started," said Vargas.

* * *

Denney stopped and turned around for one more look at the squad room. Was it worth it? Had he made a difference? He had witnessed the highs and the lows in his twenty-five years. Unfortunately, the highs topped the charts in crime rates, homicides, poverty, teen-pregnancies, unemployment, and the lows were in literacy, high school graduates, home values, morale, and honesty among public officials. The lists went on. At the rate the tax base was falling he wasn't sure whether his pension was secure. Detroit was on a downward roller coaster ride to hell. Two broken marriages, a teen-age daughter who was gang raped by seven fifteen and sixteen-year olds. They ended up spending just a couple of years in juvenile detention, while his daughter was doomed to spend the rest of her life in a prison without bars. Her eyes were vacant and her vocal cords no longer produced sound. And then there was his son. A sixteen-year old whose last resting place was a gurney in the morgue. His arms covered with so many track marks they resembled the puncture wounds that a den of rattlesnakes would have left after using his arms as a buffet line.

The balance sheet was definitely in the red. But what the fuck, he was only forty-eight years old, and maybe he could start over after a year or two of fishing in Texas.

He turned off the light and took the artist's sketch to the office clerk and asked her to fax it to Ronstadt. She placed it on her desk next to another sketch, checked the clock, and decided to do it after lunch. When she returned from lunch she was swamped with other requests and didn't remember to fax the drawing to Ronstadt until she was ready to leave for the day. She wasn't exactly a hundred watt light bulb, so it wasn't difficult to understand why she faxed the wrong drawing to Ronstadt's office.

CHAPTER THIRTY-NINE

Tucson, Arizona
Thursday, March 11, 1993.

RONSTADT WAS THE sole male in a household of six females—Elena, his three daughters and two golden retrievers—seven, if you counted their housekeeper Anna. He was severely outnumbered. He prayed he would never have to contend with four women experiencing PMS at the same time. Anna was past the age. He wondered if dogs ever had PMS. It didn't matter, they had been spayed. Elena was the most beautiful, sensitive, logical person he had ever known, but when those red blood corpuscles started their monthly pilgrimage south, it was best to avoid her. She was still beautiful, but became hypersensitive and totally illogical.

Because of her uncanny ability to think outside the box she could see solutions to complex problems with just a snippet of information. If you asked her, she would say she was never in the box. Ronstadt, on the other hand, was a linear thinker. Last week was not a good time to ask Elena her opinion. When she screamed and swore in Spanish it was not a good time. When she sang and purred passion in Spanish, it was a good time. She was humming *por un amor*, her favorite love song, when he entered the kitchen. She smiled and wrapped her arms around him, purring passion in his ear. "*Te amo vaquero,* I love you cowboy." It was a good time.

She opened the refrigerator and handed him a long neck Dos Equis. "Talk time?"

He nodded.

"The twins are at tennis, and Jennifer is taking a riding lesson. I asked Anna to prepare a late dinner."

They locked hands and strolled toward the gazebo. The sun was just starting its descent behind the Tucson Mountains. "Stop," she said. "Look through the branches of the mesquite tree."

He positioned himself so he could see what she saw. The bare branches of the tree were arranged in a lace-like pattern, and through them he could see a blanket of clouds shimmering with varying hues and intensities of yellows and pinks, changing constantly through the lens of the swaying branches. "They're never the same are they?"

"Just like snowflakes, each more beautiful than the one before.

"You've been pacing a lot more than usual. No progress?" she said.

"Hopefully we may have something." He told her about his conversations with Shea and Denney. "It's been over two years, and so far we're no further ahead than we were two years ago. First it was the women who initiated the lawsuits, now it's the lawyers who represented them. The murders are obviously connected to the lawsuits, as are the threats that were made to disfigure the other women. It makes no sense. There are thousands of women and hundreds of lawyers that are involved in these suits. The only common thread is that the murdered women and the one attempted murder were all patients of Devin Powers. And the three lawyers who represented them were members of the Centurion Counsel."

"Three? I knew about the Houston lawyer who was murdered at the Westward Look, but who are the other two?"

"I was getting to that." He explained what had happened in Detroit and Atlanta and why he was he was going to Atlanta. "Powers certainly had the motive. I don't know about Atlanta and Detroit yet, but we can place him in every one of the other cities at the time of the murders. However, there's not an iota of evidence that can implicate him, and he has a solid explanation for being in those cities at the times of the murders.

"The only other person that we've been looking at is Neal Mink. He was involved sexually with the women who were murdered in

Cleveland and Las Vegas, and he discovered the body of the lawyer murdered here in Tucson. There are just too many coincidences with him. In fact there are just too many coincidences in the entire goddamned case."

"Crimes of passion with Mink?"

"We looked at that, but we can't tie him to the other women, and what reason would he have to kill the lawyers?"

"Misdirection? But then again maybe the killer is neither of them, and he's purposely directing you toward those two."

He contemplated what she had just said. "That's a possibility, but it would take a tactical genius to set up something like that."

"So go find a tactical genius with a motive. And why did he stop killing women and start killing lawyers? Not your run-of-the-mill serial killer, is he? You've got five women murdered, and an attempt on a sixth, and now three lawyers. Does that mean he's going to kill three more lawyers from the Counsel to make it an even dozen?"

"I thought that he might be starting to target lawyers after Band was killed. It's obvious now that he's targeting lawyers who are members of the Centurion Counsel. Band was the first, and both the lawyers from Detroit and Atlanta were members as well. So yes, I believe we can expect the next ones on his list will come from the remaining ninety-seven. They were put on high alert after Band was killed, but it doesn't seem to have stopped the murders. Why those three lawyers? And, why those six women? If it was Powers, why did he pick them? He had dozens to pick from." He opened the file that he had brought to the gazebo, and handed her the list of the women that had sued Powers, underlining the six who had been murdered, and the list of lawyers who had also been murdered.

Elena scanned the lists. "That's odd," she said.

"What's odd?" he asked.

"Give me a pen and a piece of paper and I'll show you." He handed her his pen and a blank paper from the file. She wrote the names on the paper and gave it back to him. "What do you see?"

"You've lost me. I see the names of the six women and the lawyers, but that's all." He returned her the list.

She read the names from the list. "Carol Andrews, Elaine Peters, Faith Greene, Brandy Evans, Desiree LaPelle, and Adele Grant. Don't you see it?" She held out the list. "Look at their first names."

He saw what she meant. Adele, Brandy, Carol, Desiree, Elaine, Faith. "Their first names are in order of letters of the alphabet."

"Now look at the lawyers," she said.

He looked at the list of lawyers who had been murdered. Lawrence Band, Houston; Charles Henderson, Detroit; Andrew Horton, Atlanta. "I see the ABC connection—Andrew, Band, and Charles—but they're not all first names, Band is the last name."

Elena had correctly identified the intent of the first half of the puzzle, but didn't understand what it meant. She didn't see the connection to the cities where the lawyers lived in the second half. It would take someone else to make that connection and solve the puzzle, but that wouldn't happen until another lawyer had been murdered.

CHAPTER FORTY

Atlanta, Georgia
Friday, March 12, 1993.

ATLANTA'S HARTSFIELD INTERNATIONAL airport has an interesting history. It had its birth in 1925, when Mayor Walter A. Sims signed a five-year lease on a tract of land that was an abandoned auto racetrack. It was named Candler Field for Coca Cola magnate Asa Candler. In 1929, it became Atlanta Municipal Airport after the city purchased the land from the Candler family for the sum of $94,400. In 1971, it was renamed William B. Hartsfield Atlanta Airport after the death of Mayor Hartsfield. Shortly after that it became William B. Hartsfield Atlanta International Airport when Eastern Airlines introduced flights to Mexico and Montego Bay, the airport's first international service. It would eventually become the world's busiest airport.

Ronstadt was jolted from his sleep by the sound of the engaging of the landing gear. He looked out the window and saw construction activity taking place on the new 1.3 million square foot international concourse E, which would become the largest in the nation. The plane touched down with a skip and a thump, and after a wait that seemed forever the engines revved up, and snail like, the pilot taxied the plane to the terminal. At the same time a Cessna 414A Chancellor was landing at Boston Logan International Airport.

With the description Shea gave him it was easy to pick out the stocky, closely cropped blond haired detective, with professorial horn-rimmed glasses. Ronstadt just had a carry-on so they proceeded directly to Shea's waiting Crown Victoria, parked directly in the no-parking zone, much to the chagrin of the airport security-cop, who was stopped from having the car towed by the *Official Police Business* sign on the dash.

"How was your flight?

"Bumpy as hell. It got very rough as we approached Atlanta."

"Well you're lucky you got here when you did. The weather report calls for heavy winds and blizzard like conditions for the next few days. We usually get a few inches of snow every year, but they're predicting a snow storm."

Calling it a snowstorm was an understatement. It would be known as the storm of the century, the '93 Superstorm, or the Great Blizzard of 1993. Airports would be closed all along the Eastern seaboard and flights cancelled, or if already underway—diverted, stranding many passengers. Every airport from Halifax, Nova Scotia, to Atlanta, Georgia, would be closed for a several days because of the storm. Highway travel would be closed or restricted all across the affected region, even in states generally well prepared for snow events. This storm complex would be massive, affecting at least 26 U.S. states and much of eastern Canada, bringing cold air along with heavy precipitation and hurricane force winds. Blizzard conditions would occur over much of the area it affected, including thunder-snow from Texas to Pennsylvania and widespread whiteout conditions.

"Did you eat anything on the plane?" asked Shea. "We can stop for something on the way to the station if you like, we've got enough time before the meeting starts."

"Thanks, but I'd rather get started on this. There's a lot of ground to cover, and I'm flying back tomorrow afternoon."

He wouldn't be flying anywhere for the next three days.

"Well, then tonight I'll take you to a place for dinner that'll tickle your taste buds if you like Southern cooking. Mary Mac's has the best that Atlanta has to offer.

"I want you to know that your offer to come here has taken a hell of a lot of heat off the department. Andrew Horton the Fourth was one of Atlanta's most prominent citizens. His ancestor, the first Andrew, was one of the city's founders. The mayor has been climbing up our asses on a spiked ladder, demanding results *yesterday*. He and Andrew were best friends, and of course the press has been relentless with its coverage—stop the press banner headlines, and Ted Turner himself non-stop on CNN. Shit, you'd think the president had been assassinated. It's only been six days, and they want to know why the killer hasn't been caught, convicted, and crucified."

"I don't think you're going to find any answers in Atlanta," said Ronstadt. "Am I correct in assuming that the crime scene was clean?"

"Just one dead lawyer with his head hanging. The snow obliterated anything useful. The ME thinks that it was a guy who batted left-handed because of the angle of penetration. He also thinks the perp was a male, based on the depth the axe penetrated from just one blow, and the strength that it would take to deliver such a blow.

"We're here," said Shea. "Normally, we'd be having this meeting in the zone division where the murder occurred, but when the victim is Andrew Horton, you do it at the Chief of Police's headquarters. The entire hierarchy will be here, including the mayor." He looked at his watch. "We've got half an hour. Will you need anything special?"

"No, just a chalkboard."

They went directly to the conference room, where the attendees were already starting to congregate. A tall, muscular, impeccably dressed, mocha pigmented detective, who reminded Ronstadt of Jerry Washington, and who was probably a football player in his other life—also like Washington—greeted them. Shea introduced Ronstadt to him. His smile was wide and genuine.

"Gary, welcome to the road show." He extended his hand to Ronstadt. His grip was firm, and could be crushing if he chose it to be, definitely a former football player. "Paul Sanderson, I rep zone five and I'm Bill's counterpart here at headquarters."

The Atlanta Police Department was made up of six zones. Shea was based in zone two, where Horton's murder took place, and Sanderson was based in zone five, where the police headquarters was located. He used the street slang "I rep"—I represent—to describe where he was based. "We haven't had this much media attention since Sara Tokars was murdered last November," Sanderson said. "It seems it's always about the lawyers."

Sara Tokars was a woman whose husband, Fred Tokars, a prominent attorney with less than a haloed background, was the prime suspect in arranging his death.

"We'll get started when chief Bell and Mayor Jackson get here. It should be quite a dog and pony show. The mayor is pounding the drums for a task force, and the chief has already made his appearances on CNN with the yachtsman Ted Turner himself. Only in Atlanta."

Ronstadt liked him immediately. "Well, when I get through with my spiel they may be a little disappointed. If our killer follows the same pattern, which I've no reason to believe he will have changed, you're not going to find him in Atlanta no matter how many task forces you employ. That's why I came here. I'll give you a complete summary of where we are with our investigation. I'm going to provide some details that haven't appeared in the press. How zippered is your department?"

Both Shea and Sanderson laughed.

"Have you ever tried to hold water in a strainer?" asked Sanderson. "Just be careful of revealing anything you don't want to share with the public. The Mayor's aide's real name is *Highly Placed Sources*, not Greg Peacock, and Jack Merriweather, the chief's aide-de-camp's name is *Reliable Sources*. So be very careful."

"Yeah," said Shea. "What happens in Vegas may stay in Vegas, but what happens in Atlanta goes on CNN, and what goes on CNN goes out to the world, or at least that's what CNN would like to believe."

"There's also the FBI to consider," said Sanderson. "Ever since the FBI got involved with the Atlanta Child Murders in 1980, our Department has slept with them a lot. And they're going to show up like ants in an open honey pot for the Olympics in '96. You've obviously tweaked their curiosity, wondering why they weren't invited to the dance. The SAC—Special Agent in Charge—of the Atlanta office is seated at the back. I suspect the Mayor's office informed him."

"I'll explain why they haven't been involved during my presentation."

At precisely 3:00 p.m. the Mayor and the Police Chief, followed by their sycophants, entered the room. Shea introduced them to Ronstadt, and after the usual niceties Ronstadt assumed a position at the lectern.

"Thank you for allowing me the opportunity to share what I have learned about the murders similar to that of Mr. Horton's." He chronicled the details of all the murders, omitting only the specifics of the breast amputations, which was the holdback, because they had no apparent relevance to the murder of Andrew Horton.

The mayor was the ventriloquist, his aide the puppet. "It sounds like you're dealing with a serial killer," the aide said. "After two years of accomplishing nothing is there a reason why you haven't sought out the assistance of the FBI? After all, they have the experts who could have created a profile of the killer, which may have allowed the killer to have been apprehended before the unfortunate murder of Mr. Horton. And with all due respects, you are only a police sergeant with no experience in dealing with serial killers."

Ronstadt allowed the aide, Gregory Peacock, to finish fanning his feathers, thinking, *this asshole wants to get into a pissing contest. I guess I'll just have to piss on him.*

"I'm sorry, I have a lot on my mind, I forgot your name…and you are again?"

It was all Sanderson and Shea could do to keep from bursting out in laughter.

His flush rivaled a Tucson sunset. "I am Gregory Peacock,

Mayor Jackson's personal assistant."

"I'm sorry Mr. Peacock, I didn't realize that you were an authority on serial killers." The sunset changed to a deeper shade of red. "First let me explain my background, and then I'll tell you why I believe the FBI would have nothing to offer in the profiling of this particular killer.

"I have a master's degree in human behavioral psychology, and I spent three months with John Douglas at the BAU in Quantico—Behavioral Analysis Unit—studying the behavioral patterns of serial killers. I am preparing my PhD. dissertation on *the behavioral effects of anatomical aberrations in the brains of serial killers*. Mr. Peacock, as an authority on serial killers, you know who John Douglas is, don't you?"

John E. Douglas was one of the first FBI profilers, and the one mainly responsible for the creation of the FBI's Behavioral Science Unit. Lightning bolts were flashing from Peacock's eyes. Ronstadt had just made an enemy of *Highly Placed Sources.*

Ronstadt continued. "None of the victims were transported across state lines, and as such, no federal crimes were committed. Therefore the FBI had no reason to be involved. In each jurisdiction the murder is being investigated as a single event. Because a murder and an attempted murder were committed in Tucson, and because of my background, we all agreed that there would fewer hoops to jump through if I were to lead the investigation, as unorthodox as it may seem.

"Is a serial killer responsible for these murders? By strict definition...absolutely, but these were not random opportunistic killings. Each murder was planned down to the last detail, which explains why there was no evidence left at the crime scenes. I know the father of forensic science, Dr. Edmond Locard, said, 'It is impossible for a criminal to act, especially considering the intensity of a crime, without leaving traces of his presence.' Well gentlemen, with this killer, Dr. Locard was wrong. Also, your textbook serial killer does not abruptly change his pattern as this one has. There's a reason why he has stopped killing the women who had filed lawsuits, and why he is now killing the lawyers who represented them. Serial killers cannot control their impulses, and the usual escalation we see is beyond their control. This killer knows exactly where and when he will strike again, and I doubt it will be in any of the cities where he has killed before. Again, this is not the pattern of a serial killer, as we understand it. Most serial killers operate in a narrow geographic zone close to where they live.

"The perfect example of this is the case of your own Atlanta Child Murders. When Wayne Williams was arrested for those murders in 1981, it was because volunteer investigator Chet Dettlinger was able to recognize a definite social and geographic pattern among the victims, which led to the ultimate arrest of Williams. There is no such pattern to the killings that we're investigating."

There was a pattern, but it would take one more killing for the pattern to be recognized. And, as with the Atlanta Child Murders, the pattern would be recognized neither by the police nor the FBI, but by a volunteer, who like Chet Dettlinger, was initially considered a suspect in the murders.

Police Chief Eldrin Bell was impressed with Ronstadt's knowledge of the Atlanta Child Murders and how easily and accurately he introduced that knowledge into his discussion. This was a man he would like to have in his department. He was equally impressed with how quickly and accurately he assessed Peacock, and how easily he tore him a new asshole. He had made a fool out of Peacock, which would end up reflecting on the mayor because Peacock was his chief-of-staff. Bell knew he'd get some heat from the Mayor…such was politics.

Bell stood and said, "Detective Ronstadt, thank you for your insight and sharing of information, but if Mr. Horton's murder is an isolated event, and you don't believe we'll find the killer in Atlanta, how can we contribute to the investigation?"

"I realize Andrew Horton was one of your most prominent citizens, but there has to be a reason why he was targeted. That reason will come from something in his background, and only you have the keys to open the doors that will provide that information. The same is true with all the other murders. The investigators in the other cities are focusing on discovering something in the background of the victims, other than the fact they were all involved with breast implant lawsuits. Until Tucson became the focal point of the killings, and until I got involved and contacted the lead detectives in the other cities, most of those cases had been relegated to their cold case files. There are thousands of women involved in these lawsuits and hundreds of lawyers. Once we discover why those persons were picked as victims, I think then we'll be able to identify the killer."

A man stood at the back of the room. "Detective Ronstadt, I'm Craig Johnson, SAC of the FBI'S Atlanta Field Office. I was an agent on TDY—temporary duty—in Atlanta at the time of the Child Murders, and worked closely with Jon Glover, who was largely responsible for the apprehension of Wayne Williams. Glover was the one who correctly predicted the child killer would be black, and he was the one who correctly profiled Williams and predicted he would attempt to dispose of his next victim's body by throwing it off a bridge. And that is exactly what happened. And, as Mr. Peacock stated, your investigation has been going on for two years with no results. The Atlanta PD went almost two years with no success until the FBI became involved. That having been said, do you still feel that the FBI could not be of assistance to you, considering the fact that we are much better at profiling than we were in 1982, and that we have considerable resources that aren't available to most police departments?"

Ronstadt thought how he could best answer the agent. He didn't want to antagonize him. "Special Agent Johnson, in most cases I'd agree with you, but as I said earlier this killer doesn't fit any profile. As was the case with the Atlanta child killer, virtually all serial killers operate within a very narrow geographic comfort zone, working from a specific anchor point within that zone; very few travel interstate, and those that do are invariably itinerants, homeless, or have an occupation, like a truck driver, which would account for the interstate geographic distribution. And it would be a linear distribution, not random like we're seeing now. Let me show you." He wrote the names of the murder victims, and where they were murdered, on the chalkboard.

Carol Andrews, Cleveland; Elaine Peters, Houston; Faith Greene, Los Angeles; Brandy Evans, Miami; Desiree LaPelle, Las Vegas; Adele Grant, Tucson; Lawrence Band, Tucson; Charles Henderson, Detroit; Andrew Horton, Atlanta.

"As you can see, the first victims were women, and the next three victims were men. There's no geographic linear pattern, and serial killers don't change their patterns, as this one has—first women and then men. It's the consistency in the choice of victims, and restricted geographic operating zone that allows us to create a profile of a killer. There's nothing consistent in this killer's choice of victims and geographic distribution. And that's why we've been unable to create a profile."

"I noticed that two of the crimes occurred in Tucson, and one of the murder victims was from Tucson. Doesn't that suggest a pattern?" said *Reliable Sources.*

"I was going to get to that," said Ronstadt. "Although Lawrence Band was murdered in Tucson he was from Houston. The common factor all the victims shared was that they were involved in lawsuits involving silicone breast implants." He chose not to reveal that all the women were patients of Devin Powers, and that the three lawyers were members of the Centurion Counsel. He would share that information when he was alone with Shea and Sanderson. "The two year time frame is easily explained. Remember, that with the exception of Tucson, all the murders took place in cities with very high homicide rates. I spoke with all the detectives. At no time did any of them suspect that the murders were anything but random. And as time went on and their caseloads increased, priorities changed."

For the first time the mayor asked a question. "If these were all thought to be random killings, in spread out locations, how were you able to make the connection with the breast implant litigation?"

"The first victim, Carol Andrews, was a client of a Tucson attorney. He learned from conversations with other attorneys that women, who had filed lawsuits, were being murdered. He brought it to my attention, and that's when we got our first indication that the murders might be attributed to a single person. I contacted the police departments in those cities, and the rest, as the saying goes, is history. That's why I am here today in Atlanta."

"Do you have any leads?" asked Police Chief Bell.

"We believe the killer is from Tucson, and we're directing our investigation there."

"Does that translate to suspects?" asked Peacock.

"We are looking closely at two individuals."

"Are you going to share their names with us?" Peacock pressed on.

Ronstadt scanned the room. There were ten people, three of whom he had not met. "I'll discuss that when I meet later with the lead investigator, Detective Shea."

"Oh really," sneered Peacock. "Are you suggesting anyone in this room is not deeply interested in apprehending this killer, and should not be made aware of any information that might lead to Mr. Horton's killer?"

That's exactly what I'm thinking. "Mr. Peacock, when I was contacted by Detective Shea, it was I who suggested we meet in person and discuss the cases. We've not had that opportunity yet. I wasn't aware until the ride in from the airport that I would be talking before a group. I'm sure Detective Shea will share any relevant information with you as he does in every homicide he investigates."

SAC Johnson smiled. *This guy knows how to handle himself and is quick. I wonder if he ever considered a career with the FBI. I want to talk with him.*

The mayor stood. “Detective Ronstadt, thank you for taking the time to speak with us. You will have to excuse us. I’m speaking at the Commerce Club this evening and must get ready. He turned and made his way to the exit. Peacock followed, as if tethered to him by an invisible chain, but not before he turned and let his eyes show Ronstadt the rancor he felt.

Chief Bell extended his hand and said, “Thank you for taking the time to speak with us. I am certain you will conduct your investigation with the utmost delicacy. The last person, Chet Dettlinger, who volunteered his services, made the APD look like a group of incompetent buffoons. I’m sure you will not allow that to happen.” His grip tightened, and his jade-green eyes conveyed the message of a politician, not a street cop.

Ronstadt said, “Of course.” He returned the pressure of the handshake.

SAC Johnson waited until only Ronstadt, Shea, and Sanderson remained before he approached Ronstadt. Johnson did not wear the stereotypical uniform of an FBI agent. There were no dark shades, nor an ear bud cauliflowering from his ear canal. He wore a dark blue blazer and gray woolen pants. Tasseled black loafers fit the outfit, but not the image. His sandy hair kissed his shirt collar, perhaps a shade longer than regulation. It was his coffee-brown eyes that told the story. Pupils dilating and constructing like the lenses of high-speed cameras, clicking and storing everything they photographed. His grip was firm, but not intimidating. “Detective Ronstadt, I’m impressed, and I’m not easily impressed.” He spoke evenly and with authority. “I didn’t mean to imply that you needed the help of the FBI...far from it. We’ve been known to trip over our own shoelaces.” He smiled, “That’s why I wear loafers.

“I thought your idea of bringing all the detectives together for a meeting was brilliant. We would’ve sent agents out to interview them individually, and then have them report back with their findings. But I’m curious, why did you feel it was necessary to come to Atlanta?”

"Telephones, faxes and e-mail are marvelous communication tools, but I always learn more with face-to-face communication."

I definitely would like him to join the FBI, thought Johnson. "Detective Ronstadt..."

"Please... It's Gary."

"Gary, would you like to have dinner with me and one of my special agents, Lionel Lavoie, tonight? He spent a great deal of time at the BAU when he was at Quantico."

"Actually, I've already made dinner arrangements with Detective Shea."

"Why don't you join us?" Shea said to Johnson. "And you as well Paul, that way the Chief'll have a direct feed from our meeting."

"Thank you, we'd love to," said Johnson.

"Count me in," added Sanderson.

"It's four-thirty now. How about six-thirty at Mary Mac's? I can drop Gary off at his hotel to give him a chance to shower and clean up," Shea said.

"Excellent choice. Just in case Bill didn't tell you, it has the best Southern food in Atlanta," said Johnson.

CHAPTER FORTY-ONE

Atlanta, Georgia
Friday, March 12, 1993.

MARY MAC'S TEA Room opened its doors in 1945, on Ponce de Leon, in Atlanta's historic Midtown District. Mary McKenzie chose the name *tea room* because it was meant to convey an air of genteelness that the word *restaurant* did not possess, and besides, southern women just did not open restaurants. Across the street, at the corner of Ponce and Myrtle was Miss Bessie's, the local brothel, whose clientele was a who's who of Atlanta's most prominent businessmen, local and state officials. After their libido had been satisfied, the next step was to stimulate their taste buds with Southern cooking at Mary Mac's. And just as it was at Miss Bessie's, satisfaction and discretion were guaranteed.

Johnson, Sanderson, and Lavoie were already seated when Ronstadt and Shea arrived. Judging by the number of people waiting to be seated Ronstadt correctly assumed that a last minute reservation on a Friday night didn't just happen. Was it the FBI or the APD who had the clout? It didn't matter. If the aromas wafting throughout the restaurant were any indication of what to expect he wouldn't have minded waiting. Johnson introduced Lavoie to Ronstadt. A waitress appeared almost immediately to take drink orders. Her smile and welcome were not affectations. Ronstadt sensed the overall experience would be much like that of Rosa's… his favorite Mexican restaurant.

After the obligatory niceties were exchanged Lavoie changed the conversation to the murders. "Craig has already briefed me on all the details…I have a couple of thoughts you might consider, if you haven't already done so."

All business, thought Ronstadt. The uniform was stereotypical FBI, from the dark suit to the wingtips. His dark hair was regulation cut; he had no excess body fat, and it was apparent that he worked out regularly, but it was his Paul Newman ice-blue eyes that made you look at him twice.

"Gary, have you considered the possibility that you may be dealing with two killers working together? As I'm sure you know, thirteen percent of serial killings are committed by two or more individuals."

"That possibility exists, and I considered it briefly, but no...I don't think so. These killings have been orchestrated and planned with military precision. The killer knew whom, when, and where, at all times. The other possibility is that there's someone who's directing the killings."

"Are you thinking of a contract killer like Kuklinski, *The Iceman*?" asked Sanderson.

Richard Kuklinski was the notorious hit man for the Mafia, who confessed to over 200 murders when he was finally apprehended. He earned the title *The Iceman* because he was known to have frozen the bodies of some of his victims.

"Yes. It makes sense. The motive centers around the breast implant litigation."

The waitress returned with the drinks. "Are you gentlemen ready to order?"

The Atlanta contingent knew exactly what they were going to order. Ronstadt scanned the menu. "Suggestions?" he asked.

Shea said, "If you're here to taste our Southern cooking, I'd start with either the fried green tomatoes with a horseradish sauce that'll bring tears to your eyes, or the mudbugs."

"Mudbugs?"

"Deep fried Louisiana crayfish, with a jalapeño sauce that'll test your palate. Then, either the fried chicken or the blackened catfish...and save some room for the peach cobbler."

Ronstadt thought of Rosa's Mexican Restaurant in Tucson. It would have to be a pretty mean sauce to challenge her hot salsa. He closed the menu. "Let's do the mudbugs and the chicken, I'll definitely have room for the cobbler."

The meal was as good as advertised, but these Southern boys wouldn't know what a hot sauce was until they sampled a Diablo salsa from Rosa's. As Ronstadt was spooning the last remnant of the best peach cobbler he had ever tasted his Nokia 1011 cell phone rang. It was Detective Washington.

"Gary, we just got a call from a Detective Earl Potvin in Boston. Another lawyer was axed…and yes, he was a member of the Centurion Counsel."

He lowered his voice. "When?"

"Last night sometime. Same M.O. No witnesses and no evidence, almost a repeat of your guy in Atlanta. Get this, he was one of Boston's Brahmins, Francis Adams…a direct descendant of Samuel Adams. Potvin was the one you spoke to when you called the cities that had a Centurion Counsel lawyer."

"I remember him. Nice guy. I almost needed a translator to get through his Boston accent."

"He told me the city fathers are screaming for answers. He said there hasn't been this much noise since Samuel Adams led the Boston Tea Party, and the heat he's getting would make the temperature in hell feel like the North Pole. I told him about Atlanta and to expect a call from you.

"And Dr. Powers has vanished. When we got the call from Potvin, Manny called his spa, and was told by the receptionist that he cancelled all his scheduled surgery for the past week. She hasn't heard from him since. We checked the airport and his plane is gone. He left Wednesday, but didn't file a flight plan."

"I'll get back to you."

He looked at the four men and said, "We need to talk."

When Ronstadt finished repeating what Washington had told him Lavoie nodded and said, "He's accelerating."

Sanderson placed his hand on Ronstadt's arm and stood up. "Don't say anything. I'll be right back." He maneuvered his way around several tables and stopped before a table where a mousey short man with ferret like eyes was seated. "Hello Sammy, enjoying your dinner?" He leaned over and whispered in his ear, "Having a hearing problem?" He yanked an ear bud from his ear and pulled the cord attached to a pencil like device pointed at their table. "Didn't your mother tell you it's rude to eavesdrop?"

"Hey! You can't do that."

"I just did." He pocketed the listening device and said, "Dinner's over. Don't forget to leave a tip."

The man sneered. "I have my rights. You should know Georgia is a one-party consent law state."

"Oh I know that very well. But tell me which one of our party gave you permission to record our conversation? I know it wasn't me."

"Who's the guy with you? I haven't seen him before."

"Weasel, do you know what number comes after nine? Hmm? It's ten. Which means you have exactly one second before I snap my cuffs on you and arrest you for obstruction of justice. And I'm sure agents Lavoie and Johnson will find some federal charge as well."

He laughed. "You know the charges'll never stick."

"Tell that to Bubba, who will be your personal cell-mate for the next forty-eight hours. I understand his last squeeze was HIV positive...Ten."

Ferris pushed his chair back and stood. His eyes narrowed to slits. "I'm leaving, but I won't forget this."

Sanderson waited until the man left the restaurant before he returned to his table.

"What was that all about?" Asked Ronstadt.

"That was Sammy Ferris. We call him Sammy the Ferret, or Weasel. He's a free-lance reporter. Occasionally he'll have an article in the Journal-Constitution, but they'll feature him only if he has documentation to back up his story. I took this away from him." Sanderson removed the device from his pocket and placed it on the table. As he did, Ferris started his car in the parking lot, and smiled as he stroked the camera-recorder hidden in his tie clip.

Johnson fingered it and said, "Primitive, but effective." He glanced at the table where Ferris had been sitting. "…At that range."

"I think we should continue this conversation in my office in the morning where the only recording devices there are mine," Johnson smiled. "What time does your plane leave tomorrow?"

"Not until the afternoon, but from the way the snow is coming down, it may not happen. Besides, I may want to go to Boston after I speak with Detective Potvin."

"Please hold that phone-call until the morning," said Johnson. "Let's meet at my office at eight." He signaled the waitress for the check.

CHAPTER FORTY-TWO

Atlanta, Georgia
Saturday, March 13, 1993.

ATLANTA'S OMNI HOTEL at the CNN Center defined elegance and style. It was located in the heart of downtown Atlanta within the bustling Luckie Marietta District. Ronstadt was treated to a spectacular view of downtown Atlanta's skyline from his room on the fourteenth floor. After a cup of self-brewed coffee he made his way down to the lobby to wait for Shea.

Ten minutes later Shea arrived and told the valet to keep the car close, he'd be returning shortly. He found Ronstadt seated in a tub chair reading the morning edition of the Journal-Constitution.

"Anything interesting?"

"I guess you haven't seen the morning paper," Ronstadt said. He folded the paper back to reveal the headline, and showed it to Shea. The headline read. "Serial Killer Strikes in Atlanta."

"Shit! So much for keeping a lid on. How much did he reveal?"

"Almost everything we talked about. Read it for yourself."

Shea sat down in an adjoining chair and read the article. When he finished he shook his head and said, "That little bastard must have had a second recording device. The Constitution would never have published an article like that without verification. Sanderson won't be happy he missed it."

The valet had not parked the car. It was waiting when the detectives left the hotel. Shea folded two Washington's in the young man's hand and banged the steering wheel with both hands when he got into the car. "The temperature in the oven has just been increased to broil. I hope Chief Bell doesn't have a stroke when he sees this article."

They exited the hotel and started toward the FBI headquarters on Century Parkway.

"I guess the FBI will be players now, after that article," said Ronstadt "How do you feel about working with them?"

"Actually it won't be too bad. We've always had a good working relationship with them. They have one of the best SWAT teams in the country, and we've had a number of joint operations. If it weren't for them, we of the APD would still be walking around with our fingers up our asses trying to find the Atlanta Child Killer."

Normally it was a short fifteen-minute drive to the FBI headquarters, but the snow was coming down in blankets, and their progress was impeded by the crashes of six cars ahead of them that were pretending to be an accordion. It was the opening act of the Superstorm of '93. As they approached the FBI headquarters the traffic and skyscrapers of downtown Atlanta were replaced with a tranquil tree-lined boulevard. The FBI building was not imposing, but it was the tallest structure in the immediate area. It's rounded corners and glass-windowed walls showed some architectural imagination. Ronstadt was impressed with the unobtrusive light-poles and total absence of overhead wires.

They parked the car and were issued visitor badges when they entered the building and signed in. "Good morning gentlemen, SAC Johnson is expecting you," the agent at the desk said. He escorted them to Johnson's office where both he and Lavoie were waiting. The morning paper was open on his desk. They had been discussing the article.

Johnson's office was located on the fourth floor. The furnishings were functional, but tasteful. They didn't appear to be Government Issue. The pictures on the walls were scenic—not hand-shaking photo-ops with dignitaries. A trolley with two carafes of coffee was waiting in the corner by a conference table. Johnson pointed to it and said, "Help yourselves."

Ronstadt picked up a mug emblazoned with the gold and blue

FBI logo and poured a cup of decaf. Shea chose regular. When they were seated Johnson said, "I presume you've seen the morning paper?"

They both nodded.

"For better or for worse, we're now married in this investigation. Gary, I know you haven't involved the FBI, but I believe we can open some doors for you without your having to jump through a series of bureaucratic hoops. I'm not looking for brownie points, so we'll not try to take over your investigation, but we will assist you in whatever way we can. The other day you asked Bill if he could find out whether a Cessna 414A Chancellor filed a flight plan to Tucson recently?"

Ronstadt nodded.

"How long do think it would take for the world's busiest airport to accommodate that request for him? And how long do you think it would take for this office to obtain that information?"

"I see your point."

"Even with our assistance you may not get the information you're looking for," said Lavoie. "If the person you're looking for flew VFR and landed at an unregulated airport there would be no way of tracking him. Even if he flew IFR you might never know if he flew to a particular airport."

"How is that possible?"

"Think about it. We have over two thousand flights per day coming in and out of Hartsfield. An air controller sees a blip on his screen, not a Cessna or a Citation. A plane identifies itself by its call letters. No one ever checks to see if those are the actual letters. They are used to direct a plane for take off or landing. So, if you were to call in and say, 'This is Sam,' the controller would have no idea whether your name was really Sam, George or Pete, and he's not going to ask for an ID when you land. It's the same thing with call letters. No one is going to check. Once you've landed it's on to the next plane. There will be a recording of your conversation with the controller, but it's meaningless if you gave him false information. If *Cessna-seven-niner-seven-Delta* were the plane's call letters and registration, and it were to identify itself as *Cessna-*eight-*niner-seven-Delta*, only the pilot would know those were the wrong call letters. No one would check the voice recording to verify the numbers. It's only a name, not a fingerprint, and in all further communication he would be identified usually by the last two or three digits…like, *Niner-seven-Delta.* Or he might be assigned a squawk number—a transponder identification code—and that's how the aircraft would be identified on radar. You would need physical proof to verify whether that plane was at a particular airport at a particular time."

Ronstadt sighed, "That makes sense. So we're back to where we started. We have two suspects, and they both own a Cessna. In two of the murders we can place them both in the same city at the same time, but there was no evidence that would implicate either of them."

"Is there anyone else who has access to their planes?" asked Johnson.

Ronstadt thought for a moment. "I don't know about Powers, but I do know that Neal Mink, one of the suspects, has an investigator, Marvin Slater, who flies his plane from time to time."

Lavoie almost fell out of his chair. "Did you say Marvin Slater?"

"Yes. Do you know him?"

"If he's the same Marvin Slater I certainly do…"

Beirut Airport, October 23, 1983, 6:22 a.m. *Captain Marvin Slater, of the Marine Second Reconnaissance Battalion, had trouble sleeping. He was concerned about the lack of security surrounding the barracks where he was staying. Here they were in the middle of a fucking civil war where the good guys were slaughtering the bad guys, and the bad guys were slaughtering the good guys on a regular basis. The problem was nobody knew who were the good guys and who were the bad guys. They all hated the Americans. The American Embassy was blown up in April, so* *security was increased around American facilities in Lebanon. The tightened security surrounding the barracks was a five foot chain-link fence with concertina wire on top, and a guard post with two Marines who were operating under Rules of Engagement with their weapons at condition four…no magazines inserted and no rounds in the chamber. They might have been able to stop a nine-month pregnant terrorist who was tripping over her burka. Maybe. But that was all. Slater was standing outside the perimeter when he saw a huge Mercedes-Benz stake truck accelerate toward the fence. The fence offered as much resistance as a ribbon holding back a runner from crossing the finish line. The truck crashed through two sentry posts, a guard shack, and smashed into the lobby of the barracks building. The explosion carried the force of 21,000 pounds of TNT. Slater's screams went unheard as the four story building first rose toward the arms of heaven, and then collapsed upon itself into the bowels of hell, taking the lives of 241 American servicemen with it, including 220 Marines of the BLT 1/8—1st Eighth Marines Battalion Landing Team—the most Marine casualties since the battle of Iwo Jima in WWII.*

He heard the distant wailing of ambulances approaching the carnage. Let them do what they did best; he was going to do what he did best. Part of the credo of a Recon Marine was, "A Recon Marine can speak without saying a word, and achieve what others can only imagine." He climbed into a jeep and headed toward the village of Ain Dara, thirty kilometers from Beirut.

"…I was a member of the FBI forensics team conducting the investigation of the terrorist attack on the marine barracks in Lebanon, in 1983. During the course of the investigation we learned of a massacre in a remote section of the village of Ain Dara that occurred the day of the bombing. Twenty-nine of the inhabitants were slaughtered indiscriminately. They were all shot first and then mutilated afterwards. The men had their penises cut off and their testicles crushed. The women had their breasts cut off. There was a witness who had remained hidden during the massacre. She told authorities that it was an American soldier. His face was blackened, but she said he had a red patch on his sleeve with the face of a skeleton.

"It was a perfect description of the arm patch of the Second Recon Battalion. The only things missing from her description were the words on the patch *Swift, Silent, and Deadly*. Everyone suspected it was Slater, but in the aftermath of the Marine deaths no one cared about what happened in Ain Dara, and no one was going to go after a Marine who had witnessed 241 of his comrades being blown up. Slater resigned his commission shortly afterwards, and that was the last I heard of him."

"Our Slater was a Recon Marine," said Ronstadt. "He came to Tucson in 1984 and enrolled in the police academy. I remember that because he was in the same class as one of my detectives, Manny Vargas. Manny never liked him. Slater was a patrol cop for a little over a year, but resigned after a situation in which his partner almost got killed when he went after two suspects without waiting for backup. He was a good cop, but couldn't accept the regimentation that went along with the job. I never would have suspected that Slater could be our killer. He never appeared on the radar screen. After he left the TPD he went to work as an investigator for the Mink brothers, and has been with them ever since."

"Why would you have suspected him? Remember the words, *swift, silent,* and *deadly.* A Recon Marine is trained to leave no trace of his presence. He is a master of deception," said Lavoie.

"Which describes our killer," said Ronstadt.

"If the killer is this guy Slater, I can understand why he did what he did in Lebanon, without condoning it, but why would he be killing innocent women and these lawyers?" asked Shea.

Johnson said, "You're the psychologist Gary, what's your opinion?"

"You can't imagine how many hours I've struggled over the same question. Not about Slater of course, but about Powers and Neal Mink. Powers had the obvious motive, but it seemed all too convenient to have everything pointing at him. He *was* in Cleveland when Andrews was killed, but he had been scheduled to deliver a scientific paper at least six months prior to her murder. There was no possible way he could've known she'd be there at the same time. Mink knew the woman, but had no reason to kill her. However, since he made the arrangements for Carol Andrews' stay in Cleveland, it's possible he told Slater.

"I don't know enough about Slater to offer an opinion about what motivates him, and I certainly haven't had enough time to process what you just told me, but I think I can explain the mutilations of Ain Dara.

"The Qur'an draws many of its teachings from the Old Testament. Muslim men are indoctrinated from early puberty in the concept of Houris—the promise that they will have unlimited sex slaves when they reach Paradise. Slater must be a student of religion, because in addition to his knowledge of the Qur'an he certainly knew the reference of Deuteronomy 23:1 which states, 'No man whose testicles have been crushed or whose male organ cut off may enter the assembly of God.' As far as the women's mutilations are concerned, he probably was using the *Hadith* of *Punishment in the grave*. He was sending a message to the Muslims."

"Would you mind explaining that last statement?" said Johnson.

"I'm sorry. I'm guilty of lecturing. *Hadith* is anything said by the Prophet Muhammad. *Punishment in the grave* was usually a mutilation carried out on adulterers after death. Women were often suspended by their breasts on hooks, or may have had them cut off if they had displayed them in such a way as to stimulate a man. Which brings another thought to mind. Muslims believe in the concept of *Haram* which is any sinful act forbidden by God. Any change in Allah's creation would be considered *Haram.* Women who've had breast implants would be guilty of *Haram*."

The other three men stared at Ronstadt. Impressed was not an adequate word to describe their reaction to his explanation. Johnson thought this was definitely a man who belonged in the FBI. He shook his head. "Gary, you have given a plausible explanation for what Slater did, but can you tell me how in God's name that information just flowed from your tongue? And are you implying that Slater is on some kind of crusade?"

Ronstadt reddened. "My occupation is that of a cop, but my avocation is the study of Eastern religions, and Christianity began as an Eastern religion. As far as Slater being on some kind of crusade…I have no idea. It's likely his mind snapped in Lebanon, and the circuits to his brain may now be wired in ways that defy conventional explanation. But one thing is clear…we have to find Slater."

CHAPTER FORTY-THREE

Boston, Massachusetts
Saturday, March 13, 1993.

THE STORM HAD not yet shut down Logan Airport. Slater was awaiting clearance for take-off to Chicago. When he was finished in Chicago he'd be going to the Bahamas to make a deposit in a numbered account. After that he would fly to Lexington Kentucky, where Adele Grant was staying with her parents, and then to Fort Worth…the final stop on his journey. He would kill two birds with one stone; only in this case it would be with one axe.

"Cessna-six-niner-seven-Romeo-Lima this is Logan tower, proceed to runway four-R…you are cleared for take off.

"Seven-Romeo-Lima, Roger that."

"Proceed to 12,000 feet—direction-two-seven-zero—await further instructions."

His take off was flawless, and when he reached cruising altitude he turned east and smiled. *Soon it will be over.*

* * *

There were several reasons why Slater chose to stay at the Chicago Ritz-Carlton. He needed a good sleep before he left for the Bahamas, it was only half an hour from the airport, and most importantly, attorney Sanford Astor's brownstone on Astor Street was less than one-half mile from the hotel. An added bonus was the fact that the *American Society of Aesthetic Surgery* was holding its annual meeting at the nearby Westin Michigan Avenue, and he knew that Devin Powers had registered for the meeting...another coincidence that Powers would have to explain. But Slater didn't know that Powers wouldn't be attending the meeting, because he was in Guatemala.

The credit card he used at check-in was a card he would use only once...real, but untraceable. He declined assistance with his carry-on. The axe was strapped to his waist, concealed under his overcoat. He scanned the lobby. The bank of elevators was not visible from the registration desk, which meant he could enter and exit the hotel from the back entrance without being seen by the desk clerk. And it was unlikely anyone would be wandering the hallways at two in the morning when he left the hotel.

He had chosen Astor from the list as his next victim because it was convenient. He could fly from Boston to Chicago without refueling, and from there non-stop to the Caribbean. He was on a strict schedule that needed to be completed before the end of the month. He still had to deal with Adele Grant and Fort Worth attorney Reuben Clark. But first he needed to get some sleep.

* * *

Sanford Astor was a direct descendant of John Jacob Astor the First, and it was fitting that he lived on Astor Street in Chicago's Historic Gold Coast, the second most affluent residential area in the United States, surpassed only by Manhattan's Upper East Side. He had everything; the name, the money, the reputation, the trophy-wife, and was a member of the Centurion Counsel. He was also a mean, arrogant bastard who never let anyone forget that he was an Astor, as if the Astors didn't wipe their asses with toilet paper like everyone else.

The hangers-on were swarming around him in the lounge of the Ritz-Carlton Club, congratulating him on the $5 million jury award he had won on Friday.

"I propose a toast to Herbert Henry Dow, without whom none of this would have been possible." He raised his tumbler of Glenfiddich. The real celebration would come later when he opened the Macallan 55-year-old Lalique Crystal Decanter, one of only a hundred released in the United States. Another Centurion. He squeezed his wife and smiled. He didn't see Marvin Slater raise his glass at the other end of the lounge.

* * *

The chauffeur dropped Astor and Mindy off at their brownstone. Mindy. A ridiculous name, but appropriate for a trophy-wife twenty-five years Astor's junior. He was proud of this stately renovated Queen Anne brownstone, originally designed by renowned architect Jon Wellborn Rootin in 1887, who claimed the Chrysler Building among his architectural achievements.

Astor had to support his wife whose blood-alcohol level hovered around .20. He wasn't going to waste the Macallan on her. She was already wasted.

They shared the same bed only when it was to satisfy his libido. His libido was raging, but she would be useless tonight...perhaps in the morning. He took her to her bedroom and undressed her. He was tempted, but better to wait until she could participate. And when she participated, it was like being attacked by a lynx in heat. He missed his last opportunity.

* * *

It was mid-afternoon by the time Mindy stirred. Her headache was as intense as the pounding on a kettledrum, and the back of her throat felt like it had been massaged with 60-grit sandpaper. She staggered into her bathroom, relieved herself, and when she was finished she wrapped a silk robe around her nude body and made her way down to the study. It took a few seconds for her to process what she saw. When she did, her stomach churned into reverse, and the remnants of the Glenfiddich she had consumed the night before made a unique blend with the Macallan and blood pooled on the carpet beside the body of her nearly headless husband.

By the time the police had arrived Marvin Slater had already checked into the Ocean Club in Nassau.

CHAPTER FORTY-FOUR

Atlanta, Georgia
Sunday, March 14, 1993.

THE ONLY THREE people at the FBI headquarters were Ronstadt, SAC Johnson, and SA Lavoie. Ronstadt's initial impression of Lavoie being a tight assed, by the book, Federal Agent, was modified when he saw Lavoie dressed in faded jeans and a bulky cable-knit sweater. Johnson wasn't wearing jeans, but he was casually dressed, that is to say slacks and a sweater...no tie.

"Gary, thank you for staying over, actually, I should thank the weather for keeping you here. After you and Detective Shea left yesterday Lionel and I spent some time discussing your investigation. We were both impressed with how you were able to coordinate all the police departments in different cities into a functioning unit. I don't know if we could have achieved the same results even within our own agency. Have you ever thought about a career in Federal law enforcement?"

"I'm flattered that you would ask. But no, I'm just a cowboy at heart. I don't own a tie, and I would look pretty silly driving a mud-splattered truck to work, or hitching a horse to a parking meter. I need to be around horses."

"We do have some of the finest breeders, rivaling those of Kentucky, right here in Atlanta," said Lavoie.

Ronstadt smiled. "But I doubt they breed working horses, or train them as barrel racers. And as beautiful as the skyline of Atlanta is, it's not like watching a Tucson sunset. And in Tucson space is measured in acres...not front-footage.

"Also, I can't take all the credit for the organization of the investigation. Despite the fact we once considered Neal Mink a suspect in the murders, it was he who really provided most of the information that allowed us to make the associations. Were it not for the organization he had set up within the Centurion Counsel it's doubtful we would've learned about the murders of the women in the other cities in a timely fashion. They were isolated murders that soon lost priority because the investigating detectives had made no progress.

"I spoke with Neal Mink last night, and he knew about the murder of Adams in Boston before we did because of the reporting system he has in place. In fact, Neal thinks he knows what the association is between the murdered women and the lawyers. I didn't tell him about Marvin Slater. He came to that conclusion on his own, and he believes he knows within a narrow range of time where and when Slater will strike next. Slater was supposed to have flown to visit a friend in Savannah, but he never showed up."

Johnson said, "Do you think he'd be willing to come to Atlanta and share this information with us?"

"I'm sure he would, but he'll have to fly commercial, or charter a plane, because Slater has his plane."

"And we have no idea where Slater is," said Lavoie.

Nassau, Bahamas, March 14, 1993.

Paradise Island was indeed paradise, and the Ocean Club was the Garden of Eden. But when Swedish Industrialist Axel Werner-Gren anchored his yacht off its virginal shores in 1939, it was known as Hog Island. He spent over twenty years developing an estate with gardens inspired by those of the Chateau de Versailles. He named it Shangri-La. In 1962, he sold the estate to Huntington Hartford II, heir to the Great Atlantic and Pacific Tea Company. Hartford converted the estate into a luxury destination resort which he Christened the Ocean Club, and convinced the Bahamian government to rename Hog Island to Paradise Island.

Hartford invested nearly $10 million in the Ocean Club, creating terraced gardens, rivaling those of Versailles. He imported fountains, bronze and marble statuary from Europe, and a magnificent 12th-century Augustian cloister, shipped piece-by-piece from France. It was Hartford's vision that allowed Marvin Slater to sit on the terrace of his suite and enjoy the endless cerulean blue Bahamian sky, whose horizon was enveloped by the turquoise waters of a tranquil sea, which gently lapped at and played with the beach's delicate white sands.

Forty-eight hours of the resort's timeless bliss was all he needed to dispel the fatigue he felt from the intensity of the past week's activities. His actions had been pre-planned, but Adele Grant's unexpected move forced him to change his strategy. It didn't matter, because she would soon be removed from the chessboard, and then he would then make his final move. He closed his eyes and thought, *God abandoned me in Lebanon, but He is making up for it here on Paradise Island.*

Atlanta, Georgia, March 15, 1993.

Lavoie kept the engine running in the no-stopping zone while Ronstadt waited for Neal at the arrival gate. The Crown Victoria was unmarked, but the blue light on the dash identified it as a law enforcement vehicle, which allowed it to override the no-stopping ordinance. The snow in Atlanta was slowing and the airport had re-opened.

Ronstadt waved when he saw Neal emerge from the gate. He was the first one off...obviously seat 1A. The two men shook hands, and Ronstadt said, "Neal thank you for coming. First I want to apologize..."

"Stop right there. I would've felt the same way if I had been in your position. The important thing is to end this shit. I'll explain when we get to the FBI headquarters. But tell me, when did you get into bed with the Feds? I thought you wanted to keep them on the sidelines. And why Atlanta?"

"It wasn't my intent when I got here, it just sort of happened. It's like the guy who wakes up in the morning in a strange bed with a strange woman and wonders how he got there. I'll explain everything later, but I'm glad they're involved."

Introductions were made, and Lavoie suggested that they stop first at the Omni so Neal could register, as it was on the way to FBI headquarters. Traffic was light and moving at a steady pace despite the snow.

"Had I known it was going to snow this much I would've dressed for the occasion," said Neal. "But on second thought, I don't own any clothes designed for snow, except for my ski clothes, and I wasn't planning to go skiing in Atlanta."

A discussion of the weather was always a safe topic when individuals were meeting for the first time. One might say it was an icebreaker.

"We usually get some snow every year, but never this much. I suspect it'll be over soon, and then we can treat you to some of Atlanta's balmy spring weather," said Lavoie.

Neal's check-in at the Omni took less than fifteen minutes. It took considerably longer than the normal fifteen minutes to reach FBI headquarters because they had to work their way around a group of cars whose drivers were unaccustomed to driving in snow. When they entered Johnson's office, as before, a trolley was waiting with carafes of coffee, only this time a tray of Krispy Kreme doughnuts had joined the party.

Ronstadt introduced Neal to Johnson, and after the customary small talk droned down to silence Johnson said, "Mr. Mink..."

"Please, it's Neal."

"...Neal, we appreciate you coming to Atlanta. Sergeant Ronstadt said you think you know where Slater will strike next."

"Actually, it was something Gary told me that made me think of it. Apparently his wife Elena noticed something that none of us had picked up on. Gary why don't you explain it."

"A little background. My wife has an uncanny ability to divine logical explanations for events or situations that sometimes seem to be totally *non sequitur.* She is a multi-dimensional thinker who is always thinking outside the box, whereas I am a totally linear thinker."

"She sounds like someone we could use in our cryptography analysis department," said Lavoie.

He laughed. "That'd never work. She's a maverick who could never be tamed. With all due respect, she's not someone who could observe the protocols of the FBI.

"Elena and I were discussing my inability and the inabilities of the detectives in the cities where the breast implant murders took place to come up with any evidence that would implicate someone in the murders. At one point even Neal was a person of interest." He explained the circumstances that placed Neal near the top of the list of suspects. "My wife saw immediately that the first names of all the murdered women and the woman who had an attempt made on her life followed the letters of the alphabet A through E, although the murders weren't in alphabetical sequence. At first she thought the same pattern was being followed with the murdered lawyers as well, but the alphabetical sequence for the lawyers' names wasn't restricted to first names, as it was with the women. She saw the sequential association, but had no idea what it meant. Neal has a theory that may explain it. Neal?"

"As you know there are thousands of women who are involved in litigation involving silicone breast implants, and hundreds of lawyers who are representing them. There was no possible way to predict which women would be targeted as victims. The alphabetical sequence makes sense when taken in context with another parameter. When Gary called me the other night and told me about the murder of the attorney in Boston, I was convinced I had the answer. The women were chosen alphabetically by their names, but the lawyers were selected alphabetically by the cities in which they practiced. Atlanta, Boston, Detroit, and Houston. All were members of the Centurion Counsel. Let me explain how the Centurion Counsel works…"

"So what you're saying is that women were chosen at random because of their names, but the lawyers were chosen because they were all Centurion Counsel lawyers representing women who were involved in the breast implant litigation," said Johnson.

"Up to a point..."

Johnson's phone flashed. "Let me take this call." He turned his back from the group for a moment and spoke quietly into the handset.

"…I see…yes, I understand." He looked at Neal as he replaced the receiver in its cradle. "Neal, it would appear your theory might be correct. That call was from the field office in Chicago. An attorney named Sanford Astor was found murdered in his home two nights ago. They just learned of it. Was he..."

"Yes, he was a founding member of the Counsel."

"If he continues his pattern that means there are ninety-five lawyers from whom he could choose his next victim," said Lavoie.

Neal shook his head. "In theory yes, but he selected only lawyers who were representing patients of Dr. Devin Powers, and that includes Astor."

"Why do you think Slater stopped killing the women and started on the lawyers?" asked Ronstadt.

"The answer to that question is so complex that I couldn't believe it until you just confirmed it," he looked at Johnson, "when you just told us of Astor's murder in Chicago. What do you know about the details of...?"

After Neal explained his theory the other three men sat in stunned silence.

Finally Lavoie said, after studying the names of the remaining lawyers and the cities in which they lived, "Which means, based on your theory, there are eleven remaining lawyers in the Centurion

Counsel who meet the city alphabetical criteria, and the next victim could be any one of them."

"I'm beginning to understand his thinking," said Ronstadt. "First, he'll want to finish off Adele Grant. She's been sequestered at her parents' farm in Kentucky so she should be safe there."

"I don't think so," said Neal. "When we decided she would be safer at her parents' until the trial started, we made certain there'd be no paper trail that could trace her to her parents' farm, but Slater knows exactly where she is...he flew her there. Her parents have a landing strip on their farm."

"I don't think we should have any immediate concerns," said Johnson. "It'll be days before all the snow can be cleared in and around Lexington."

"That won't stop Marvin Slater," said Lavoie. "He'll find a way to get there even if the roads are closed. One way would be with a helicopter. He's ATP—Air Transport Pilot—certified, and is licensed to fly any class of helicopter. One of the many skills he acquired as a Recon Marine. I suggest we get her out of there. Now!"

CHAPTER FORTY-FIVE

Lexington, Kentucky
Monday, March 15, 1993.

LEXINGTON KENTUCKY WAS known as the *Horse Capital of the World.* It lay in the heart of the Bluegrass Region, which got its name from the blue flowered Poa grass that grew there. In several different Indian languages the name *Kentucky* meant *meadowlands* referring specifically to the Bluegrass Region, and it wasn't until many years later the name Kentucky was adopted for the entire state. By 1800, farmers noticed that horses that grazed in the Bluegrass Region were of heartier stock than those that grazed in other regions. The difference was because of the high calcium content of the soil.

The Crawford horse farm, originally Winfield Farm on Athens-Hill Walnut Pike, sat on eighty-two of the finest of those bluegrass acres. The main house was built from cut stone, and the four horse barns had a total of fifty-four stalls. Thirty-two were occupied. Adele Grant's parents, Jack and Roberta Crawford, were in Louisville for the weekend at a horse auction. They were supposed to have returned to the farm the next day, but the weather had other ideas. At first the snow was a minor curiosity, but soon it became a major problem. The '93 Superstorm was an uninvited guest, and within twenty-four hours it shut down the entire city. By the time it left, three days later, its venom had paralyzed the entire city.

The Crawford farm, which was isolated by design, became inaccessible by chance. It was only eighty miles from Louisville, but after the storm it would have been easier to scale Mt. Everest than to access the farm. The county was simply not equipped to handle a snowfall of this magnitude.

Louisville, Kentucky, Monday March 15, 1993.

Marvin Slater had already completed his morning workout at the Crown Plaza Airport Hotel fitness center when he received the news that one runway had been opened for operations. He hadn't planned on being in Louisville this long, but then again, no other visitors had either. His original plan had been to rent a car and drive to Crawford Farms, but the snow squelched that possibility. He didn't like daylight operations, but he could helicopter into a remote area of the farm in the predawn hours. He had already made the arrangements for the rental at Eifler Helicopter Service.

Atlanta, Georgia, March 15, 1993.

They knew earlier in the week that the storm was coming, but had no idea of its magnitude. Spring was officially less than a week away, so the ever-optimistic Atlantans concentrated on the Cherokee Rose, the state flower, as it started to unfold from its winter blanket. They should have concentrated on the barometer. It was in the tuck position heading straight downhill.

The FBI agents and Ronstadt were frustrated. They were unable to make a move, but then again, neither could Slater. It was a stalemate. The phone lines were down at Crawford Farms, and they could only hope they would get there before Slater. Atlanta's airport had just opened.

They had thought that Slater would most likely fly to Louisville, but they didn't know he was already there. On his return from the Bahamas he developed engine problems with the Cessna and was forced to divert to Miami, where he rented a Beechcraft Baron, while repairs were being made to the Cessna. He was able to leave

Miami before the storm reached its full intensity, and he arrived in Louisville undetected. Lavoie had alerted all airports within a 100-mile radius to report any landing of a Cessna 414A Chancellor.

"We're good to go," Lavoie announced. "The weather's broken in Lexington, and I'll have us there less than two hours." He hung up the phone and said, "Gary, you're welcome to join us, but this will be an FBI SWAT operation, and you'll be there strictly as an observer. APD has turned the operation over to us. The storm has left their plate completely full."

"Understood. One question...did I hear you correctly when you said, 'I'll have us there in less than two hours?' "

He addressed Ronstadt's puzzled look. "Yes. I'll be flying the chopper, I'm ATP certified. All FBI fixed wing and helicopter pilots are trained agents. We have to have five years field experience before we're allowed behind the controls." He grinned, "It wouldn't do to have civilians involved in hush-hush FBI operations. J. Edgar would turn over in his grave if we did."

It took less than half an hour before they airborne. They would arrive at Crawford Farms in ninety minutes. Marvin Slater would arrive in seventy-five.

Lexington, Kentucky, March 15, 1993.

The sky was clearing at Crawford Farms. Below it was a Currier and Ives Christmas, except for the absence of a horse-drawn sleigh. The snow was virginal. When Slater landed he would be the first to violate its chastity. There was no activity on the ground below. He knew the landing was going to be difficult. The helicopter was equipped with snow skids and bear paws, but there was still a real risk of the tail assembly sinking into the snow, with a chance that the copter could flip. He performed a high-hover landing maneuver, remaining stationary, until the rotors had blown away enough snow for the craft to be eased down safely. He turned off the rotors, and when they stopped he jumped out of the craft, took a shovel, and cleared enough snow from around the 'coptor to ensure a safe take off it.

He tucked his Beretta into his waistband. The Beretta M9 was his choice of weapons because of its short recoil and its 15-round staggered box magazine that had a reversible magazine release button that could be positioned for either right or left-handed shooters. He was left-handed. It was unlikely he would need the weapon, but there was always the possibility of collateral damage. He clipped on his Red Feather Stealth snowshoes, which featured a live action hinge that sprang back after each step, allowing a natural fatigue-reducing stride. These shoes would allow him to walk at a brisk speed. It was about half a mile to the main house, which he estimated he could reach in about six to seven minutes. He checked his watch. Mickey mouse was waving at him. 06:38. His estimated time to complete the operation and become airborne again was twenty-six minutes.

Overcoming the security code was simple. Once inside he removed his snowshoes, and made his way up the stairs. He didn't hear the Blackhawk approaching from the south because it's rotors had been modified to make it into a stealth aircraft. Only the horses reacted to its approach.

* * *

Adele hadn't slept well. She was alone...well, almost alone. Manuel Ortega, the groom, and his wife Petra, were the only ones in residence in the employees' quarters. The rest of the staff was unable to get to work because of the snow. Her parents were in Louisville, and Greg couldn't get there for the weekend as planned, because the airport had been closed. The phone lines were down.

She sensed, rather than heard, a presence in her room. She fumbled under the covers and clicked on the remote for the lights.

"Hello Adele. Trick or treat."

Her eyes widened when she saw the axe. His eyes were lifeless. She sat up in bed. The comforter slipped off, revealing the outline of her breasts beneath her negligee, but not her hands beneath the comforter.

"Such nice breasts, Adele. Were they really worth it?"

He approached the bed and raised the axe.

The first shot shattered Mickey Mouse's and Slater's wrists. The axe dropped onto the bed. The second shot shattered his larynx. He staggered backwards grasping his throat with what remained of his wrist. The third shot exploded his heart. Her gun was also a Beretta M9.

* * *

They saw the helicopter and the tracks leading to the house. "Shit, he's here, I hope we're not too late," said Ronstadt. They didn't hear the gunshots. The Blackhawk hovered at the front of the house as the six members of the SWAT team fast-roped to the ground. The helicopter wasn't equipped with landing skis so two of the team began clearing an area of snow so it could touch down. The other four entered the house and went directly to Adele's bedroom.

The scene they saw was not what they had expected. A frail, five-foot-two, hundred twelve-pound woman had just taken out a Recon Marine.

* * *

Ronstadt touched her arm and said, "It's over Adele."

"Over? It won't be over until the nightmares stop. Will I have a new nightmare to deal with now? I just killed a man. Do you think I will ever forget that? Have you ever killed a man Detective

Ronstadt?"

"No, Adele, I've never killed a man, but I do know the nightmares will stop."

"I forgot, you're a psychologist as well as a homicide detective. I hope you're right. It's funny; when I grew up here on the farm my father taught me how to shoot. I was a marksman, I could bag a possum from a hundred yards, but I never thought I'd have to shoot a human being."

No, they weren't really worth it.

CHAPTER FORTY-SIX

Tucson, Arizona
Thursday, March 18, 1993.

INGRAM WAS THUMBING through Adele Grant's file when Neal came into his office. He sat down and stared at his brother.

"It's too bad she asked me to drop the suit," said Ingram. "I'm sure I could've easily got a nine figure award."

"I'm sure you could've," said Neal. "But that was never your plan, was it Ing?"

He removed his glasses. "I don't understand. What are you talking about?"

"Please don't try to patronize me. You never had any intention of going to trial…did you?

"Why did you do it Ingram? *Why?* All those senseless murders… *why*?"

Their eyes locked. Ingram's face contorted into something Neal did not recognize.

"*Why*? I'll tell you *why*. But first tell me. How did you figure it out? There was nothing to tie me to the killings. Nothing. Slater would never have said anything."

"No, Slater never said anything. But you made one mistake early on, and Slater made another. And as soon as I realized them, everything else fit into place."

"Go on."

"November 19, 1992. Does that date mean anything to you?"

"No. Should it? But I'm sure you'll you enlighten me. You're the one with the encyclopedic memory."

"On November 19, Slater met with us and delivered his report about the additional killings he'd uncovered in Los Angeles, Miami, and Las Vegas. Do you remember that conversation?"

"Vaguely. But what significance does it have?"

"Think about it. Slater never said anything about a murder in Houston in his report. Why he omitted that detail we'll never know. Yet, you knew about it because you said, after Slater left, 'Why would he kill the women in Cleveland, Los Angeles, Houston, and Las Vegas, and make threatening calls to the others.' *Houston.* I didn't know about the murder of Elaine Peters in Houston until December 4, when Lawrence Band told us about it at the Counsel meeting at Westward Look. But yet *you* did on November 19.

"I recalled that comment when I fit together the other pieces of your plan, which I may never have noticed if it hadn't been for an observation made by Gary Ronstadt's wife, Elena."

"And that was?"

"The first names of the murdered women and the attempted murder. All followed the sequence of the letters of the alphabet, A through F. Adele, Brandy, Carol, Desiree, Elaine, and Faith. Elena didn't understand the significance, but when I saw the same alphabet pattern repeated for the cities in which the murdered lawyers practiced, Atlanta, Boston, Chicago, Detroit, and Houston, I understood the significance. The letters and sequence of numbers referred to positions on a chessboard. The first murdered woman Carol was C1, and the first murdered lawyer, Lawrence Band from Houston, was H1. They were all chess moves. "It was a chess game…a fucking game of chess! You were playing chess with these people's lives! *Why*, Ingram...why?"

Ingram smiled. "And what was Slater's mistake?"

Neal glared at him. "On December 30, when we met with Slater, he said, 'I thought you were out of the loop.' I never told him about my conversation with Ronstadt…you were the only one I told. The only way he could've known about that conversation was if you had told him…in a meeting *without* me. After that it was easy to figure out the rest, especially when I learned of Slater's background as a Recon Marine in Lebanon."

"Bravo, Neal!" He clapped his hands. "Bra—vo. You're the only one who could've figured it out. *Why*, you ask?" His smile morphed into a sneer. "Why? They were pawns in a war."

"War...pawns? You're insane!"

"Insane? I don't think so. Calculating? Yes. I knew what I was doing at all times. You can't remember how it all started because you buried it. But I know it's locked in your mind, unable to surface, because it's too painful to face…the source of your nightmares. No one could bring it out. Not psychiatrists, therapists, hypnotists…no one. Your mind refuses to relive that day—the day that has haunted me every waking hour of my existence. The day that Polish peasant slaughtered our mother and father with an axe—the axe that burned an image in my brain, and would not go away and leave me in peace! And then I saw it. The axe you were so enthralled with in Powers' office the day we took the first deposition. The axe on his wall—it was *that* axe.

"I had Slater check him out. It was easy. Powers was *not* Powers. He was born Dariuscz Palowski. His father emigrated from Przytyk Poland to Pittsburgh in 1936. *Emigrated*? He fucking ran away from Poland. The bastard murdered our parents. He eventually drank himself to death, but I was determined to make his son Dariuscz pay…for the sins of the father. That arrogant bastard deserved whatever I'd planned for him.

"We knew Carol Andrews was going to Cleveland, and when Slater discovered that Powers was going to be there for a speaking engagement at the same time I couldn't believe it. That's when I decided on my plan. I was going to set up Powers, or should I say *Palowski,* for her murder. Slater broke into his office, took the axe, used it on Andrews, and then replaced it while Powers was still in Cleveland.

"From then on it was easy. There were so many women on whom Powers had operated… and so many lawsuits. All I had to do was find women whose names started with A through H. They were the ranks. It was the same with the lawyers from the Counsel. I selected them from the cities in which they practiced. They were the files. A through H and one through eight, the rank and file, the foot soldiers. It was war. I wanted to annihilate Powers.

"Don't you see the irony? The women were pawns. Expendable. Their lawyers were the knights, castles and bishops...the protectors. They were sacrificed in order to reach the king."

"And how did you get Slater to agree to be your hatchet man?"

Ingram smiled. "Ah, *hatchet man*, a paronomasia...intended... or did it just come out that way? *Slater.* In addition to being a superb investigator Marvin was a trained killer. The Marines trained him to kill, but they didn't train him to enjoy killing. That was something he came to on his own. After the incident in Lebanon the Marines cut him loose. You were at Oxford when he was with the TPD. I represented him when he killed two gunmen during a Circle-K robbery. IA determined it to be a righteous shooting, but there was always the suspicion that he executed them. He hadn't followed procedure, and his partner almost lost his life because of his cowboy antics. Shortly afterwards he resigned from TPD... no one would partner with him. I recognized his skills and hired him as an investigator. When you returned from Oxford he was on our payroll. Didn't you ever wonder why he was such a successful investigator?"

Neal didn't answer.

"I thought not. Did you think the success of our law firm was due entirely to your brilliant research, and my oratorical skills? Of course not; Slater had ways of obtaining information that you never thought of questioning."

"Was it part of your plan to make me appear guilty as well?"

"Strictly diversionary. Planned obfuscation. I knew that you'd eventually be dismissed from the list of suspects. It would've been far too obvious and convenient if everything pointed to Powers. My intent was to keep Slater from ever appearing on the radar screen, and it would have succeeded were it not for that FBI agent

Lavoie who made the connection. A most unlikely and unfortunate coincidence."

"There had to be more than just wanting to destroy Powers. The women you chose to kill may have been selected randomly, but the lawyers were targeted weren't they?"

"Very perceptive little brother. Yes. The ones I chose were the only ones of the one hundred Counsel lawyers who were capable of obtaining a larger judgment than I. That was not going to happen."

"Bullshit. There's more to it than that. What's the real reason Ingram?"

"The *real* reason? I don't think you could possibly understand. How could you? You…the libertine. Your only pursuit in life has been the pursuit of pleasure. How many women you could bed. Despite your brilliance you never saw the larger issue. Those Counsel lawyers deserved to die. They propagated the sins of their ancestors. Their goal was never justice. It was self-aggrandizement. I know what they thought of me and what they said about me. All were anti-Semites. Sanford Astor. I could never have belonged to his clubs because I was a Jew. Did you know the original Astors were believed to be Jewish? A fact conveniently buried by the original John Jacob Astor.

"Were the massacres of the Creeks by Andrew Horton in the 1800s any different than the pogroms of history? All these men were brigands, and their progeny were no better."

"So you decided to be judge and jury? You decided what was justice?"

"*Justice*? Don't make me laugh. There's no such thing as justice. These men weren't interested in justice. They manipulated the law to serve their own interests."

Neal shook his head. "One last question Ingram, the first five women you had murdered were all single women, why did you choose Adele Grant who had a husband and three children?"

"The Polish Sacrifice. The best sacrifice in the history of chess was from the *Polish Immortal Game* between Glucksburg and Najdorf...Warsaw 1929. Najdorf won the game because he sacrificed his queen in the Dutch Defense. Adele Grant was the Queen, the other women merely pawns. They were all sluts and deserved what they got.

"Now that I've bared my soul to you little brother what are you going to do? Slater is dead, and there's no way to prove that I had anything to do with the murders. I made certain of that. Who would believe you?"

"Bared your soul? *You have no soul.* Who would believe me?" He unzipped his jacket to reveal a wire. "I believe Detective Ronstadt and a jury would."

Ronstadt entered the office. "Ingram Mink...you have the right to remain silent..."

Neal started to walk out of the office as Ronstadt was cuffing his brother. He turned and said, "Oh, by the way big brother... checkmate."

EPILOGUE

Three months later, June 1993.

THERE WERE A lot of unanswered questions that Ronstadt and Neal Mink felt could best be answered if the detectives were to meet again in Tucson. The Mink Foundation offered to pay their travel expenses. Lavoie would have to travel courtesy of the FBI, because as a federal employee he could not accept gratuitous funding from outside the agency. Ronstadt hosted the meeting at his ranch. It wasn't exactly the way murder cases were closed, but then again the way in which the entire investigation was conducted after the initial meeting in Tucson wasn't exactly how homicides were approached. The complexity of Ingram Mink's plan created a new chapter in the profiling of serial killers.

The investigating detectives who were involved were all invited. Detectives Sadowsky and Scalpone from Cleveland, Martin and Saffer from L.A., Berkson from Houston, Lasky and Forman from Miami, Dubois from Las Vegas, and Denney from Detroit. Shea and FBI Special Agent Lavoie from Atlanta had been briefed prior to Ronstadt's return to Tucson. Shea declined the invitation, but Special Agent Lavoie accepted. It was he who suggested that Neal be wired when he confronted his brother.

After more than two very frustrating years of being tethered to the original starting point, the detectives were more than happy to close their murder books.

Ronstadt spooned his glass to catch their attention while the detectives were devouring the remnants of the *flan* his housekeeper Anna had prepared. "Gentlemen, thank you for coming. Before we start, I'd like to propose a toast to my lovely wife Elena whose insightful observations led us to a more rapid solution of this case than otherwise would've been possible, if she hadn't recognized a pattern, which I'll explain shortly."

They raised their glasses and cheered, much to the embarrassment of Elena. After the cheering had tapered, Ronstadt proposed a second toast to Neal Mink, who acknowledged the toast with a nod of his head. Ronstadt then explained everything from the time Carol Andrews was murdered until the final confrontation that Neal had with his brother.

The first question came from Lasky. "Gary, you're to be complimented on the way you conducted this investigation, but there's still one thing that I can't figure out. It probably has nothing to do with the investigations, but why would a Recon Marine like Slater who timed everything to the second be wearing a simple Mickey Mouse watch?"

Neal stood up and raised his wrist to show his watch. "We've all used the expression 'That's Mickey Mouse'—to mean bullshit. Well Slater, my brother Ingram and I all wear, or wore, Mickey Mouse watches, gifts from Slater to us. It was a statement of his opinion of the legal system, which he believed was nothing but *Mickey Mouse*. I guess it was his way of showing his disdain for the rule of law. My brother and I wore them because we thought they were kind of cute."

Denney said, "I feel like a complete idiot. If I hadn't fucked up like a rookie, this case might've been solved a lot earlier. First of all, the message that Scalpone sent to me about axe murders went unnoticed until I cleaned out my desk the day I retired. So when I finally contacted him and told him we had an eyewitness to the murder of the lawyer *and* we had a composite, he asked me to fax the picture to Gary. Normally, I would've done that myself, but I was in such a hurry to get out of the building I had a temp-clerk send it. I didn't learn until Gary invited me to this function that the composite faxed to him was of the wrong guy." He shook his head. "If anyone on my squad had created a FUBAR like that on my watch, he would've ended up supervising a speed-trap."

Ronstadt said, "Stop beating yourself up. If you hadn't squeezed that guy Dufour, in Hemlock, we might never've been able to prove that he made the acid threats.

"I forgot to mention that Bob learned it was Thomas Dufour, the head of security for Sherman-Hall, who made those threats. Dufour had contacted Powers asking him to provide the names of women with Sherman-Hall implants who were suing him. He told Powers he'd make the lawsuits go away. Powers, the poor schmuck, probably thought that Dufour was going to pay them off."

SA Lavoie stood up and said, "We've arrested Dufour and his employer William Sherman of Sherman-Hall. Sherman devised the acid threat scheme in an attempt to save his company. Sherman said he had no intention of harming anyone...he said he just wanted to scare them. They've both been arrested and charged federally because the calls were made across state lines."

"Whatever happened to Powers?" Saffer asked.

"The lawsuits would've forced him into bankruptcy," said Ronstadt. "He would've been wiped out financially, so he liquidated his assets and sold his spa to another Tucson Plastic Surgeon, Dr. Theodore Aragon, before the shit hit the fan. The last I heard was that Powers was in Guatemala performing plastic surgery under the auspices of Doctors Without Borders."

"There's still one thing that bothers me," said Berkson. "Gary, you said the acid threats had nothing to do with the murders, yet Desiree LaPelle who'd been threatened with acid disfiguration was murdered. What's the connection?"

"I don't think there was one. It was probably pure coincidence that she'd received an acid threat. Remember, Dufour and Slater weren't working together. She sued Powers, and he probably used Sherman-Hall implants with her. So I suspect he provided her name to Dufour. Slater obviously had her already targeted, and he wouldn't have known about the acid threat because she never told anyone until she told Neal the night she was murdered."

"I think Gary's right," said Neal. "Desiree's name wasn't on the list of women who'd been threatened by Dufour. She hadn't revealed that information until she told me. So neither Slater nor my brother knew that fact. I had dinner with Desiree in Las Vegas the night she was murdered. She told me she wanted to withdraw from the lawsuit because of the acid threat. Ingram knew I was going to be in Las Vegas that night, and because he was trying to make it appear that I was involved in the killings he chose her. He probably would've had Slater kill her anyway because Powers was at a meeting in Las Vegas that weekend. The fact we were both there at the same time assuredly sealed her fate."

"If Slater'd been using Powers' axe, don't you think he would've reported the theft, knowing he was a suspect in the murders?" Dubois asked.

"Powers never knew the murder weapon was an axe, because the press never knew that fact until it was revealed after the Horton murder in Atlanta," said Ronstadt. "Also, the axe was never missing as far as Powers knew. As painful as it is for me to say, I will concede the brilliance of Ingram Mink. He made certain the murders were committed on weekends, or on days Powers was out of town. It was easy for Slater to break into Powers' office and steal the axe and replace it before Powers returned.

"If it hadn't been for FBI Special Agent Lavoie I don't know if we would ever have linked Slater and Ingram Mink to the murders."

Sadowsky said, "Gary, both Steve and I can trace our ancestry back to Poland or Russia, and have heard stories of the pogroms in those countries. I have no fucking love for either of those countries because of the unchecked pogroms. Can you put on your psychologist's hat and give us some insight into what tipped Ingram Mink over the edge after so many years?"

"Neal and I discussed this at length. After I arrested Ingram he was quite cooperative, but offered no apologies for his actions.

"He created the Centurion Counsel with the noblest of intentions. But, after a number of years he realized a significant number of the members didn't share his idealism. They were interested only in dollar signs. And even worse, he discovered some of them were rabid anti-Semites. When the Connie Chung show aired in December 1990, he saw the perfect opportunity to show them all how far superior he was to them, by going for multi-million dollar awards. And when he saw the axe in Powers' office, during the first deposition, he recognized it immediately because its image had been permanently etched in his mind. Unbeknown to Neal, he had Slater find out how the axe came to be in Powers' possession. Once he learned Powers' background, all his repressed emotions percolated to the surface and his mind snapped. He saw the opportunity to avenge his parents' death by destroying Powers, and at the same time eliminate the lawyers who had a family history of anti-Semitism. For example, when he had Sanford Astor murdered, he believed he was avenging the actions of Sanford's mother Lady Astor, known as the *Mistress of Cliveden,* whose anti-Catholic and anti-Semitic views caused comment and the origin of the term 'Cliveden Set,' which became, probably unjustly, a synonym for 'Nazi'. And so it was with the other lawyers."

The final question came from Scalpone. "When we were at the autopsy for Carol Andrews, the pathologist suggested that her breasts had been 'meticulously cut off with a surgical instrument.' Where the hell do you think Slater learned how to do that?"

Ronstadt shook his head…"I have no idea."

Neal looked at Scalpone and said, "I never would've thought of it until you just brought it up…my brother probably taught him how to do it."

"Your brother?"

"Yes, his hobby was taxidermy. He prepared all the stuffed animals in our office. I watched him once skin one of the mink that he stuffed…he could've been a surgeon. So I'm sure he taught Slater how to do the skinning…and Slater was a very quick learn.

"And in case you're wondering what will happen to my bother… he was just diagnosed with advanced inoperable pancreatic cancer, and will never make it to trial." His eyes moistened, "It will not be a pleasant death."

Ronstadt said, "I want to thank you all for coming, and for all your help in bringing this case to a close. We were lucky. I think our collective experience underscores the need to have a national database for these types of crime. We might have been able to save some lives if we had had this resource available."

Lavoie said, "As you know, the FBI has developed the ViCAP program to address this very issue. At the present time it's available only to the FBI for the profiling of serial killers. We hope within the next few years to have the ability to embrace all law-enforcement agencies nationwide. Until then I encourage you to report all unusual homicides to ViCAP, so we can develop a database."

In 1996, Ronstadt would be dealing with another series of killings. ViCAP would still be floundering.

THE END

Author's Note

THE CONTINGENCY FACTOR is a work of fiction. Actual events, dates, and lawsuits resulting from purported problems with silicone breast implants have been blended with fictional cases. The details involving real people have been taken from public records. On December 10, 1990, TV journalist Connie Chung did air an interview with several women and two medical experts on her program *Face to Face.* The excerpt I used in my novel was taken directly from that transcript.

The Mink brothers are fictional, but the Przytyk Pogrom did occur on March 9, 1936. The shoemaker, Josek Minkowski, and his wife, Chaja, were real, and were murdered with an axe by a peasant during the pogrom, and they did leave two orphaned sons. It was those events that provided the inspiration and background for my story.

The details I have written about the breast implant litigation that preceded the Connie Chung show were taken from the actual cases. The litigation that followed the show was indeed like a snowball that became an avalanche. Personal injury lawyers had discovered the *mother lode* in the form of a silicone breast implant. In May 1995, Dow Corning filed for Chapter 11 bankruptcy. Dow was faced with more than 20,000 lawsuits, some with multiple plaintiffs, and about 410,000 potential claims that had been filed in the global settlement. The bankruptcy essentially halted all litigation.

The final amount approved by Judge Pointer to settle hundreds of thousands of claims of injury from silicone breast implants exceeded $4 billion.

After being asked by the British minister of health to review the safety of silicone implants, a seven-member panel of scientists reported no convincing evidence that they caused any of the purported diseases. The U.K. has never removed silicone implants from the market. Subsequent studies throughout the world have shown conclusively that silicone implants did not cause the diseases claimed by the litigants. In June 1999, The Institute of Medicine released a 400-page report prepared by an independent committee of thirteen scientists. They concluded that although silicone breast implants may be responsible for localized problems, such as hardening or scarring of breast tissue, implants did not cause any major diseases, such as lupus or rheumatoid arthritis.

The Institute of Medicine is part of the National Academy of Sciences, the nation's most prestigious scientific organization. Congress had asked the Institute to set up the committee. The committee did not conduct any original research; they examined past research and other materials and conducted public hearings to hear all sides of the issue. Studies subsequent to that report concluded there was no scientific evidence to support the claims that silicone implants caused any of the diseases claimed in the lawsuits. Nevertheless, the settlements from the mass tort will continue through 2014.

So what was Dow Corning guilty of? I personally believe that it was stupidity and arrogance. But, one could argue that describes our U.S. government, because the FDA was certainly complicit in the whole affair with its lack of oversight. But, an individual cannot sue the Government, unless the Government grants permission to do so, because the Federal Government is protected from lawsuits under the doctrine of Sovereign Immunity. The details described in the novel were taken from direct quotations and court transcripts.

And what has happened with breast augmentation surgery since Connie Chung aired her show? Before her show aired in December, 1990, breast augmentation was the number one cosmetic surgery procedure performed in the country, and according to the American Society of Plastic Surgeons, in 2011, it was still the number one cosmetic surgery procedure in the country, with 307,000 women undergoing the procedure. This is a four percent increase from the previous year and a forty-five percent increase since 2000.

The only things that have changed since 1990 are the amounts of money that changed hands and the amount of regulations that have come into force. A few women became millionaires and a lot of lawyers became multi-millionaires, and as a result, the cost of breast implants and the cost of breast augmentation surgery skyrocketed. The first informational product disclosure for breast implants consisted of one paragraph. Today, Mentor's informational brochure consists of twenty-three pages.

For readers who may be interested in following the chronology of the breast implant controversy I recommend the articles written by Harvard Law Student Ellen Connelly *From Regulation to Litigation: An Analysis of the Silicone Breast Implant Controversy,* and *Fatal Litigation Part II: Dow Corning Succumbs,* by Joseph Nocera, Fortune Magazine. Call me cynical, but based on my personal experiences during the breast implant litigation era, my conclusion is; *Only God and lawyers can create a new disease.*

Acknowledgements

THERE WERE MANY people who helped bring the Contingency Factor to its present form. It's risky for an M.D. to write a medical/legal thriller, especially when his two sons are lawyers. But David and Michael gave me a passing grade with all matters relating to the law. My daughter Susan, an ICU nurse, was an ardent cheerleader. Judi White, John Terry, and Clare Hamlet read the first draft and were a constant source of support. They saw things that I missed, and their suggestions resulted in changes that made for a better story. Karen Phillips, my cover artist, turned my vision and ideas for a gripping cover into a reality. Russell Phillips (no relation), my editor, was relentless in finding ways to improve the story. His patience and guidance can only make me a better writer. Retired FBI agent, Stuart Silver, provided me insight into the workings of the FBI and ensured the accuracy of my descriptions of Atlanta and the Atlanta FBI Field Office. Retired Marine and Delta pilot, Benny White, taught me about the Marines and how to fly a plane. (Figuratively) Any errors or inaccuracies are mine…for those I apologize. My closest friends were brought alive as characters in the book…ensuring they will live forever. My closest friend, lawyer Larry Band, assured me he was never attracted to underage redheaded females and he would forgive my libelous comments if he gets a free copy of the book. My bride of fifty years, Jane, tolerated the trail of coffee drips on her carpeting as I staggered into my library at 4:00 a.m. each morning to resume writing. During that time the *honey-do* list got longer, but her support never waivered. To all, I say…thank you.

Also by Philip Fleishman

Available at:
amazon.com and
philipfleishmanmd.com

About the Author

Author Philip Fleishman M.D. is a retired Plastic Surgeon who, in addition to writing thrillers, has been creating wood art for over forty years. His works include complicated intarsia, fretwork, custom furniture, delicate inlay, and some of the most creative and unusual pepper mills you will ever see.

While practicing Plastic Surgery he received many awards and honors for his work with burned patients. In 1973 the Centurions in Tucson Arizona named him "Physician of the Year" for his dedication to burn care in Southern Arizona. He is one of a very select group to ever receive the award of "Honorary Firefighter" by the Tucson Fire Department. His writing and wood art reflect the same precision and attention to detail that he brought to the practice of Plastic Surgery.

He lives in Tucson, Arizona, with his wife, Jane, and their two golden retrievers, Rosie and Sassy.

Made in the USA
Middletown, DE
21 June 2015